The Burnt Ones

The Burnt Ones

by Patrick White

New York · The Viking Press

First published in 1964 by The Viking Press, Inc.
625 Madison Avenue, New York, N.Y. 10022

Published simultaneously in Canada by
The Macmillan Company of Canada Limited

Library of Congress catalog card number: 64-20679
Printed in U.S.A. by The Colonial Press Inc.

ACKNOWLEDGEMENTS

Thanks to the following magazines in which stories have appeared:
Australian Letters for "Willy-wagtails by Moonlight," "Miss Slattery and Her Demon Lover," and "The Woman Who Wasn't Allowed to Keep Cats"; *Overland* for "Clay"; *Quadrant* for "The Letters"; *Meanjin* for "Being Kind to Titina" and "Down at the Dump"; *The London Magazine* for "A Cheery Soul," "Clay," "The Evening at Sissy Kamara's," and "Miss Slattery and Her Demon Lover."   —P.W.

For Nin and Geoffrey Dutton

οἱ καυμένοι . . .

the burnt ones
(the poor unfortunates)

Contents

The Burnt Ones

The Blunt Ones

Dead Roses

Val Tulloch liked to look at her husband while he was reading, and not exactly chat—a word dangerously close to chatter—she liked to think of it, rather, as speaking her thoughts. She spoke them, too, with appropriate softness. Sometimes she wondered whether she irritated Gil by doing so, but she had never asked, because she did not want to find out for certain.

Now she was going over the house-party she had arranged for the Island that Christmas, speculating again on the desirability of those she had invited, and Gil Tulloch was frowning slightly as he read. His wife was of the opinion that a frown suited his otherwise flawless face, giving it authority.

Val was saying: "The Furfields are always good value. Helen doesn't jib at the washing-up, and Doug is so handy in the boat. We're so used to them, darling, don't you think? It's restful. Though I can't say I'll ever take to Marcus. Bashing up poor little Jeremy. But after all, that's life, and Jeremy had better find out."

Gil Tulloch, who was giving *Tristram Shandy* another go, increased his slightly authoritative frown.

"And Mollie Aspinall—certainly one has to take some trouble with Mollie, one has to listen to her—but she does love children."

If she had been all like this, all the time, Gil Tulloch could not have put up with his wife, but here and now Val's social speculations were hardly more boring than the battle with Sterne.

"And Barry Flegg."

3

"Why did you invite Barry?" Gil Tulloch asked, reading.

"To balance Mollie Aspinall."

"Isn't Mollie a bit leathery, a bit long in the tooth for Barry?"

"But she's grateful just for the smell of a man."

Val Tulloch was so pleased, she laughed. Shortly before their discussion she had begun to accept the presence of their fifth and unexpected child. She was still dazed, but very happy.

Her husband turned the page, and waited. He could skim books professionally. And really did enjoy his wife.

"No," said Val, sitting forward, her face growing dark with purpose. "I'll tell you why I asked Barry. I've invited Anthea Scudamore."

"But isn't she pretty awful?"

"How?"

"Nothing you could put your finger on."

"Exactly! And it isn't all her fault. She's just a bit brought-up and not brought-out."

"Barry'll do his best by her. But I've always had the impression Anthea knows exactly where she's going."

"I don't think she does. She knows what she ought to know, and where she ought to go," said Val. Then she added: "That won't stop me giving her a push in what her mother will consider the wrong direction."

Turning in what was for her the obvious and only possible direction early in life, Val Tulloch was a woman who believed that all others must accept the one way to happiness.

[II]

Mrs Scudamore was an arranger too, but in her case she had never allowed herself to consider whether she was *un*happy. There was no reason why anyone should be, no one in Australia at least, if they were well provided for, and of a happy social level. After that, if a person started complaining, she was morbid, or neurotic. Or something. So Mrs Scudamore never allowed herself to complain— unless she had good reason to.

Though she managed to conceal it to a decent extent, her happiness was immense on hearing of Anthea's invitation for

Christmas on the Island. Certainly the Tullochs were lax, intellectual, and in appearance often downright shabby, but they wore the aura which only inherited wealth and station can give. The afternoon the invitation was issued Mrs Scudamore made four telephone calls, one of them to that woman on the *Clarion*.

"Of course it will mean I shall have to take a great deal extra on my own shoulders, here, at Christmas," Mrs Scudamore did not complain to her daughter. "But I am so pleased for you, dear. I am sure you will have lots of fun. The Tullochs belong to such a jolly set. I wonder whether Gilbert Tulloch is as red as they make out. Probably is. Like all those university men. Atheists too. His mother was a Briscoe—property in her own right. I do wonder which of their friends you'll meet. Minnie Briscoe didn't always remember hers, but one had to make allowances; she led a very busy life, and her mind gave out before the end. It just occurred to me, Anthea dear—put in your blue. I know summer on the Island is what people call informal now, but one should go prepared for all eventualities. I mean—it is so much more agreeable—don't you think?—not to get caught out."

Mrs Scudamore would have been deeply hurt if anyone had suggested she had never paused to consider what her daughter might *think*. Why, it was too obvious. They were more like two *sisters*. So, as nobody had ever drawn her attention to the reality of the relationship, Mrs Scudamore continued to think, for Anthea, and everyone. The tempo of life today being what it is, and she married to a leader-writer who kept such odd hours, she was forced to take so much on her own shoulders. As it were.

"Anthea," she would call, "do see whether there is an egg for Daddy, and run down to the corner for a dozen if there isn't. I have my appointment at ten."

Slight acquaintances might have wondered whether Bill Scudamore existed at all, though they heard about him, and read the headings of those unreadable leaders in the *Clarion,* and his hats were on the pegs in the passage outside the downstairs lavatory. Mrs Scudamore's close friends, who knew that everything was aboveboard, remembered him as a wry, skinny, silent man, who rose late, and breakfasted principally off newspapers. Late in the afternoon he would dawdle down to the *Clarion* office, and return to a refrigerator phase of life after others had gone to bed. Mentally he appeared to exist on political abstractions and a convincedly pessimistic attitude to all human endeavour. This, together with his "hours," meant that he was not missed by his wife's friends, who knew that life is what you make it, and whose paths lay between its brightly-enamelled, concrete details.

Mrs Scudamore, who was puzzled, not to say distressed by nonconformity of any description, dismissed it from her mind whenever it affected her closely. So she assured herself: Bill cannot be *un*happy. Temporarily, perhaps, she was right. Her husband suffered more from foreboding and irritations, the kind begotten by President Sukarno and ingrown toe-nails, or the egg he spilled on his dressing-gown. Anthea would boil him his egg before going off to one of her courses, and as Bill Scudamore took the knife, and scraped off the spot of offending egg, it would sometimes sadly occur to him: There goes Anthea, and again I haven't thought what to say. Regret would ripen into guilt, until he remembered her mother, who took so much upon herself. Anthea would be taken care of.

"Anything more, Dad, before I go?" his daughter—his *daughter* —might call from the end of the veranda.

She was so bright, so thoughtful, so damn pleasant. She had learnt it all. Squinting through the glare of the veranda Bill Scudamore thought to see Betsy, or at least the wax which still had to be worked up into the replica. Some men, he understood, allowed themselves to experience twinges of renewal or desire on recognizing the past in the present, but his was a disbelieving nature, and this, surprisingly, his child. This white wax which sense of duty was moulding into a smile. This greenish, girlish flesh under a large summer hat. It made him examine his own hands.

Mrs Scudamore once said to Mrs Vesey who was known as her great friend: "It is thrilling to watch the blossoming of a young girl, particularly when she happens to be one's daughter. One's very own act of creation."

There were moments when Mrs Scudamore suspected she was verging on the intellectual. That sort of thing was permissible provided one took care not to become involved with intellectuals. Seeing so little of her husband she forgot to count him, and as for the Tullochs, now that they hove in sight, property reconciled her to their aberrations of the mind.

Mrs Scudamore was downright thrilled by Anthea's invitation to the Island. She could not help going over and over all its satisfying implications, while remembering the afternoon at Government House Minnie Briscoe, Gil Tulloch's potty old mother, failed to recognize her. For that reason Mrs Scudamore moistened her lips at the airport and hesitated before kissing her daughter good-bye.

Then she said: "Always remember who you are, darling. Both sides are in the Book."

As there was nobody close enough to hear, Anthea need not have blushed for her mother. But she did. And felt frightfully disloyal as she lowered her head and crossed the tarmac. At least the equally regrettable frown which had come to her with the warmth of shame helped to keep her hat on in the wind.

[III]

The day was almost upon them when Val Tulloch remembered they must expect Anthea Scudamore.

"Oh, God!" Gil complained.

Everyone else had arrived, and settled down into one of those temporary communities far closer knit than most of the lifelong relationships.

"I know," Val decided. "I'll get Ossie Ryan to fetch her out on the mail run. Then nobody need be disturbed."

By nobody she meant her husband, who had always been her first preoccupation.

So Anthea was met at the plane by Ossie Ryan, a sandy man who knew what was happening anywhere on the Island, and who ran one of those loosely-connected bombs which rattle between fixed points in the remoter parts of Australia.

"All set?" Ossie asked of this spotless girl from the city who dusted the seat before sitting down.

"Yes. Lovely, thank you." She was so composed, agreeable.

Ossie had never been seen without a kind of straight scar of a grin. Now he grinned at the vaccination mark which glared white from the girl's passive arm.

They began to drive across the Island, through the gold blur of barley crops, past mobs of turkeys blown sideways by the impetus of Ossie Ryan's car. Wherever they occurred, the little runty island trees appeared to have accepted a permanent deformity forced upon them by the wind.

The girl sat holding her summer hat. She was very lush, white, imported, beside her red, skinny, indigenous companion. In her mind she composed a letter to her mother, which would in fact never be written because they had promised each other to ring through every evening after dinner. But in the girl's mind the letter began: *It is all rather an adventure.* . . .

She sat offering a smile in place of the words she did not find for the mail-man, while the adventure continued in bursts of sun, and a bashing of wind, and the blaze of ripe barley. Sometimes Ossie Ryan would widen her experience by telling what was happening in the stone cottages they passed:

"That's Mrs Crane. 'Er old man got took over to the mainland Thursday. Operation for hernia. That house up there—the woman runs a baby-farm, they say. *They,* mind you. I don't say nothun about no one, but mind me own business. That place is Mr Isbister's. From Glenelg. Looks like 'e brought a different wife with 'im this year."

As the car clove the dust Anthea Scudamore drifted through the penetrable houses. She opened drawers and looked inside. Or she settled herself in the chairs, her rather wide hips, her large thighs arranged in that oblique position she adopted for sitting. Only when she was completely composed would she allow the owners of the houses to approach and tell her their closest secrets.

This indulgence was something Anthea would never have admitted to her mother, for whom life was bright and unconcealed. Perhaps it was a vice the daughter had inherited from a father she scarcely knew.

"I think it's all fascinating," she remarked, turning to Ossie Ryan with an expression of such sincerity he wondered whether it meant anything.

He cleared his throat, and spat over the side, and the spittle was flung into the light in a fine, glistening curve.

"I reckon people are about the same," he said sheepishly, "wherever they happen to be."

But he was pleased at her interest, and would continue to exert himself.

"Mrs Tulloch's ordered the turkey. She's expecting again." He laughed. "Gil keeps 'er busy."

Then Anthea Scudamore, large and white, began to tremble, not that she was afraid exactly, or shy, but at the thought of the people she would meet, and in particular those she might learn to know too well. She had never known anyone intimately, at least in the way she imagined people did get to know one another, nobody except her mother, and that was different. In the circumstances, the image of Mummy in her straw from Martin's, and her substantial shoulders, not unlike Anthea's own, was comforting. But not comforting enough. The girl's arms, flushed by the sun, had got the goose-flesh, and it did not leave her.

[IV]

Usually Ossie Ryan slung the mail into the box, and planked down a packing-case of groceries in the sand beside the post, but this morning, as it was an occasion, he ran the car up the stony lane, through the scrub, to Tullochs'. As the Chev slung them around Ossie was grinning his scar of a grin.

Because they had expected, and finally heard, all, with the exception of the Furfields who had withdrawn somewhere to deal with children, could be seen waiting on the corner of the veranda, against the skyline, preparing officially to proffer friendship—an attitude which can look so hostile.

Mollie Aspinall giggled, stroking her easy, sea-bitten skin. She said: "Mummy hasn't let her come without the hat."

And Val Tulloch couldn't resist: "She's probably left the gloves on the plane." She felt a beast, however.

Anthea Scudamore had begun to wave, and smile, or grimace at the glare, and extricate her thighs from the car. She was feeling very large and exposed.

"A regular Juno," said Barry Flegg, going over his chin with his fingers.

"Probably not so explosive. But that's up to you, Barry." Gil Tulloch had given the game away at forty. "You may discover a time-bomb."

"Dammit!" cried Val. "How perfectly beastly we all enjoy being!"

She began to walk down the stony slope with that long, casual stride she adopted naturally on the Island, her figure spoiled by pregnancies. Gil Tulloch never tired of looking at his wife.

"Here at last!" Val heard her voice swaggering idiotically. "And isn't it always alarming—one's first contact with the natives!"

Her impulse was to embrace the girl, but the cheek looked so immaculate, she found herself holding out her hand, hardened by the iron frying-pan and a morning spent reeling in.

Anthea was for the moment all motions, none of which mattered greatly, and words, none of which was distinguishable, until she bent to smooth a crease:

"I'm looking the most *ghastly* mess."

The most colourless, Val Tulloch decided; I must do something for Anthea.

But for the moment all she could manage was to submit her to the terrors of introductions. As the Furfields came out of the house, Val was glad to realize they were some of her more negative friends.

Soon it was actually over, and when she had been taken inside Anthea Scudamore could tell the goose-flesh was leaving her arms. A crushed survivor in a room of her own, she already felt she would be happy there, because at least she could close the door. In her small stone cell she began to open drawers on yellow newspaper and the smell of somebody else's powder. She was listening to the leaning tea-tree continue to saw at the gutter—it must have been the one which had let in the water—while the wrinkled mirror reflected a face sufficiently unlike her own to encourage a burst of vanity.

When she had unpacked her things, and hung her blue on the plastic hanger her mother had advised taking, she flopped down, and lay for a moment on the bed, on the washed-out Indian counterpane. Probably Anthea Scudamore had never indulged in a gesture quite so free, in a position so unorthodox. Certainly if anyone had seen her she would have felt ashamed—for her tumbled, white opulence. For the moment she suspected uneasily it might only be possible to come alive in secret positions, in other people's houses. Or would a house of her own be someone else's? She had a hankering after ornaments in jade, for the cool, sensuous throb which breaks through their remoteness of form. She would have enjoyed perching them on their neat ebony stands.

She lay there only for a moment or two, enough to feel guilty about it. She got up quickly, and glanced through the window, as though she expected her mother might approach along the stone-flags of the veranda. But the sea glaze had sealed Anthea Scudamore off. Down in the bay gulls were squabbling over the heads of the fish Doug Furfield was filleting. Down around a grey, lop-sided dunny, two little boys were having a fight. Anthea Scudamore watched them briefly with the conventional interest she took in her friends' children. She was relieved to feel she need not investigate, and probably would never hear the reason for this ritual quarrel. After all, it was not what went on at other people's houses which invested those houses with peculiar life. It was what she herself brought into them. It was only the receptacle of which she was in desperate need, in which her uncommunicative nature might spill itself, if silently. So she was hungrily grateful for this stone cell, for the sound of the bent tea-tree as it sawed at iron and silence. And sawed.

[v]

After dinner at the house on the point, in the acceptably disordered living-room, the children of two families buried their differences, and stood to sing by lamplight round the old worm-eaten upright. The little boys' voices were exceptionally pure and clear. They're really rather sweet, Anthea Scudamore decided, throwing back her arms as she sat sprawled in the chintzy chair from which the springs had gone. Except for the straggle of veins, she was at her whitest in the crooks of her arms, Barry Flegg observed. Objectively. Even warmest she was cold. And Anthea was perspiring by now, after the couple of gins, and the washing-up, and conversation with Doctor Flegg. They had discussed in such unusual detail dish-washing machines and God, that Anthea had plunged her arms almost up to the elbows in the sink, and the yellow water had risen up, and over onto her raw silk. What a *disaster,* Mollie Aspinall shrieked, from beside her droopy cigarette. Anthea laughed, and looked at herself, and said it didn't really matter. Nor did it, except that Mummy. All the other women were wearing haggish, spotty slacks. Doug Furfield, drawing a tea-towel out of a tumbler as he discussed trolling techniques with Gil, thought perhaps this girl wasn't such a bad sort. But as a solicitor in real life he would know how to keep his distance.

Afterwards in the living-room, while the little boys, accompanied by Helen Furfield, sang what could have been their wordless songs, Anthea remembered Mrs Meadling's saying which irritated her on most occasions. *I love people,* Mrs Meadling used to say, several times every Thursday, as she turned out the house for Mummy. *Oh, but Mrs Meadling, how can you be so general?* the irritated Anthea had once exclaimed. *Eh? I was never a general, only ever went out daily.* Anthea murmured: *What I mean, Mrs Meadling, is, there are reservations in everything.* Now in the Tullochs' disorderly room, so obviously a place for living, she rubbed her head against the back of the chair, and felt that she clung less, perhaps, to the principle of reservation.

Poor thing, Val Tulloch concerned herself; one has to remember she is younger. What can one do for Anthea? Out of her fullness Val continually felt the need to be doing things for people, when people, her husband reminded her, didn't wish to have them done.

Anthea sat rubbing her hair against the Tullochs' perennial chintz.

Pale hair loving itself, Gil saw round the edge of *Tristram Shandy,* which, he had come to the conclusion, must remain his great stumbling block.

Suddenly Val had thought of something.

"I know——" she said. "Who'd like to feed the possums?"

There was an immediate barging of little boys as they ran for stale crusts.

"What about you, Anthea?"

Anthea Scudamore remarked: "I don't think I've ever touched a possum!"

But got up, though, a grinning girl whose hockey stick might have been standing in the hall.

Barry Flegg announced he would fetch a supply of bread, and made for the bin, while Anthea waited, embarrassed, touching the stain on her frock. His return removed her, not exactly from her isolation, but together they went outside. The furry darkness was full of the distinctive noise made by possums, and the giggles of little boys.

"Gee!" Marcus Furfield was reminded. "Did you hear that breezer Doctor Flegg let out, while they were washing-up? It shook the whole kitchen."

Doctor Flegg squatted down, and began offering bread to darkness. He told Anthea about a winter he had spent at the point, after an illness, alone except for a roofful of possums.

"There was one old girl," he said, "you would have thought somebody was emptying a quart jug on the ceiling every time she made water."

Anthea decided to accept coarseness as part of the situation, but did pause to wonder what Mummy, as she copied her companion's attitude, and squatted. Her smile, her dress was unnaturally tight, while sufficiently adapted, she hoped. Anyway, in the darkness, nobody would be able to see.

"What did you do that winter, here, alone, after you had been ill?"

Barry Flegg had not expected to rouse interest.

"Nothing," he said. "Lay about, and watched the sea. I was too weak at first for anything else. Later on, when I got back my strength, I found I just wanted to look at things I hadn't ever noticed before."

The little boys had wandered off. The young man's voice, separated from his hitherto obtrusive body, surprised her by its intimate, its gentle tone. She had never cared for the name "Barry."

In the darkness, apparently, he had continued offering crusts while speaking, for the immediate neighbourhood was moving and clutching. She suddenly felt a cold claw grasping at a crust she held in her hand as a token of what they had come there for.

"Oh!"

"What?"

"I didn't expect! I nearly toppled over!"

Anthea Scudamore wobbled, and giggled most foolishly, she heard. But it frightened away the animal's too human claw, and secretly she was glad.

"It was only a possum."

It was only a man's, flat, ordinary voice, but trying to help her, she realized, and his hand, to keep her balance. Along her arm she felt the man's rather shaggy arm, which she had noticed already by lamplight with unresolved feelings. Nor did she wish now to explore a sensation which had begun to affect her too closely. At least there were only possum witnesses of her engagement in the musky darkness with this hard, human body, which, she had been taught, it must be her duty to resist.

In the moments of her indecision she heard her shrill, unnatural voice: "If I came here alone I should probably explore. And collect things. Shells and things. Seaweed. Plants. Make little collections."

Never before had she considered anything of the kind. Though her wobble was now more controlled, thanks to the clamp of Barry Flegg's hairy hand, she knew her voice sounded absurdly unconvincing. Instead, she should have dared tell him: This afternoon I lay on the Indian counterpane, and my real, secret self was half-waiting for a door to open—but quickly. It was exciting, and perfectly ghastly, at the same time.

Perhaps a good thing that one of her legs was shooting with pins and needles. Then she was deafened by the telephone.

"The telephone!" She shouted to be heard above the whispers of her own thoughts.

"What about it?"

"Isn't it deafening!"

When he answered he sounded surly enough for her to remember that lower lip. Sun and wind had worked on it to what looked a painful extent, yet she could not visualize intentions ever weakening under the scaly skin.

"In places like this," he mumbled, "they ought to tear the telephone out."

Then Val's full figure was standing in the lit doorway, her voice calling: "Anthea? The telephone. It's your mother."

Anthea Scudamore was relieved, not exactly glad, but relieved.

"I must go and speak to her," she explained superfluously to Doctor Flegg. "We promised to ring each other every evening. To save writing."

When she went into the house her hand remained in possession of a certain salt stickiness, a roughness of crumbs, though she translated at once into affectionate pleasure any exhilaration that lingered. In the full room where the telephone stood, all her agreeable friends, as she glanced round, were again the strangers she would never know.

"Oh, yes. It was lovely. But over quickly . . ." She was echoing her own voice in the depths of the telephone. "A man met me. In a car . . . A *man* . . . The mail-man . . ."

Nobody in the room was listening, but mildly enjoyed hearing: Mollie Aspinall scratching her salty scalp, with nails she glanced at afterwards, Helen Furfield waiting for children to cry, from a distance, out of their sleep.

"Oh, yes, it's lovely. So unspoiled," Anthea Scudamore was saying expectedly. "Well," she said, looking round, apologizing, smiling, "the ones we were told . . . Yes . . . And Barry Flegg . . . *Flegg* . . . Yes. It *is* a short name . . . Yes . . . At the University . . . A physicist . . . No, I don't know whether his aunt . . ."

What to do about Anthea? Val Tulloch was obsessed.

"I don't know . . . Go to bed, I suppose . . . Yes . . . Yes . . . The view's lovely . . . Yes, I hung it up as soon as I unpacked . . . on the hanger . . ."

After that, when the telephone had been silenced, they went to bed. Barry Flegg had already gone. There was nothing left, though Gil Tulloch imagined that, if he had not been a married man, he would have come back, and got drunk, alone.

When she had gone with her to her room, Val managed to kiss Anthea at last, and promised as she closed the door: "Tomorrow you'll have to see something of the Island."

Anthea thanked for everything.

But most of all she was thankful for her own stone cell, in which she might flower again—a full, distinct white. She was never *un*happy, as Mummy liked to say. Tomorrow she would be shown, she had been told, an estuary of black swans. She could not remember whether she had ever come close enough to hear the hissing, to watch the writhing of the black necks. Did she altogether want? Or touch the papery bark, flaking, down around the grey dunny, into opalescent scales. Sun and wind, to say nothing of moonlight, had worked upon the paper-barks. Better to watch without becoming involved in any process of skin. She withdrew her hand, finally, out of reach of further experience.

[VI]

Anthea Scudamore fished, rowed, shot at a wallaby, drove with Val Tulloch in the elegant ancient rattly Railton to fetch supplies from cottages. Her arms became red and ugly. Pickled in brine. She was doing everything expected of her. She was becoming a Different Person.

And at night, usually at eight-thirty, Mummy telephoned from the mainland, on which life was led by positive rule.

Mrs Scudamore reminded: "The skin can dry up if you don't attend to it, dear, leading that kind of life, and nobody admires a chapped skin. Nobody of any taste, that is, though today there are those who haven't been educated in what is nice. Anthea, the young man, the Doctor Flegg, nobody has heard of. He must be a decent young fellow, though, or the Tullochs wouldn't have invited him. Tomorrow I start my treatment. Dad only laughs. If I ever see him. He's decided to take his holiday. His friend Hessell Mortlock is arriving unexpectedly. They knew each other in Brisbane. Mr Mortlock lives in Sydney now. Or nearby. At Sarsaparilla. Anthea? Oh dear, this *line!* Anyone would think you were trying to throw me off. Mr Mortlock is driving over in his Riley. I believe he's wealthy.

Cement tiles. But related to the Eardley Browns. Do you hear me, Anthea? I thought that woman was cutting us off. . . . There they sit, in those country post offices, and when they feel they've extracted the juice from the orange, they . . ."

In the house on the point they would all sit round, after dinner, hands on their stomachs, waiting for Mummy. It had become their ritual.

Anthea would have liked to protect her mother from her friends, but was no longer capable, she suspected, of protecting even herself. She seemed to have gone with her smooth skin. Her skin which she couldn't be bothered to do anything about.

The will slackened in the slack air, the conscious grew unconscious. Worst of all were the early afternoons, when people tended to disappear, and at such a time of suspended continuity Anthea Scudamore allowed the wind to carry her along the arc of beach, her feet eliciting slight felted protests from the quilted sand.

If she had been honest—but it did not matter being dishonest with oneself, only with others—she would have admitted watching him set off after lunch for an undisclosed point beyond the rocks. Now, in the circumstances, she only saw out of the corner of her mind's eye the blurred image of his young man's body, in trunks, carrying a book, and wearing the rag hat with the iron-mould on it. The mind itself had covered up her purpose, if she had ever had one, as the wind had covered his foot-prints with sand.

Barry Flegg was lying just the other side of the rocks. On his back. He had taken off his trunks. From the absence of a visible line dividing his public from his private skin, this must have been a habit with him, she realized in a flash of light, wind, sand.

"Sorry," he said, pulling on the trunks without any awkwardness. "Nobody's come this way before."

"Oh!" she cried, then mumbling, blown this way and that, it seemed, on the edgy rocks: "In another direction. I didn't mean to intrude."

Never had she been so powerless to express, never had she stood longer waiting for guidance of some kind.

"Come on down, then," he encouraged, "now that we're more conventional, and make appropriate conversation."

His teeth were glaring up at her.

"You're reading," she contributed, with an obviousness which would not be avoided.

But he threw the book aside as though it were something they might not be able to discuss, and as she planted herself in the sand beside him, he was looking at her from under those thick eyelids, detaching from the light whatever was necessary to stimulate a changed relationship. She wondered how much of her would have been necessary to Barry Flegg. She wondered, in fact, intensely, as everything she did, said, now, was happening out of curiosity. The innermost part of her was pulsing with daring, like the sound of footsteps approaching through thick sand.

"I hate to barge in on people." Her clumsy words lurched after sincerity. "Particularly when they're reading."

"I hoped you weren't barging in," he said. "I hoped it might have been part of a delicate plan."

His flippancy, unexpected in one who had conveyed earnestness till now, confused her slightly. She confessed: "I was at a loose end. After lunch. Everybody their own occupations. Just for the moment I couldn't think what to do."

Her blotting-paper voice flapped uncontrolled around him in the wind.

"What do you do, Anthea?" he asked.

"What do I do?"

"I don't know anything about you."

She wished it had been easier to answer.

"Well," she said desperately, "I'm taking the course at Mrs Treloar's Secretarial College." He was watching her as closely as she felt it necessary to examine the fragment of cowrie she held in the palm of her hand. "For a time, I," she gulped, and laughed, "I thought I might have a talent for acting. I started a drama course. I thought that, later on at least, there might be some parts for me. I saw myself playing older women. But I," she hesitated, "I was too self-conscious, I suppose. Daddy said I was too big. That most men wouldn't like acting with me."

She was suddenly annoyed he didn't interrupt, even more so

because she suspected him of staring into her shirt where it flapped open unbuttoned lower because of summer and the beach.

Then she did what she didn't know properly how to do. She lay back on the sand, stretching out her bare thighs, to allow herself the luxury of confessing something she had only just that moment thought of.

"Of course what I'd really like to do," she said, "is take up something like physiotherapy. Or nursing. I'd like to feel I was helping *people*."

For a moment she honestly believed it. A voluptuousness of self-sacrifice swam at her out of the drained sky, and she had to make an effort to contain the tears which would have been shameful for Doctor Flegg to witness. Because he was still looking at her so intently. Could he have noticed her expression, self-indulgent in her act of service, as she bent above the bed-sores of old, flaccid men?

Suddenly Barry Flegg opened his mouth and yawned like a horse.

"I expect you'll marry some bloke, and he'll take you to bed, and get children with you. That's what happens to most girls. The normal thing."

Nobody had spoken so coarsely to her before. The shock of it convinced her that her mother was mostly right.

She lay there trying not to frown, trembling although she gripped the sand.

"Poor old Anthea!" Barry Flegg was saying, and began gently to stroke her thigh. "It's my common origins. Dad's the stationmaster at Buckleboo. Mother used to clean out the toilets at the Black Bull before she married. They're a bloody boring pair, but good. I go down there from time to time, when my sense of duty needs refreshing, and learn about truth at its source. And eat baked parsnips, which I don't particularly like."

All the time gently stroking her thigh. And she let him. Petrified with curiosity.

Gulls were flying overhead in slow, white, unabashed sweeps, looking, and lulling, and swooning, and wooing.

When he eased his arm, harder than the pillow of sand, underneath her neck, she was no longer so very surprised, nor at the stench of male body and whorls of tingling hair with which the gulf in her experience was now filling. She lay rigid, though, unyielding while unresisting, allowing the theory of it to play upon her breasts and ear.

"Poor old Anthea!" he kept on saying. "This is the course the Vocational Guidance Officer prescribes. Believe *me!*"

Her vocation! If she had had faith she might have believed in voices, particularly those of men. Or she might have offered up her pale hair, instead of submitting her cheek to razors. Some of it was excruciating.

"Lie still! I want you." He had changed key to give an order.

But the hoarser voice and the weight and extent of his body growing on hers, undermined her daring.

Then the one great gull swooped, intense of beak, intent of eye, as though about to strike.

"No-ooh!" she screamed.

Beating her head against the sand.

At least he respected her distress. He raised himself, and lay along the ridge of shells which were becoming sand, but close beside her, and without any attempt to disguise the true state of his affairs.

She sat up dusting her still comparatively white shins.

"I'd always hoped," she said, "I'd fall in love."

"Why not?" he replied, looking at her without resentment. "That's what we're all trying for. But have to learn it."

"Not like animals."

"We are, aren't we? With instincts for decency thrown in."

She preferred to nurse, not so much her bruised sides, as a moral injury she might have enjoyed sustaining.

"It's not the way I look at it," she said. "It's more," she said, "something finer."

He kept on looking at her from under the heavy eyelids, so that she had to turn to him at last, and smile, restoring him to a position where they might meet socially. But could not return his stare for long, because she was too conscious of his throat.

Lumping herself up, she said: "I'd better go. They may be wondering what's happened to me."

She was rather pleased with the prudence which had enabled her to handle the most difficult situation of her life, and looked back only once, to see his arm waving with the slow detachment of a gull.

When she got in and found nobody had missed her, Anthea went to her room which, for the present, was what she loved most. She began panting, for consolation, crying for the comfort of it, as she persuaded the indifference out of an old pillow-slip. Presently she fell asleep. She dreamed about her father, who was smoother than fact, or perhaps she had just failed to meet that secret man in the course of their less actual lives. In any case she woke smiling from a dream too garbled to remember. She was glad. And rose to comb the knots out of her painful hair.

[VII]

That night at dinner the Furfields told the story of their courtship and marriage, and everybody pretended to be interested—or perhaps everybody was; the fable revealed such a touching banality.

"We found that on winter mornings we both chose the east side of the bus, in summer the west," Doug Furfield explained.

"We gathered first of all that we were climatically suited," Helen added.

Their plant lives showed too clearly in their faces as they leaned out towards each other from the past, entwined even now, across the table. Anthea could not look at them at last. She was afraid she might never be able to offer to the lamplight proof of even a plant existence. Or she looked unintentionally at Barry Flegg. She had already rejected the animal proofs too firmly to hope for a position in an animal world. If she had wanted it. Which she didn't.

Val Tulloch watched *that Anthea* digging her table-cloth, old though it was, with the prongs of a fork, wounding, or wounded.

Mrs Scudamore rang with the punctuality they had learnt to expect. Everyone sitting round seemed to be waiting for it. Anthea ignored the possibility that it might be somebody else, and fitted her revived face to the archaic receiver.

"A disaster!" Mrs Scudamore could not wait because it was hers. "Fell on the veranda steps, and sprained my wrist. I had always heard it is cheaper for *drunks* to fall."

"Oh, darling, how dreadful for you! How painful!"

The two voices slipped into one of those duets in which empathy and practice almost totally disguise technique.

"Just when I was beginning to benefit from the Treatment. Well, we shall get through somehow—a one-armed Christmas. Mrs Meadling, of course, is expecting her daughter and family from Mildura, and no part of her will be available. But we shall get through it. The frightening thing is that Mr Mortlock is due tomorrow evening, and I cannot very well put him off. I mean, he is a person of a certain level, and where levels exist nowadays they have to be respected."

"Mr Mortlock?"

"I told you, dear. But you don't always remember. Mr Mortlock is Daddy's friend."

"Yes, yes. Who is driving over in the Riley. Of course I remember. Perfectly."

Awfulness thickened the air in the Tullochs' over-crowded room. Distress was making Anthea Scudamore frown, and suck her upper lip. Anyone present could only have regretted the difficulty of the situation in which the girl found herself placed. But in fact Anthea, for almost the first time since coming to the Island, perhaps even in her whole life, saw clearly what she must do.

"Mummy," she said, "we shall ring through early in the morning. To book. I'll come by the afternoon plane."

"Oh, but darling, what about your Christmas?"

"Christmas is Christmas anywhere, and I can't think of you suffering. In difficulties. With Mr Mortlock."

"He writes such affable letters. I can see no reason why Mr Mortlock should turn out difficult. It is just the fact that . . ."

As though her voice had outlived its purpose Mrs Scudamore died away.

Everything had been arranged, then, and there was really no need for Anthea to inform anyone else who had to know; they were all there, and all knew.

"What shall we do without Miss Scudamore at Christmas?" asked Mollie Aspinall of Jeremy Tulloch, whom she had sitting in her lap.

But Jeremy was sucking a lolly.

In the morning Val Tulloch drove Anthea across the Island to the airport, and was determined to say something to the girl, something sympathetic and helpful. Yet could not find the moment or the word. As Anthea sat upright in the car, her half-smile flickered in the shuttered light the tunnels of scrub allowed to reach them, and during the open stretches, whenever Val sneaked a look at it, the smile appeared no less equivocal, directed inward even while greeting the blaze of ripened barley.

[VIII]

On arriving home, Anthea was thrust together with her parents' guest far more precipitately than she had bargained for, or liked. After paying off the taxi, she had run up the veranda steps and in by the living-room door. It was so familiar she could have sung. Except that a gentleman who had been sitting there, rose from the sofa and explained:

"I am Hessell Mortlock, your father's friend. Your mother is taking it easy for a bit upstairs, and your father hasn't come in."

Then he cleared his throat, and looked.

"Oh, yes!" she flustered. "Of course!"

Surprise had made her snigger and blush regrettably. In Mummy's room, she realized, everything was too polished, too arranged, for her chapped skin to be acceptable. But she longed to be received back, and hopefully touched one of the little Chinese bowls which were kept filled with potpourri on the cedar table.

The little bowl was merciless. It overbalanced.

Anthea Scudamore snorted and giggled.

"Did you have any punctures?"

"Any what?"

"Punctures. In that car."

"Why," he said, "no. You've upset the bowl," he pointed out.

"Its proportions are not very good," she said, glad to have thought of such a rational explanation.

He had come forward, to help her gather the spilt petals. Perhaps it was the situation which made them copy each other. Their fingers held as for using chop-sticks, they were conveying the brown rose-

petals back into the Chinese bowl. It was all most solemn and
stilted. For Anthea at least, the faint scent of the dried petals turned
the moment into a distinguished one.

"Roses are something of a speciality of mine," Mr Mortlock was
confessing. "I grow, but I don't exhibit them. Human beings tend to
lose sight of whatever they happen to be exhibiting," he added
rather effectively.

"Yes," Anthea agreed. "I am told the cage-bird world is worst of
all."

It was curious the sense of experience Mr Mortlock gave her. His
hands, returning the potpourri to the bowl, had a masculine
elegance which began to obtrude. He was wearing a blood-stone
ring.

"So I don't show my roses," he said. "But have received
compliments from several people who know what they're talking
about."

"Roses can be glorious." She sighed, and wished she could
remember one or two names. "Even here."

Because Mr Mortlock's presence disposed her to apologize, for
their house, for their city, which was dwindling into a provincial
town.

In the pause which follows the close of a phase in conversation,
the visitor was taking another look at her. She could sense that, very
strongly, although she had turned her face, and stood dusting the
last specks of potpourri from her mother's waxed table. His
appearance had remained with her. Out of her first embarrassed,
fragmentary impressions, she could have described with exactness
the expression he must be wearing at the moment.

Mr Mortlock was a man, if not old, well, older. She wondered
briefly, how in the blurred Queensland past, he had come to be
Daddy's friend, and where the tailor existed who could mould that
style of suit so beautifully to his still impressive figure. For he was
not of the present. If anything she was touched by the fact, and
would have been ready to defend his entry into a roomful of
contemptuous strangers—the shaggy destroyers, the Mollie As-
pinalls and Barry Fleggs, even the Val and Gilbert Tullochs. For
Anthea Scudamore Mr Mortlock was not a stranger.

Yet, at this point, she had been with him long enough.

Showing him her face, she said earnestly: "I expect my father will come soon. You will have a lot to talk about." She smiled.

"I bet Bill hasn't any more to say than he had in Brisbane," Mr Mortlock answered.

Then it was one of those relationships, which she imagined, and at times hoped for, in which words did not matter.

"In any case, you must excuse me," she said. "I must go up to my mother."

He was very gallant in his not so old, but elderly gestures. His smile had practised on many faces.

"I'll be happy to sit a little," he said, stirring up his money. "This is the right time of day."

"I hope you've got soap and towels," she murmured, imitating her mother.

It was not the sort of thing one answers, so Mr Mortlock made a little motion with one of his legs, bending the knee, meant to assure. If she had not felt so full of respect, she might have been reminded of some old terrier dog lifting his leg on lavender in the sudden presence of a bitch.

But she was much too respectful of this most respectable visitor. As she left the room.

Upstairs, Mrs Scudamore was propped on her bed, in her dress, with a pink chiffon sling supporting her hurt wrist. She looked exhausted, but satisfied, for her. When the two of them had embraced with an affection which was delicious to the daughter after some of the horridness she had lately undergone, the mother asked:

"Do you think he has everything he wants? Of course your father wasn't here to help me. But I pointed out both the lavatories."

"Isn't he rather old?" Anthea said.

"A man isn't old if he has his health and his interests," Mrs Scudamore was of the opinion. To that she added: "His wife left him, you know. I believe she behaved very badly."

"How?"

Mrs Scudamore frowned.

"I don't know."

"And he lives all alone at Sarsaparilla?"

"He has an unmarried sister who keeps house for him."

"I wonder whether she is like her brother."

Anthea doubted there could be two of such a kind.

Once again this was a question on which Mrs Scudamore had not become informed, so the two women grew silent, in the shuttered room, at a distance from the city noises. It was a ruminative hour, and although they did not communicate in words, a general softness suggested that their thoughts were in agreement.

[IX]

Later, when they went downstairs in their changed dresses, men's voices were coming from the veranda. Dad had returned, apparently. He had got the whisky out, and seemed to be finding it a help.

Mr Mortlock was telling about the old days in Brisbane, when his friend Bill Scudamore had been a reporter on the *Courier Mail,* and he, Hessell Mortlock, of some unspecified business importance.

"This young feller brought a lot of gaiety into an old man's life," Mr Mortlock announced.

He would obviously have enjoyed sinking into a warm bath of recollection, but at once restrained himself, and looked at Anthea.

"Yes," he said, pursing his mouth in a certain way. "He was acquainted with the highspots!"

"I'm sure he was!" said his wife, and laughed, not quite jolly, not quite bitter.

She went out sighing, into the kitchen, on some further stage of a domestic martyrdom.

Mr Mortlock had rounded his eyes into knowing marbles, and this time Anthea did catch sight of the old terrier dog, though drove the idea almost immediately out of her head.

Dad was looking embarrassed, playing with his wrist-watch strap, which was old and sweaty, she noticed. Because it was both fascinating and repulsive, she half remembered the dream of the afternoon before. She would have liked to change the strap for the benefit of Mr Mortlock, whose every detail seemed flawless in its way, in spite of the long drive in the Riley.

"Doesn't Anthea tipple?"

He was looking at her, sipping his own drink as he addressed her.

"No," she answered breathily. "Only sometimes, that is."

For she remembered the gins she had drunk on the Island.

"All to the good," said Hessell Mortlock. "Moderation in everything."

Dad kept looking at his own feet. He was at his wriest that evening, as though his family embarrassed him—or was it his friend?

Anthea would have liked to make some witty remark in the presence of two men, but Hessell Mortlock seemed content to set out again into the past, this time on a journey he had made with Bill to Mount Isa.

Presently she excused herself.

"I must go in," she explained, "and help with the meal."

All her remarks seemed to her that evening breathier than usual, more colourless. But she sensed he was looking at her calves when she did not actually see.

From the kitchen she noticed the car standing beside their own in the garage. By comparison it looked most exotic. It was a bottle-green, and must have been freshly washed. She could imagine Mr Mortlock take out a note from a crocodile—yes, a crocodile—wallet, and hand it to an anonymous attendant in overalls.

"Is that the car?" she asked her mother, hoping to involve her.

But Mrs Scudamore might not have heard. She continued having difficulty with a shape, trying to unmould it, ostentatiously single-handed, while her daughter failed to offer assistance.

The evening proceeded. It was what her friends on the Island, Anthea was sure, would have found a boring one, but that did not prevent her enjoying the figure Mr Mortlock cut. In his moulded suit. His rather broad shoulders. His hair of that sandiness to which grey is kind, merging and fading into the original shade. Where the scalp showed through, besides, the hair was so sensibly arranged. Not even Mollie Aspinall could have turned Mr Mortlock's head into a sarcastic joke.

"I expect you are tired," Mrs Scudamore said at last, as though she had a sore throat.

"Not exactly," Mr Mortlock replied, "but ready."

He was so tactful. With his hands, and the blood-stone ring, spread on his knee-caps.

That night Anthea Scudamore cleaned her teeth with energetic gaiety. She was glad she didn't go in for make-up, not enough to notice; she had nothing to hide.

Were her parents hiding something, though?

"He's your *friend*," Mummy was saying.

"The old coot! Can't think what I ever saw in him."

"But a successful man. Of some distinction."

Mummy at least valued distinction.

"Flattered a poor Brisbane clot."

"And so considerate. Very few men of Mr Mortlock's age would take trouble with a young girl."

Anthea could not resist pausing in the passage.

"Brenda was quite a bit younger than old Hess. Brenda walked out on him because. . . ."

"I understand she behaved very badly." Mrs Scudamore repeated a lesson learnt.

Anthea realized she was listening in, and went immediately to her room.

[x]

She would remember the days following as days of dry summer heat in which Hessell Mortlock drove her along undistinguished streets expressing an interest, however, in their city and allowing her to take the wheel in particular the day they wound up to the Summit a slightly delirious breeze streaming out behind them like a scarf or music in a dated film.

When they were parked in front of what people went to see, Mr Mortlock laid his arm along the back of the seat, and confessed: "I'm never all that interested in a view. It's the company that goes with it."

He was so gallant, making it clear he accepted her as his equal in sympathy and understanding.

"My wife Brenda," he said "—you know I have been married,

Anthea—Brenda was incapable of extracting the little pleasures out of daily life. That is what is important," he said, "in life."

It made her feel so serious. She understood the predicament he must have been in—with Brenda who walked out.

Before Mr Mortlock started back east he came in on a hot morning bringing Anthea Scudamore the largest bunch of crimson roses. They were quite an armful.

"Oh!" she cried, receiving them, regardless of the thorns.

She stood holding them.

"Well," he said, "I can never resist buying roses."

And went upstairs.

Anthea began to arrange her roses, which were of the overpowering kind.

"Aren't they fabulous, Mrs Meadling?"

It was a Thursday.

"I'll say!" Mrs Meadling said. "The Queen of Flowers."

She was turning out the living-room for Mummy—only Mrs Meadling would refer to it as *lounge*.

"Yairs. Roses," Mrs Meadling said. "There's a glut of 'em this year. They can't *give* 'em away down at the stalls."

"It's not a question of money," Anthea Scudamore pointed out.

"It plays its part," Mrs Meadling said.

Anthea went on arranging roses. Even after she had carried them into the living-room, she could not resist one more effort to achieve the perfect cumulus of crimson. She liked to look up and catch sight of herself in the glass. She remembered a photo she had seen, of a film star, her bust brushing a bowlful of enormous roses.

All that morning Hessell Mortlock was packing, because, as he said, he was a methodical packer. Almost forgot his after-shave, which Mrs Meadling brought from the bathroom. All his luggage of the highest quality. Genuine pigskin, Mrs Meadling reported.

Mr Mortlock came down finally to where Anthea Scudamore was sitting against her arranged roses. To some extent they had infused her greenish, girlish skin. He began to tell her about his sun-room at Sarsaparilla, and the view from it which was still unspoiled although development had set in.

He said: "I let the paddock to a sort of horse-coper. Because what's the point of its lying idle?"

She agreed.

Then he took her hand, and she was not so surprised at his action as she was at the object of her own hand, with its long, passive, uncoloured, but polished nails.

It was one of the serious moments in life, which the scent of roses attempted to intoxicate.

After lunch Hessell Mortlock started back on the long drive in the bottle-green Riley, and Daddy went out at once, and they forgot they had stopped seeing him.

"Well!" Mrs Scudamore let out her breath.

She was glad to be able to put her feet up, only figuratively, that is.

"I think I ought to tell you some news," Anthea began, quietly, though soon. "Mr Mortlock asked me to marry him."

"That is certainly news!" said her mother, arranging her pink chiffon sling. "And what did you answer?"

"I said I'd accept," said Anthea.

"Oh, darling!" cried Mrs Scudamore.

And at once they were together. They had never been closer. The mother's scent, far subtler than anything out of a bottle, arose from ritual and several layers of conviction. It was what the daughter had always known, and although she loved, she did also, momentarily, envy this scent of permanence, which made of her mother a reality, a force.

"I hope I am not making a mistake!" the girl almost cried in her stifled position. "But I think I can do the best by him. I do respect him! I do love him!"

"He is a distinguished man," Mrs Scudamore said. "Yes, I am glad, Anthea," she added more thoughtfully. "So many people lavish money—and love—on their children, only to have it thrown back in their faces."

Anthea recovered herself from her mother's embrace, and blew her nose, which had grown soggy.

"I don't like what is nasty," she admitted.

Her mother patted her hand.

"I expect we shall soon hear from Mr Mortlock himself," she said. "He is the kind of man who respects formalities. Then we can go ahead with arrangements for the wedding."

[XI]

Mrs Scudamore arranged for Mr Mortlock to return soon, to a ceremony which, without being ostentatious, was much talked about in nicer circles. Mrs Scudamore was lucky enough to have got Philippa Canning and Charmian Reid for bridesmaids in spite of the fact that neither of them was a close friend of Anthea's. Lady Reid, in addition, gave a Doulton tea service.

Mr Mortlock stepped from the plane on arrival looking, not exactly years younger—so alert, Mrs Scudamore put it; one saw how he could not help being a success in business. The face of the man she had begun not to know made Anthea suddenly shy. But he was all kindness, all attention, offering his arm on the way to the car.

"The little lady isn't in need of support," Mr Mortlock joked, "but an arm is always cosier."

By coincidence, on arrival at the house, the bridegroom's present was waiting—he had sent it by rail because of the weight—a real crocodile dressing-case with silver fittings. She kissed his cheek, so closely shaven he must have seen to it on the plane and finished it off with something which smelled of camphor. The texture of the skin was closer than she had expected from the look. Anthea Scudamore drew in her breath for the situation which had taken hold of her with inevitability. She might have found confidence by fiddling with her engagement ring, but was not wearing it yet—one which had belonged to Hessell's mother, it was being reset in more up-to-date style.

As it turned out, the jeweller let them down, and she found herself with her wedding ring on before she could show off her diamonds. Apart from the unfortunate business of Hessell's mother's engagement ring, everything went so smoothly, expertly, needless to say, tastefully. The bridegroom wore morning dress, and a perfect gardenia, in the manner one would have expected of him. Anthea Mortlock looked sideways to see whether her friends Val Tulloch and Mollie Aspinall appreciated.

"It *would* be *grandiflora*," Mollie whispered to Val.

Just then Gil Tulloch came up and said: "Who was right? If Anthea doesn't know where she's going!"

"I hope she does, poor girl," replied his wife, "otherwise I shall have to feel sorry for her."

On top of everything else it was something of a triumph for Mrs Scudamore to have got the Tullochs inside her house. Her colour was higher today, not altogether from triumph, for Dad refused to make a speech.

"I bloody won't!" Bill Scudamore said.

"People will hear you," his wife reminded him from behind her teeth.

It was fortunate for Mrs Scudamore that her husband was a fairly silent drunk. Thanks to his taciturnity, his wry character, and his sleight of hand, only she knew when he was.

It would have been more provoking on the present occasion if Hessell Mortlock had not behaved with such urbanity. He cocked his leg at several ladies, with the result that all but the most cynical stopped trying to calculate his age. It was more or less agreed that he was *rather fun*.

When suddenly the bridegroom looked at his wrist-watch, and said: "Anthea, we'll be hard put to it! Unless you change your togs quicker than most."

For he had decided to return east with his bride that same evening; business matters demanded it.

Anthea was not so much unfeeling as relieved to escape those of her incapacities which tended to follow her around in their house thrown open to the public.

At the airport her teeth almost collided with her mother's.

"Good-bye, my baby!" Mrs Scudamore blubbed through her lipstick.

But it was Dad who looked awful—silent, yellow, down at one shoulder, in his hired clothes. Anthea promised herself that one day she would give some thought to her father, to discover what it was they had in common. But for the moment there was too much else to explore. And then they were strapped into their seats. She lay back happily enjoying the lingering smell of weddings. And looked at her—husband. It was a relief to feel it was not imperative any more to think of something to say.

[XII]

As he had left the Riley at the airport they were able to drive out to Sarsaparilla in comfort, though comfort did not protect her from foreboding as other people's suburbs filtered through the darkness.

"It is late, of course, but perhaps your sister will have got something ready for us to eat," she ventured.

Hessell was having trouble with his gears.

"You can never tell with Grace," he answered.

So she tried instead to talk about their house, making a certainty of what she had not seen.

"That second spare room, which probably we shall never use, might be converted into a kind of work-room," she suggested.

"What would we do with all that stuff—all that furniture?" he asked.

Perhaps it was the late hour which seemed to have made him grumpy.

The house was at least a solid, if dark reality, which they approached, for some mechanical reason by little jerks, down a formidable gravel drive. She tried to identify the shapes of shrubs, to show her intention of belonging.

"Aren't those photinias?" she asked, with such a degree of pleasure nobody would have guessed at her allergy.

But he was not altogether pleased.

"The garden isn't what it ought, or used to be," he said. "Used to pay a fellow to come in a day or two in the week. It wasn't worth it, though. Doing me such an honour, at such a price."

"They are like that," she murmured as though she knew.

Whereas all she knew, in fact, was that her husband's house was looming awfully in the darkness. It would be better perhaps when they got inside, which they did in some awkwardness, lugging luggage, and bumping into formal obstructions, fom which, in one instance, she heard an outraged tinkling. She feared she must have put her elbow through one of the panes of one of those cabinets which serve as a repository for useless glass.

Finally Hessell Mortlock found the switch, and they were standing amongst furniture.

"Grace must have gone out," he mumbled. "It's late," he kept on saying, but more for himself in the deserted house. "It's late."

While he stamped through the rooms, as though it had been winter, switching on lights, and looking for some spirit-deputy of his sister's, which his companion already felt he needn't bother to do, she strayed hesitantly, amongst all that brooding furniture. And the roses. The neglected roses. For somebody had filled the rooms with silver vases and cut-glass bowls of roses. There they were, the brown roses, in some cases almost turned to metal, to bronze. The petals of the dead roses creaked as she passed.

And he came out of a room, his face quite red and blank, saying, again for himself: "Grace has gone. Her wardrobe's empty."

"Perhaps she's been called away. Perhaps she's left a note in the kitchen."

But as she went past him, in a fit of possessive curiosity, into what had been her sister-in-law's room, she knew that Miss Mortlock had not had, and would not have any intention of writing. In one of the drawers which he had pulled out she observed a reel of dental floss, and the corpse of a blow-fly, so very frail.

Then Mrs Mortlock began to affect cheerfulness. After all, vows had been made. She began to elbow her way about.

"At least we've got to eat," she said. "At least she must have left something to start us on."

She went out, thumping the carpets in her resolution, her size accentuated by foreign surroundings, the petals of entombed roses falling, as she passed in the probable direction of the kitchen. Although he knew, he did not direct, but followed, as though the shock had been too much for him.

Mrs Mortlock rooted round in the way she had seen her mother do. She tossed together an omelette, which, in her eagerness, she burned, and opened a tin of spaghetti, which, she soon realized, she had forgotten to warm. But Mr Mortlock sat and, to her surprise, accepted whatever nourishment she had to offer.

"I'll tell you a trick we learned," he said, manoeuvring his toast past his denture. "We buy a whole side of mutton and put it in the fridge. That way you don't have to bother, just eat your way through the mutton, and it's a little economy into the bargain. I don't begrudge money. But some of these butchers charge fillet prices regardless of the cut."

"Some of them are incredible," she agreed.

Already she saw her fridge filled with the frozen-rose tints, the bluish tendons of special-offer mutton. Well, one had to protect oneself.

In between their thoughts they listened to each other's toast. At least the butter was easy, not to say economical, to spread, because Miss Mortlock had left it on the dresser, where it had turned soft and warm.

The bride loved her house, her husband. She would have liked in some way to express her love as she unpacked her tooth-paste and laid out her pale-blue nylon. She said: "I am going to like it here."

Hessell Mortlock was less impressive in his underclothes, with the red line dividing his neck from his shoulders. But he was a man, she reminded herself, of station, of an age to respect.

The Mortlocks lay beside each other in the Beard Watson bed.

He said, after putting his hand over hers, as though remembering she was a young girl: "We ought to get a good night's sleep. It's late. Then we'll wake fresher tomorrow."

It was very reasonable.

So she shuddered deeper into the unaired sheets, into an unexpected roughness, and recalled how she had escaped, by that same grace of reason, the brutality of sand.

Mrs Mortlock cried very briefly and furtively for the happiness she was experiencing. As she fell asleep she was holding in her arms a world in abstraction. Or slack gas-balloon. And soon the gulls were lashing at the metal petals of Egyptian roses. While she was sunk in safety. The creaking of roses, their knife-edged wings, grew silenter for distance.

[XIII]

It took Mrs Mortlock some time to realize she was Mrs Mortlock. To realize and forget about it. Which is when marriage becomes marriage. It took her some time because of the furniture which had belonged to someone else.

"It's Brenda's taste—mostly," Hessell explained. "But what can you do with a lot of stuff? When you've paid for it."

She would be the last person to react unreasonably. She would get to know Brenda's stuff. Which was hers now.

"What has become of Brenda?" she asked, to begin with.

"I wouldn't know," he said. "Only that she cashes her cheque."

"But you must know. Or somebody. Your accountant, or solicitor."

"I believe she lives at Denistone," he said, wiping some marmalade off the wind-jacket he wore when he didn't go to business.

Because Hessell Mortlock was semi-retired. That is, he had a manager he didn't altogether trust, and would go down to the works to try to catch the manager out. Hessell liked best to work amongst his shrubs, and to come in to a light lunch which his wife had prepared. After a certain age, a man can't be too careful about his heart.

In the beginning, as she looked after what the estate agents would have called *this well-appointed residence,* Mrs Mortlock remained Anthea Scudamore, opening drawers and peeping inside. Or depositing herself in a chair to receive other people's secrets. Only in this instance, the secrets were too carefully kept. Or did not exist. And whereas in the past she had brought into other people's houses a whole secret life, a mystery of girlhood, in this one she failed to conjure, perhaps because she was a married woman, and officially the house had become her own.

At first she longed for the company of her mother, hoping the latter might know how to fill an emptiness. But Mrs Scudamore wrote:

. . . perhaps when it is spring, Anthea dear, perhaps when you have settled down. I do not feel it is altogether right for a mother to intrude shall we say immediately on a

—she had crossed out *young* and written: *married couple.*

I am sure, dear, on thinking it over, you will agree with me that this is a reasonable attitude—to say nothing of all the little things you will have to do to put your house in order—I must confess I do rather itch to have a peep at his first wife's furniture—perhaps it is frightful! Do you think about your mother, darling? I cannot help feeling you have changed towards me since Hessell Mortlock carried you off. I suppose it is natural for a girl to alter. We are experiencing such a torrential autumn. Oh dear, the gales! The thought of trees falling on those electric wires—and killing people in a blue flash! Your father is well, but has developed the habit of not answering. I am suffering from my neuralgia, and have a cold. . . .

Mrs Mortlock was not exactly put out by her mother's scruples. She had begun to feel guiltily irritated at being treated like a child, still she would have enjoyed the luxury of playing at childhood in her mother's presence. But her mother did not come.

I have my husband, Mrs Mortlock consoled herself.

She made him a sponge cake, and watched him fill his cheeks with it, munching and munching. Some of the crumbs fell down his plaid wind-jacket, and he looked down, to see, without his glasses, brushing the crumbs frowningly off. The wind-jacket, or the woollens he wore under it, made him bulge more than she had noticed.

She adores her husband, she could imagine people saying.

She did adore him, too. They were early-to-bed, of course, and sometimes then, they would hold each other most touchingly. Mrs Mortlock almost cried for the tenderness she could have given to the world. As she held her husband in her opulent arms, she could feel his stomach, stirring, rumbling, against her, but distant. There were times when her arms could not eliminate the distant sadness which possessed her. Lying, for instance, listening to the soft snoring which issued out of his slack mouth. For he would no longer have the protection of his teeth.

Mrs Scudamore wrote:

I have some news. You remember that young man you met on the
Island—that Doctor Flegg? Well, he is married. She is not from
here, and, I am told, won some kind of competition—of no importance—purely local. I understand she is—or was, that is—Miss
Toowoomba. Her name was Cherie Smith. Oh, my darling, I am
so relieved to think you are married to such a substantial man. . . .

If her mother had been at hand Mrs Mortlock might have hinted
at indelicacy. Certainly she would have protested that the information did not interest her. To discover that her mother was not
always right had come as a shock. Like the shock of distance. At
first, in the sadness of separation, she had kept her mother's letters
in a bundle, but now she began to tear them up.

She had her husband.

On Sunday he would call out: "If you don't put the finishing
touches, we'll miss the sermon."

She would go outside to the car, and he would be shouting,
laughing. On Sundays he was particularly jolly. In one of his
moulded suits. In the shirt she had laundered so beautifully for him.
The women you pay to iron, he used to say, *don't take pride in what
they are doing.* Funnily enough she found she enjoyed ironing. To
dress her husband in those slightly starched, made-to-order collars.

She would go out to him and know that he was pleased. She
moved well, in that large hat, and of all the things she had brought
with her, the grey frock, drawn frothily across her somewhat full
bosom, her arms showing in white flashes through the slashes in
the long filmy sleeves.

The service would have started by the time they arrived. She
enjoyed their progress down the aisle, the warden whose deferential
face she was beginning to recognize, the loud accents of those who
informed one another: "There's Mortlocks!" If they were late their
clothes showed they could afford to be. She would kneel down,
however, so meekly, it was in itself an act of worship. While the old
boy would stick his bottom on the edge of the seat, and shade his
eyes for a second or two. You couldn't expect old men to go all the
way; they mightn't get up again.

Once Mrs Mortlock, from behind her Gothic hands, was horrified to receive a vision of the bodies of Barry Flegg and Cherie Smith lashed together by ropes of hair. Lashed and lashing. She was so horrified with herself, she felt faint. She would have gone out if it had not been for her husband blocking the way from the pew. Nobody noticed that Mrs Mortlock was perspiring. All she could do was bow her head and suffer the blasphemy which had been thrust upon her. Endure it to the last convulsive shudder.

"Are you all right?" he asked at last, noticing something, leaning towards his perhaps valuable possession.

"Yes." She smiled.

She was calm again by the time they left the church, walking with the fine carriage of her assured young-womanhood, while he followed, easing his bones. *You can see she's a lady,* voices were heard. Some of the women, of his own age, smiled at Mr Mortlock without composing their mouths at all, because they had known him for years, and been disappointed, and got over it.

Hessell Mortlock was the kind of man who couldn't resist making a fool of himself, the elderly women had decided long ago, so they invited him and his young wife to eat their chicken à la king and sherry trifle, without any rancour, while smiling at her in a certain fashion, asking her to have another helping when conversation failed—she was so large, too.

"I couldn't! It was lovely—lovely," the amiable Mrs Mortlock would reply sighing. "You must put something special in it, that we ordinary mortals know nothing about."

Then Hessell Mortlock would approach, in his dark, best suit, and the monogrammed cuff-links, hooking his arm to his wife's white arm, examining her, asking: "She's doing well, isn't she? Am I looking after her?"

Some of the women experienced a twinge on glimpsing the youthful situation which existed between the Mortlocks.

[XIV]

It was almost five years before Mrs Scudamore flew over to visit her daughter. One thing and another had intervened. There was Mummy's Operation, for one, and then Dad spent a few months in

That Home. During their separation Mrs Mortlock genuinely grieved for her ailing parents, and would have liked to go to them. She hardly dared tell herself the reason she didn't.

"I'm sure you won't find her a nuisance," she told her husband as the visit became imminent. "I'll drive her about and show her the different gardens. That is, when you're not using the car."

"Why should I find her a nuisance?" Hessell Mortlock asked.

There were moments when he took refuge in a pinker transparency of skin, in a completely shadowless blue stare, which made him less even than a boy. He was so assured in his innocence.

Mrs Scudamore came, and was different from what her daughter remembered. The enamel had cracked. She seemed to have shrunk, was older, naturally, and colder; she was always chafing her hands and talking of slipping a cardigan on. Upon seeing each other the two women proceeded to embrace, grappled almost, making little noises which a third person might have had difficulty in interpreting, but which they themselves understood perfectly. The daughter seemed to tower now above her shrivelled mother, to whom she longed to give something from her own excess.

Just then Hessell Mortlock came in.

"I'm glad to see you haven't altered, Betsy," he said, gallant as always.

"Oh! I?" Mrs Scudamore laughed it off. "But I am glad to see *you,* both of you, looking so well and *happy.*"

Because she had never forgotten that *happiness* must be her philosophy of life.

"You ought to be happy, too, in this charming house, full of such lovely things."

She was soon walking through the rooms, aiming little sideways glances at the "things."

"What a priceless escritoire!" she exclaimed. "It is genuine, isn't it? Your wife must have had very good taste."

"Oh, Brenda!" Mr Mortlock said. "That was before her time."

He went away, and his wife was not sure, but felt he might be irritated by her mother's exploration of the house.

One day Mr Mortlock came to his wife and said: "There's something I wish you'd tell her, Anthea."

"What is it?" she asked gently.

"I wish she wouldn't close the lid of the lavatory bowl. Not after the thing's been in use."

"It seems to me a harmless habit," Mrs Mortlock suggested.

But he wrinkled up his face, and she couldn't help seeing an old resentful baby, puzzled by some logic of the world.

"Bottles up the smell!" he persisted, and his resentful face was smelling it.

Although Mrs Mortlock found the matter most distasteful, she mentioned to her mother: "Mummy darling, after you've used the lavatory, would you mind please not closing the lid?"

Mrs Scudamore was offended, not to say disgusted.

"In the first place he needs a new seat. The hinges hardly serve their purpose. But quite apart from that, Anthea, you know we've always kept the lid closed!"

It was obvious that she alone might defend refined custom from vulgar assault.

"Otherwise the room becomes—well, without wanting to be crude—frankly—smelly."

"I would rather you didn't," Mrs Mortlock begged.

Mrs Scudamore did not answer, but screwed herself up inside her twin-set.

Mrs Scudamore continued to close the lid and Mr Mortlock to open it. Their principles made it difficult for them to face each other any more. And Mrs Mortlock realized her hair was falling out; she discovered handfuls of it in her comb.

By this time she found it necessary to devise little jobs and pastimes for her mother. She would produce some peas, and a colander, and say: "There, Mummy, it will help me a lot if you shell the peas."

Once Mrs Scudamore shed some tears which fell into the colander.

"I am not complaining, Anthea. I am not *un*happy. But some of us have our crosses to bear."

"Is it my father?" Mrs Mortlock asked, stiffening.

"I am not saying," Mrs Scudamore said.

Then it was Mrs Mortlock's turn to feel unhappy. Spasmodically she felt deeply so. Now it was for that dark man her father. If she had only been able to touch him, they might perhaps have pooled their secrets and discovered the reason for human confusion. But as that wasn't possible, she went outside, into the garden.

Thinking and frowning, she walked, and presently called absently: "Daddy, where are you? There are several things I want to ask."

"What's that?" answered Hessell Mortlock, who had been in hiding amongst his shrubs.

His expression of suspicion and astonishment increased her own feeling of shame.

"Oh!" she said, laughing, blushing—she had never called him that before, and rarely by any name. "I wasn't thinking!"

"What is it you want to ask?" he demanded in ever greater suspicion.

He was afraid it might be about the lid of the lavatory bowl.

"I forget," she said, and went away.

Her slip of the tongue, however, shocked her out of her unhappiness, and soon she was giving further orders to her mother.

"If you're going to change your frock, darling, the roast will be ready in a quarter of an hour."

Through the bars of the kitchen window she called to her husband: "Aren't you going to wash-and-brush-up, dear? You know how you hate it when the mutton turns dry."

Mrs Mortlock's brand of reasonableness had probably come from long experience in dealing with children. But there were times, too, when she let herself go and entered into the fun of things. Then she would become a large, lolloping girl teasing and joking with her friend, who also, only incidentally, happened to be her mother.

On one occasion, for instance, they were fossicking through a cupboardful of junk which provoked a joint hilarity.

"What's this? Who is it?" Mrs Scudamore asked.

"I haven't the vaguest!" Mrs Mortlock replied, and giggled. "Unless it's Brenda."

They both grew giggly over the old photograph.

"What sights we looked in those days!" Mrs Scudamore

protested. "Well I never! Look at that hair—the shingle! The shaven neck!"

"I adore the kiss-curl!"

They both shrieked.

"And the mmm—" Mrs Scudamore roared, and could not get it out except in the end, in a tremendous rush "did you ever" she screamed "see such a—MOUTH!"

Their eyes were staring, bursting out of the fires of mirth as they examined the passive photograph, in which the victim had attempted her timid version of the cupid's bow.

When suddenly the two friends realized it was time they returned to their senses.

"Oh, dear!"

Mrs Mortlock wiped her eyes.

Mrs Scudamore blew her nose.

Mrs Mortlock took the limp photograph, by instinct rather than with purpose, and shut it up in the writing-desk her mother had so much admired. She intended perhaps to do something with it—but what?—later on. Perhaps after Mummy had gone.

Mrs Scudamore, who was booked to return home that Thursday, grew sad accordingly. She said: "You have everything, Anthea. I only hope you are happy. I wonder whether there is anything. Whether I could advise you. I am your mother."

"Oh, yes, I am happy," Mrs Mortlock said, and sighed. "There is perhaps a certain matter."

But there she hesitated because it would have embarrassed her to tell.

Mrs Scudamore thought better not press; it might be something physical.

And soon she had flown off.

[xv]

Mrs Mortlock would have felt relieved to find herself once more alone with her husband in the house she had grown used to, if her mother had not roused to rankling point what might otherwise have lain a dormant grudge.

In the circumstances she began to speak to her husband, practically without deciding, at breakfast, over some of the chops from the special-offer side of mutton it was their habit to buy.

"There's one thing I've been meaning to mention," the young woman said. "Although there were the clothes I brought with me when I came here—quite a wardrobe—when we were married—it is now five years." She began to feel foolish. "Certainly there were the one or two dresses I ran up myself, in between. But nothing to speak of."

She was dwindling wretchedly. And he continued to masticate the cooling chop, the pleats round his mouth opening and closing.

"Well?" Hessell Mortlock asked.

"Well," she said, "over and above the money you give me for housekeeping I have hardly a bus fare in my bag. I couldn't go anywhere even if I wanted to. Or take anyone to lunch."

Although he sat straight and square, very impressive for his age, she could sense that inwardly he was curving.

"If you don't allow me something to dress on, soon you will see me in rags," she told him.

He put down his knife and fork.

"Nothing lasts for ever," she added, almost in anger.

Hessell Mortlock cleared his throat and went outside.

That evening, however, as she was putting the dishes away, he came to her without speaking, and slipped into her hand a five-pound note, new, and folded small. When he had done it he went again, steadying himself on the kitchen table. Seeing how he stooped, and his blotchy hand with its several patches of New Skin taut against the table, the anger which was rising in her became pity for this old man she had promised to cherish. While the dusk flowed down amongst the well-established evergreens, she was softly crying, she realized, for them both.

But at least she would breed a virtue with him, she decided, fiercely, remembering certain of her own mother's attitudes. So she bought some tins of paint. She set to work to paint the kitchen, and particularly the ceiling where the flies had spotted, which would prove her severest test. She stood on a table, and the paint fell into her hair and eyes.

Hessell Mortlock had to applaud his wife's initiative and industry.

"You're certainly an energetic young woman, Anthea." He stood by, admiring as he looked. "You've got taste," he said; it cost him nothing.

"Do you think I might set up in business?" she asked, fiercely plying the roller and bitterly enjoying the dribble of paint.

He laughed softly, not to disturb.

"That might be carrying it a bit too far."

[XVI]

Mrs Scudamore wrote less than before.

There is so little happens nowadays (*she found*). So many people have gone away. It is sad to live in a town one no longer knows. Oh one thing, Anthea, you will be interested to hear. Doctor Flegg —you remember—who has been doing something nuclear, was given a fellowship by the Americans. He, too, will be going away, with his wife who won the competition. To Tennessee—is it? They have two young children, I am told—or perhaps three . . .

Mrs Mortlock was unable to share her mother's interest in strangers. Only the image of that strange island in which, it seemed, almost the whole of her youth had been spent, disturbed her by returning through the mists of sleep, with a crying of gulls, and that milky sea, sucking at and troubling her ample breasts.

At least it was always morning after sleep, and as soon as she woke she would force herself out of the bed in which she might have been tempted to remain. She flung herself at activities now, whether the house-painting, or merely driving to the Centre to buy the vegetables, or, when the old one was finished, the next side of special-offer mutton. The ladies of the Mortlocks' acquaintance— they never developed into anything else—smiled at one another and remarked: "So economical, she has his interests at heart." It was only the purely malicious who added: "He'll see she doesn't get the opportunity for anything else."

She was devoted to her husband, to her home, and on a second occasion, but never again, surreptitiously, with exquisitely pained old movements, he slipped her a fiver. They did not discuss money after that.

As for Hessell Mortlock he was pleased enough to have supplied her needs, after he had recovered from the shock caused by direct approach and the general indiscretion of the situation. Women never understood the significance of money. Women he had known —mind you, he was not in any way accusing Anthea—but he had known other women hack into capital as though it were only a material matter, as though they were not also involving themselves morally by such an act.

Hessell Mortlock went less than before to the factory to catch out the manager who was running it. Not that he would have derived less pleasure from the discovery of dishonesty—it was simply that the physical strength had begun to trickle out of him. Nothing alarming, or noticeable, yet. He hoped. He could still get himself up in his suits, and present to the world a fine figure of a man, and cock his leg at the ladies as he stood with a plateful of chicken à la king. At such times his wife would grow proud again of her distinguished, elderly husband. His thinning, his silvery hair filled her with love and pathos.

For Mrs Mortlock had learnt the way of happiness which her mother had practised before her. She *ordered* her life—dared it perhaps, in any case kept a firm hand on any of the loose bits which might fly out and hit her in the eye. She was fortunate indeed in having her health, her strength, to buoy her up. Even in the old, patched, paint-spattered slacks she wore about her husband's hoovered house and gardenful of polished shrubs, she was not without a physical magnificence. On winter afternoons she became almost conscious of it herself as she bore down the grassy slope to give her husband a message, or assure herself that all was well. How the blood rushed through her firm flesh, daunting the atmosphere; the warmed air returned to rub against her like a swath of furs she didn't own.

"You aren't overdoing it, darling?" She would peer, and call formally, frowning with anxiety.

For he had taken to wheeling manure up the hill, in a barrow, from the paddock the horse-coper rented.

"Can't let all this good stuff go to waste," he said, "when the shrubs are crying out to be fed."

"But you might overdo it. Your heart," she protested.

He grunted, still pushing. Hessell Mortlock liked to be reminded of what he should not do. It was when he wasn't that he grew surly.

"I'm not a crock. And I'm not an idiot," he replied, as he struggled with the arms of the barrow, his feet slipping on the fat turf.

She grew anxious finally, and cast about for a plan. Then one afternoon she hit on it, and came down the slope carrying a coil of stout cord she remembered noticing in the shed.

"Now we shall see," she said, laughing.

"See what?" He had stopped pushing to satisfy his curiosity, as well as to pause for breath.

She did not answer, but uncoiled the cord and attached it by its two ends to the barrow. Then she stepped inside the loop, wound it once round her body, plaited her arms with the tautened cord, and announced to her husband: "You will push. And I shall pull."

Already she had begun, and as he caught on, he struggled forward on the arms of the barrow. Pushing.

"That's something like a bright idea!" He snorted, and laughed.

Sometimes he would look up, at his wife's back arched against the hill. Or at her shoulders, momentarily straightening themselves, throwing off the weight of labour.

Then he would chortle: "Gee up, Neddy!" this aged schoolboy enjoying the game.

And she would bend and exert herself again.

With Mrs Mortlock it was all seriousness, part of the necessary ritual she must evolve by inspiration to help her bear her chosen existence. So she bent and heaved. Her ribs strained. Her neck grew ugly. Sharp daggers of pain stabbed at times into her back. As she pulled, and bit her lips. To suffer thus enduringly was to ensure her continued happiness.

And afterwards they would sit and eat buttered toast with swollen fingers. Stuffing it into their mouths. Breathing too heavily.

"Who wouldn't remain independent," Hessell Mortlock once remarked, "of all, bludging, hired labour!"

That afternoon the bell sounded, and it was the boy from the post office. He smiled at Mrs Mortlock in the manner of those who know, and handed her the telegram.

When she returned into the darkened sun-room she said simply: "It is Dad. He has died."

Hessell Mortlock sat there in the almost darkness, his neck thickening from the very personal news which had been forced on him with so little thought or warning. It wasn't as if he had entertained any affection for his father-in-law, except perhaps briefly, when the latter was a young man. Youth, or more candidly, the theory of it, stimulated Hessell Mortlock.

But his wife, he could just see, had continued standing in the position in which she had been abandoned.

"They never ought to telegraph it," he protested. "You can't *undo* anything by telegraphing. And you can adjust yourself if you hear decently, by letter."

Or let someone else adjust.

But his wife's obscure figure appeared permanently arrested.

Mrs Mortlock would have been unable to do or say anything for anyone, least of all for her father, with whom she had not succeeded, and now would never succeed, in communicating.

The image of her mother, swimming out of darkness and the islands of material possessions amongst which both had hoped to escape, suddenly merged with herself in a common wretchedness.

"I shall have to go," she whimpered, "home."

If it had not been for the dark, her broad shoulders might have looked grotesque.

"What am *I* going to do?" he complained, but succeeded in transposing his querulousness into a lower key. "I mean, when a woman accepts a husband, it isn't to down tools and fly off half across Australia the minute something unpleasant happens."

But I am not flying *away* from unpleasantness, she almost answered, only at the final instant her tongue resisted what might, after all, be true.

She remained for a little, crying softly, crouched in a wicker chair, until she remembered the sister-in-law she still hadn't met.

"Perhaps your sister would come to look after you while I'm away."

"Grace isn't good for an emergency. Not again. Anyway, that's how she put it last time I saw her."

Although Mrs Mortlock had stopped crying there was hardly silence in the obliterated sun-room; it was full of the protests of wicker, and the old man's breathing.

"And how," he continued truculently, "how am I to know you'll come back to me?"

She could not bring herself to answer that.

Seeing that he had subdued her, he tapped her on the knee, and proposed with a fatherly thoughtfulness: "I'm going to put the jug on. And see about getting us a meal. We're the ones who have to go on living."

It was never good policy not to make the peace.

And Mrs Mortlock continued to do the things which were expected. Her mother wrote at last in detail. Dad, to humiliate her as never before, had taken his life one wet evening in the yard of the Black Bull. If the daughter's feelings remained unexpressed, it was perhaps because, in her chilled condition, she dared not submit herself to the unpredictable terrors of grief. She was now at all times numb, at moments pinched and snuffly. Otherwise silent. And in that silence, little tremors of suffering seemed to reach out to her, from amongst the furniture, from far past occasions.

In the course of it all she went one day to the writing-desk and deliberately found the photograph of Brenda. The pearl ear-rings, the kiss-curl and unsteady cupid's bow treated the face, almost archaic, to a brutality which no longer seemed hilarious.

It was about the time of afternoon her husband left off forking round his perfectly-tended shrubs the manure gathered from the horse-coper's paddock.

"Poor Brenda," she could not avoid mentioning, "her eyes have something sad in them."

"Who?" he asked.

"Brenda," she said. "Your wife."

Holding out the warped photograph.

He was an honest man by some standards, but perhaps it wasn't that, perhaps he was caught in one of those situations where the truth takes over.

"That isn't Brenda," he said. "That's Alice."

"Who is Alice?" she asked.

"Alice was my wife. My first wife."

The present Mrs Mortlock was almost overcome by the sadness of it.

"Did she die?" her swollen tongue was forced to inquire.

"No," he said without bothering any more. "She left me."

After that they had their tea.

It began on a clear day, August 27—why Anthea Mortlock noticed she did not know, only that she must leave her husband, and the date was blazing at her from the calendar.

It could have been a conspiracy in that house of defection, which belonged incidentally to Hessell Mortlock. His wife went to her handbag and found she could muster seventeen-and-sixpence. Then she thought of using cunning. By skimping on the housekeeping, and he always commended her for her economy, she could hope to increase the sum by slow degrees. But she grew impatient. And on the last day of the month, went and looked in his handkerchief drawer, and took the necessary from his wallet.

The voice on the telephone as she booked the air ticket to her home city was so warm and masculine she was almost persuaded she had committed a willing adultery.

After that it was a simple matter of packing the little she cared to take with her. She was surprised to find she was unperturbed on meeting the inquiries of the old man she had married. But of course she had already left him.

"Where are you going?" his shocked voice was asking.

"I am going," she said, "just going."

She went on arranging her hair in the reproduction mirror in the hall, and tried not to see his face, what it had become.

"I took fifteen pounds eight-and-sixpence out of your drawer," she said. "But have not stolen it."

"What else," he had begun.

"I'll pay it back."

"Do you know what you're doing, Anthea?"

Oh, too well! She could have screamed it at this stage.

"Because I don't think you do," he was saying as well as a shivering and a breathlessness allowed him. "I'll see Simpson on Monday. You won't get a penny, you know. Not a penny. For such behaviour. They all think they can behave."

Then, caught in the intricacies of what was by now pure behaviour, for the taxi had arrived, she was looking back at him through his door. Her half-filled suitcase dangled from her hand.

"I shall pay it back," she kept on uttering. "I shall pay it back. The money. If I am in your debt in any other way, I am sorry. It wasn't meant dishonestly."

So, turning on what must remain her substitute for the great set speech, she bundled into the taxi, and was brought momentarily to her knees by bashing her forehead on some metalwork.

[XVII]

Mrs Mortlock could not afford a lengthy convalescence from her marriage, on account of the sale of her mother's house, and the settling into a smaller one.

"Do you think anyone will come to see us," Mrs Scudamore speculated, "in such a small house, so out of the way, and on top of Everything Else?"

Because, for decency's sake, daughter's separation from her husband was now referred to as Everything Else.

"What am I going to tell Them?" Mrs Scudamore would repeat.

"Tell them," said Mrs Mortlock with a tired simplicity, "tell them I have separated from my husband."

But the idea of such candour made Mrs Scudamore screw herself up inside her cardigan. She preferred a mystery—which everyone might solve, provided it was not in her hearing.

"My daughter is here on a visit," she said. "Well, she will be staying with me for quite some little time."

Then Mrs Mortlock saw that something practical must be done. She said: "I am arranging to take a refresher course at Mrs Treloar's school. Because I must get a job. It is necessary now. And you will be able to look after yourself, won't you, Mummy?

Provided I see to the shopping—early, or late. You will not be lonely, will you, out here at the end of the road? The view of the mountain is lovely."

Whether lovely or not Mrs Scudamore had reached an age where she was glad to surrender her authority. If she pouted at times she secretly admired the officious motherliness of her child.

"I can't always rely on you, you know, to do what is best for yourself," Mrs Mortlock once heard her own voice.

She enjoyed it, too. Most of all she enjoyed ringing from the city to make sure her mother had started thawing the meat. Almost invariably Mrs Scudamore hadn't.

And in far too short a time Mrs Mortlock had finished the refresher course at the School, and would have to take the position she began to dread looking for.

But before this she revisited the island of her youth.

Val Tulloch explained to her husband: "I ran into poor old Anthea Scudamore—Mortlock, or whatever—looking so terribly downcast, that bastard can only have beaten or left her. Anyway, I'm giving her the key to the house. She can work some of it off on the Island."

"I still think Anthea will get what she wants," Gil Tulloch insisted. "Her voice is the echo of her awful mother's."

"Poor old Anthea!" said Val. "Not that she's all that old. And her mother's not all that awful. They're both really a bit pathetic. I don't believe either knows what she wants."

"They're out to reach a state of impregnable negation," Gil Tulloch stubbornly claimed, "where there are no questions, only answers. No husbands, and no fathers. Bill Scudamore's worst fault was to hint at the unanswerable question, all his life, most unforgivably by his way of leaving it."

Gil did not feel his wife could better such a round statement, nor did she attempt, but went away to supervise the feeding of her many children. She had done what she could for Anthea.

And Mrs Mortlock was all packed to leave for the Island when the letter from Hathaway and Simpson came.

Mr Simpson wrote:

. . . apologies for not communicating with you sooner . . . difficulties in ascertaining your present whereabouts.

Mrs Mortlock arrived presently at Mr Simpson's point:

. . . My client and your husband Mr Hessell Mortlock died on the 7th September following a car accident and a seizure. Already on the 4th he had set out, alone, and driving his own car, to keep an appointment with me, when, apparently as the result of an attack, he collided with a telegraph pole. I proceeded the following day to his home, but Mr Mortlock was unfortunately incapable of conveying the nature of his business. Three days later he was carried off by a second stroke. Perhaps it was all for the best considering the vigour and independence of his mind. Please accept the warmest sympathy of myself and senior partner, Mr K. Y. Hathaway, in your loss. . . .

Mrs Scudamore had been out to pay a call on someone she suspected of not wishing to receive her. When she returned her daughter was in bed.

"What is it, Anthea?" she asked, afraid it might be something she would not want to face.

But when she heard: "There!" she said. "That is retribution! For that horrid man. Whom I found smarmy before he turned mean and rude. I never liked him."

She seated herself by the bed in the room which Mrs Mortlock had expressly darkened.

"But," said Mrs Scudamore, "is that all they told you?"

"Who?"

"The solicitors, silly! Where is the letter?"

"I tore it up."

"Any document of that kind," Mrs Scudamore gasped, "should be kept to produce if necessary."

Here was this daughter suddenly become a child again.

"I don't want to be reminded," the latter said. But added for her mother's information: "Mr Simpson did tell me at the end I am the sole beneficiary."

"Then he did not change it!" Mrs Scudamore cried. "But was on his way to do so. That wicked man! It's as I said. A retribution! Oh dear, Anthea, I'm so glad! For you, I mean."

For two days longer Mrs Mortlock kept to her bed, partly because her legs remained feeble from the shock, partly because she wished to luxuriate in what she felt could be the only possible moral decision. To renounce Hessell Mortlock's beastly money. The money he hadn't intended her to have. To rise above the humiliation their life together had imposed on her. Sometimes, however, Mrs Mortlock wavered miserably before the prospect of her ethical triumph, particularly after a glass of wine. She would burst into tears, and Mrs Scudamore say:

"I can understand, darling, after all you have suffered, that your feelings must be a little mixed. In any case you served him loyally for ten whole years. You deserve repayment."

"I can't accept it!" Mrs Mortlock nobly cried.

"But it is all yours," her mother almost shouted, "the whole quarter of a million—less what the probate people grab."

In the circumstances it was useless to argue. Mrs Mortlock enjoyed her silence. There was also the melancholy image of that old man, stumbling as he pushed a barrow-load of horse manure up the damp and darkening hillside. Or again, the more horrifying one of his same but different face, choking now on words and blood, looking skyward, at the foot of the telegraph pole.

Two days after Mr Simpson's important announcement Mrs Mortlock received a second: Miss Mortlock, his client's sister, proposed to contest the will.

Mrs Mortlock rose from her bed.

"But surely you won't let the wretched creature get away with it?" All considered, Mrs Scudamore might permit herself a vulgarism.

Her daughter went on dressing.

"After all," Mrs Scudamore said.

"I am too tired, Mummy," Mrs Mortlock answered. "I shall go to the Island. It was so kind and thoughtful of Val Tulloch to suggest it. After that, perhaps, I shall feel strong enough to work things out."

She really looked quite ill and tragic.

[XVIII]

Ossie Ryan drove her as before. He had not exactly aged, but dried out. This time as he crouched over the wheel he seemed to take her for granted. He was silenter, as though the narrative of life had slackened in his grasp.

At one stage she asked feebly: "What has become of the baby-farmer?"

"The what?" he asked. "Oh! 'Er."

But he did not answer her question. Only later, he smiled and said: "You remembered, then!"

It was enough really. She was grateful for it.

And for the shabby, rambling house, the ochre of its now conventual walls rubbed and scored by the leaning tea-trees. On letting herself in she sat a while, in her hat and gloves, her knees slewed obliquely, her suitcase standing on the floor beside her. She could simply have lacked further strength, or else she feared the inevitable order to resume some mission she had left unfinished.

Days slipped easily away for Mrs Mortlock. Her island, balanced in its bubble, floated between seasons in an air which was neither hot nor cold. She clumped like an animal through the scrub. Or stalked birdlike over the sand. So deserted was her desert beach that she took off her clothes once, without even looking over her shoulder, and walked into the milky sea. Exquisite skirts of foam clung to her ankles, and began to soothe her thighs. It was so gently perfect in the healing water that she closed her eyes and almost understood which direction was the right one. But it floated out of her grasp, together with the capsules of weed, as though almost is the most.

At least she did not expect complete enlightenment, and rose, content enough to re-enter the solid sculpture of her body. To put on the clothes she found. To notice the remote rocks which hid the wrestling-match of her girlhood. What she had regarded then as ugly, monstrous, frightening, she now saw as merely undesirable, or absurd. And went away along the hard sand, thoughtfully combing out her hair with her fingers, to let it dry.

Absurd. Yes, absurd. That night Mrs Mortlock realized her

condition was easily curable. As conviction set in her mind, she might have found herself walking through the house, throwing open doors to rooms she would not need. She could not remain there; that was as clear as banging doors.

Shortly after, Mrs Mortlock made two telephone calls, the second of them to her mother.

"Yes, darling. It is," she said. "Are you well?" she asked, as though she had been wondering. "Perhaps it is the weather. . . . Livery weather. I have just booked my seat, dear, in tomorrow morning's plane. I shall be with you for lunch. . . . No, darling, a salad will do. Listen, I have decided," she said, "I have decided not to let Miss Mortlock have her way. I don't see why she should keep the money. . . . The *money!*" she shouted across the distance.

Once she had been diffident even of mentioning a word which had such a sound metallic ring.

[XIX]

After that, a very short time after her return from the Island, Mrs Mortlock flew east, and was not seen for how many months people did not bother to count; they were dealing with lives of their own. Mrs Scudamore might have resented her acquaintances' indifference if she had had less to announce.

"It has been decided, and quite rightly, in my daughter's favour," she was able to mention, and murmur in discreeter key: "I would not know how much, but it will leave her, well, comfortably off."

To her daughter she said as they lingered reunited over that first, delicious cup of tea: "I have never known you paint your nails. Do you think, Anthea, such a vivid red is in the best of taste?"

Mrs Mortlock glanced down, at her lovely, dripping nails.

"People," she said, "will learn to accept what they are expected to." Then she looked up, because she had developed a habit of delivering the ping-pong balls of words pat at the opposite wall. "And why should one go on doing what one has always done?"

Mrs Scudamore went, and stooped, to pick up the swath of silver-foxes which had slipped off the arm of an empty chair.

"What will you do, Anthea, now?"

"I expect I shall travel."

"Where, dear?" Mrs Scudamore did not protest.

"Perhaps everywhere. I haven't thought. Provided I travel."

Mrs Scudamore, who might have resented an answer on a smaller scale, was full of admiration for such an expensive decision.

"I think you are very wise," she said.

[xx]

So Mrs Mortlock, it was learnt from the press, began to travel. If the details of her voyage were not recorded, it is because the details are never of importance, not even always to the traveller. Except that Mrs Mortlock stayed in many, and the best, hotels, glanced into the windows of the most exclusive shops, bought expensive objects for which she had no need, often abandoning them afterwards because of their excessive weight. Incidentally, she crossed oceans, climbed mountains, was carried down great rivers, and considered remaining for ever on a Greek island, only the haphazard plumbing put her off. In the course of her travels, naturally, she received several proposals of marriage, and even more indecent propositions, but was always prudent enough to lock her door on retiring.

Then, in Athens, she suddenly grew bored, and it occurred to her to return to her native city, to bask in the glory of achievement.

So it was settled. She was packed. And although she was sick to death of being driven through the dust to make conversation with other tourists on historic sites, she did, to pass the time, by herself, take the dreadful ordinary bus along the coast, that last afternoon, and got down just anywhere to stroll amongst the scrubby pines. In her white, rather heavy dress. Which accentuated her substantial figure, and intensified the impression that here was a statue in motion.

Mrs Mortlock strolled, and the stones were intolerable to her stilted heels. Lightly she touched the trunks of the pines. She frowned slightly to find that some of the white milk had oozed out onto her fingers, and probably the dirty, sticky stuff would refuse to come off.

However, the light washed her, and the sea rose up at her feet, and higher, so that she was forced to sit down on a rock. She was so dazzled by Saronic blue that she did not at first notice the four children. Then—there they were. Playing, or just being. She had never really had cause to study the habits of children, unless the aged ones.

"Arr, go on! Cut it out!" ordered the eldest, an already leggy boy, slapping down his younger sister, who had mixed sea with some of the dust, to make a mud, with which to anoint her round, brown, serious face. "You've mucked yourself up enough!"

The little girl began to cry.

There was something, but something, about the voices. Then Mrs Mortlock realized she was understanding every word. She was understanding the drawn-out, monotonously convinced, yes, the Australian voices. She became so excited.

"Oh," she cried, she almost ran, "where are you from?"

The little girl had stopped crying. All the children looked shocked.

Then an elder girl toyed with one of her plaits, and answered.

"From the States," she said.

But her elder brother, who had intended to have no truck with the strange, wealthy-seeming woman, was compelled to tell the truth.

"That's only because Dad was working there," he said, quite angry. "We're Australians," the boy proclaimed aggressively.

"How interesting that we should all meet like this. Beside the sea," she blurted anxiously, not to say ridiculously, and in spite of the fact that she could tell from the children's faces it would be of minor interest. Embarrassing was perhaps the word.

But Mrs Mortlock was too shaken to be able to organize her remarks. She was obsessed by the boy's eyelids, and the mouth, not yet conscious of an inherited sensuality. She knew now.

"*She* was born in America, wasn't she?" Mrs Mortlock asked, touching the hair of the smaller girl.

"Yes," they said, suspiciously, quivering on stiffened necks.

"Because I had been told, earlier on, there were only three."

The peculiar woman, vague with thought, might have been terrifying for the children if the light had not driven any look of evil out of the bosom of her white dress. As it was, she had strayed out of some other category, of divinities and statues.

"I thought I'd take a walk," she was saying, "but find I have come in the wrong heels."

"You could take your shoes off," said the second of the boys.

"Yes," she mumbled. "I could take them off."

For a moment they all stood staring at the offending pair of shoes, but she did not follow the boy's advice, and they began to walk, shod and barefoot, all in somewhat stilted fashion, though moderately contented.

Until Mrs Mortlock caught sight of the man, rising above a ridge of rocks, to become by degrees the children's father.

"Here!" he called, indolently rather than angrily. "What've you kids been up to? Your mother's started worrying."

It was, naturally, Doctor Flegg. Mrs Mortlock did not even feel flustered since her initial shock on discovering traces of him in his child. In her anonymity she even had power over this unknowing man, his youth's body hardened, scored, and already grizzled, by participation.

He began squinting, shading his eyes, to protect them from the unexpected sight of the strange woman in her blinding dress.

"We met," she explained, "the other side of the point. And strolled a little."

As he came up she could see his tongue beginning to try the feel of words, preparatory to manoeuvring them over the obstacle of his lower lip.

Then Mrs Mortlock took aim.

"It was a great surprise and pleasure for me, Barry Flegg."

As she watched the mystification dissolving in his now unguarded eyes, she continued conscious of her own strength, no longer dependent on anonymity, rather on the image which, she knew from countless hotel looking-glasses, she must present. So she held herself erect, and smiled, out of the lipstick which she could tell was still in pretty good repair.

"Anthea Scudamore!" he said. "Whaddayaknow, eh?" And again in an expiring breath half amusement, half disbelief: "Anthea!"

His diffidence to believe in the incontrovertible reality of herself filled Mrs Mortlock with ironic pleasure. If she had been staying longer she would have cashed a cheque to buy presents for his children. Not so expensive as to spoil the child. But enough to convince this doubting father.

"Oh, just travelling," she explained as they strolled. "But now I'm heading for home. For no particular reason. Just that there comes a time."

"Yep. We're on our way back, too. Because we gotta," said Barry Flegg. "Back to the sticks! It'll be good," he said, and then: "I suppose."

For a moment he paused to settle a children's argument. A little boy and a little girl were threatening to gouge out each other's eyes.

"Well, Anthea," he said, "did you find what you were expecting?"

She hesitated. It was too long since she had been asked such a direct, not to say indiscreet, question. Then she raised her head, and smiled, with that approach to a dimple which she never succeeded in bringing off.

"Oh yes," she said. "I have everything. I am very happy."

They continued walking.

"Are you content?" she asked, because it was her turn.

"No," he said. "Not all that. But I reckon we're not intended to be."

She did not quite giggle for one of those extravagances which polite associations had taught her not to take seriously. At least there was no need to answer.

Over the ridge, in a clump of pines, they came to the minibus in which the Flegg family must have quarrelled across Europe. To one side a tent-contraption had been attached.

"It's the only way," Doctor Flegg explained. "Four kids eat the bottom out of your pocket."

"I ate a thing in Athens," told the elder girl, "and the cream squashed out in all directions. It was a sort of pastry. It was gorgeous," she remembered.

From under the canvas flap, stooping first, then straightening, came a woman. She narrowed her eyes, perhaps out of suspicion, or perhaps because she needed glasses. She hitched up her leopard-skin matador pants.

"Cherie, this is Anthea Scudamore. I used to know in Adelaide. She just turned up along the coast."

Mrs Flegg muttered something about an Australian under every stone. She had those very clear blue eyes surrounded by a blaze of golden skin. They were disconcerting eyes, not for what they saw, but for what they didn't.

"My name is Mortlock now," Mrs Mortlock thought it was the moment to remind.

"Husband not with you?" asked Doctor Flegg.

"My husband died," she said. And although there was no necessity for it, she felt she must explain: "We had already separated."

Cherie Flegg, who was fiddling with the tips of her uninhibited blue-black hair, thought she had better do, well, something, dispense some kind of hospitality.

"We've got a drop of that *ouzo* stuff," she said, "left over from last night's drunk. Or I can make you a cup of tea. An authentic Australian cuppa tea."

Anthea laughed, and said she'd simply adore the tea. Cherie Flegg made her feel she should act in some way differently. But how? She hoped good nature would see her through.

While her hostess was boiling a battered aluminium kettle on a primus and buttering enough slabs of bread, the Flegg family disposed of themselves all around. A stool was produced for Mrs Mortlock, who was glad of it—on account of her dress. So there she sat, all of them looking up to her, and she began to accept it as her due.

"Damn you! Damn you! Damn you!" Mrs Flegg started to shriek in her rather thin, tin-opener voice.

The little girl only laughed, who had been sticking her fingers in the butter to smear her face.

"I'm sorry, darling, but you do do it, don't you? *All* the bloody time!"

Having first admonished, the mother caught up her youngest child, and appeared to be finding her edible. While the little girl laughed and laughed.

They must be very buttery together, decided Mrs Mortlock.

The stains of carelessness and haste had superimposed their own more abstract pattern over the formal leopard spots of Cherie Flegg's fabric pants. Her clear eyes could not have seen, nor would they notice much else beyond the behaviour of her children, and the approach of other women. Mrs Mortlock experienced a sadness on recognizing the professional carriage, the figure from which nature had not yet exorcised the grace, of Cherie Smith. When Mrs Flegg lay down on the ground, her blue-black hair spread itself naturally around, her long legs plaited themselves together in the most expressive twists.

"Tell me something abour your work," Mrs Mortlock asked of the doctor, though she did not want to know.

As he told about the fellowship, and their life in the States, she was greedy for the tone of his voice, droning outside her partitioned thoughts. She examined his hands, to see what she could remember of them. Their male skin was incredible. But the hands remained withheld, unless responding to some joky demonstration of affection on the part of his younger children, or in the case of his elder girl, overt sallies of love.

"And now we gotta settle down in *Can*berra," Barry Flegg brought his story to an end.

"I was never cut out for any sort of academic wife. No sirree!" grumbled Mrs Flegg, though it was obvious she would not have relinquished her position.

Mrs Mortlock had eaten half a slice of bread, with its fairly rancid, sandy butter, and burnt her mouth on the metal cup. Although enthroned on the camp stool, familiarity had begun to make her status suspect.

"Why do you go around in a hat?" the younger boy thought to ask.

So, she was preparing to leave, when the old Greek came along the path with the bunches of roses, the crimson-purply, country bunches. Because he was asked, Doctor Flegg bought a bunch, giving too much, Mrs Mortlock saw—she was quick to master the currency of any country she visited—and tossed the roses into his wife's leopard-skin lap.

"What'll I do with a bunch of roses?" Mrs Flegg complained, and laughed. "Give them to Mrs Scudamore."

"Oh no! Please!" Mrs Mortlock protested.

Her lips were trembling unaccountably under the last flakes of lipstick.

"Or perhaps one," she begged.

And pinned the rose with a brooch, which seemed, rather, to draw attention to the diamonds, though she had not intended it that way.

"Flowers die on me," she apologized, "very quickly."

She spoke more softly than was her habit, almost childlike, while glancing sideways at Mrs Flegg, who continued sitting for a moment abandoned in time, it might have appeared, but for the evidence of children, and the crimson roses, glowing and spilling from her stained lap.

Soon after that Mrs Mortlock left, accompanied by Doctor Flegg, with a string of children tagging behind, less from a sense of duty than to allay an evening boredom. There was a smell of dust and roses, as sea and sky began to purple over, and shadow deepened dust at the roots of the pines.

On their reaching the top of the ridge, Barry Flegg's reluctant pace showed that he planned to go no farther with his guest. So that she could only feel their uneventful meeting in such uncomfortable circumstances, in the presence of his wife—to whom Mummy would have referred as Such a Common Little Person—must remain for ever a meaningless occasion.

Perhaps for that reason, as they stood amongst the rocks, Mrs Mortlock could not resist: "I went across to the Island, Barry, not so very long before I left. I was alone. I lived on eggs. And bread. I tramped about the bush. I was pretty miserable at the time. I swam."

She was surprised at the directness, the candid softness of her own voice. Did she, perhaps, hope he might watch her rising from the sea? But he was looking down, his eyelids weighed with heavy copper. Frowning. His eyes saw inward, she realized, preoccupied no doubt with some more important matter, of an explosive conscience.

Then he glanced up, and laughed, and said: "Oh yes, the Island!" just for a moment looking at her.

She understood he was embarrassed. So she went away, leaving him to clothe a secret part of him which she knew by heart.

Once or twice Mrs Mortlock turned to confirm that no one was aware of the thoughts she was indulging in so recklessly, and found the landscape empty of all but its serene perfection. Into which her mind, putting on distorted flesh, lumbered and lurched, the lips of thought parted to receive. In her silence she gave little gasps, or grunts, of anticipation or surrender. Once she even laughed aloud.

It was at this point that she chose to notice the young Greek, his body scarcely less naked than his face, poised on the wall she had barely passed. Mrs Mortlock looked away in order not to see, what, she suspected, he would expect her to. On that side, she drew down the brim of her hat, forcing it scratching against her cheek. Above the uproar of straw and emotion, the sinewy Greek, balancing almost on one hand, on the stones of the irregular wall, was calling to her, in short, foreign, though expressive words. Before jumping. She heard. She heard, she fancied, the rubber soles thumping the earth. In any case, his breath, trumpeting a monstrous urgency, into the evening, behind her back, was made clearly audible.

Mrs Mortlock was running holding her hat. The landscape of dust and stones streamed. From now on, all her strength must be poured out in an effort to outdistance rubber. Her splitting dress ridiculed her. By luck, or misfortune, she had left off her foundation garment, with the result that her breasts were dealt out in great dollops. They had stopped being part of her. Running and jumping. As she ran from the rubber Greek, she was terrified by the glistening veins in the sinewy arms she could not see.

Oh the reeling cypresses. The purple evening threatened to suck her under.

Two incredulous faces, of two peasant women in black, stared at Mrs Mortlock out of a hovel.

"Can't you," she rasped, calling in a gush of tears, "won't you DO?"

But for the two faces she might have been a hurtling stone.

So, in the end, still running, she had only herself to rely on. If she had expected more in the beginning. Her own hat, even, had fallen amongst the yellow thistles.

The sighing of dry thistles pursued her as she burst out into the main road.

"A man," Mrs Mortlock stood, whimpering into a policeman's face, "following, running, horribly, every intention of molesting. Do you understand? To *molest?*" she asked, in doubt.

The policeman got off his motor-bike. His eyes followed this crazy *Engleza*'s finger, pointing back, into the exhausted evening, at a peaceful emptiness of dusk.

Mrs Mortlock herself was rather surprised at its emptiness, and as there was nothing further which she could do personally, she allowed the policeman to help her aboard the rackety bus.

Considering the ghastly nature of her experience, she was fairly composed by the time she entered her well-starred hotel. In the foyer, in the press of strangers, she passed for normal. Nobody examined her split seam, everybody took it that her tousled hair was fashionably dressed.

On reaching her room she took off her clothes, dropping into the basket a wilted rose she had accepted from those people against the warning of her better judgment. She bathed. She ordered a cup of iced consommé. Her ritual made her almost scornful, and after she had hidden the air ticket and her travellers' cheques, under the pillow for safety, she lay down with the Mrs Parkinson Keyes she had been lucky enough to find in an otherwise ghastly shop. Almost immediately she fell asleep.

How long Mrs Mortlock remained dead to the world would have been difficult to estimate. The clocks of Athens were standing still. But at some point in that incalculable night, she awoke to her own face. The glass was overflowing with it. The grey face, emerging from the wastes of sleep, had been mutilated unmercifully. Extinct terrors caked her lips, choked her long, dusty throat. But it was not the isolation of her own reflected and reflective face of which Mrs Mortlock was chiefly conscious. She began, with a slow distaste, to accept that she had been dreaming of Cherie Flegg, of her stained leopard-skin matador pants.

It was only then that Mrs Mortlock's face forced itself on her, out of the glass, and the breath went *crrkk* in her throat, and she fell back, and switched the light off.

Willy-wagtails by Moonlight

The Wheelers drove up to the Mackenzies' punctually at six-thirty. It was the hour for which they had been asked. My God, thought Jum Wheeler. It had been raining a little, and the tyres sounded blander on the wet gravel.

In front of the Mackenzies', which was what is known as a Lovely Old Home—colonial style—amongst some carefully natural-looking gums, there stood a taxi.

"Never knew Arch and Nora ask us with anyone else," Eileen Wheeler said.

"Maybe they didn't. Even now. Maybe it's someone they couldn't get rid of."

"Or an urgent prescription from the chemist's."

Eileen Wheeler yawned. She must remember to show sympathy, because Nora Mackenzie was going through a particularly difficult one.

Anyway, they were there, and the door stood open on the lights inside. Even the lives of the people you know, even the lives of Nora and Arch look interesting for a split second, when you drive up and glimpse them through a lit doorway.

"It's that Miss Cullen," Eileen said.

For there was Miss Cullen, doing something with a brief-case in the hall.

"Ugly bitch," Jum said.

"Plain is the word," corrected Eileen.

"Arch couldn't do without her. Practically runs the business."

Certainly that Miss Cullen looked most methodical, shuffling the immaculate papers, and slipping them into a new pigskin brief-case in Arch and Nora's hall.

"Got a figure," Eileen conceded.

"But not a chin."

"Oh, hello, Miss Cullen. It's stopped raining."

It was too bright stepping suddenly into the hall. The Wheelers brightly blinked. They looked newly made.

"Keeping well, Miss Cullen, I hope?"

"I have nothing to complain about, Mr Wheeler," Miss Cullen replied.

She snapped the catch. Small, rather pointed breasts under the rain-coat. But, definitely, no chin.

Eileen Wheeler was fixing her hair in the reproduction Sheraton mirror.

She had been to the hairdresser's recently, and the do was still set too tight.

"Well, good-bye now," Miss Cullen said.

When she smiled there was a hint of gold, but discreet, no more than a bridge. Then she would draw her lips together, and lick them ever so slightly, as if she had been sucking a not unpleasantly acid sweetie.

Miss Cullen went out the door, closing it firmly but quietly behind her.

"That was Miss Cullen," said Nora Mackenzie coming down. "She's Arch's secretary."

"He couldn't do without her," she added, as though they did not know.

Nora was like that. Eileen wondered how she and Nora had tagged along together, ever since Goulburn, all those years.

"God, she's plain!" Jum said.

Nora did not exactly frown, but pleated her forehead the way she did when other people's virtues were assailed. Such attacks seemed to affect her personally, causing her almost physical pain.

"But Mildred is so kind," she insisted.

Nora Mackenzie made a point of calling her husband's employees by first names, trying to make them part of a family which she alone, perhaps, would have liked to exist.

"She brought me some giblet soup, all the way from Balgowlah, that time I had virus flu."

"Was it good, darling?" Eileen asked.

She was going through the routine, rubbing Nora's cheek with her own. Nora was pale. She must remember to be kind.

Nora did not answer, but led the way into the lounge-room.

Nora said: "I don't think I'll turn on the lights for the present. They hurt my eyes, and it's so restful sitting in the dusk."

Nora *was* pale. She had, in fact, just taken a couple of Disprin.

"Out of sorts, dear?" Eileen asked.

Nora did not answer, but offered some dry martinis.

Very watery, Jum knew from experience, but drink of a kind.

"Arch will be down presently," Nora said. "He had to attend to some business, some letters Miss Cullen brought. Then he went in to have a shower."

Nora's hands were trembling as she offered the dry martinis, but Eileen remembered they always had.

The Wheelers sat down. It was all so familiar, they did not have to be asked, which was fortunate, as Nora Mackenzie always experienced difficulty in settling guests into chairs. Now she sat down herself, far more diffidently than her friends. The cushions were standing on their points.

Eileen sighed. Old friendships and the first scent of gin always made her nostalgic.

"It's stopped raining," she said, and sighed.

"Arch well?" Jum asked.

As if he cared. She had let the ice get into the cocktail, turning it almost to pure water.

"He has his trouble," Nora said. "You know, his back."

Daring them to have forgotten.

Nora loved Arch. It made Eileen feel ashamed.

So fortunate for them to have discovered each other. Nora Leadbeatter and Arch Mackenzie. Two such bores. And with bird-watching in common. Though Eileen Wheeler had never believed Nora did not make herself learn to like watching birds.

At Goulburn, in the early days, Nora would come out to Glen Davie sometimes to be with Eileen at week-ends. Mr Leadbeatter had been manager at the Wales for a while. He always saw that his daughter had the cleanest notes. Nora was shy, but better than nothing, and the two girls would sit about on the veranda those summer evenings, buffing their nails, and listening to the sheep cough in the home paddock. Eileen gave Nora lessons in making up. Nora had protested, but was pleased.

"Mother well, darling?" Eileen asked, sipping that sad, watery gin.

"Not exactly *well*," Nora replied, painfully.

Because she had been to Orange, to visit her widowed mother, who suffered from Parkinson's disease.

"You know what I mean, dear," said Eileen.

Jum was dropping his ash on the carpet. It might be better when poor bloody Arch came down.

"I have an idea that woman, that Mrs Galloway, is unkind to her," Nora said.

"Get another," Eileen advised. "It isn't like after the war."

"One can never be sure," Nora debated. "One would hate to hurt the woman's feelings."

Seated in the dusk Nora Mackenzie was of a moth colour. Her face looked as though she had been rubbing it with chalk. Might have, too, in spite of those lessons in make-up. She sat and twisted her hands together.

How very red Nora's hands had been, at Goulburn, at the convent, to which the two girls had gone. Not that they belonged to *those*. It was only convenient. Nora's hands had been red and trembly after practising a tarantella, early, in the frost. So very early all of that. Eileen had learnt about life shortly after puberty. She had tried to tell Nora one or two things, but Nora did not want to hear. Oh, no, no, *please*, Eileen, Nora cried. As though a boy had been twisting her arm. She had those long, entreating, sensitive hands.

And there they were still. Twisting together, making their excuses. For what they had never done.

Arch came in then. He turned on the lights, which made Nora wince, even those lights which barely existed in all the neutrality of Nora's room. Nora did not comment, but smiled, because it was Arch who had committed the crime.

Arch said: "You two toping hard as usual."

He poured himself the rest of the cocktail.

Eileen laughed her laugh which people found amusing at parties.

Jum said, and bent his leg, if it hadn't been for Arch and the shower, they wouldn't have had the one too many.

"A little alcohol releases the vitality," Nora remarked ever so gently.

She always grew anxious at the point where jokes became personal.

Arch composed his mouth under the handle-bar moustache, and Jum knew what they were in for.

"Miss Cullen came out with one or two letters," Arch was taking pains to explain. "Something she thought should go off tonight. I take a shower most evenings. Summer, at least."

"Such humidity," Nora helped.

Arch looked down into his glass. He might have been composing further remarks, but did not come out with them.

That silly, bloody English-air-force-officer's moustache. It was the only thing Arch had ever dared. War had given him the courage to pinch a detail which did not belong to him.

"That Miss Cullen, useful girl," Jum suggested.

"Runs the office."

"Forty, if a day," Eileen said, whose figure was beginning to slacken off.

Arch said he would not know, and Jum made a joke about Miss Cullen's cul-de-sac.

The little pleats had appeared again in Nora Mackenzie's chalky brow. "Well," she cried, jumping up, quite girlish, "I do hope the dinner will be a success."

And laughed.

Nora was half-way through her second course with that woman at the Chanticleer. Eileen suspected there would be avocados stuffed with prawns, chicken *Mornay,* and *crêpes Suzette.*

Eileen was right.

Arch seemed to gain in authority sitting at the head of his table.

"I'd like you to taste this wine," he said. "It's very light."

"Oh, yes?" said Jum.

The wine was corked, but nobody remarked. The second bottle, later on, was somewhat better. The Mackenzies were spreading themselves tonight.

Arch flipped his napkin once or twice, emphasizing a point. He smoothed the handle-bar moustache, which should have concealed a harelip, only there wasn't one. Jum dated from before the moustache, long, long, very long.

Arch said: "There was a story Armitage told me at lunch. There was a man who bought a mower. Who suffered from indigestion. Now, how, exactly, did it . . . go?"

Jum had begun to make those little pellets out of bread. It always fascinated him how grubby the little pellets turned out. And himself not by any means dirty.

Arch failed to remember the point of the story Armitage had told.

It was difficult to understand how Arch had made a success of his business. Perhaps it was that Miss Cullen, breasts and all, under the rain-coat. For a long time Arch had messed around. Travelled in something. Separator parts. Got the agency for some sort of phoney machine for supplying *ozone* to public buildings. The Mackenzies lived at Burwood then. Arch continued to mess around. The war was quite a godsend. Arch was the real Adj type. Did a conscientious job. Careful with his allowances, too.

Then, suddenly, after the war, Arch Mackenzie had launched out, started the import-export business. Funny the way a man will suddenly hit on the idea to which his particular brand of stupidity can respond.

The Mackenzies had moved to the North Shore, to the house which still occasionally embarrassed Nora. She felt as though she ought to apologize for success. But there was the bird-watching. Most week-ends they went off to the bush, to the Mountains or somewhere. She felt happier in humbler circumstances. In time she got used to the tape recorder which they took along. She made herself look upon it as a necessity rather than ostentation.

Eileen was dying for a cigarette.

"May I smoke, Arch?"

"We're amongst friends, aren't we?"

Eileen did not answer that. And Arch fetched the ash-tray they kept handy for those who needed it.

Nora in the kitchen dropped the beans. Everybody heard, but Arch asked Jum for a few tips on investments, as he always did when Nora happened to be out of the room. Nora had some idea that the Stock Exchange was immoral.

Then Nora brought the dish of little, pale, tinned peas.

"Ah! *Pet—ty pwah!*" said Jum.

He formed his full and rather greasy lips into a funnel through which the little rounded syllables poured most impressively.

Nora forgot her embarrassment. She envied Jum his courage in foreign languages. Although there were her lessons in Italian, she would never have dared utter in public.

"Can you bear *crêpes Suzette?*" Nora had to apologize.

"Lovely, darling." Eileen smiled.

She would have swallowed a tiger. But was, *au fond,* at her gloomiest.

What was the betting Nora would drop the *crêpes Suzette?* It was those long, trembly hands, on which the turquoise ring looked too small and innocent. The Mackenzies were still in the semi-precious bracket in the days when they became engaged.

"How's the old bird-watching?"

Jum had to force himself, but after all he had drunk their wine.

Arch Mackenzie sat deeper in his chair, almost completely at his ease.

"Got some new tapes," he said. "We'll play them later. Went up to Kurrajong on Sunday, and got the bell-birds. I'll play you the lyre-bird, too. That was Mount Wilson."

"Didn't we hear the lyre-bird last time?" Eileen asked.

Arch said: "Yes."

Deliberately.

"But wouldn't you like to hear it again? It's something of a collector's piece."

Nora said they'd be more comfortable drinking their coffee in the lounge.

Where Arch fetched the tape recorder. He set it up on the Queen Anne walnut piecrust. It certainly was an impressive machine.

"I'll play you the lyre-bird."

"The *pièce de résistance?* Don't you think we should keep it?"

"He can never wait for the lyre-bird."

Nora had grown almost complacent. She sat holding her coffee, smiling faintly through the steam. The children she had never had with Arch were about to enter.

"Delicious coffee," Eileen said.

She had finished her filter-tips. She had never felt drearier.

The tape machine had begun to snuffle. There was quite an unusual amount of crackle. Perhaps it was the bush. Yes, that was it. The bush!

"Well, it's really quite remarkable how you people have the patience," Eileen Wheeler had to say.

"Ssh!"

Arch Mackenzie was frowning. He had sat forward in the period chair.

"This is where it comes in."

His face was tragic in the shaded light.

"Get it?" he whispered.

His hand was helping. Or commanding.

"Quite remarkable," Eileen repeated.

Jum was shocked to realize he had only two days left in which to take up the ICI rights for old Thingummy.

Nora sat looking at her empty cup. But lovingly.

Nora could have been beautiful, Eileen saw. And suddenly felt old, she who had stripped once or twice at amusing parties. Nora Mackenzie did not know about that.

Somewhere in the depths of the bush Nora was calling that it had just turned four o'clock, but she had forgotten to pack the thermos.

The machine snuffled.

Arch Mackenzie was listening. He was biting his moustache.

"There's another passage soon." He frowned.

"Darling," Nora whispered, "after the lyre-bird you might slip into the kitchen and change the bulb. It went while I was making the coffee."

Arch Mackenzie's frown deepened. Even Nora was letting him down.

But she did not see. She was so in love.

It might have been funny if it was not also pathetic. People were horribly pathetic, Eileen Wheeler decided, who had her intellectual moments. She was also feeling sick. It was Nora's *crêpes Suzette,* lying like blankets.

"You'll realize there are one or two rough passages," Arch said, coming forward when the tape had ended. "I might cut it."

"It could do with a little trimming," Eileen agreed. "But perhaps it's more natural without.

Am I a what's-this, a masochist, she asked.

"Don't forget the kitchen bulb," Nora prompted.

Very gently. Very dreamy.

Her hair had strayed, in full dowdiness, down along her white cheek.

"I'll give you the bell-birds for while I'm gone."

Jum's throat had begun to rattle. He sat up in time, though, and saved his cup in the same movement.

"I remember the bell-birds," he said.

"Not these ones, you don't. These are new. These are the very latest. The best bell-birds."

Arch had started the tape, and stalked out of the room, as if to let the bell-birds themselves prove his point.

"It is one of our loveliest recordings," Nora promised.

They all listened or appeared to.

When Nora said: "Oh, dear"—getting up—"I do believe"—panting almost—"the bell-bird tape"—trembling—"is damaged."

Certainly the crackle was more intense.

"Arch will be so terribly upset."

She had switched off the horrifying machine. With surprising skill for one so helpless. For a moment it seemed to Eileen Wheeler that Nora Mackenzie was going to hide the offending tape somewhere in her bosom. But she thought better of it, and put it aside on one of those little superfluous tables.

"Perhaps it's the machine that's broken," suggested Jum.

"Oh, no," said Nora, "it's the tape. I know. We'll have to give you something else."

"I can't understand"—Eileen grinned—"how you ever got around, Nora, to being mechanical."

"If you're determined," Nora said.

Her head was lowered in concentration.

"If you want a thing enough."

She was fixing a fresh tape.

"And we do love our birds. Our Sundays together in the bush."

The machine had begun its snuffling and shuffling again. Nora Mackenzie raised her head, as if launched on an invocation.

Two or three notes of bird-song fell surprisingly pure and clear, out of the crackle, into the beige and string-coloured room.

"This is one," Nora said, "I don't think I've ever heard before."

She smiled, however, and listened to identify.

"Willy-wagtails," Nora said.

Willy-wagtails were suited to tape. The song tumbled and exulted.

"It must be something," Nora said, "that Arch made while I was with Mother. There were a couple of Sundays when he did a little field-work on his own."

Nora might have given way to a gentle melancholy for all she had foregone if circumstances had not heightened the pitch. There was Arch standing in the doorway. Blood streaming.

"Blasted bulb collapsed in my hand!"

"Oh, darling! Oh *dear!*" Nora cried.

The Wheelers were both fascinated. There was the blood dripping on the beige wall-to-wall.

How the willy-wagtails chortled.

Nora Mackenzie literally staggered at her husband, to take upon herself, if possible, the whole ghastly business.

"Come along, Arch," she moaned. "We'll fix. In just a minute," Nora panted.

And simply by closing the door, she succeeded in blotting the situation, all but the drops of blood that were left behind on the carpet.

"Poor old Arch! Bleeding like a pig!" Jum Wheeler said, and laughed.

Eileen added:

"We shall suffer the willy-wags alone."

Perhaps it was better like that. You could relax. Eileen began to pull. Her step-ins had eaten into her.

The willy-wagtails were at it again.

"Am I going crackers?" asked Jum. "Listening to those bloody birds!"

When somebody laughed. Out of the tape. The Wheelers sat. Still.

Three-quarters of the bottle! Snuffle crackle. *Arch Mackenzie, you're a fair trimmer!* Again that rather brassy laughter.

"Well, I'll be blowed!" said Jum Wheeler.

"But it's that Miss Cullen," Eileen said.

The Wheeler spirits soared as surely as plummets dragged the notes of the wagtail down.

But it's far too rocky, and far too late. Besides, it's willy-wagtails we're after. How Miss Cullen laughed. *Willy-wagtails by moonlight!* Arch was less intelligible, as if he had listened to too many birds, and caught the habit. Snuffle crackle went the machine. . . . *the buttons are not made to undo* . . . Miss Cullen informed. *Oh, stop it, Arch!* ARCH! *You're* TEARING *me!*

So that the merciless machine took possession of the room. There in the crackle of twigs, the stench of ants, the two Wheelers sat. There was that long, thin Harry Edwards, Eileen remembered, with bony wrists, had got her down behind the barn. She had hated it at first. All mirth had been exorcised from Miss Cullen's recorded laughter. Grinding out. Grinding out. So much of life was recorded by now. Returning late from a country dance, the Wheelers had fallen down amongst the sticks and stones, and made what is called love, and risen in the grey hours, to find themselves numb and bulging.

If only the tape, if you knew the trick with the wretched switch.

Jum Wheeler decided not to look at his wife. Little, guilty pockets were turning themselves out in his mind. That woman at the Locomotive Hotel. Pockets and pockets of putrefying trash. Down along the creek, amongst the tussocks and the sheep pellets, the sun burning his boy's skin, he played his overture to sex. Alone.

This sort of thing's all very well, Miss Cullen decided. *It's time we turned practical. Are you sure we can find our way back to the car?*

Always trundling. Crackling. But there were the blessed wagtails again.

"Wonder if they forgot the machine?"

"Oh, God! Hasn't the tape bobbed up in Pymble?"

A single willy-wagtail sprinkled its grace-notes through the stuffy room.

"Everything's all right," Nora announced. "He's calmer now. I persuaded him to take a drop of brandy."

"That should fix him," Jum said.

But Nora was listening to the lone wagtail. She was standing in the bush. Listening. The notes of bird-song falling like mountain water, when they were not chiselled in moonlight.

"There is nothing purer," Nora said, "than the song of the wagtail. Excepting Schubert," she added, "some of Schubert."

She was so shyly glad it had occurred to her.

But the Wheelers just sat.

And again Nora Mackenzie was standing alone amongst the inexorable moonlit gums. She thought perhaps she had always felt alone, even with Arch, while grateful even for her loneliness.

"Ah, there you are!" Nora said.

It was Arch. He stood holding out his bandaged wound. Rather rigid. He could have been up for court martial.

"I've missed the willy-wagtails," Nora said, raising her face to him, exposing her distress, like a girl. "Some day you'll have to play it to me. When you've the time. And we can concentrate."

The Wheelers might not have existed.
As for the tape, it had discovered silence.
Arch mumbled they'd all better have something to drink.
Jum agreed it was a good idea.
"Positively brilliant," Eileen said.

A Glass of Tea

Malliakas decided to use the introduction only on his second visit to Geneva. He had come there in connection with property belonging to an aunt, a rich Alexandrian who had spent her widowhood, and died finally, at Lausanne. On his first visit he knew for certain he would have been bored, and even now, as he heard his letter flutter and fall inside the box, he wondered what had possessed him—to use the introduction Ellison, the elderly Englishman who had known Philippides in the Levant, had as good as forced into his hand. Days of grace made Malliakas hope a mistake might have been corrected, when Philippides wrote, in engraved words, expressing a wish to receive his friend's acquaintance. Although the note was brief and dry, its appearance suggested the inevitable. Malliakas was horrified, but caught the bus to Cologny the day before he was due to leave.

There were other forces at work, too. It was perhaps melancholy, or the luxuriant somnolence of the Swiss landscape, or the mottled acres of Swiss flesh which had in the end persuaded him. A bachelor in his early forties, Malliakas was moved in general by impulse and his liver. Not rich enough in material or spiritual ways to make the grander gestures of life, he was still too rich to have achieved the work of art, which, in the beginning, had been expected of him. But he continued to try. His pen would threaten the paper, heavy with that unfulfilled promise. At least a talent for the fragment did not prevent Malliakas from deriving pleasure from his own fragments.

Though what satisfied him most, of course, was to lounge away the morning on the balconies of the best hotels he could afford, sipping early coffee, and playing with a *komboloyi* inherited from a relative. Contentment need not content less for being minor, and at such times he would ease his thighs, and peer from under black lids at a tousle of hair, a tumble of buttocks under the plane-trees in the square. If Malliakas sometimes also sighed it was because he had experienced a succession of mistresses, all of them adequate, though none of them memorable for that lingering brilliance on which his imagination still insisted.

Imagination—of all his qualities it was the one he cherished most, yet was unable to boast of what his friends were only able to guess at. On the way to Cologny, to the meeting with Philippides, he sat toying with this secret jewel. Churned around in the sturdy bus, he regretted finding that every Swiss seemed to have achieved a balance, while he, the Greek, could only oppose his undemonstrable inner life and a certain soft elegance. Annoyance tasted bitter in his mouth as he put up his hand and discovered he had forgotten to shave. His chin would be looking its bluest.

By the time they put him down in the lane Malliakas was what his English governess used to call *grumpy*. Remembering Ellison had referred to Philippides not only as a *hearty octogenarian* but as a *grand old gentleman,* the gravest doubts slowed him up. Rain had fallen that morning, and pools of water still lay. Clouds hung in summery abundance above the green cumulus of trees. Malliakas sneezed. There was no avoiding anything now. Mud spattered his Italian shoes, as he went on, and into the yard of the house in which Philippides lived, still in some affluence, it seemed, though Ellison had suggested the old man's fortunes had suffered a decline.

In the wisely proportioned Swiss doorway of this ample though unpretentious house, an appropriate girl informed the stranger that Madame Philippides had been called away to a sickbed. One would find Monsieur, however, in the little garden-house at the end of the alley. She began at once to lead the visitor along the gravel, talking amiably of the weather. Malliakas, rather gloomy, examined the contours of the girl's behind.

Arriving at the garden-house the maid raised her voice to its loudest.

"Here," she shouted, "is this Greek gentleman you were expecting, Monsieur Philippides."

Sitting in the little garden-house, of frail white lattice which had become untacked in places, was a shrivelled, yet very bright old man.

"Yes," he said, addressing the visitor in English, in one of the quiet, but convinced voices of the deaf, "we have received your note. Also, several years ago, a letter from Tillotson warning us of your possible arrival. Ellison—he will have told you—was my friend in the Smyrna days, even before that, at Konya. I spent several years at Konya. I was sent for by a cousin who had made a mess of a carpet-weaving concern. In three years I had increased the number of looms from thirty-three to three hundred and twenty."

So very pleased at remembering, old Mr Philippides laughed, and the guest wondered what to do.

"You will take tea?" Philippides asked.

Although Malliakas did not care for the stuff, he accepted the offer of an occupation.

"Geneviève, a pot of tea. Tillotson would drink a pot of tea. A whole pot. In the old days."

The girl had already gone down the steps.

"But you are not English," Philippides remembered, and slipped thoughtfully into Greek.

He now looked most extraordinarily bright, seated at a little garden-table, in a poacher's cap, a plaid across his shoulders, his purple bird's claws emerging from brown hand-knitted mittens. On the table in front of him, on a pewter salver, stood a glass half-filled with tea.

"My wife will be sorry to have missed you." Philippides stirred his tea, and the spoon sounded against the glass. "She was called away, to some lady—I forget whom—who is sinking," he said, "sinking."

Without apparently disturbing his host's train of thought,

Malliakas sat down. The iron chair pinched his thighs. There was a smell of mould in the summer-house.

"They are always sending for her," Philippides explained, but suddenly altered course. "Now *you*," he accused, "must have the gift of languages. Like any Alexandrian. My wife was taught languages. All the governesses of the Levant were brought to bear on her education. And that of her sisters. Almost everyone in Smyrna had heard of their accomplishments. Constantia—would you believe it?—learnt to shoot out a candle flame while standing at the opposite end of the court. With the ivory pistol her uncle gave her."

If Malliakas did not express in words appreciation of such a talent, it was because he had begun to recognize in his host a portraitist he might respect.

"In embroidered dresses, amongst the pomegranate bushes, on summer evenings—all those girls, waiting to be picked."

Mr Philippides took a mouthful of tea, extracting the utmost from it, from under his almost dandified moustache. A slight breeze starting up stirred the damp green thickets of the garden. Malliakas had to look over his shoulder, momentarily nervous of approaching skirts and introductions. But it was only the maid, who put down his pot of tea, and left.

"Tea!" Philippides sighed. "It is one of the few remaining pleasures. Everybody dies, you know."

Respecting his host's abstraction, the guest began to help himself. His fingers, he saw, bungling the sugar, were swollen and tufted. A presence of girls in embroidered dresses had made them clumsy.

"If you gave me time, I would tell you about my wife," Philippides confided. "Constantia. A passionate, a difficult woman. But worth the suffering involved."

He laughed with a slight inward tremor.

"The best hater I have ever known. How she got to hate these!" he said, tapping his glass.

"Oh?" Malliakas murmured.

He felt drowsily, willingly enchanted, listening, scenting the past, and the omnipresent smell of mildew, as he sipped tea from a bluish cup.

"Yes. You have only a cup," Philippides noticed. "Because this is the last of the glasses. Of the twelve I bought from the Russian who was leaving Konya. Which my wife brought with us in the destroyer, in a cardboard box. I will tell you everything if you give me time."

"Then I shall give you it!" said Malliakas, who suddenly, sincerely, wanted to.

For the visitor realized by now it was most important that all the fragments should fall into place, even more important that he should await the return of Mrs Philippides.

"Oh, but it is not always possible to give. With the best will it is not possible," Philippides remembered. "There was the gipsy. Did I mention? That was in Chios. After we escaped. The gipsy promised to tell me my fortune, and Constantia was furious because it hadn't happened to her."

The old man began to laugh enormously.

"And did she tell?" asked Malliakas in the thick voice listeners develop.

"In the end. The gipsy said: 'First you must pull a hair from your chest, and I shall take it, and dance, bare in front and bare behind, amongst the rocks at Ayia Moni.' "

Malliakas was listening to his own breathing.

"Did you?" he asked.

"In the end," Philippides said. "It was not easy. Because, as you see, I am rather smooth."

Through a conglomeration of woollen garments he began to scratch at his old chest. While smiling for the past.

"And what did the gipsy say?"

"She said," said Philippides "—I was drinking tea at the time, out of one of these glasses—she said: 'You will live,' she said, 'till the last of the twelve glasses breaks.' "

"Well now," Malliakas prepared to indulge this amiable, aged child, "you have lived! Just as the gipsy prophesied."

"I wonder," Philippides considered quietly, "or whether one dies before one's time." But quickly added in lighter tone: "Constantia was so angry when it happened. She said it was a lot of nonsense, that the gipsy must have known about the twelve Russian glasses from Kyria Assimina, who was stupid, and a babbler, and who had broken two of her most valuable dishes. Whether Constantia was right, or not, in all her charges, Kyria Assimina was a breaker. She broke, I think, four of the glasses before she was got rid of."

Malliakas was fascinated by the glass which had survived.

"That Russian," Philippides told, "at Konya, would give receptions for men, with vodka, and many *mezedes*—both hot and cold—and afterwards tea from a big silver samovar." He paused, and confided: "Constantia was jealous of this Russian. She was jealous of Kyria Assimina, who had fine eyes, certainly, but a hairy mole just above her dress."

The evening was darkening. On the slaty sky an aeroplane had begun to write something which might have been in code.

"I remember a storm was brewing the night Kyria Assimina broke the Sèvres dishes. A shutter kept on banging. Constantia was ailing. It was her time of life. Though she was always quick-tempered, I can tell you! She said she would go away to Athens. And stay. Well, she went. When she came back—as I knew she would—she brought a girl. A young peasant from Lemnos. Aglaia, too, broke one of the glasses, but that was later."

"With such competition to kill you," Malliakas could not resist, "you have been very fortunate."

Philippides loved that.

"Oh, I will tell you everything," he promised, "if you will have the patience. It was a wonder Constantia did not kill me. From love."

Philippides coughed. Then he said, with sudden sweet innocence: "People are like that, you know."

Malliakas leaned forward. He heard the shutter banging. In Chios. Or was it inside Constantia's head? It was most important that he should hear, see, all. And as he sipped his tea out of the opalescent cup, Philippides wove the muslin gauzes, only too willingly. Stirring his dead glass.

Later on, as he sensed he would, Malliakas became so obsessed by Constantia that he wrote her story, finished it too, and almost felt pleased. But this was still only the beginning of the affair, in the garden-house at Cologny, as he sat forward in the iron chair, and heard what he must expect, and waited quite fearfully for the return of Mrs Philippides.

In the beginning the family in Frankish Street had been unwilling to confer the daughter they valued so highly on a young man of modest breeding and uncertain means. Constantia was doubtful, too, whether to accept a lover a head shorter than herself. She would look down from under her eyelids while dismantling a pomegranate flower. Whole mornings she would spend copying extracts from Dante and Goethe into leather notebooks, or dabbling in water-colour landscapes, the English landscapes she had never seen. But listening for the steely step of the small, undesirable, muscular man. Her sisters would lean out of windows and tell her when to expect. She was furious then.

She said, still looking down—she had a perfect nose: "Don't you find the difference in height makes us look ridiculous?"

"I had never thought about it," he replied.

"Oh, but please don't touch me! I hate to be touched," she confessed, "by someone who means so little to me. Even my sisters, of whom I am fond, respect my feelings."

She spoke tremblingly.

"And yet you are not cold."

She blushed, or it was the pomegranate flower reflected in her cheek.

"Oh, leave me! Who knows what I am? *I* don't!" She sounded to herself as though she were positively shouting.

But he touched her. He had small, rather compelling hands.

The young couple were married from the house in Frankish Street, and almost before the design of the *bonbonnières* had ceased to delight the guests, the bridegroom was summoned by the cousin at Konya.

Constantia wrote: "What are you doing down there, Yanko, amongst all those Turks? And the Russian you mention. I dislike parties gentlemen give for gentlemen. At times there is something secretive about the behaviour of men."

She wrote: "Will you not send for me? I do not mind dirt, flies, Turks, boredom—it could hardly be boredom! I shall organize our lives. I shall bring the nicest of the five tea-sets we received at our wedding. If you will send for me! I have my eye on the stuff for curtains. Oh, Yanko, I can no longer sleep! You won't write, excepting about the wretched carpets!"

When the weather grew cooler he came and fetched her, and at the *lokanda* where they changed horses, she threw back her veil and announced: "I can smell camels!" with such distaste he wondered whether her feelings for him would survive.

Later, a moon in an autumn sky provoked her to remark: "Do you see that moon? Such a splinter, such a little *icicle* of a moon!"

She would hold his head in her arms, as though it no longer belonged to him, as though she intended to protect it from the whole world, and might succeed, excepting from herself. By morning light they would glance sideways at each other's mouths for the bruises they suspected a third person might discover. Whole evenings they used to listen to dust and voices the length of their potholed provincial street, yet he no longer feared they might find themselves in the position of couples at separate tables, reading the label on the wine-bottle, and moulding bread. Instead they moulded silences, they became familiar with each other's uncommunicated thoughts.

After this existence at Konya, life in Smyrna tended, they found, to float them apart. It was not so much the business trips, which took him to Athens, Alexandria, sometimes Marseilles—if anything they were closer then, by correspondence—rather it was their social obligations, which required them to shine each in an individual orbit. So they found themselves noticing each other across other people's rooms, a face which each had thought to possess, but which had in fact remained public property. In these circumstances he admired her for her figure and her jewels, while she reassessed with a twinge the merits which flatterers claimed to discover in her husband.

Sometimes it even happened they danced together, ironically, in the houses of acquaintances.

Whether she ever took a lover he did not care to conjecture. She, on the other hand, accepted her husband's mistresses, on the grounds that convention allowed for some degree of dishonesty in a man. Besides, she said, he will never leave me.

Nor would he. They loved each other.

They rode, sometimes together, more often with company, through the olive groves above Bournova. From the chestnut mare he had bought her for a birthday she would look back to locate her husband yet again. But without appearing to. Then when she had caught the sheen of leather, of leggings as they lagged amongst the rougher black of olive trunks, she was free to turn once more, to discuss literature, with the Frenchman, the Italian, and the Pole. So languid on her burnished horse as her glove flicked at flies. Of the three men she favoured the Frenchman, because his insincerity enabled her to feel secure.

It was Nétillard who carried her down to the road the morning she was thrown.

"I hate you to see me like this," Constantia Philippides complained to no one in particular. "So grotesque. But then one is, in almost all situations where reality intrudes."

She was suffering a good deal, more so when she lost the child for which they had both been hoping.

She set about convincing him. She said: "Yanko, this isn't our last chance."

But it might have been.

At least they had their décor, the house in rose-coloured marble along the Quay, through which, when the doors were folded back, the breeze careened out of the blue blaze of the Aegean. Strangers observing the *kyrioi* through the grille envied them their perfection.

At first it was impossible to believe their personal lives could be reduced by a shuffle of history, which is what happened, momentarily at least, on the deck of the destroyer, after the sack of their city. Because it had been personally theirs, which was now burning by bursts, and in long, funnelling socks of smoke, and reflections of slow, oily light. As he ran looking for that other part of him which was lost, he gashed his shin on a companionway. But did not know. Calling her name. None of that rabble of sufferers— wet, dry, singed, bleeding, deformed by the agony of their first historic situation—none of them *knew* any more, as they stood in their fashionable rags and watched their city burn. At least they had succeeded in bribing their way on board the French destroyer. But for what purpose? Certainly a small man, running amongst them, pushing, in dishevelled English herring-bone, could not rally them back to reality by repetition of a name. In a boater, too, the brim chewed like a biscuit. *"Constantia,"* he called, *"Constantia!"* As he pushed and pummelled, the eyes of others turned in his direction only slowly, and a certain figure, blacker, more ponderous, more respectable than the rest, detached itself, and punched the distraught gentleman, perhaps unable to endure the irony of constancy.

Philippides, as he struggled and burrowed, scarcely paused to reason why Kykkotis—was it? a chemist, was he?—had attacked him on the iron deck of that vessel of doubtful mercy. In later years he preferred not to remember the incident at all. But at the time, when it was so important to focus, all his attention was needed to climb the rope ladder *again,* to steady her body on the rope web, inside the bubble of hostile air. Before they were so unaccountably parted.

"Constantia?" he begged, to call her back, to what remained of life.

He saw her come towards him then, out of the shadows, and light from the burning town struck the colour of verdigris out of her helmet, from the bird's wing she was wearing unsuitably on her head. But convention had stuffed it there as she ran. The once soothing silver of her dress had been ripped streaming open while remaining soft to touch. She stood against him, calming him.

"But Yanko," she was apologizing, "I almost lost our box. I put it down. Just for a second. When I found it again, somebody was sitting on it."

He half-remembered the cardboard box, frail and dispensable, if it had not been necessary as their one surviving possession, to be manoeuvred up a rope ladder.

Now she was standing, surrounded by the unnatural light, in her idiotic little plumed hat, holding the recovered cardboard box.

"What the devil," he shouted in relief, "whatever could you think of bringing along in that box?"

"The tea glasses," she answered. "Of the Russian from Konya."

"But which, for all I care, could have followed him to Russia! Or smashed in Konya! The box! My God, the glasses!"

The rage of fire had grown too much for her. She was blinded by it. So she burst into tears on the public deck, where private scenes were no longer even interesting.

A last barge drifted empty and abandoned. A corpse floating face down was nuzzling peacefully at the water. Anonymous voices were calling: *"We are moving, we are saved"*—as if that were really possible, more likely: *risen from the dead*.

In any case, he put his arm through the crook of her arm to watch the death of Smyrna, and the cardboard box jumped against her dress with her continued gulping. She was determined to hold on to it, though.

In the little garden-house outside Geneva Philippides sat stirring the dregs of his tea. Malliakas had drunk too much of the stuff. His otherwise empty stomach began to turn against him. He was feeling sick.

"Not the greatest of all disasters," Philippides said, "except that it was our own."

The old man in the poacher's cap was perhaps by now too far distant from even his own disasters. He was obsessed by present minutiae. Looking at his watch he remarked:

"It is tiresome my wife is late. We had decided on the *avgolemono*. She makes an excellent *avgolemono* soup, which she learned, I believe, though she won't admit it, from Kyria Assimina, a housekeeper she disliked, who came to us in Chios."

Philippides' eyes were focusing again. His vision had been refreshed by the healing promise of his wife's soup tureen.

"We lived at Chios for some time," he said, "in my grandfather's house, which I believe I still own."

"The house in which the shutters bang."

"Yes!" said Philippides. "You remember then?"

But his guest did not answer. He was living it.

"Whenever the *meltemi* blew," he heard Philippides murmur.

It blew through the over-furnished rooms. The over-stuffed furniture was sown with a grey grit of pumice, while Constantia Philippides walked through the greyer rooms, to control, to control.

"Aglaia? Kyria Assimina!" she called, unable to control lives or shutters. "They are *banging!*" She complained, and the wind added a stridency to her voice. "Two women," she shrieked, "and not a thought between you, unless I actually put one in your heads. Quick! Help me! My nails are breaking!"

And the two servants came running in their slippers to avert disaster, Kyria Assimina, who would grow resentful, and the girl from Lemnos.

"Aglaia is strong," Mrs Philippides used to tell her husband. "She is an ox."

He might be eating cherries, and would not reply, but slip the stones into the palm of his hand in a way which made her bite her lips.

"But good." Mrs Philippides sighed.

The strong, yet gentle, brown girl was so good at controlling the rusty old catches of the hateful old Chios shutters. Mrs Philippides was glad she had brought her, because often her husband was absent in Alexandria or Marseilles.

Sometimes, when he was present, and they were sitting together at evening, he with his foreign newspapers, and she had laid out a game of patience, they would fall back on English, that legacy of governesses and childhood.

"As much as anything I bought Aglaia for company," Mrs Philippides once remarked.

"Bought?" He laughed.

"Brought!" she corrected, noticeably angry, and repeated: *"Brought! Brought!"*

So he did not pursue a matter which drew him closer to their maid.

"Shall I brush your hair, *kyria?*" the girl would ask on gentler mornings.

Constantia enjoyed that. Aglaia's stroke, strong but gentle. Constantia Philippides sat in a wrapper, reading the grandfather's books, the poems of Heredia and Leconte de Lisle, the letters of Paul-Louis Courier; she read *Ivanhoe*. In her husband's absence she was often bored, bored.

She would get up and walk through her empty house. Oh, she loved him—even if he did not love her—nobody ever really loves.

"Do you understand how he can love the Devil?" Constantia overheard.

It was Kyria Assimina. Then Mrs Philippides overheard the silence. Which was Aglaia's.

"The Devil!" muttered Kyria Assimina.

Once Kyria Assimina had screamed: "If she's not the Devil, who else is she? The Empress of Byzantium?"

Kyria Assimina stuck a chamber-pot on her head. Mrs Philippides had to remark: "Such a disgusting habit! I am surprised at you, Kyria Assimina—a person of some refinement."

When the glass got broken, one of the Russian tea-glasses, which were so precious for a certain reason, Mrs Philippides had rushed certainly, at Aglaia, and slapped her face. But in those days girls expected it. So Aglaia was silent as before.

"My God! Thank you, Aglaia!" Mrs Philippides overheard.

"I would have shrieked, I know," Kyria Assimina confessed. "The silly old ugly glasses! As if there weren't plenty left. She has given me nerves. She makes things fall out of my hand."

Aglaia was silent.

And Mrs Philippides sent for her maid at dusk. She did not

apologize, because one could not apologize. Not to a brown girl from an island.

"Bring your sewing," she said, softer, "and sit here a little. While I read. Because it is lonely."

So they sat together, and it was most unorthodox, but there was nobody to know.

And that Mrs Philippides, of the house which stood behind the ficus hedge, would peer out through the large windows with the blistered shutters at the summer visitors, the rich from Athens whom one did not accept, and they would return her glances from under their hats. At the mercy of daylight she appeared a grey woman, but one whose bones refused to allow elegance to desert her.

In the absence of her husband she would walk at evening in the garden of the grandfather's house, cracking almonds, and eating the sweet kernels. Usually she was attended by her maid, a thick-set girl with frizzy hair, whom she had brought back after a visit somewhere.

For Mrs Philippides, too, would stay away. After the gipsy, she left for Athens.

When the gipsy came Mr Philippides had been sitting with a glass of tea on the terrace. Kyria Assimina had brought the tea. Because undoubtedly Aglaia, the girl from Lemnos, had not yet arrived on the scene.

"For a *taliro, kyrie mou,* I shall tell your fortune," the gipsy promised.

She had long leathery breasts under a cotton frock, and smelled of the smoke from charcoal fires, and a particular little cachou sold at the kiosk at the corner of the park.

"But a hair! You must give me a hair," the gipsy insisted, "out of your chest."

And the small smooth Philippides searched.

How long the gipsy danced, bare in front and bare behind, amongst the rocks at Ayia Moni, only the saints knew. But dance she must have. She walked with a long, dancing step, and her clothes were too easy on her. The shabby bodies of some women are quick to lose possession of themselves. Mrs Philippides could just imagine the gipsy's dance, the detached shadow of it, under the ripe, indifferent moon.

That is why Constantia was so annoyed at the gipsy's prophecy, why she went, and why she might have stayed away—she might have gone to Paris—with her husband resurrected in a silver frame —but came back, bringing the girl from Lemnos for her own comfort.

"You see," she said to her husband, "life arranges itself for other people as well as for you."

Voices carried in the grey house.

On the night of her return, however, voices choked each other.

"*Ach!*" she cried. "Yanko! You are mad! *Mad!*"

Laughing for his madness. Fastening her teeth in it.

Kyria Assimina, who had not yet been dismissed, could not listen enough.

"We shall leave, then. We shall go to Athens," he said at last, when he had given it enough thought.

"Oh, I don't *ask* you to!" She hurried to defend her weakness, which by now he took for granted.

"But if it is a matter of your health."

"It is my age," she replied, composing her mouth. "I know women of my age are a traditional joke, but that doesn't alter the situation." ·

He put his hand over hers, with the gesture she almost couldn't bear, wanting to take his hand, withering as it was, and lock it up in her bosom for ever. Where all things keep fresh.

It was not her indifferent health, although that played its part. There were the many other reasons: there was the gritty house in which the shutters banged, and which the light from the lighthouse the other side of the mole would gash open at night, there were the deep ruts of the island roads, there was the long mountain in grey pumice, there were the evenings in which ladies sat spooning up jam from saucers and thinking of the hand-bags they must order from Athens. Oh, the long, sighing Chios evenings, in which moisture fell without watering. Worst of all, Mrs Philippides could have felt, there was her husband's fate, which might be escaped somewhere else.

So, instead of a hand-bag, Constantia Philippides ordered them a new life. Her mouth quivered with success, in the silver-backed looking-glass, with its lovers' knots and irises.

"But you mustn't look," she protested, putting the mirror down when he had swum up over her shoulder. "Don't you know that a woman's face in the looking-glass is more private than in actual life?"

What was her *actual life?* he wondered. Confusion had cracked her voice. The place under her left eye had begun its twitching. He loved her for the mysteries they had solved together, still more deeply for those he could never help her solve.

After that they went away in the little steamer, which all the town always met, hoping for something it never brought.

The Philippides went to Athens, to the apartment at the foot of Lycavitos. As an address it was not all that unfashionable, though it could have been better. In any case, Mrs Philippides had withdrawn more or less from the society of those she might have been expected to cultivate for pleasure.

"I am too content," she said in defending her attitude, "too selfish, if you like, to bother."

She spoke with such conviction she might have been expecting someone to take her up on it. But her husband never reacted. And the servant was the servant.

Mrs Philippides had resigned herself to being alone while her husband was away on those business trips to Mediterranean ports. He suspected she was happiest after he had gone. Distance, or so it seemed in her letters, allowed her mind to rest.

Dearest Yanko,   (*she once wrote*)
   Whenever you are away I am able to relive the past without any of the interferences—none of those jagged incidents which continue to strew the present! You may say: What about the jagged incidents of the past? Well, one is no longer cut by them.

I must tell you, incidentally, Aglaia broke one of the glasses. I slapped her. She did not cry. I have often wondered whether that girl is altogether without feeling, but have come to the conclusion she is too considerate to allow herself such a luxury. I think I value her, Yanko, almost more than anything. And may never tell her. How embarrassed we should both be! But she *broke the glass*—and now there are only two, of all those you bought from the Russian at Konya. Of all the casualties we have experienced these are without a doubt the worst. On losing anything so solid, so *unbreakable,* one suffers quite a physical shock. . . .

Such a shock that Mrs Philippides had taken to her bed. He found her there on his return.

"It is nothing," she said. "Or nothing more serious than a migraine."

But her voice had dried out, and raised itself only with an effort.

"Well," she told, "nothing happened while you were away. Excepting the glass. The wretched old Russian glass which broke."

They laughed together for what had happened, and he touched her lightly, not intimately, but in the way he had seen doctors. She was glad he did not contemplate a greater intimacy.

Soon Mrs Philippides was up and about. She was walking on the terrace in her dressing-gown, watering the brittle pelargoniums, to say nothing of the gardenia, which heaved its heavy heads into the late summer air.

"It is too heavy, the perfume," Constantia complained. "I must get rid of it." She paused. "Give it away, *Yanko mou,* to one of your smart lady friends."

Although she took pains to turn it into a joke, it was implied that she would face facts, with tolerance, even sympathy.

For he was still dapper, in his English suits and clipped moustache. Sometimes she would take the nail-scissors and snip at one or two of the hairs which showed at his nostrils.

"To make you more attractive," she explained, "to your smart lady partners at bridge."

He used to arrive back late from the bridge occasions she shunned, and she would call to him from the terrace, until he came and sat at the end of the wicker day-bed on which she had been lying. Perhaps it was then that she possessed him most completely.

"Who was there?" she used to ask.

Though she did not care to know, nor he to remember.

He felt agreeably tired, while she would rise refreshed, and walk, almost stride, in a sound of imperious loose silk, amongst the plants of the terrace which evening had revived. Constantia still wore her hair piled high. Because it suited her. And as she moved, the light from the city or the moon would strike her face, breaking its form into a glittering mosaic, fragmentary, but immemorial.

"Now that I am thin and ugly," she used to say, and pause.

But they both knew she was not. She was the work of art which only passion can create, on the many evenings of late summer added up to make a life.

"I am hungry," he might say. "I shall ask Aglaia to give me something to eat."

"Yes, our Aglaia will prepare you something. If you are in need of it." And here she would play upon her voice, making it the instrument of a viciously raucous vulgarity: "If you haven't stuffed at bridge, on a hundred little nastinesses."

In the split darkness he could hear her shifting the groups of flower-pots into other grating groups.

"At least Aglaia will make you something *real*. And here am I, never even learned to cook!"

"You could have," on one occasion he reminded her gently, "if you had wanted to."

As he went away.

"And bore myself to death stirring and stirring? No, thank you!"

She was so furious she laughed.

"Boring! Boring! Do I ever bore you, Yanko?" she called.

Because he did not answer she presumed he had not heard, but in any case he could never have satisfied her with answers, and because of that, she took the crumpled handkerchief out of her bosom, and blew her nose.

She used to listen to them—she detested overhearing a dialogue which remained just the other side of distinctness—she would listen to their voices in the kitchen, the light metallic fall of inconsequential communication. Not even conversation. The voice of that stolid girl would grow lighter with other people, other people. Not even a girl any more, but thickened out, and grizzled over.

"*Yanko mou,*" Constantia would call, "ask Aglaia to bring it out on the terrace. Then we can chat a little while you eat."

She would be standing in the darkness, listening to her own voice. Or listening.

She liked to shake out the napkin for him, and with her own hands, bring him his glass of tea.

The evening Aglaia went to the country with the policeman from Menidi—whom it was healthy for her to know, although *oh no, kyria,* she insisted, *this man can't be taken seriously he is just another*—Constantia had brought the two glasses, which were all that remained to them of the set.

"There!" she said, putting them down. "Although I cannot cook, I am domesticated to this extent."

He watched the excited motion of her ankle as she sat sipping her glass of tea.

"But you will be hungry," she regretted, "after the bridge, and I am not Aglaia."

"I am not hungry."

"Not hungry? So late! But it isn't natural!"

The small man, her husband, sat sipping slowly. Was he looking at her? Was he thinking of her? In her over-eagerness she must have burnt her throat. A long, incautious finger of light dared to touch her frown.

Then, on recovering her voice, she asked: "Tell me, at least, who was at the Sarandidis' bridge?"

"I don't know," he answered. "I forget."

It was too exhausting.

The heat of August was so intense the darkness smouldered garnet-red. As for any artificial light, it could turn malicious on August nights. It pointed out the blemishes. Day, she saw bitterly, had edged her gardenia flowers with brown.

"Ah," she cried, tearing one off, "why, I wonder, does one find it necessary to deceive others?"

Tearing up those petals of wrinkled, yet intoxicating kid, she could not have answered for the words she had to speak.

"Do *you*," he asked, "find it necessary to deceive?"

"One doesn't know! One doesn't know!" she kept repeating. "It happens in spite of oneself."

"I can answer for *my*self," he assured her.

"But can you?" she asked, sitting very upright; he could see the shape of her piled-up hair.

"Can you be aware," he heard, "of the effect you have on other people?"

Her voice had reached splintering point. Light from the rooms slashed through the darkness at the tiled terrace.

"All those women in Paris clothes! The cigaretty women! Clawing at a handful of cards! Rapacious, bridge-playing women!"

She had stood to deal her *coup de grâce*.

"That is one thing," she said. "But Aglaia. Even Aglaia."

"For God's sake!"

"Yes," she cried, and daring made her whirl, "Aglaia! You are so drunk with your success, you cannot resist, must court, inspire love even in a servant."

The long, silky, timeless skirt whirled the darkness round in dancing out its hate. The voice of darkness choked with hate.

"For God's sake," he repeated. "What if Aglaia comes in and hears your lies?"

"Oh, yes! Lies! Lies! Aglaia is the honest one. She is true. Yes. She is the rock that will never break unless God strikes her hard enough."

Then Constantia, who had gone so far she could not return, took the glass from which she had been drinking, and pitched it at a corner of the terrace. The fragments hissed, and slithered bright across the tiles.

Afterwards, when he was raising her up, she believed she heard him say: "You will never kill what I feel for you, Constantia, however hard you try."

She did so very much wish to believe, to hear tell of constancy. She longed to reach the plane on which he stood. Too far distant, finally.

"I think, perhaps," she said, "I have killed. *Myself*. And that. Was the best way."

But he raised her up, and held her, to pour into her hollow body something of his own strength.

Presently, with the little that remained of her, she took the surviving glass, and Aglaia came in, in her hat, and received the glass from the hands of her mistress, and rinsed it, and put it away.

Malliakas had lived so long in the garden-house at Cologny that the iron chair had eaten into his buttocks and hips, and signs of livery distress had appeared in patches round his eyes. Not that he regretted the time spent. In fact, he had allowed himself to be possessed to an extent that had never happened before.

He began to cough now, though, and look at his expensive Swiss watch.

"She is late," said the old man, staring out across the sad lake. "It is her good heart. She allows them to make use of her."

But almost as the visitor's chair grated in the preliminaries of departure, an approach was heard, along the gravel, from the direction of the house.

Unable to force himself to look, Malliakas stood hunched in the constricted space of the latticed pavilion, and listened to the breath rattling in his anxious chest.

Then, when the footsteps had advanced to the point of no avoidance, the old man repeated: "To make use of her," and added with conviction, still without looking: "She has come, though, and you shall make her acquaintance, and I shall have my soup."

The visitor glanced at the brown woman approaching the little garden-house. Stolid, but sure, she came on, crunching over the wet gravel, avoiding any mud or puddles.

"Aglaia," Mr Philippides said at last, "this gentleman is the Alexandrian. The friend of Tillotson, who wrote us. You remember? From Smyrna. Tillotson was in figs, I believe. He plays an energetic game of tennis."

In Mrs Philippides' confident approach, only her smile revealed some slight diffidence. It was very white and pleasing, though, framed in her rather brown face.

Relief did not prevent Malliakas' murmuring about his bus.

"Yes, yes, we shall catch the bus," Mrs Philippides promised, but first had to touch her husband. "It is damp," she said, rearranging the plaid. "Your tea is cold."

"And should be a whole lot colder, considering the time we've waited," Philippides said peevishly. "What about the *avgolemono*? We discussed it enough to be hungry for it."

"Yes," she consoled. "You shall have the *avgolemono*."

Her broad hand with the gold ring remained unhurried in its rite of reassurance.

She announced calmly: "I shall take the gentleman to the bus." But began to coax: "Won't you walk with us as far as the house? Geneviève shall light a fire."

"Fire! I shall stay a little longer. By myself," Philippides insisted in his dry voice. "And watch the sunset. If there is one."

For all those Swiss clouds denied the possibility.

As Mrs Philippides appeared about to lead, Malliakas prepared to follow.

"Come again," said the old man. "And I must tell you about my wife. We had always meant to go back, to look for the property in Smyrna. But she did not care to face the Turks. We were always intending to do this and that. To learn to cook. Or keep our tempers."

But the other Mrs Philippides had begun to lead the visitor away, and he obeyed, following her squat figure, under the wide summer hat.

The fact that her back was turned on the gentleman—the path made this unavoidable—possibly emboldened her. She began to talk.

"He will sit there for hours," she said. "It is his favourite place. It is his greatest pleasure. Drinking tea out of that glass. He told you about them."

She did not ask.

"Won't he catch cold?"

"He can stand, oh, any amount of fresh air. And has his thoughts."

She continued plodding. Silenter.

"He told you about Her?" she asked. "She would have known how to entertain you. What to say," Mrs Philippides said.

Crunching always.

"She was the *archontissa*," she explained. "I am a peasant. A servant. But have also done my duty as a wife. Because I loved her. I hope, I *think* she would not have disapproved. Not of everything."

"Is it long since Mrs Philippides died?" Malliakas asked prudently.

"Long? Oh, yes. How long? But long!" The second Mrs Philippides sighed, as though the gap between then and now was too great for her to measure.

"Her health, it appears, was not of the best."

"Oh, it was not her health!" Mrs Philippides answered. "The *kyria* died violently. Oh, violently! I had expected it."

And suddenly the words began to slip from this peasant throat as never before, in bursts at first, then in bitter streams, so much so that the stranger himself was caught up, and whirled with her down from the upper story, round the spiral, and into the street.

The maid running in her slippers. Slapping the marble stairs.

It was the hour of reddish summer dusk, which tightens round the skull. They stood shoulder to shoulder on the pavement. He could smell the anxiety of her strong but helpless peasant body.

"Kyria mou! Kyria!" the maid cried.

Then she stooped.

Her great buttocks were quivering in distress, her great breast would have given up its breath.

Bending over the figure in the gutter.

Constantia Philippides was just able to move her head. Her body was broken, though, which the maid arranged under the tumbled gown. It was still too soon for anyone to have gathered, excepting a dog, and the two ladies from the ground floor.

"Aglaia," Constantia began, issuing her order against that little trickle of darkening blood.

To the maid kneeling, rocking.

"Kyria! Ach, kyria mou! What shall we do now? But what shall we do?"

Rocking and lamenting, already in her black.

"I am glad, Aglaia," said Constantia Philippides, "that *you* will never break. Never. You must never!" Then, when she had risen for a moment, above the mounting tide of blood: "I am the one, you see, who broke."

A policeman carried her up the stairs, though the maid would have attempted it.

When it was over, the two figures walking through the passive landscape had almost reached the bus stop.

"You won't miss it. Although the Swiss are punctual," Mrs Philippides reassured.

She was again herself—decent, stolid, and composed.

"It is good the *kyrios* talked to you," she said. "It must have pleased him. There is so little to interest him now."

Then she paused, thinking, as some of her anxiety returned.

"You know," she said, in quick, panting whispers, "it is the last of the glasses—and if it breaks, what shall I do? I shall have nothing left then."

Suddenly Mrs Philippides halted, aware, it seemed, of her nakedness, and turned, and lumbered back, into the damp, choking garden. Nor did Malliakas find the courage to watch her go. There was the bus, besides. Regular and Swiss. He ran to mount. Away from silence. Smiling tautly. He could not have endured it if called upon to listen to a last shivering of glass.

Clay

For Barry Humphries and Zoë Caldwell

When he was about five years old some kids asked Clay why his mother had called him that. And he did not know. But began to wonder. He did, in fact, wonder a great deal, particularly while picking the bark off trees, or stripping a flower down to its core of mystery. He too, would ask questions, but more often than not failed to receive the answer because his mother could not bring herself to leave her own train of thought.

Mrs Skerritt said: "If only your father hadn't died he'd still be putting out the garbage the bin is too much for me the stooping not to mention the weight in anyone short of breath but you Clay I know will be good to your mum and help when you are older stronger only that is still a long way off."

So that it was Clay's turn not to answer. What could you say, anyway?

Mrs Skerritt said: "I wouldn't ask anything of anyone but there are certain things of course I wouldn't expect a gentleman to stand up for me in the tram while I have my own two legs only it's the sort of thing a gentleman ought to do and ladies take Mrs Pearl for instance what she expects of her husband and him with the sugar-diabeties too."

Clay mooned about the house listening to his mother's voice boring additional holes in the fretwork, for fretwork had been Dadda's hobby: there was fretwork just about everywhere, brackets and things, even a lace of fretwork hanging from tabletop and doorway. Stiff. Sometimes while his mother's voice bored and sawed further Clay would break off pieces of the brown fretwork and hide it away under the house. Under the house was full of fretwork finally.

Or he would moon about the terraces of garden, amongst the collapsing lattices, flower-pot shards crackling underfoot, legs slapped by the straps of dark, leathery plants, lungs filled with suffocating bursts of asparagus fern. He would dawdle down to the harbour, with its green smell of sea-lettuce, and the stone wall, scribbled with the white droppings of gulls. The house itself leaned rather far towards the harbour, but had not fallen, because some men had come and shored it up. There it hung, however.

So Clay mooned. And would return often to the photograph. It was as though his childhood were riveted to the wedding group. There was his father, those thick thighs, rather tight about the serge crutch (unlike the Dadda he remembered lying Incurable in bed), and the influential Mr Stutchbury, and Auntie Ada, and Nellie Watson (who died), and someone else who was killed in action. But it was to his mum that Clay was drawn, before and after all, into the torrential satin of the lap, by the face which had just begun to move out of its fixture of fretted lace. And the shoe. He was fascinated by the white shoe. Sometimes its great boat would float out from the shore of frozen time, into the waters of his imagination, rocking his cargo of almost transparent thoughts.

Once Mrs Skerritt came into the room and caught him at it, though she did not exactly see Clay for looking at herself.

"Ah dear," she said, "in the end things is sad."

She would often half cry, and at such moments her hair would look more than ever like so many lengths of grey string, or on windy days, a tizz of frayed dish-cloth.

On this particular day when she caught Clay looking at the photograph, his throat swelled, and he dared to ask:

"Why is my name Clay, Mum?"

Because by that time he was seven, and the kids were asking worse than ever, and bashing him up (they were afraid that he was different).

"Why," she said, "let me think your father wanted Percival that is after Mr Stutchbury but I could not bring myself I said there are so many things you don't do but want take a name a name is yours take pottery I said I've half a mind to try my hand if I can find some feller or lady you never know I may be artistic but didn't because well there isn't the time always so much to do the people who have to be told and who have to be told and then Dadda's incurable illness so I did not do that only thought and thought about it and that I believe is why you was called Clay."

Then she went out the back to empty the teapot on a bed of maidenhair which tingled perpetually with moisture.

So the kids continued to bash Clay up, and ask him why he was called that, and he couldn't tell them, because how could you even when you knew.

There were times when it got extra bad, and once they chased him with a woman's old cast-off shoe. He ran like a green streak, but not fast enough in the end—they caught him at the corner of Plant Street, where he had been born and always lived, and the heel of their old shoe bored for ever in his mind.

Later, when he had let himself in, into the garden of the leaning house, lost amongst collapsing lattices and the yellow fuzz of asparagus fern, he cried a bit for the difference to which he had been born. But smeared his eyes dry at last, and his nose. The light was rising from the bay in all green peacefulness, as if the world of pointed objects did not exist alongside that of the dreamy bridal shoe.

But he did not embark. Not then. His ribs had not subsided yet.

Once Clay dreamed a dream, and came down into the kitchen. He had meant to keep the dream to himself. Then it was too late, he heard, he was telling it to his mum. Even though his mouth was frozen stiff he had to keep on, to tell.

"In this dream," he said, "the steps led on down."

His mum was pushing the rashers around, which went on buckling up in the pan.

"Under the sea," said Clay. "It was beautiful."

He was sorry, but he could not help it.

"Everything drawn out. Hair and things. And weeds. The knotted ones. And the lettucy kind. Some of the fish had beards, Mum, and barked, well, like dogs."

His mum had put the fried bread on a plate to one side, where the little squares were already stiffening.

"And shells, Mum," he said, "all bubbles and echoes as I went on down. It felt good. It felt soft. I didn't have to try. But just floated. Down."

He could see his mother's behind, how it had begun to quiver, and he dreaded what might happen when he told. There was no avoiding it, though, and his mum went on prodding the bacon in the pan.

"When I got to the bottom," he said, "and the steps ended, you should have seen how the sea stretched, over the sand and broken bottles. Everything sort of silvery. I don't remember much else. Except that I found, Mum," he said.

"What?" she asked.

He dreaded it.

"A cloud, Mum," he said, "and it was dead."

Then Mrs Skerritt turned round, it was dreadful, how she looked. She opened her mouth, but nothing came out at first, only Clay saw the little thing at the back. Raised. When suddenly it began to act like a clapper. She began to cry, she began to create.

"Whatever are you gunna do to me?" she cried, as she pummelled and kneaded the moist grey dough of her cheeks.

"On top of everything else I never ever thought I'd have a freak!"

But Clay could only stand, and receive the blows her voice dealt. It was as though someone had taken a stick and drawn a circle round him. Him at the centre. There was no furniture any more.

The bacon was burning in the pan.

When Mrs Skerritt had thought it over, and used a little eau-de-Cologne, she took him up to McGillivray's. It was late by then, on a Saturday morning too. All the way Clay listened to her breathing and sometimes the sound of her corset. McGillivray was already closing, but agreed to do Mrs Skerritt's lad. McGillivray was kind.

"We want it short short Mr McGillivray please," Mrs Skerritt said.

As the barber snipped Clay could hear his mum breathing, from where she sat, behind his back, under the coloured picture of the King.

Mr McGillivray did his usual nice job, and was preparing to design the little quiff when Mrs Skerritt choked.

"That is not short Mr McGillivray not what I mean oh no oh dear but it is difficult to explain there is too much involved and I left school when I turned fourteen."

McGillivray laughed and said: "Short is not shorn!"

"I don't care," she said.

Clay could only look at the glass, and suck his cheeks in.

"Short is what I said and mean," Mrs Skerritt confirmed. "I was never one for not coming to the point."

McGillivray was a gentle man, but he too began to breathe, he took the clippers, and shore a path through his subject's hair. He shore, and shore. Till there Clay was. Exposed.

"That suit?" McGillivray asked.

"Thank you," she said.

So meek.

Then they went home. They crunched over the asphalt. They were that heavy, both of them.

As they went down the hill towards the turn where the milko's cart had plunged over, Mrs Skerritt said:

"There Clay a person is sometimes driven to things in defence of what we know and love I would not of done this otherwise if not to protect you from yourself because love you will suffer in life if you start talking queer remember it doesn't pay to be different and no one is different without they have something wrong with them."

Clay touched his prickly hair.

"Let me remind you," she said, "that your mum loves you that is why."

But Clay could no longer believe in love, and the kids bashed him up worse than ever, because his no-hair made him a sort of different different.

"Wot was you in for?" the kids asked, and did windmills on his stubble. "Old Broad Arrer!" they shouted, and punched.

Actually Clay grew up narrow. He was all knuckle, all wrist. He had those drawn-out arms. He had a greenish skin from living under too many plants. He was long. And his eyes overflowed at dusk, merged with the street lights, and the oil patches on lapping water.

"Are you lonely, Clay?" Mrs Skerritt asked.

"No," he said. "Why?"

"I thought perhaps you was lonely you should get out and meet other young people of your own age you should get to know nice girls otherwise it is not normal."

Then she drew in her chin, and waited.

But Clay stroked his prickly hair. For he went to McGillivray's every so often since it was ordained. When his voice broke the others no longer bashed him up, having problems of their own. The blackheads came, the pimples and moustaches.

Sometimes Mrs Skerritt would cry, sitting on the rotten veranda overlooking the little bay in which cats so often drowned.

"Oh dear Clay," she cried, "I am your mother and have a responsibility a double one since Dadda went I will ask Mr Stutchbury but cannot rely totally do you know what you want to do?"

Clay said: "No."

"Oh dear," she moaned worse than ever, "how did I deserve a silent boy who loves what I would like to know himself perhaps himself."

In fact Clay did not know what he loved. He would have liked to think it was his mother, though it could have been Dadda. So he would try to remember, but it was only cold yellow skin, and the smell of sick sheets. When he had been forced to approach his father, lying Incurable in the bed, his heart could have tumbled down out of the belfry of his body.

Once his mother, it was evening, clutched his head against her apron, so that she must have pricked her hands.

"You are not my son," she clanged, "otherwise you would act different."

But he could not, did not want to. Sometimes, anyway, at that age, he felt too dizzy from growing.

"How?" his voice asked, or croaked.

But she did not explain. She flung his long body away.

"It's not a matter," she said, "that anybody can discuss I will ask Mr Stutchbury to see what we must do and how."

Mr Stutchbury was so influential, as well as having been a mate of Herb Skerritt's all his life. Mr Stutchbury was something, Mrs Skerritt believed, in the Department of Education, but if she did not clear the matter up, it was because she considered there was not all that necessity.

She bought a T-bone steak, and asked him round.

"What," she asked, "should we do with Clay I am a widow as you know and you was his father's friend."

Mr Stutchbury drew in his moustache.

"We will see," he said, "when the time comes."

Then he folded his moist lips over a piece of yellow fat from the not so tender T-bone steak.

When it was time, Mr Stutchbury thought up a letter to some fellow at the Customs and Excise.

Dear Archie,   (*he composed*)
This is to recommend the son of an old friend. Herb Skerritt, for many years in the Tramways, died in tragical circumstances —of cancer to be precise . . .

(Clay, who of course opened the letter to see, got quite a shock from a word his mother never on any account allowed to be used in the home.)

. . . It is my duty and wish to further the interests of the above-mentioned boy. In brief, I would esteem it a favour if you could see your way to taking him "under your wing." I do not predict wonders of young Skerritt, but am of the opinion, rather, that he is a decent, average lad. In any event, wonders are not all that desirable, not in the Service anyway. It is the steady hand which pushes the pen a lifetime.
I will not expatiate further, but send you my
Salaams!

The young lady whom Mr Stutchbury had persuaded to type the letter had barely left the room, when his superior called, with the

result that he forgot to add as he intended: "Kindest regards to Mrs
Archbold." Even persons of influence have to consider the ground
they tread on.

But Clay Skerritt started at the Customs, because Mr Archbold
was not the sort to refuse Mr Stutchbury the favour he asked. So
Clay took the ferry, mornings, in the stiff dark suit his mother had
chosen. His long thin fingers learned to deal in forms. He carried the
papers from tray to tray. In time he grew used to triplicate, and
moistened the indelible before writing in his long thin hand the
details, and the details.

Clay Skerritt did not complain, and if he was ignored he had
known worse. For he was most certainly ignored, by the gentlemen
who sat amongst the trays of papers, by the young ladies of the
Customs and Excise, who kept their nails so beautifully, who took
their personal towels to the toilet, and giggled over private matters
and cups of milky tea. If they ever laughed at the junior in particular, at his tricky frame, his pimples, and his stubble of hair, Clay
Skerritt was not conscious of it. Why should he be? He was born
with inward-looking eyes.

That all was not quite in order, though, he began to gather from
his mother.

"When I am gone Clay," she said—it was the evening the sink
got blocked up, "you will remember how your mother was a messer
but fond she only scraped the dishes into the sink because her mind
was otherwise engaged with you Clay your interests always some
practical young lady will rectify anything your mother ever did by
good intention I would not force you but only advise time is not to
be ignored."

But on days when the wind blew black across the grey water Mrs
Skerritt might remark, peering out from the arbours of asparagus
fern:

"Some young woman clever with her needle lighter-handed at the
pastry-board will make you forget your poor mum well it is the
way."

Her son was bound to ignore what he could not be expected to
believe. He would take a look at the wedding group. All so solidly

alive, the figures appeared to announce a truth of which he alone could be the arbiter, just as the great white shoe would still put out, into the distance, for destinations of his choice.

His mother, however, continued in her mistaken attempts to celebrate the passing of reality. There was the day she called, her voice intruding amongst the objects which surrounded him:

"Take my grey costume dear up to the dry cleaner at the Junction tomato sauce is fatal when a person is on the stoutish side."

Clay acted as he had been told. Or the streets were acting round him, and the trams. It was a bright day. Metal sang. The brick homes were no longer surreptitious, but opened up to disclose lives. In one window a woman was looking into her armpit. It made Clay laugh.

At the cleaner's a lady finished a yarn with the young girl. The lady said from alongside her cigarette:

"I'll leave you to it, Marj. I'm gunna make tracks for home and whip me shoes off. My feet are hurting like hell."

Then the bell.

Clay was still laughing.

The young girl was looking down at the sheets of fresh brown paper, through the smell of cleaning. She herself had a cleaned, pallid skin, with pores.

"What's up?" she asked, as the client continued laughing.

She spoke so very flat and polite.

"Nothing," he said, but added: "I think perhaps you are like my mother."

Which was untrue, in a sense, because the girl was flat, still, and colourless, whereas his mother was rotund, voluble, and at least several tones of grey. But Clay had been compelled to say it.

The girl did not reply. She looked down at first, as though he had overstepped the mark. Then she took the costume, and examined the spots of tomato sauce.

"Ready tomorrow," she said.

"Go on!"

"Why not?" the girl replied. "We are a One-Day."

But flat and absent she sounded.

Then Clay did not know why, but asked: "You've got something on your mind."

She said: "It's only that the sink got blocked yesterday evening."

It sounded so terribly grey, and she looking out with that expression of permanence. Then at once he knew he had been right, and that the girl at the dry cleaner's had something of his mother: it was the core of permanence. Then Clay grew excited. For he did not believe in impermanence, not even when his mother attempted to persuade, not even when he watched the clods of earth tumble down on the coffin lid. Not while he was he.

So he said: "Tomorrow."

It sounded so firm, it was almost today.

Clay got used to Marj just as he had got used to his mum, only differently. They swung hands together, walking over the dead grass of several parks, or staring at animals in cages. They were already living together, that is, their silences intermingled. Each had a somewhat clammy palm. And if Marj spoke there was no necessity to answer, it was so flat, her remarks had the colour of masonite.

Marj said: "When I have a home of my own, I will turn out the lounge Fridays. I mean, there is a time and place for everything. There are the bedrooms too."

She said: "I do like things to be nice."

And: "Marriage should be serious."

How serious, Clay began to see, who had not told his mum.

When at last he did she was drying the apostle spoons, one of which she dropped, and he let her pick it up, on seeing that it was necessary for her to perform some therapeutic act.

"I am so glad Clay," she said, rather purple, after a pause, "I cannot wait to see this nice girl we must arrange some we must come to an agree there is no reason why a young couple should not hit it off with the mother-in-law if the home is large it is not so much temperament as the size of the home that causes friction."

Mrs Skerritt had always known herself to be reasonable.

"And Marj is so like you, Mum."

"Eh?" Mrs Skerritt said.

He could not explain that what was necessary for him, for what he had to do, was a continuum. He could not have explained what he had to do, because he did not know, as yet.

All Mrs Skerritt could say was: "The sooner we see the better we shall know."

So Clay brought Marj. Their hands were clammier that day. The plants were huge, casting a fuscous tinge on the shored-up house.

Mrs Skerritt looked out of the door.

"Is this," she said, "I am not yet not yet ready to see."

Clay told Marj she must go away, for that day at least, he would send for her, then he took his mother inside.

Mrs Skerritt did not meet Marj again, except in the mirror, in which she saw with something of a shock there is no such thing as permanence.

Shortly after she died of something. They said it was her ticker.

And Clay brought Marj to live in the house in which he had been born and lived. They did not go on a honeymoon, because, as Marj said, marriage should be serious. Clay hoped he would know what to do as they lay in the bed Mum and Dadda had used. Lost in that strange and lumpy acre Clay and Marj listened to each other.

But it was good. He continued going to the Customs. Once or twice he pinched the lobe of Marj's ear.

"What's got into you?" she asked.

He continued going to the Customs. He bought her a Java sparrow in a cage. It was a kind of love poem.

To which Marj replied: "I wonder if it's gunna scatter its seed on the wall-to-wall. We can always spread a newspaper, though."

And did.

Clay went to the Customs. He sat at his own desk. He used his elbows more than before, because his importance had increased.

"Take this letter away, Miss Venables," he said. "There are only two copies. When I expected five. Take it away," he said.

Miss Venables pouted, but took it away. She, like everybody, saw that something had begun to happen. They would watch Mr Skerritt, and wait for it.

But Marj, she was less expectant. She accepted the houseful of fretwork, the things the mother-in-law had put away—sets of string-coloured doilies for instance; once she came across a stuffed canary in a cardboard box. She did not remark, but accepted. Only once she failed to accept. Until Clay asked:

"What has become of the photo?"

"It is in that cupboard," she said.

He went and fetched out the wedding group, and stuck it where it had been, on a fretwork table. At least he did not ask why she had put the photo away, and she was glad, because she would not have known what to answer. The bits of your husband you would never know were bad enough, but not to understand yourself was worse.

So Marj stuck to the carpet-sweeper, she was glad of the fluff under the bed, she was glad of the pattern on the lino, the cartons of crispies that she bought—so square. Even light is solid when the paths lead inward. So she listened to the carpet-sweeper.

All this time, she realized, something had been happening to Clay. For one thing his hair had begun to grow. Its long wisps curled like feather behind his ears. He himself, she saw, was not yet used to the silky daring of hair, which formerly had pricked to order.

"Level with the lobes of the ears, Mr McGillivray, please," Clay would now explain.

McGillivray, who was old by this, and infallibly kind, always refrained from commenting.

So did the gentlemen at the Customs—it was far too strange. Even the young ladies, who had been prepared to giggle at first, got the shivers for something they did not understand.

Only when the hair had reached as far as Mr Skerritt's shoulders did Mr Archbold send for Clay.

"Is it necessary, Mr Skerritt?" his superior asked, who had the additional protection of a private office.

Clay replied: "Yes."

He stood looking.

He was allowed to go away.

His wife Marj decided there is nothing to be surprised at. It is the only solution. Even if the fretwork crackled, she would not hear. Even if the hanging basket sprouted hair instead of fern, she would not see. There were the chops she put in front of her husband always so nicely curled on the plate. Weren't there the two sides of life?

One evening Clay came up out of the terraced garden, where the snails wound, and the sea smells. He stood for some considerable time in front of his parents' wedding group. The great shoe, or boat, or bridge, had never appeared so structural. Looking back he seemed to remember that this was the occasion of his beginning the poem, or novel, or regurgitation, which occupied him for the rest of his life.

Marj was certain that that was the evening he closed the door.

She would lie and call: "Aren't you gunna come to bed, Clay?"

Or she would stir at the hour when the sheets are greyest, when the air trembles at the withheld threat of aluminium, Marj would ungum her mouth to remark: "But Clay, the alarm hasn't gone off yet!"

From now on it seemed as though his body never stayed there long enough to warm the impression it left on the bed. She could hardly complain, though. He made love to her twice a year, at Christmas, and at Easter, though sometimes at Easter they might decide against—there was the Royal Agricultural Show, which is so exhausting.

All this is beside the point. It was the sheets of paper which counted, on which Clay wrote, behind the door of that little room, which his wife failed to remember, it was soon so long since she had been inside. One of the many things Marj Skerritt learned to respect was another person's privacy.

So Clay wrote. At first he occupied himself with objects, the mysterious life which inanimacy contains. For several years in the beginning he was occupied with this.

". . . the table standing continues standing its legs so permanent of course you can take an axe and swing it cut into the flesh as Poles do every once in a while then the shriek murder murder but mostly nothing disturbs the maps the childhood journeys on the frozen wave of wooden water no boat whether wood or iron when you come to think satin either ever sails from A to B except in the mind of the passenger so the table standing standing under an

electric bulb responds unlikely unless to determination or desperation of a Polish kind . . ."

One night Cay wrote: "I have never observed a flower-pot
intimately until now its hole is fascinating the little down of green
moss it is of greater significance than what is within though you can
fill it if you decide to if you concentrate long enough . . ."

Up till now he had not turned his attention to human beings,
though he had been surrounded by them all his life. In actual fact he
did not turn his attention to them now, he was intruded on. And
Lova was not all that human, or not at first, a presence rather, or
sensation of possession.

That night Clay got the hiccups, he was so excited, or nervous.
The reverberations were so metallic he failed to hear his wife Marj,
her grey voice: "Aren't you gunna come to bed, Clay?"

Lova was, by comparison, a greenish-yellow, of certain fruits,
and plant-flesh.

"Lova Lova Lova," he wrote at first, to try it out.

He liked it so much it surprised him it had not come to him
before. He could have sat simply writing the name, but Lova grew
more palpable.

". . . her little conical breasts at times ripening into porepores
detachable by sleight of hand or windy days yet so elusive fruit and
shoes distributed amongst the grass . . ."

In the beginning Lova would approach from behind glass, her
skin had that faint hot-house moisture which tingles on the down of
ferns, her eyes a ferny brown that complemented his own if he had
known. But he knew no more than gestures at first, the floating
entanglement of hair in mutual agreement, the slight shiver of skin
passing over skin. She would ascend and descend the flights of stone
steps, inhabiting for a moment the angles of landings of old moss-
upholstered stone. The leaves of the *Monstera deliciosa* sieved her
at times into a dispersed light. Which he alone knew how to
reassemble. On rare occasions their mouths would almost meet, at
the bottom of the garden, where the smell of rotting was, and the
liquid manure used to stand, which had long since dried up. She was
not yet real, and might never be. No. He would make her. But there
were the deterrents. The physical discords.

Marj said: "My hands are that chapped I must ask Mr Todd's advice. You can enjoy a chat with a chemist, doctors are most of them too busy pushing you out."

And Lova got the herpes. Clay could not look at her at first. As she sat at her own little table, taking the fifteen varieties of pills, forcing them into her pig's snout, Lova would smile still, but it was sad. And soon the sore had become a scab. He could not bring himself to approach. And breath, besides.

For nights and nights Clay could not write a word. Or to be precise, he wrote over several nights:

". . . a drying and a dying . . ."

If he listened, all he could hear was the rustle of Lova's assorted pills, the ruffling of a single sterile date-palm, the sound of Marj turning in the bed.

Then it occurred to his panic the shored-up house might break open. It was so rotten, so dry. He could not get too quickly round the table, scattering the brittle sheets of paper. Motion detached itself from his feet in the shape of abrupt, leather slippers. Skittering to reach the door.

Clay did not, in fact, because Lova he now saw locking locking locked it, popping the key afterwards down between.

Lova laughed. And Clay stood. The little ripples rose up in her throat, perhaps it was the cold key, and spilled over, out of her mouth, her wet mouth. He knew that the private parts of babies tasted as tender as Lova's mouth.

He had never tried. But suspected he must.

She came to him.

"Bum to you!" Lova said.

She sat in his lap then, and with his free hand he wrote, the first of many white nights:

"At last my ryvita has turned to velveeta life is no longer a toast-rack."

"Golly," said Lova, "what it is to be an educated feller! Honest, Clay, it must be a great satisfaction to write, if only to keep one of your hands occupied."

She laughed again. When he had his doubts. Does every face wear the same expression unless it is your own? He would have

liked to look at the wedding group, to verify, but there were all
those stairs between, and darkness. All he could hear was the sound
of Marj breaking wind. Marj certainly had said at breakfast: "It is
the same. Whatever the manufacturers tell you, that is only to sell
the product."

But Lova said: "It is different, Clay, as different as kumquats
from pommygranates. You are the differentest of all perhaps. I
could lap up the cream of your genius."

She did, in fact, look at moments like a cat crouched in his lap,
but would close at once, and open, like a knife.

"I would eat you," she repeated, baring her pointed teeth, when
he had thought them broad and spaced, as in Mum or Marj.

Although he was afraid, he wrote with his free right hand:

"I wood not trust a razor-blade to any but my own . . ."

When Lova looked it over.

"Shoot!" she said. "That is what I am!"

He forgot about her for a little, for writing down what he had to
write.

". . . Lova sat in my lap smelling of crushed carrot tops she has
taken the frizz out of her hair but cannot make it smell less green I
would not trust her further than without meaning to cast aspersions
you can't trust even your own thoughts past midnight . . ."

"Chip Chip Chip chipped off his finger," Lova said. "Anyway it
begins with C."

"Oh dear," C began to cry. "Oh dear dear dear oh Lova!"

"When does D come in?" she asked.

"D isn't born," he said, "and pretty sure won't be. As for A, A is
in bed. No," he corrected. "A am not."

Suddenly he wished he was.

He realized he was eye to eye with Lova their lashes grappling
together in gummy agreement but melancholy to overflowing. They
were poured into each other.

After that, Clay finished, for the night at least, and experienced
the great trauma of his little empty room, for Lova had vanished,
and there were only the inkstains on his fingers to show that she had
ever been there.

There was nothing for it now but to join Marj in the parental bed, where he wondered whether he would ever be able to rise again. He was cold, cold.

Actually Marj turned over and said: "Clay, I had an argument with Mr Tesoriero over the turnips. I told him you couldn't expect the public to buy them flabby."

But Clay slept, and in fact he did not rise, not that morning, the first in many years, when the alarm clock scattered its aluminium trays all over the house.

Clay Skerritt continued going to the Customs. They had got used to him by then, even to his hair, the streaks in it.

He realized it was time he went to McGillivray's again, but some young dago came out, and said:

"Nho! Nho! McGillivray gone. Dead. How many years? Five? Six?"

So Clay Skerritt went away.

It was natural enough that it should have happened to McGillivray. Less natural were the substances. The pretending houses. The asphalt which had lifted up.

Then he saw the pointed heel, caught in the crack, wrenching at it. He saw the figure. He saw. He saw.

When she turned round, she said.

"Yes. It's all very well. For you. With square heels. Bum bums."

Wrenching at her heel all the while.

"But Lova," he said, putting out his hands.

She was wearing a big-celled honeycomb sweater.

"Oh, yes!" she said.

And laughed.

"If that's how you feel," he answered.

"If that's how I *feel!*"

His hands were shaking, and might have caught in the oatmeal wool.

"I'm not gunna stand around exchanging words with any long-haired nong in the middle of Military Road. Not on yours!"

"Be reasonable," he begged.

"What is reasonable?" she asked.

He could not tell. Nor if she had asked: what is love?

"Aren't you going to know me then?" he said.

"I know you," she said, sort of flat—two boards could not have come together with greater exactitude.

"And it is time," she said, "to go."

Jerking at her stuck heel.

"I've come here for something," he remembered. "Was it birdseed?"

"Was it my Aunt Fanny!"

Then she got her heel free and all the asphalt was crackling up falling around them in scraps of torn black tinkly paper.

If he could only have explained that love cannot be explained.

All the while ladies were going in and out, strings eating into their fingers together with their rings. One lady had an alsatian, a basket suspended from its teeth, it did not even scent the trouble.

It was Saturday morning. Clay went home.

That evening, after they had finished their spaghetti on toast, because they were still paying off the Tecnico, Marj said: "Clay, I had a dream."

"No!" he shouted.

Where could he go? There was nowhere now.

Except on the Monday there was the Customs and Excise. He could not get there quick enough. To sharpen his pencils. To move the paper-clips the other side of the ink-eraser.

When what he was afraid might happen, happened.

Lova had followed him to the Customs.

The others had not spotted it yet, for it could have been any lady passing the day at the Customs in pursuit of her unlawful goods. Only no lady would have made so straight for Mr Skerritt's desk, nor would she have been growing from her big-celled oatmeal sweater quite so direct as Lova was.

She had those little, pointed, laughing teeth.

"Well," she opened, "you didn't reckon on this."

She was so certain of herself by now, he was afraid she might jump out of her jumper.

He sat looking down, at the letter from Dooley and Mann, Import Agents, re the Bechstein that got lost.

"Listen, Lova," he advised. "Not in here. It won't help find the piano."

"Pianner? A fat lot of pianner! You can't play that one on me."

"You may be right," he answered.

"Right!" she said. "Even if I wasn't. Even if I was flippin' wrong!"

She put her hand-bag on the desk.

"If anyone's gunna play, I'm the one," she said.

Sure enough the old black upright slid around the corner from behind Archbold's glassed-in office, followed by the little, leather-upholstered stool, from which the hair was bursting out. Lova seemed satisfied. She laughed, and when she had sat down, began to dish out the gay sad jazz. Playing and playing. Her little hands were jumping and frolicking on their own. The music playing out of every worm-hole in the old, sea-changed piano.

Clay looked up, to see Archbold looking down. Miss Titmuss had taken her personal towel, and was having trouble with her heels as she made her way towards the toilet.

When Lova got up. She was finished. Or not quite. She began to drum with her bum on the greasy, buckled-up rashers of keys of the salt-cured old piano.

"There!" she shouted.

She came and sat on the corner of his desk. She had never been so elastic. It was her rage of breathing. He was unable to avoid the pulse of her suspender, winking at him from her thigh.

One or two other of the Customs officials had begun to notice, he observed, desperately through the side-curtains of his hair.

So he said: "Look here, Lova, a scene at this stage will make it wellnigh impossible for me to remain in the Service. And what will we do without the pension? Marj must be taken into account. I mean to say, it is the prestige as much as the money. Otherwise, we have learnt to do on tea and bread."

Lova laughed then.

"Ha! *Ha!* HA!"

There is no way of writing it but how it was written on the wall. For it was. It got itself printed up on the wall which ran at right angles to Archbold's office.

Clay sat straight, straight. His Adam's apple might not endure it much longer.

"Scenes are so destructive," he said, or begged.

So his mum had told him.

"If that is what you want," said Lova, "you know I was never one for holding up procedure for the sake of filling in a form."

And she ripped it off the pad from under his nose. Her hands were so naked, and could get a whole lot nakeder. He was afraid he might be answerable.

"I would never suggest," she shouted, "that the pisspot was standing right end up when it wasn't."

But he had to resist, not so much for personal reasons as for the sake of public decorum, for the honour of the Department. He had to protect the paper-clips.

Because their hands were wrestling, troubling the desk. Him and Lova. At any moment the carton might burst open. At any. It happened quite quickly, breathily, ending in the sigh of scatteration.

"I will leave you for now," she said, getting off the corner of the desk, and pulling down her sweater, which had rucked up.

Almost every one of his colleagues had noticed by this, but all had the decency to avoid passing audible judgement on such a very private situation.

When it was over a little while, Miss Titmuss got down and gathered up the paper-clips, because she was sorry for Mr Skerritt.

He did not wait to thank or explain, but took his hat, treading carefully to by-pass the eyes, and caught the ferry to the other side.

Marj said: "Aren't you early, Clay? Sit on the veranda a while. I'll bring you a cuppa, and slice of that pound cake, it's still eatable I think."

So he sat on the veranda, where his mother used to sit and complain, and felt the southerly get inside his neckband, and heard the date-palm starting up. Sparrows gathered cautiously.

Marj said: "Clay, if you don't eat up, it'll be tea."

You can always disregard, though, and he went inside the room, which he did not even dread. There she was, sitting in the other chair, in the oatmeal sweater. Her back turned. Naturally.

"Lova," he began.

Then she came towards him, and he saw that she herself might sink in the waters of time she spread before him cunningly the nets of water smelling of nutmeg over junket the steamy mornings and the rather shivery afternoons.

If he did not resist.

She was just about as resistant as water not the tidal kind but a glad upward plume of water rising and falling back as he put his hands gently lapping lapping. She was so gentle.

Marj began to knock on the door.

"Tea's getting cold, Clay," she announced.

It was, too. That is the way of things.

"I made you a nice devilled toast."

She went away, but returned, and held her ear to the dry rot.

"Clay?" she asked. "Don't you mind?"

Marj did not like to listen at doors because of her regard for privacy.

"Well," she said, "I never knew you to act like this."

It could have been the first time in her life that Marj had opened a door.

Then she began to scream. She began to create. It was unlike her.

She could not see his face because of all that hair. The hair and the boards between them were keeping it a secret.

"This is something I never bargained for," she cried.

For the blood had spurted out of the leg of the table. Just a little.

And that old shoe. He lay holding a white shoe.

"I never ever saw a shoe!" she moaned. "Of all the junk she put away, just about every bit of her, and canaries and things, never a shoe!"

As Clay lay.

With that stiff shoe.

"I don't believe it!" Marj cried.

Because everyone knows that what isn't isn't, even when it is.

The Evening at Sissy Kamara's

At that instant Mr Petrocheilos probed the nerve, and in spite of her rigidity Mrs Pantzopoulos bounced, the paper covering the head-rest grated, the hair grew moist round the edges of her face.

Would she care for an injection? Mr Petrocheilos asked.

"Oh no, we are Greeks, aren't we?" Mrs Pantzopoulos said, and laughed.

Mr Petrocheilos did not reply, and she blushed for what must have sounded pretentious to anyone who did not understand. For much as she hated the nagging of the little metal probe, and the gnawing of the still more brutal drill, Mrs Pantzopoulos felt it her duty to test her capacity for suffering while extended in the dentist's chair.

Now she watched, with fascinated languor, from beneath her eyelids, the dentist's strong and hairy wrists, as he stopped, and breathed, and prepared the drill. Mr Petrocheilos was a bony, uncommunicative man. Did he perhaps enjoy torturing his patients? Mrs Pantzopoulos wondered. That would have been going too far. She wondered why she had not changed her dentist.

Then Mr Petrocheilos was opening her mouth as though it were a rubber slit. He was inserting an enormous finger. He was introducing the dreadful drill. How very much to the point she might have been some some peasant. Mrs Pantzopoulos' gurgle was half-scream half-laughter. Though she could bear it of course. She lay with her eyes closed, her body slack. To submit. Oh it was moooo*ohn*strous what one was expected to endure.

And as if the physical frightfulness were not enough, all the unpleasanter recollections chose to torment her in the dentist's chair. More often than not incidents of no significance. For example, the evening at Sissy Kamara's. Yes, the evening at Sissy Kamara's.

Mr Petrocheilos breathed fire into Mrs Pantzopoulos' face. The caverns of black, wiry hair threatened to engulf.

"Sissy Kamara rang," Poppy Pantzopoulos decided at last to mention to her husband.

Basil made that little noise.

"She's invited us—I must say I was rather touched—because, she says, she wants to talk about old times."

"Anatolian Nights!" She recognized Basil's cutting-edge. "None of you Smyrna breed can resist the opportunity to wallow."

"I am not to blame for my origins, am I?"

"Not," he agreed, "for your origins. *But.*"

Basil touched his black pearl, the one he always wore in his tie. He had grown so flawless he could afford to forget his original grain of Piraeus sand. Every morning he put on his trousers still warm from the pressing-board. Every morning he walked to the bank, just to make certain of his figure. Those not his equals in precision were inclined to consider Basil cold, but his wife was convinced that the observances had brought him the Kolonaki branch.

"But," he said, and bored with his finger, "you *are* responsible for accepting the evening at Sissy Kamara's. You could have avoided something each of us is bound to regret."

"Oh!" she cried. "You are unjust! As if poor Sissy! You can attack *me!* I know what I am. But Sissy is such a brilliant woman."

"So we are told," Basil said.

Often Poppy Pantzopoulos refused to forgive her husband's still perfect profile until she found it on her pillow.

"Well, there are the poems," she offered.

"Printed so privately nobody has read them."

"There was the *epic* poem," Poppy Pantzopoulos mumbled on.

On occasions her mind became the victim of her plumpy body.

"There was the epic poem." Basil sighed. "On a theme nobody can remember. Which Sissy Kamara declaimed. On a mountainside. To a group of women, most of them by now dead."

All their life together Poppy Pantzopoulos had refused to admit that her husband's opinion of women, even those women he used, might embrace herself.

"Well," she apologized, "there was her other work. There was the weaving. She organized *Greek Peasant Crafts* at a time when nobody—nobody nice—took any interest in such things. And persevered almost unassisted. At the expense of her health. Because everyone knows Sissy Kamara is not strong."

"Sissy Kamara is one of those with a talent for bullying others into works for which she takes the credit."

"Oh, you are so very wrong! Not to say wicked! I cannot deny Sissy is forceful. But where would she be without her forcefulness? Considering all she has to bear. Not only her poor health, but reduced means, and that husband."

"Certainly," said Basil, "one wonders how she came to marry Sotos."

"For that matter," answered Poppy, "one wonders why most people married the husbands or wives they have got."

Basil did not have to look. He knew she knew. She knew he had married her for her Aunt Danae's house in Ploutarchou and Uncle Stepho's Euboean estate. She knew about Hariklia, and Phroso, and possibly Smaragda Thiraiou. But she was not bitter, because she loved him.

Basil touched his black pearl.

"Sotos Louloudis!"

"Yes," she said. "Yes. With all those family obligations Sissy was forced to marry late, and by then she was too poor, I suppose, to get herself anything better."

Poppy Pantzopoulos could have cried.

"But Soto Louloudis! No one even knows what he does!"

"Something very discreet, I expect. I have heard he's some kind of clerk. Or perhaps already *was*. He appears to stay at home a lot."

"But what a man! One can't think of her as being *married* to that Sotos. Nobody can. To everyone Sissy is still Sissy Kamara."

"That is true," Poppy Pantzopoulos had to admit. "Because everyone knows that Sissy Kamara of Smyrna . . ."

"Oh, dear! There we go! We Anatolians!"

"Isn't it late?" she asked.

"Yes," he said, and frowned. "It is late."

She had admired him for his conscientiousness, which perpetually accused her own superficiality. In museums, for instance, he would read the legend under every piece while she sat at the end of the hall and rested her swollen feet.

"We shall see what we shall see," Basil said. "Whether Mrs Kamara Louloudis can give us an eatable dinner. At least, until Thursday, we may hope."

That morning he had not kissed her, and although she was usually restored by ritual, she was glad he had not offered it, knowing that her chin was beyond repair, and that her eyelids wore their black-greasy look.

Then Mr Petrocheilos said: "You can't always tell, but I think it is going to be worse than we expected."

His breath almost scorched her ear.

"How frightful!" Mrs Pantzopoulos replied through a mouthful of instruments, but her words were sucked down by the tube in a stream of ineffectuality.

"I am a coward," she added. "The least pain," she seemed to scream in opposition to her ear-drums.

And hoped that distortion had prevented the dentist from interpreting.

Sotos Louloudis had come to the door. They must excuse Sissy, he said, or rather suggested, she was in the kitchen attending to things. She had sent away the girl, who was made nervous by guests, which made Sissy nervous in turn. Poppy longed for the power to protect Sotos' excuse from her own husband's smile.

In any case, there stood Sotos. He was so thin. There was little to remember of Sotos except his thinness. Certainly not his opinions, which were an echo of the dying fall in other people's remarks.

He said: "Welcome. Will you come with me? Sissy thinks we should sit on the balcony. Will you come out?"

It could only have been Sissy who had arranged the chairs, amongst the jasmine and the pelargoniums, as though for the passengers in a ship. They were so strictly aligned on deck.

"Will you take a drop of something?" Sotos asked.

There was, indeed, what remained of a bottle of *ouzo*.

"Do you care to smoke a cigarette?"

He did not add: if you have brought one. Basil, of course, had his presentation case. Sotos himself did not smoke. Was it perhaps as a reproach to Sissy, who carried her cigarettes around as though they were her luggage for the journey?

Soon they were sitting in the grating chairs, and Sotos Louloudis was prepared to fill the gaps people leave in conversation.

"Yes," he said. "You wouldn't believe, would you? Not unless you were told."

"Is it, now? Is it a *fact?*" he would inquire from above his plaited hands, and add perhaps: "I suppose it is, isn't it? It only goes to show!"

Twisting his thin legs together inside their inferior cloth.

Only towards the end of an evening Sotos Louloudis might suddenly look out at those others who had been in possession of it. His eyelids would twitch, and he would appear to emerge from the end of the tunnel, no longer so very perplexed and surprised. Each time it happened Poppy Pantzopoulos would remember having been fascinated by Sotos on similar occasions, by the sudden closeness of his distance. It was something one quickly forgot, however.

She certainly did not think of it now, because here was Sissy Kamara coming out. And then Sissy's cheek. And not so much a perfume as a recollection of doors opening into the house on Frankish Street.

"Oh dear," Sissy Kamara exclaimed, "here you are! I am so terribly glad to see you, darling Poppy!"

If Poppy Pantzopoulos had not *known* Sissy she might have wondered. She could hear Basil making that little noise, the clicking sound at the back of his throat.

"And Basil too. That goes without saying," Sissy added, and put her luggage on the table. If she did not notice Sotos, it was because he was her husband, and always there.

"Do you care for pelargoniums?" she asked. "I wonder whether I do. Too straggly. They refuse to be guided."

Even so, her hand could not resist an attempt.

"Well, we shall eat, at least. We hope." She laughed, and blew out some smoke. "Are you hungry?"

She did not expect an answer.

"I have discovered a young man, an *action* painter," Sissy Kamara said.

Poppy was terrified, a little for herself, more for Basil, but most of all for Sissy Kamara.

Sotos Louloudis only smiled, who knew that his wife must always do right. He went and left her to it.

"Your young man, I hope he isn't a genius," Basil was protesting.

"I shall show you," promised Sissy Kamara, "afterwards. Oh dear, there is so much to tell and hear! *Poppitsa!*"

She clapped her hands together, and all the little oriental bracelets chattered.

Sissy Kamara was a dry-feverish woman, of an ugliness accentuated by the attention she drew to herself, Basil used to say. Basil was not so much uncharitable as the victim of his own fastidiousness. That voice, that laugh, he said, the cigarettes of course were half to blame. The dash of dry rouge she gave to either cheek certainly made her look rather hectic, added to which her high hair, it must have been designed that way, though it gave the impression of having got squashed, as though Sissy Kamara had just risen from sleep and a couple of aspirin.

"He is so kind, he has brought us some *mezedakia*," * Sissy was saying.

* *Mezedakia:* hors d'oeuvres.

They began, in fact, to notice Sotos had returned, with plates. There were olives. There were *dolmadakia** out of a tin.

"Food is of so little importance," Sissy said, "its necessity becomes humiliating."

Poppy was afraid that Basil, she was afraid for Sissy, that she might begin one of her clever conversations. Basil hated Sissy when she talked about the sado-masochism of the Greeks.

But Sissy took the plate as though she were about to consecrate.

"You *like dolmadakia*," Sissy ordained.

"*Ach, dolmadakia!*" Poppy cried, and was again a girl. "I adore *dolmadakia!*"

She did not look at Basil for confirmation of her silliness—she had heard that with her own ears—as she smelled the smell of, as she anticipated the distinctive, the metallic, the almost bad taste of *dolmadakia* out of a tin.

"The plate was my mother's," Sissy told, against the chink of her mother's rings. "Do you remember, Poppy? In Smyrna?"

Then Poppy Pantzopoulos and Sissy Kamara were staring together at the plate, not so much at its ingenious ugliness—for it was in the shape of a double eagle ringed with snakes of writhing gold—they were drawn, rather, beyond the excrescences and cavities and the little parcels of *dolmadakia* scattered in moist, toppling heaps, to contemplate what might have been a common lover whom time and distance now allowed them to share with diminished bitterness.

Poppy Pantzopoulos had remembered the drawing-room on Frankish Street, the summer stealing through iron shutters, by stealth of light and grace of jasmine, to flirt with the neo-Byzantine plate. Which the old woman had brought in.

"Here are a few *kourabiedes*," † said old Vangelio. "Specially for Poppaki. Who is so good."

"I am not good," said Poppy Pesmazoglou, who had called to see her friend, and who was irritated besides by the sentimental deference of old family servants.

* *Dolmadakia:* stuffed vine-leaves.
† *Kourabiedes:* biscuits dusted with icing-sugar.

"But you *are* good. I can see," Vangelio insisted with that rather cloying, sweet smile.

"I am not! I am not!" Poppy insisted, almost shrieked.

Vangelio had cracked hands, usually stained by the vegetables with which she was still allowed to help. She was so old and useless, though.

"Do you like *kourabiedes?*" Sissy Kamara asked.

She had come in. The feathers of her hair had fitted out her head in a cap of inky light.

"Oh, I adore *kourabiedes!*" Poppy Pesmazoglou replied, and giggled.

"You are not afraid of moustaches then."

For already the two girls wore the white down of powdered sugar. Again Poppy giggled, and wiped off her ridiculous moustache. She would have liked to do or say something people might remember. But had never yet succeeded. She paid morning calls, and feared that no one noticed when she went.

"I shall tell you something," Sissy Kamara said as they sipped at the *soumada*** Vangelio had left.

Poppy Pesmazoglou could not wait to hear.

"I am writing a novel in the first person."

Poppy was breathless, with admiration, and the sudden rush of scentiness out of her cold glass.

"It is about a flying officer," Sissy Kamara confided, "who crashes behind the lines, and is taken prisoner by the Turks."

"Oh but Sissy, how do you *know?*"

"One knows." Sissy sighed. "I shall be perfectly confidential. On the second of the month I expect to visit the Front. To distribute comforts."

"How is it possible?" Poppy Pesmazoglou gulped *soumada.* Her admiration was too intense.

"Between ourselves," Sissy said, "Pouris has arranged it. We shall drive to K——, where we shall find horses and mules waiting to take us across the mountains. It will be so good for the troops' morale."

Poppy Pesmazoglou realized she was slopping *soumada* out of

* *Soumada:* nonalcoholic drink made from almonds and orange-flower water.

her glass. She was suffocating in orange-flowers as she wiped the sweet stickiness.

"But does your mother?" Poppy asked.

"Mother is too exhausted," said Sissy. "It is the influx of metropolitan Greeks!"

Then the two girls laughed together, for they had been set apart in the shuttered drawing-room on Frankish Street, in an Anatolian reality, on which certainly no Greek, not even a war which armies of men were fighting out, might possibly intrude.

And all the time—how many years?—Sissy Kamara sat holding the few *dolmades* on the ugly neo-Byzantine plate.

"Isn't it beautiful?" Sissy Kamara asked.

"It is beautiful!" Poppy Pantzopoulos agreed.

Each knew that she was watched by her husband, but that neither of the men would dare intrude on the slightly immoral relationship the past must allow them to enjoy a few moments more.

"Do you know that that plate," said Sissy Kamara putting it down with solemnity, "is almost the only material possession I succeeded in rescuing at the time of the Catastrophe. And I might not have brought that if Vangelio hadn't wrapped it. You remember poor old Vangelio—my uncle's wet-nurse?"

Poppy nodded, and looked down, as she did for anyone who had died.

"If Vangelio had not wrapped the plate, and practically put it into my hands, after the Turks had set fire to the town."

Then Sotos Louloudis, Sissy Kamara's husband, ventured to remark, to whisper rather: "I took the veal, Sissy."

"My God, did it burn?"

"No, but it was drying up."

"My God," said Sissy Kamara, "doesn't veal dry up! Not only behind one's back, but under one's nose!"

"I watched it, Sissy," said Sissy's husband. "It is not, I think, what you would call dry."

Poppy Pantzopoulos got up before she had been asked, knowing Basil's contempt for humility in a man. She said, in the little voice which was hers from girlhood, and which sometimes she made even smaller:

"I am sure Sissy's veal will taste delicious."

It sounded, she heard, so ridiculous, yet Sotos smiled in sympathy.

It was afterwards, when they had gone inside, and Sotos was doing things for the dinner, that Sissy Kamara, who had sat down, began to talk about the sado-masochism of the Greeks, and Poppy, without looking at Basil, wished that Sissy would not.

"We are a brutal, detestable race," said Sissy Kamara, and some of the sauce shot into her lap as she helped herself to the veal Sotos had brought. "If we care to admit, we are little better than Turks turned back to front. By the way," she added gravely, "there is no first course, because I forgot about it, and we are all such old friends I knew nobody would mind."

Poppy Pantzopoulos did not look at Basil, but heard him shifting his cutlery.

"To return to what I was saying," Sissy Kamara said, "put a knife into a Greek's hand, and he has to use it, more often than not, against himself."

Then Poppy Pantzopoulos heard Basil in his tightest voice: "I will not sit, Sissy, and hear myself lumped with *all* Greeks, to say nothing of the Anatolian *loukoumia*." *

"Admittedly," said Sissy Kamara, between mouthfuls of her own innocent veal, "there are the active and the passive. But at a certain point, any Greek will bare his breast. It is in the heroic tradition," she said, and added as though she loved it: "the heroic tradition, but ingrown. Like a toe-nail."

"The average Greek," Basil was shouting, "is too busy scratching a living from amongst the rocks, or holding down his job with the Department, to lend himself to your generalizations."

"Average!" screeched Sissy Kamara, with an expression of triumph and a gold bridge. "Who is average?"

Poppy Pantzopoulos could not bear it. For perhaps the same reason Sissy's husband had gone, or scuttled, out. His veal abandoned, his knife and fork. Sotos, Poppy could hear, was some-

* *Loukoumia:* Turkish delight.

where on his wife's terrace, amongst the unruly pelargoniums. She could hear the infinitely fragile sound of a handful of glasses being gathered up.

"But Basil," Sissy had placed her fingertips upon her breast, in such a very awkward position her elbows looked quite exposed, "I would give my *soul* for Greece. It is my love for *all* Greeks that opens my eyes to weaknesses."

"It is your joy in tortures."

"I?"

Poppy too would have protested if she had known how. She should have cried: Oh no Sissy here am I your shield shall turn the most savage blows of truth. Instead she sat looking through the window onto the terrace, her unhappiness less sharp than sensuous. Her fleshy body could have been to blame. Plumpy plump to fat fat. Outside on the terrace Sotos Louloudis stood holding his handful of glasses. Was it a corrosive light, or the shadow of anticipation, which had reduced Sotos further still? He appeared thinner than ever, a hank of sinews, a puzzle of veins.

Then for the second time Poppy Pantzopoulos would have cried out, or perhaps did, and nothing escaped. For Sotos was stooping stooped. As Poppy protested: Only my hands are insensitive enough to bear the plate it cannot break.

But already it had. As it must. As she and Sotos had known several instants in advance.

Poppy Pantzopoulos sat and watched the fragments of the Kamaras' double eagle whitening the terrace. The spatter of *dolmadakia* on marble had sounded faintly human, but at once they had lain, even more humanly inert. The bones of Sotos' behind were carving his trousers cruelly as he bent.

It was so sad, her throat was a gulf in which she might soon drown. Her eyes were threatening. It was so excruciating, Poppy Pantzopoulos had begun to laugh. Or grunt. Or hiss. It was so reckless, so awful. Basil, she would have liked to command—between gulps—you shall not look you are not in need of additional weapons.

But Basil looked, of course. He saw Sotos' thin behind. He heard the slither of pottery bits.

Sissy Kamara had leant across the table. She was grappling with her tower of hair.

"Oh, it is brutal," she complained, "how one's best intentions are ambushed before they can declare themselves. All my life I have been misinterpreted. And yet I cannot say I really care. I have just that saving faith in my own integrity."

But Poppy Pantzopoulos could only laugh. It was killing her. And Basil began to laugh too, but in better taste, because drier. It was the twisting of dead palm-leaves on their stems, while Poppy herself was churned, rather, like a sackful of little sucking-pigs let fall on deck by a peasant. Provided something did not give split soon against the kicks.

If Sissy had not yet noticed perhaps it was because she had been sucked too far back. She tortured her already wounded cheeks, and told:

"The greatest unkindnesses have never made me cry. Because I have always expected them."

As the spasms of Poppy's mirth threatened the space in which she had compressed them, she heard Basil's dry titter twist at its moorings in that cruel wind. Her eyes, no longer hers, were a pair of detached, yet painful eyeballs permanently pinned to a window-pane, beyond which stood Sotos Louloudis, raking together the pieces of the Kamaras' old plate. Gathering the spilt *dolmades*. Since they had failed to fulfil an intended purpose, the little vine-leaf parcels were growing yellow and obscene. Which rocked Poppy and Basil Pantzopoulos. One remembered that smell of tinned *dolmadakia*. And laughed.

But Sotos Louloudis straightened up. His wrists were older, longer, thinner.

Then Sissy Kamara noticed, it could have been this, her husband's age, his grotesque figure accusing all three of them. For she screeched at the window from where she was sitting:

"What have you done, Sotos? You haven't broken my lovely plate?"

Sotos had come in. He had made a nest out of his hands in which to carry the sharp fragments, and the soft wet *dolmadakia* were squeezing oozing between his fingers, to escape.

"Yes," he said. "I broke. The plate."

Then he went out, into a secret part of the house, walking as though in canvas and rubber, and might in fact always have been thus shod, one had never noticed.

At least the passing of Sotos Louloudis allowed Poppy Pantzopoulos to release the laughter she contained. From heaving she began to wobble, gobbling, she felt, most uglily. Basil, who was drier and a man, rocked and tottered.

"By my plate!" screeched Sissy, before she too began to laugh. "My eagle!" Sissy laughed. "I was so fond of him! And you go and drop *drop* of all things my lovely eagle!"

Sissy Kamara's fever had broken. Dew lay amongst the dust. Water gushed from the corners of her eyes. Her face, screwed up in normal circumstances with the ideas she worried, was cracking open.

"Almost my last possession of importance," Sissy laughed, "when one had hoped with age to grow less attached when age itself is the arch-disappointer a final orgy of possessiveness of of of a gathering of minor vanities."

Basil stopped laughing. He who had not looked at himself all the evening would have done so now if he had been able to find a glass.

Sissy Kamara all but supplied him with one.

"Oh, I shall not deny some of us are well-preserved," Sissy laughed and dabbed, "and beauty is so often a guarantee there is nothing further to lose."

Last gasps were battering Poppy Pantzopoulos against the ladder-back of her chair—she had been thrown down that far—when Sotos Louloudis returned.

Sotos sat in his place, and began to cut his cold veal with long, oblique strokes. He ate behind pale lips.

"It is wrong to be afraid," Sissy Kamara subsided, "to face old age. I find it more or less normal. Only my arthritic thumb. I have an arthritic thumb, Poppy. It cannot support weights."

Here Sissy Kamara held up her maimed claw.

"I am always afraid of dropping things." She sighed. "My plate! My pretty plate!"

Although she did not want to, Poppy Pantzopoulos watched

Sotos' eyelids twitch, and he looked out from his position right at the end of the tunnel, facing the light, as he would at certain moments. Poppy would have liked to know what Sotos saw. She was glad she had stopped laughing. All by now had stopped.

Poppy said: "Aleko Philippidis has a theory ocean fish are more nutritious than our Mediterranean ones because of the exercise they are forced to take. He told me at Elly Lambraki's."

Saying good-bye the night air makes it easier, less a duty, to feel sorry for whatever has happened.

"Wrap up well," Sissy Kamara advised, standing with her husband in the doorway. "The weather is still treacherous."

Light had isolated Sissy and Sotos. They were, in the one case, smaller, in the other thinner, than anybody had ever supposed. Like those of aged dogs, their dry noses, sniffing the air, hoped against scenting desertion behind departure.

When Basil and Poppy Pantzopoulos were seated in their nice car, and had made sure the windows would ventilate without admitting a draught, Basil opened:

"That was a disgraceful episode, Poppy. Though I have to admit I took part. Laughter is catching. What can one do but follow?"

"Yes," said Poppy Pantzopoulos, turning her head, addressing the corner.

"Poor Sissy! At least we shall probably not be able to face her again," suggested Basil.

"No," said Poppy.

While believing that everything happens again, just as, to some extent, it has happened before.

"Irrrhhhh!"

The wall had given, and Mr Petrocheilos' drill had blundered through, straight into the nerve of Mrs Pantzopoulos' tooth.

"That's it!" the dentist shouted in some triumph. "There's no doubt about it!"

Mr Petrocheilos lowered his great, dreadful nose.

"It smells, too. It ought to come out."

"No! No!" Mrs Pantzopoulos cried and protested, gripping the chair's sweating arms. "On no account shall I part with a tooth. Whatever the circumstances. Patch it up, Mr Petrocheilos, please. It's my own. It's what I was given."

If necessary change her dentist, but not her tooth. If she could have expressed herself through the mouthful of paraphernalia. Her legs, feeling for a foothold on the metal step, were far too short, fat, flabby, in fact, the Anatolian *loukoumia*.

Mrs Pantzopoulos closed her eyes.

"I shall suffer anything," she said, "short of losing my rotten tooth."

All the maids had tied up their hair, their island faces, in the kerchiefs they had brought with them into service. They were holding their bundles, waiting in the hall behind the grille for Monsieur Leclerq to take them to the French destroyer.

From time to time the girls asked: "My God, will he come, though?"

"Of course he will come. He has been paid to!" Poppy Pesmazoglou assured.

Responsibility had thinned her, darkened her, made her stern. There were times when she could not believe in what she saw when she opened her passport. Only her parents, sending telegrams from Lausanne, reminded that she was still their silly, dimpled girl.

"My God," moaned Panayota, "Mr Phitilis said they've set fire to the town. They're burning Smyrna."

"Do you believe everything?" it was Miss Pesmazoglou's duty to ask.

Until it was no more surprising that Monsieur Leclerq did not come to keep a paid promise, or that the party should be setting out for the Quay, the three girls strung out hand to hand, the cook lagging.

Miss Pesmazoglou strode ahead on her suddenly longer legs.

And Smyrna was burning. The night had drawn its daggers, a playful chiffon of smoke choked.

Ahhhh, they were crying, or laughing, lowering their heads to run at the distance.

Miss Pesmazoglou ran because the panicky darkness groped at stationary, isolated figures. All was running fire and glass. A horse's wet bowels flopped out through the traces and over the paving. A hand hung from the doorway of a tram.

"The dirty Turks!"

The whole darkness heaving with men's tufted bodies. Men's nipples winking at the sweat which blinded them. She stripped the streets as never before running in pursuit of a ball. She trod on a face which accepted pressure. Ran.

At the corner of Independence Street the Turk holding the short knife was, she saw, the fig-seller from Konya, so mild, if rather smelly—one never spoke to them of course—weighing out the purple figs on dusty mornings under acacias. Now this elderly Turk appeared to have caught fire. The flames were twisting his seamed face. And Vangelio, the old nurse, Sissy's uncle's wet-nurse. Vangelio kneeling on the cobbles offered her expression of resigned faith and goodness to the Turk. Her sweet gift of a face wrapped in its white kerchief. To the Turk's amazing knife.

"O God!" screamed Miss Pesmazoglou and it fell back in a shower of glass splinters.

What can one do running jumping faces? Sieze the knife the flesh parting bone wincing? Oh no, not that! Or would it have hurt less than the omission?

Running throttled thought, and there in the Gulf were the electric skeletons of ships waiting to receive refugees, and the refugees themselves clinging to the barges from which they had refused to be pushed off.

So she ran, and with the last of her breath she must ask to be allowed to send a telegram to Lausanne.

Mrs Pantzopoulos lay at the dentist's. It was the exhausted hour at which ladies taste ices and tell about their maid. But Mrs Pantzopoulos, in her sopping, and still rather jagged condition, was languidly elated to find she had survived.

That her dentist was not even looking at her irritated her temporarily, and she opened her hand-bag, and might have appeared to bear a grudge against the objects she found inside.

While Mr Petrocheilos of hairy wrists stood sorting his instruments.

For all he knows, Mrs Pantzopoulos told herself, I might have a knife hidden in my hand-bag, though for this Petrocheilos no doubt I am the kind of silly woman who spends her life paying calls.

Mrs Pantzopoulos had to frown at the thought of it, but smiled immediately and said:

"I am going to settle, Mr Petrocheilos, now."

"But there is no need," the dentist replied. "There will be the account! As usual. I trust you, you know."

"Oh, I am so glad you trust me!" Mrs Pantzopoulos said, seeming genuinely relieved, though laughing a little to make it sound decently frivolous. "So very, very glad! But I shall pay you, all the same. Why, a bus could crush me as I cross the square."

She bit her mouth.

"My legs might wobble at the critical moment. They won't, of course, but might. One can't be absolutely certain. Not even of oneself."

Then Mrs Pantzopoulos paid the dentist, and left. She went on slowly down the stairs, looking just ahead of her feet, for the trap which might have been set for her.

A Cheery Soul

That evening Mrs Custance decided to tell her husband they must do something about Miss Docker.

"*That* old ratbag," Ted Custance began.

"She is such a cheery soul," his wife hurried, over-bright. "Always so helpful. Doing for others what is never done for her."

Ted Custance, who was finishing his thirtieth summer with the bank, could not have felt gloomier.

The whole of Sarsaparilla knew something of Miss Docker's present circumstances: how, since old Miss Baskerville died, and the niece had decided "Lyme Regis" must be sold, there was Miss Docker, soon to find herself without a roof. Almost everyone had been the object of the poor woman's thoughtfulness. One need only mention the Christmas presents she could not afford. Miss Docker was a gift to the gift-shops: all those little ash-trays with gum-nuts in relief, the shepherdesses of dusty lace, the miniature boomerangs, with the holes to hold the toothpicks, to spear the chipolatas with. Everybody knew, but almost everybody forgot. It was more convenient to remember she had her pension and her health.

"And what do you propose to do?" asked Mr Custance, when it seemed he must surrender.

Mrs Custance watched her own hands cutting a piece of recalcitrant crust.

"Well," she said, "I will tell you. What I would like to do is to ask Miss Docker to accept"—she chose the word with particular care—

"to come and live in our little glassed-in veranda-room. She could repay us by helping with the chores. Not *rigidly*," she hastened to add. "I would not make a slave of anyone. Otherwise she would be quite free. And is in such demand. She is always hemming and mending, and sitting with the old or young. We shall hardly notice she is here."

Ted Custance freed his teeth. It had to be admitted he was not so well acquainted with Miss Docker. He was a silent, grizzled man, above all suspicious of the human animal.

"No one else in Sarsaparilla," Mrs Custance continued to persuade, "can equal Miss Docker at doing good."

Mr Custance made a tired noise through his moustache.

"Provided it is not you," he said, "who are having a fly at doing good, I shall not worry all that much."

Mrs Custance blushed, for it was her secret wish to justify herself in the eyes of God, and this, she suspected, promised to be her greatest opportunity.

"Oh, Ted!" she said.

Her blush made her look younger, not that she was old, somewhere midway. Mentally she went and sat in his lap, and began to stroke his roughish skin. She had never done such a thing, of course, but would wait for those occasions when he reached out, then she would submit to whatever Ted decided on.

Now they were both a little chilled by apprehension.

"We must not expect our lives to remain unchanged," she ventured.

Ted Custance grunted.

Their lives. Hitherto they had remained intact. No children, thanks to an absent-minded surgeon. Could have sued, I expect, said Ted. But they hadn't. They were too decent. Besides, all the embarrassment. The reporters. They had continued to live, in the one envelope, as it were, which nobody had bothered to tear, because no one was sufficiently interested.

"Oh dear, I am really quite excited!" Mrs Custance exclaimed in a rush. "At last we are doing something!"

He did not answer. Could it be that her husband was selfish? She looked at the hard skin round his nails. Ted Custance was so handy he could never get his nails cleaned up by Monday, to start counting out the notes again at the Wales.

The same Sunday, as the light was growing a deeper green, she called to him:

"Ted? What are you doing?"

He did not answer till she went to see. Then he said: "I was sticking up some sort of shelf for her to put her bloody books on."

Then he was not selfish, and she was riotous with gratitude.

"How clever!" she said, as though she had just that moment discovered.

He was hitting the hard of his palm with the hammer. His manner almost suggested she had put him to shame.

"But supposing she doesn't read!" she said. "At least I've seen her *sitting* with a book. And then I expect there are a few she is fond of. Things she must have inherited."

Because his wife had embarrassed him, Ted Custance began shouldering her out of the room, and again she was surprised at the hardness of his body. What made their uneventful marriage so rewarding, was the fact that it was filled with little surprises. Sometimes Ted would not reach for the reading-lamp cord. Oh dear, she would protest, do you think we ought? But he would not answer. And although she hardly dared look, it always left her quietly younger.

Then it was Thursday, and it could only be the hire-car she heard, for Miss Docker had announced she would hire a car, on such an occasion, and a little van to fetch her oddments: a rocker, and a chest, and so forth, which could stand in the garage if not convenient, provided they were inspected regularly for white-ant.

Mrs Custance was so excited she shook the whole side of the house in running at the window.

It was, in fact, the hire-car, and Miss Docker's behind was getting out.

Mrs Custance rushed to make her welcome.

"Well, now," Miss Docker was saying, "isn't it lovely to be amongst friends? What would we do without them? I, for one, would be homeless in the world. Neat place they've got"—she was addressing the hire-car man—"only, as a matter of personal taste, I would have painted it cream and green."

The hire-car man was laughing, because, well, this was Miss Docker.

"Here," she said, thrusting a box, "help yourself to a lolly. Don't tell me there's a man who hasn't got a sweet tooth."

Miss Docker, too, helped herself. The foil fell tinkling at her feet. And Mrs Custance stood. It was all in order, because Miss Docker had not yet finished with the hire-car man.

"Ah dear, it is lovely," the visitor repeated, turning at last towards her friend.

Such loveliness as she implied remained this time in the abstract. Nor did Mrs Custance demand a clue. She realized how very shy she was feeling. Confronted with Miss Docker's munching face, on which the hairs stirred, and the dust of a beige powder trembled, and the chaps were indenting the purple lipstick, Mrs Custance was altogether at a loss, except that, somewhere in the distance, she knew, lurked the other, dark-brown woman, under everything else, like the truth.

Now the substitute Miss Docker was staring back through expert eyes.

"You are looking peaky," she decided. "What have you been up to?"

"I?" asked Mrs Custance, shocked.

"Who else? Not Fisher's Ghost!"

Here Miss Docker shrieked. She had walked inside the home. She had laid a hand on her friend's arm.

"It's my sense of humour," she apologized. "You and I will have a laugh together. Oh, not all laugh," she said. "Wait till I get me sleeves rolled up. I was never one to avoid showing gratitude. You will not regret your good deed."

Mrs Custance and the hire-car man, between them, managed to drag the boxes inside. Mrs Custance suspected she had ricked something. And soon the little van had arrived, with the rest of Miss Docker's oddments: the rocker, the chest, as well as a tallboy and half a dozen cane-bottomed chairs, which Mrs Custance had not bargained for.

"I was never a nuisance to anyone," Miss Docker said, "but shall take what is offered, whether garage, or outhouse."

"Oh," replied Mrs Custance, hurt, "we had agreed on the little glassed-in room."

"Well," said Miss Docker, peeping inside, "if that was *agreed*. But these few poor sticks can stand somewhere outside. The rocker on the front veranda, of course, where we shall often sit and chat. But no one could object to the tallboy at least in my own room. There is not that much furniture. In fact, it is fairly bare. You men —won't you?—will help move the tallboy in."

When it had been squeezed through, and all the panting and sweating was over, Mrs Custance had to protest:

"Oh, but Miss Docker, don't you see, it will be standing in front of the louvres!"

"You can't have it all ways," Miss Docker replied, gloomily for her.

She gave the thing an extra shove, with the result that something splintered down.

"What is that?" Miss Docker asked.

"That," Mrs Custance replied, who had fallen immediately on her knees, "is nothing. Nothing of importance. A little book-shelf."

"I am sorry," Miss Docker said, "but accidents will always happen."

So Miss Docker had arrived.

She began to walk about soon. Mrs Custance could have sworn she heard comb-and-paper, but it was only the sound of Miss Docker humming. So she roamed, and the purple-brown strains of evening filled the house with steady treacle.

"Wouldn't you like to take off your things? I must get the tea," Mrs Custance called.

"I am settling in," Miss Docker replied. "Everybody has their different methods. Nobody will tell you I am not cheerful. *Normally*. But there are the moments in life which are not normal. When you are dislocated, so to speak. Won't you agree?"

"Yes." Mrs Custance did, feebly.

She was attending to the macaroni cheese.

"Macaroni cheese," Miss Docker observed.

She had come in. She was standing over.

"Remind me," she said, "to tell you of a trick I learned with that."

Mrs Custance promised she would.

"And a nice piece of rump. Tender, I bet. Nice and thick."

"That is for my husband," Mrs Custance explained. "After a hard day's work, I consider a man is in need of meat."

"I'll say!" Miss Docker said, and laughed.

Mrs Custance wondered.

"Ah, the men!" Miss Docker said. "One day I'm going to tell you all about the men in my life. There are some will not believe, but I am not forcing anybody to accept the truth. It is like religious faith. Take it or leave it, I say. Yes," she sighed, "the men! Now is that a hydrangea? That staggy, sickly thing over by your rotary clothes-line?"

"Yes," Mrs Custance had to admit.

"I bet you did not prune it in July, leaving the requisite couple of eyes."

"I never prune it," Mrs Custance dared.

"What," said Miss Docker, "you are not one of those who are afraid to prune?"

Mrs Custance almost might have been, though that was not, in fact, the case. She said: "It is useful for drying things on, when they overflow from the line."

"But that is not a hydrangea's purpose."

Miss Docker was so depressed.

> "Hy-der-range-y
> hy-der-range-y
> hy-der-range-y-er!"

she breathed and hummed.

In the dark brown light her cheeks were turning a chocolate-purple.

"Oh dear," she suddenly shrieked, "whatever will you think of me? Everyone will tell you I'm nothing if not cheerful. And helpful. Here," she said, "give me a towel."

She flung a few dishes together.

"Where does the tea live?" she asked.

"But it is far too late and still too early," protested Mrs Custance, who could stick to principles.

"It is never too early for a cup of tea," Miss Docker had to contradict.

Oh dear—Mrs Custance had herself in hand—I must on no account begin to sulk.

"No one is installed," said Miss Docker, "till after her first cup of tea."

When Ted Custance returned he crunched across tea and sugar, and realized it had happened.

"It is me!" called Miss Docker, to emphasize.

Mr Custance looked at her.

"Well," she said, "no one can deny, Yours Truly least of all, it makes a difference having a man in the house."

Ted Custance walked through. His footfall followed him in tea and sugar.

> "Where skies are blue,
> And hearts are true . . ."

Miss Docker sang.

"Tea in the dinette, I presume, when we are *ong fameel*."

She began to lay the cutlery. She continued humming.

"Wouldn't know I had a voice," she said. "Only amateur, of course. Chorus work. But there has to be a chorus too."

Mrs Custance did several things very firmly.

"I say," Miss Docker said, "do you people really go for these hard lights?"

"We have nothing to hide," said Mrs. Custance.

"Now! Now!" Miss Docker reproached. "Sharp tongues give unkind answers."

So that Mrs. Custance was most terribly mortified.

"Tea is ready, Ted," she had to confess to her husband.

Ted Custance made up his mind there was one corner of the

kitchen his eyes should avoid in future. Miss Docker had taken out her teeth before coming to table. She sat munching, breathing, holding up her jaw, as though to resist death by drowning. She had decided, apparently, to live on bread.

"Not all that much," she said, when offered her helping of macaroni cheese. "Just a teeny weeny bit for *me*. Because, you see, I have to resist gluttony. Oh yes, you wouldn't believe. There was never such a glutton, and worst of all for meat."

So Miss Docker masticated bread in virtuous lumps.

"Is it tender, Mr Custance?" she asked.

He did not answer.

"Not very talkative, is he?" she said.

"Some people are not," said Mrs Custance.

She would have liked to do something of a positive nature to protect her husband, but had never been positive—except through him.

"Well, it takes all kinds," Miss Docker said. "Personally, I like a good discussion, amongst friends, on a metaphysical theme."

The Custances had started on their chocolate mould.

"We are inclined to be book-worms," Mrs Custance apologized.

"Oh, I read, too. A lady lent me *Manong Lescoat*. I once read the Bible from cover to cover. That was when I was at the end of me tether. A whole fortnight it took me. I lay in bed, and read, and read. It was raining cats and dogs. Never stopped. Before that I was a pagan. But suddenly I saw."

"What did you see?"

Ted Custance was looking at her now.

"Don't be silly!" she said. "You can't say what you see. But *see!*"

He was looking at her. His eyebrows and moustache were hanging over, like someone famous and unpleasant, she could not remember.

"You know what's the matter with you, don't you?" Miss Docker asked, lowering her eyelids.

Now that the powder had left her cheeks, her face was the colour of brown pears, the stewing ones.

"Your posture is all wrong," she said. "And posture is nine-tenths. According to Indian philosophy. Mind you, there's a lot of that that isn't altogether healthy, but you can pick up a wrinkle here and there. Now, posture," she resumed. "Remind me to show you. Some other time."

There she paused.

"I've got to be without me corsets!"

She nearly burst, and before she had recovered, Ted Custance went outside. Certainly he looked rather hunched.

"Moody type," Miss Docker said.

"Ted is the most even-tempered of men," his wife protested.

"When you only want to help a person. When there are so many people waiting to be helped. So much Christian love waiting to be poured out on those who are unwilling to accept it. The world would be a wonderful place."

Mrs Custance took a pinch of bicarb in warm water, and began the washing-up.

But Miss Docker was a dedicated soul. You could not deny that.

"There is that Mrs Florance," she said the following morning. "Pernicious anaemia. Though if you ask me she is starved for love. Do you know what I am going to do? I'm going up to the butcher's to buy a couple of mutton shanks. I'm going to make Mrs Florance a basinful of broth. There are so many professing Christians. Mind you, I think a lot of things just don't cross their poor minds. If only they could be awakened."

Miss Docker went.

And returned.

"I—tiddly—i—tie,
pom—pom!"

Miss Docker sang.

She sat in her rocker on the front veranda, waving at those she knew amongst the passers-by. Some of them stared back in pale surprise.

At night Miss Docker would turn and turn as she lay in bed. The Custances could almost feel her, rubbing against the dividing wall, before switching her transistor on.

"You should invest in a transistor," she would call through.

"We don't need to!" Ted Custance had once gone so far as shouting back at the dark.

But Miss Docker did not hear. There was an awful lot she did not hear.

"Ah, the lovely music!" she called. "It does you good. And talks. Educational. Though what I go for most of all is the man who says good night. Always so friendly."

The Custances lay in rigid alignment in their bed. He would pinch up the skin along her arm with the tips of his rather rough fingers.

Long before the Epilogue, with those vibrant voices and English accents which did things to Mrs Custance in normal circumstances, Miss Docker was sucked under. The Custances lay and listened to the surf roaring into the caverns of sleep.

Then, to synchronize with the time pips, Ted Custance would nip the skin of his wife's arm with precise, but quite brutal bravado.

Till Mrs Custance dragged away her arm. The Presence would have allowed her very little respite from guilt.

One Sunday Miss Docker had an admission to make. They had fetched her from church, where she sang in the choir; the Custances were vaguely Baptist.

"That woman," she said, casually, for this was not yet her admission, "that Miss Scougall has something against me. She cannot bear that I should improve on my part. She is all the sopranos rolled into one. She won't admit that anyone else might be artistic. And of course her sister sides with her. She plays *flat*."

Each of the Custances was toying absently with the last of the apple Betty. They were exhausted, but no longer destructible. Perhaps, by now, they had learnt to withdraw far enough.

When Miss Docker stopped munching, and leaned forward, and announced quite ominously, the beige powder trembling on her darker jowls: "There is something that has been grieving me."

The Custances returned at once, knowing they must suffer a blow.

"For some time," Miss Docker said, "I have wondered why, amongst good friends, there seems to be a ban on Christian names."

Ted Custance could have been warding it off.

"I was christened Gertrude," Miss Docker told. "But everybody calls me Gee. Gee would feel she really was your friend to hear her name occasionally."

Mrs Custance hung her head.

"I expect we are not that kind," she confessed. "We are not exactly cold people, not formal in any way, but stiff"—here she made the greatest effort—"yes, I suppose, too, we are shy."

"A name is friendship's sweetener," Miss Docker coaxed.

Mr Custance was sweating.

"I'm buggered if I will!" he said, very quiet, and quickly went outside.

Miss Docker did not seem to hear.

"Ah well, it was only a suggestion," she said. "*Nemo* will remain *nemo*. That means *nobody*."

When Mrs Custance went in search of her husband, she found him pinching out the tomato shoots instead of starting his Sunday nap. But cool by now. She noticed the green reflections on his skin. They were both splotched with patches of green, both cool people. Not that this precluded passion. It meant, rather, that each needed identical, cool, greenish flesh to twine around. Their leaves opened only to silence.

Mrs Custance saw something must be done at once. Desperation helped her to remember that she knew somebody, who knew somebody, who knew a bishop. So the matter was arranged with greater speed.

"Miss Docker," she announced, when it could no longer be avoided; it sounded almost savage to Mrs Custance herself, "we have decided, Mr Custance and I"—because she needed some support—"that at our time of life, we are too set in our ways, too *selfish* perhaps, to share our home with a third person. It is dreadful, I know, *dreadful*," Mrs Custance said quite honestly.

But Miss Docker smiled, as if she knew, as if from the very beginning she had known.

"People," she said, "cannot help theirselves."

But broke into a shapeless sobbing.

Mrs Custance launched at once into a deplorable, but necessary, recitative.

"You know what a privilege it is to enter the Sundown Home at Sarsaparilla. You should just see the waiting list. Many of them well-connected couples. Single ladies too."

Nothing would restrain Mrs Custance now. She might always have been playing that game.

"Well, to cut it short, a friend, or acquaintance, has spoken to Bishop Agnew, and the home has decided to accept you, overlooking prior claims."

Miss Docker had stopped her crying. It had been of a mercifully dry variety.

"Will Thursday suit?" she asked.

So, on the Thursday, the hire-car arrived, together with the little van, to fetch those few oddments, how long or how soon after her arrival neither Mrs Custance nor Miss Docker herself was prepared to calculate.

"I will not speechify," Miss Docker said, "only to say that Christian kindness is a rare thing, and never too easy learned, even by those of other virtue. Well, dear, you will gather I am grateful, though not one to make a mouthful of it. Okay, Fred," she said, "drive on in this lovely car, which you have spat on extra hard, I see. For me. Some men claim that face powder. Ordinary face powder. Did you know?"

So Miss Docker was driven away to the Sundown Home at Sarsaparilla.

"It is only next door! We shall be neighbours!" Mrs Custance called.

"Well?" asked her husband when he came home from work.

"It is done," she said.

She might have been the serpent. Or Lady Macbeth.

Already he breathed more freely. He loved her for it. She was so thin, but he loved her even for her salt-cellars.

Then Ted Custance did an extraordinary thing. With the flat of his hand, he began to beat up the bob of his wife's brittle, neutral-coloured hair. His arm rising as though by levitation, he beat and beat, ever so lightly, till the hair fanned out and stood on end.

"Ted! Oh, Ted!" she cried and protested. "Whatever would people say?"

Laughing.

He flopped down silent then, on the broken springs of the kitchen chair, and she was drawn towards him till caught between his thighs.

Silence made it seem natural enough: her familiar knees, the rough material of his trousers—though on looking out through the green gloom of staked tomatoes, they saw the daylight accusing them, and Mrs Custance, for one, suspected she must always stand condemned in any trial by goodness.

Perhaps her husband was reading her thoughts.

"She'll be there by now. She'll have started the next round. Poor devils," he tempted her to think, "they haven't a hope in hell!"

[II]

After the evening meal of mince collops and bread pudding, the old ladies and gentlemen too, would retire to the Chinese Room of what had been the cement millionaire's mansion. There was still a largeness, if not actual magnificence. There were the enormous *cloisonné* vases, there were the remains of the Chinese rugs which the heirs had thrown in with the house. By now almost predominantly string-colour, the rugs had retained a border of embossed opulence, a skeleton of their original splendour. That particular make of rug was commonly referred to as "carved," somebody had recently told the inmates—it could have been Miss Docker—and signified the extreme of luxury and wealth. The old people had derived immediate comfort from the information. They sat and stirred their coffee essence in the dusty shadow of luxury.

Miss Docker had soon adapted herself to the routine of the Sundown Home. Like all those whose lives are episodic, she ended by failing to see the joins. She came in on the second evening, into the Chinese Room, carrying the shoe-box which contained her photographic record, and at once began to gather her flock.

"Where are the men?" she asked. "There are several men, aren't there? Where have the old boys toddled off to?"

"To their rooms. To die. Perhaps," suggested Mrs Hibble from her corner.

"What a thing to say!" Miss Docker exclaimed. "And in a Church of England home. We are here by the grace of God."

Mrs Hibble wondered whether all her life she had been an agnostic without knowing.

"When it is only ever my intention," Miss Docker said, "to give a little pleasure to all and sundry. Thought we might have played a game, only I was shown at the start we are not exactly a gamy lot. Still, Animal and Vegetable helps to pass. Or the Truth Game. Some object to the Truth Game. Then some do not care to face the truth."

Mild rumbles from the tepid ladies seemed to sound agreement of a kind.

"Seeing as there is no inclination to spend a jolly, communal evening, I fetched down my box of photos," Miss Docker said. "Maybe a few of us could look through those. Though mind you, it is not compulsory."

As she fumbled with the shoe-box in her lap, Miss Docker noticed that Mrs Hibble depended in some way on a second lady, still shadow, seated in a state of elderly acquiescence on her right. Mrs Hibble barely turned her face. But Miss Docker saw. Or sensed. Her capable hands were fumbling with the lid. Dependence rattled Miss Docker, since she had failed to achieve anything so undesirable.

"I will not bother you," she said, and tore a corner of the cardboard overlap; the box had never been so unmanageable before, "I don't want to thrust a lot of pictures on people who are not acquainted with the subjects, but thought you might be amused to see what Yours Truly looked like at different stages."

Here she hooted, and several of the photographs shot out in yellow abandon. When she had stooped, and strained, and risen purpler, she exploded:

"There! You wouldn't believe! Now would you? I ask! Or would you?"

Two or three contiguous ladies craned old, felted necks, but did not dare give an opinion. Opinions had wilted for the most part at the Sundown Home. Though the ladies were interested enough to see what was indeed a peculiar phenomenon: the young, velvety girl, with butterfly bow restraining her fall of hair, the nice lace collar on the gentle bosom, the modest, crocheted sleevelets standing starched on the supple arms. The peculiar thing about it was, the ladies saw, the girl in the photograph could have been Miss Docker before the wind of time blew her up over-life-size.

"There must have been a great deal we didn't understand," Miss Docker decided, scratching with a thumb-nail at something on the girl's face. "Young girls like that! We must have been real ignorant." She shrieked to think of it. "Well, we were! A lot of silly young things! Age, you see, has its compensations."

But the silence ached in the ears of the inmates of the Sundown Home.

"Can everybody see?" Miss Docker asked, and frowned. "The light is that dingy."

"Oh, yes. Well enough," said Mrs Hibble.

Miss Docker hated Mrs Hibble. To say nothing of Mrs Hibble's established, yet so shadowy friend. Then Miss Docker, squinting through the shadows, did at last begin to see enough to put an end to anonymity.

"Well!" she cried. "Waddayaknow! Isn't that Mrs Lillie? Mrs Millicent Lillie?"

The shadow stirred evasively.

"I am Mrs Lillie," it admitted.

"Well now, what a contrary thing! Not to make yourself known to a friend!"

"It didn't occur," said Mrs Lillie, "I thought there would be time enough."

"In a place like this, never leave undone. Wouldn't you agree?" Miss Docker looked around at the others. "Time can play tricks," she warned.

Mrs Lillie sat.

"Who would believe," Miss Docker continued, "it is two—or is it three years?—since your poor husband passed on."

Mrs Lillie continued to sit, evidently waiting for the moments to carry her out of reach. At her lowest she would even decide time was her only infallible protector. Her friend Mrs Hibble, they were silently agreed, could do nothing for her now.

"Wait. As a matter of fact. I do believe," Miss Docker was saying, and scrabbling. "It couldn't be coincidence, could it? There is a snapshot. Somewhere. There!"

She brandished, before settling to devour.

Mrs Lillie moistened her lips.

"Tom and Millie Lillie."

Again Mrs. Lillie wet her lips. Never had Miss Docker referred to them with less respect. Was time, after all, the infallible protector?

"And there is Me!" Miss Docker pointed. "Holding his hand. He had begun to need attention. That was after the first stroke. Do you remember how I would come in? Voluntarily. I was never one to refuse assistance to anybody who needed it. Was I?" Miss Docker asked.

"No," Mrs Lillie answered faintly.

But her skin was unquenchable. It glowed still through the dingy light with the secrets of experience.

"Later on I used to help you turn him. I don't know how you would of managed. He was that heavy. A big man."

A no-hoper, Millicent Embery overheard before becoming engaged to him. But his shoulders were magnificent, his head the rubbing from a Roman plaque. At least on the mother's side Tom Lillie passed the genealogical test, though did not come up to the Emberys, of course. What to do with Tom, provided Millicent married him—that had been the subject of discussion. Till Mrs Embery, overnight, turned him into a landscape gardener, and Tom never looked back. He was so rude to his clients, they accepted his dismissal of the golden cypress, they had never dared refuse the rocks with which he strewed their suburban lawns.

"I was afraid at first," Miss Docker meandered, "I must admit, Mrs Lillie, your aquiline nose put me off. Do you care for it yourself?"

"I have never thought about it," Mrs Lillie answered.

Millicent Lillie had taken her beauty for granted. It had been so indisputable, she had never analyzed the details.

"A nose can cut, you know," Miss Docker accused. "He, though, he was *bluff*—I think I have heard them call it. A lovely man. His speech was gone by then. But does speech make all that difference?"

Mrs Hibble laughed, and glanced deliberately at her friend. But Mrs Lillie did not notice.

"I would turn him in the end on my own. Like he was a baby."

So that several of the old ladies grew fascinated by the nurse's hands.

As for Miss Docker, she swaddled and coddled still. She loved her log. Which was all that was left of the man who had blown an inheritance.

In the sordid little house to which they were reduced. So Mrs Lillie remembered.

"You, my dear, never had the strength," Miss Docker reminded.

No, indeed. She remembered how Miss Docker's strength had rocked the fibro. She remembered the smells and stains of sickness.

Even at her apogee, Millicent Lillie suspected it was age which evolved the figures of the dance. The hieroglyphs on ancient stonework might lull her back into a sense of security. But only briefly, and only false. So her aigrette trembled, long before the palsy overtook her, and the single strand of diamonds that she wore almost severed her head from her throat. What the deuce, asked Tom, kissing her eyelids, kissing her throat. It was, of course, too irrational, not to say perverse, to explain. So she joined her mouth to his. And drank his kisses, drunkenly, which smelled of claret. As the dahabiah plunged them deeper awash in the uniform moonlight of Egypt, they were sculptured in the same marble, and at the same time deliriously dissolved. There were the days, however, when the dust would play upon the deck, reaching out from the eroded shore. Then her lips tasted of the desert.

"But how can you possibly see from there?" Miss Docker realized. "You want to take a proper look."

Oh, but I have seen, Mrs Lillie would have protested, if the object of her protest had not reached her side. Are truth and goodness the knouts from which we suffer most? She had even known such weapons turn at last on those who wield them.

"It's not all that much to *me*," Miss Docker claimed. "You are the one."

In the uncertain light, the snapshot seemed to suggest the reverse. It was Miss Docker's potato shape which dominated the photograph. Protecting the sick man from what? In his tweed cap, of a style which had never altered, flat on the top, Tom ignored, as rocks will ignore the arabesques of lichen. Only his wife knew that rocks will open at a touch. Driving in the Pincio at dusk, she floated while he sat. Horses had always terrified her—those flaring nostrils in the carved heads. Oh, my hair, she cried, as the branches of trees matched their dew against her spray of diamonds. Her long amethyst sleeves tangled with the shadows of trees. Wheels tilting at a corner. Supposing they should overturn? But he steadied her as always by putting out an arm. In age it had been Miss Docker who put out an arm to Tom. She herself, Mrs Lillie saw, was an old head blurred on its shoulders by perpetual motion.

"Would you like to keep it? As a memento?" Miss Docker menaced.

Mrs Lillie was aware of the avalanche of kindness, waiting at her elbow, to engulf.

"No," she answered. "Thank you."

"It was only a thought," Miss Docker said. "One can only offer."

And really she had so much to do. There were lots of other pictures.

"Oh, this," she shouted, "will kill you!"

Flying at several ladies at once.

"This is Me! As Aladdin! At a ball!"

Her legs had been quite remarkable.

"I could kick up my heels with the best," she screamed. "At the Charleston. And all that."

Here we go, oh-de-doh! The Chinese Room reeled. At least the drunken cabinet—genuine lacquer, too—had learnt to waggle in its day. A brass *jardinière,* tarnished now, shouldered what there was of light. Fringes drizzled their sour music from the lamps. Broken springs bulged in bass.

But Mrs Lillie, she had been set on a sea of amethyst music. How it swelled, and swirled, in ever rosier shawls. Once his shirt-front had broken open, and there they were together on their knees, laughing for the unimportance of a vanished pearl.

Again Miss Docker rummaged in her box.

"This. And this," she clattered.

"And that one?" asked an old lady whose life suddenly depended on it.

"That is private. Somebody who died," Miss Docker mumbled.
And put it away.

Somebody who died! Was death so very private? Mrs Lillie almost laughed.

Instead she had stood there smiling the morning Tom died. Miss Docker had come in. Miss Docker was sitting beside the bed, her legs apart, on the lid of that commode which somebody had lent.

"I am talking to him," Miss Docker explained. "You never know with a stroke, you might get through to them. You don't mind, now do you, dear? I have what they call an intuition. I have been telling him about the process of digestion, which I read about in a medical journal, in a doctor's home, where I was invited recently."

Mrs Lillie smiled for the hate she saw in her husband's eye.

"Humour the sick," Miss Docker said. "Keep their interest alive."

Fanning all the while with the *Herald*.

"A norrible fly is threatening to land on the patient's nose."

So Miss Docker fanned the prisoner.

"You, dear," she said to his wife, "are the kind that dispenses passive charm. I am the practical one. Perhaps there should be two women," here she turned to laugh at her friend, "in the life of every man."

But Mrs Lillie only smiled.

For here was Miss Docker, hitting Tom's nose with the folded *Herald*. Hitting. Hitting. While she, Millicent Lillie, was only able to smile and tremble.

"One to bear the brunt," Miss Docker shouted.

Smack.

Oh, Mrs Lillie should have cried, my darling, my breath, my life-blood is flowing out of me. Love, she should have said, is dead.

For it was.

She saw that the life had gone out of her husband's eye. But she was still only able to stand and smile.

"The other to radiate!" Miss Docker laughed.

And swung.

How she wrung the dead man's hand.

"Well," she said to the old Chinese ladies, "everyone must die, only it does not do to talk about it in an institution like this. Some have even died in my arms."

She put away another photograph.

Horrible though the morning of her husband's death had been, Mrs Lillie remembered his funeral as worse.

Miss Docker looked at Mrs Lillie. She could not quite forgive her Tom Lillie's manner of dying. But the funeral, that had been the worst.

Mrs Lillie remembered how her sister Agnes had come, and the Trevelyan girls, always so dependable, even after one's fortune had gone. They had huddled in the close, chintzy pretence of a room, listening to the dry scratching of magpies on the iron roof. Agnes was helpless enough, but Baby Trevelyan had produced the little flask, the five-and-threepenny size, from her bag, and suggested, not without colour:

"I think we should all take a good strong nip. Don't you? In the circumstances?"

Violet Trevelyan fetched the glasses. As for Agnes and Millicent, their hands would not have been capable. And Baby poured.

Conspiracy sustained the mourners. Refinement lay lighter on them as brandy seeped through the labyrinths.

"Do you think it is the right shade?" asked Agnes Pinfold, eyeing the smear on her sister's tumbler.

"Oh, that was Miss Docker," Millicent Lillie explained. "She told me lipstick strengthens the morale. I accepted, because it pleases her. You know," she said, slowly—she had, in fact, only just discovered, "her goodness is a disease. She is sick with it. One must try to be kind to her."

As Miss Docker meant very little to those who had come, they kept their silence. While Mrs Lillie was tempted again to look in the glass. She saw that what had once been a cool statue, impeccable marble, had melted to soft, palpitating, white kid, except that someone had replaced what should have been the beige strips of lips with a bow of scarlet patent leather. It was quite terrifying. Miss Docker had kindly done it, because Mrs Lillie herself had not known how.

All three visitors jumped when Miss Docker came in. Her advent as usual shook the fibro.

"Expect you had given me up," she panted. "But I wouldn't let a person down. Beat the car by a toot of the horn."

There, indeed, was the long, black, incredible car, which could not have belonged to anybody. It was a blessing really, because Agnes and the Trevelyan girls were not given time to take fright at Miss Docker.

The young man was so polite.

"Thank you," the elderly ladies said, tottering with grief and brandy.

Miss Docker had begun to organize.

"Mrs Pinfold get in first," she ordered. "Then, you, dear, in this nice, comfy corner. The two ladies—twins I'd say at a guess—will take the collapsible seats. But Little Me will squeeze into the middle of the back. You see," she said, turning to Agnes, "your sister is used to lean on me. I have seen her through so much. And understand. Understanding is everything."

So they were arranged.

Anticipating friction with Miss Docker's steamy trunk, Mrs Lillie's tremulous fragility quailed. Miss Docker was holding Mrs Lillie's hands, as though she feared they might fly away. Mrs Lillie's smile struggled to the surface through the heavy impasto of scarlet grease. She would concentrate on the Trevelyans' backs. For their age, they sat very upright, in spotted voiles and balibuntals.

The service in the church was quickly over. The spirit was not absent from Mr Wakeman, but lack of words made him favour works. So that when he put his hand beneath her elbow, the widow was almost lifted off her feet—not unpleasant—in her return passage to the car.

"Now, Mrs Lillie," Mr Wakeman consoled, "you must look to your friends. Of whom you have a fair share. And God," he added, as if he were embarrassed.

But his eyes, so blue, so crinkly at the corners, strained to convey a fervour which was more perhaps than expected by the parish.

"Friends all right!" said Miss Docker; she was still there, even if forgotten. "There are friends and friends, though. Some do not always stick."

If Miss Docker was a plaster to her friend's side, the rector was a soothing salve.

"I shall be just in front, Mrs Lillie," he explained in simple, unnecessary words. "In my car—look—the Morris. You will only have to follow."

Then he made the little noise which suggested someone had got past his guard, and in spite of his strength, punched him in the ribs.

It would have been hot in the funeral car without the addition of Miss Docker. The springs on which Mrs Lillie functioned, inside her cloud of suspended belief, resumed their gentle quivering.

The cortège began to trickle, trickle. At first there was a man, a kind of major-domo, very stately, in a pair of gloves, walking ahead to regulate the traffic. Then he got inside the hearse. She noticed the rector in his unaccommodating little car. Agnes began softly to cry. Her sister, Mrs Lillie knew, had never much cared for Tom. The Trevelyan girls were nodding gravely beneath their black balibuntals.

So the procession trickled, and at length ran, oilily, almost as though it were the organized intention to get the business over.

"There is Mrs Cartwright," Miss Docker observed. "Thought she might at least have come. Seeing you were customers."

The splendid car was only just audible.

"There is that blue cattle-dog," Miss Docker remarked. "Get run over if it isn't careful. Wonder who the owner is. Some people and their dogs."

Mrs Lillie had never owned a dog. For some reason, she remembered the infinite kindness of her young, her beautiful husband, before he had grown rude to people who wanted to plan their own gardens, and the knife which stabbed her side was so agonizingly painful, her smile grew demonstrative.

"You can depend on me, dear," Miss Docker assured. "At all times. Even in the middle of the night, you can give me a tingle on the phone. That is what the alcoholics do."

Mrs Lillie was surprised her hands had not been broken off. But was grateful in a way. The actual, physical pain in which Miss

Docker dealt, prevented her from stooping, and kissing once again her husband's dead lips. She did not think she could have borne that.

When the procession halted. Jarringly. Something had happened over which the expert young chauffeur had no control.

"What is it? Eh?" Miss Docker demanded. "Want to break a person's neck?" She wound and wound at the window. She began to crane. "There is Mr Wakeman. He has got out. And that fellow from the funeral establishment. Have they lost their bearings? Don't tell me! You can see Mr Wakeman is every inch an ex-army padré! He can't give up those army boots. A proper man's man. I would of thought a professional funeral establishment would of known the roads from anywhere to There."

They had halted uncertain at a signpost, somewhere in a suburban scrub. The soil could not have been sandier.

"But I can tell them," Miss Docker said. "Everybody knows the way to the Northern Suburbs Crematorium. We are going there every other week."

For it had been decided that Tom Lillie should not be laid beneath the grass and broken bottles.

"I say! Mr Wakeman!" Miss Docker called through the open window, her veins growing thick and distended.

But the rector and the funeral person did not recognize Miss Docker.

"Mr Wake-*murn!*" she called, her skin all mottled. "Ohhhh! How stupid can some men get!"

The Trevelyan girls were withdrawing themselves as far as was physically possible from a scene.

When out leaped Miss Docker.

"I cannot bear it!"

She began to march forward, in the direction of what Agnes Pinfold and the Trevelyans would not have dared call the hearse.

The door of their car stood open. A bee flew in, and pinned itself, a jewel of gold, to Mrs Lillie's stifling silk.

Miss Docker butted at the air. Pointing. Calling.

When, just as suddenly as she had jumped out, the two men jumped back, in.

The cortège resumed its interrupted itinerary, Miss Docker laughing into space, for the joke was clearly against her.

"At least I meant well," she called, easing, and turning, and laughing, and gulping.

As she stood for a moment alone, the empty sky cruelly distorted her already inflated figure.

What exactly happened then, Mrs Lillie had never been able to decide. Not that she had really attempted. Her instincts persuaded her that research might prove too painful.

For the door of the widow's car had shut. Or was it slammed? Unfortunately, or perhaps fortunately, Mrs Lillie could not remember by whom, or how. The polite young chauffeur? Too distant. The Trevelyan sisters? Too discreet. Agnes? Too helpless. She herself, undoubtedly, would have been much too weak.

But the door had slammed.

And there, outside, was Miss Docker's face.

"Hey! Wait a mo!" it called.

As the faultless young chauffeur smoothly drove.

Miss Docker, too, remembered faces. Distinctly now. In the Chinese Room at the Sundown Home. She remembered the absent expressions of the women. She remembered the widow's chalky face, and that lipstick she had been kind enough to contribute.

But the enormous car slipped slowly out of her control. Others dared not submit to it. The other cars were gathering speed. In some cases she heard a hostile grinding of metal teeth. Along the line, several drivers seized on difficult hand-brakes as an excuse for bowing their heads. So important was it to preserve a continuity.

"Hey!" called Miss Docker, ambling first, then running. "Have a heart! Mr Gartrell! Mr Custance? Mrs Fitzgibbon! Mr Galt!"

Running and running as they sped, she held her hands outstretched to catch—no longer cars, no longer people—something which was escaping her.

It was curious, but, in the grip of procedure or grief, none of the faces in the procession even recognized Miss Docker. Although, it was true, all examined the object running red along the ditch.

"Commander Clapp!" Miss Docker cried. "Colonel Ogburn-

Pugh! Mr Thompson! Mrs Jones! Miss Ethel Jones, Miss Dora! Mr Lickiss!"

But the cars were dedicated to a mission.

"Mr Lickiss! For God's sake! Mr Lick-iss!" Miss Docker did not quite whimper.

At one point she fell upon a knee, missing the jags of bottle, though tearing her stocking on an almost equally vicious stone. Then, when her surroundings had been reduced to dust and silence, and the hoarding which announced: 2 MILES TO SARSAPARILLA, THE FRIENDLY SUBURB, she began the walk back.

Miss Docker remembered, she remembered in the Chinese Room of the Sundown Home for Old People, her hands shuffling the photographs, her jaws munching as she masticated all that was bitterest in memory.

"Surely the photographs are not all finished?" somebody was kind enough to inquire.

"Oh dear, no!" Miss Docker replied. "Nothing is ever finished."

As for Mrs Lillie, she had got up by stages out of her chair, and was hobbling and trembling her way towards the threadbare stairs.

"What is up with *her?*" Miss Docker asked.

"I expect she is turning in. The past has been too much for her," her friend Mrs Hibble explained.

Miss Docker appeared somewhat mollified, though nothing would atone for the incident by which Tom Lillie had eluded her. Only in her mind had she watched his polished casket slide shakily behind the curtain.

"Won't you show us another?" the old voices continued to beg; even Mrs Hibble's joined in.

Then Miss Docker gleamed.

"Will anybody recognize in this," she asked, flourishing a faded picture, "the true portrait of Little Me?"

Mrs Hibble got up very slowly, and when she was in the shape of a half-open knife, advanced to make sure she would not miss anything of what Miss Docker had to reveal.

Certainly the baby naked on the rug was horribly like its exhibitor. So Mrs Hibble saw.

"I was a bed-wetter too, they say," Miss Docker informed.

Several of the dim faces recoiled.

"Somewhere I read, I believe in a medical journal," she had grown very grave, "that bed-wetting is a sign of parental discord."

The old heads shook in disbelief.

"But the funny part of it is," Miss Docker began to explode "—if it isn't a joke you'll tell me—I was a, I was a *norphan!*"

Here she fairly shrieked.

[III]

Almost all the life of the Sundown Home was conducted in the cement millionaire's Chinese Room. Certainly during the fortnight of spring, when the blossom burst out of quiescent branches, and sap seemed momentarily to moisten the driest of the talcum-powdered skins, the old bodies would stumble through the damp grass and sun themselves against espaliered walls. Always returning to the Chinese Tomb. It was not that the mansion failed to offer a variety of communal rooms, but this was closest to the telephone, and even though it seldom rang, closeness inspired arthritic limbs with hope.

Sometimes Miss Docker—more athletic—would jump up and drop a few pennies in the box. She would ring the rectory.

"The Reverend Wakeman, is it?" Miss Docker would ask. "It is a pity," she said, "but this evening I shall have to miss my Bible class. Thought I would inform you. A poor soul is in need of attention. I will sit with her," she said, "while I have the strength."

"That is, indeed, charitable, Miss Docker," the rector's voice replied. "I commend you for your Christian act."

He could have been searching for further words. And Miss Docker waited. But he did not find them. She was disappointed.

"Never was able to express himself," she said. "Fatal in a parson."

On another occasion Miss Docker rang, and was answered by some young person she failed completely to identify.

"Is it the night for Bible class?" Miss Docker inquired.

"No, it is not, Miss Docker," the young girl's voice replied.

"Oh. Then I was not out in my calculations. Though if I was, I would still have time to toddle down."

The silence on the phone remained the silence of a second person.

"Who is that?" Miss Docker asked, flat out. "Is it Charmae? Or Glenyse?"

The truth was: she was dying to know.

But the young person hung up.

"Some young girls are that uncivil" Miss Docker complained to the Chinese ladies. "It was only sociable to inquire. But at least Bible class is not tonight."

"Oh, but Mrs Woolnough and Miss Perry," Mrs Hibble insisted, "left for the rectory immediately on finishing their tea."

"Without telling?"

Miss Docker could not believe.

When Mrs Woolnough and Miss Perry returned later from Bible class, they were ever so refreshed and meek.

"I hope you enjoyed it," Miss Docker reproved. "Were there many? Was there some young girl?"

"There were several," said Miss Perry.

"But the one who answered me on the phone?"

"I cannot think," said Mrs Woolnough.

"Did you have the savoury boats?" Miss Docker asked.

Yes, Mrs Wakeman had handed round savoury boats, afterwards, with a pot of tea.

Wednesday evenings there was choir practice.

"Have you given up the choir?" Mrs Hibble asked.

"I haven't given up the choir," Miss Docker confessed, "the choir has given up me. To be more exact, there is now no choir at all. It is those women," she said. "That Miss Scougall is a ball of ego. Called herself a choir-mistress, too. Of course, when she walked out, Mrs Knight—she was the organ—could only follow suit, depending as she did for a lift in her sister's Austin. So we are disbanded."

Mrs Hibble realized the situation was a tragic one, though Miss Docker appeared to be absorbed in sorting stamps for her collection. She sat munching her gums, since it was past the hour when she took out her teeth. For comfort's sake, she would explain again.

"Oh, but I shall sing," she suddenly announced. "How I shall sing! I shall be the whole choir. Nothing should prevent you praising God. Now, should it?"

Mrs Hibble refrained from comment, because Miss Docker was a, not to say *the,* pillar of the church. Devoted to the rector, too.

Miss Docker went to the rectory Thursdays to mow Mr Wakeman's lawn. As a labour of love.

"It is Miss Docker's day," Mrs Wakeman always remembered.

Miss Docker did not care for Mrs Wakeman ever since the latter accused her of pruning Crimson Glory to death.

"I only did it as a gesture," Miss Docker had defended herself, "and nobody knows for certain the rose did not die a natural death."

"We do not know by scientific proof," Mrs Wakeman conceded. Which was unorthodox in a clergyman's wife.

Miss Docker had knitted Mr Wakeman a balaclava, heather mixture, to wear between the rectory and the vestry when the frosts set in. She herself, in anticipation, could feel it grating on his square, cleft chin.

"You know the trick of wearing it?" she asked.

"Oh, I know! I *know, Miss* Docker!" the rector said, and laughed.

Men were all boys really, silly at times. It took a woman's subtlety to direct their otherwise innocent lives.

So Miss Docker laughed a certain laugh, and ran the push-mower at the grass.

Mrs Wakeman left off peeling rhubarb. She looked out and saw the balaclava Miss Docker had knitted. If the rector's wife experienced a twinge, it was because her calling required her to outgive. An upright young woman of earnest calves, who gave away her winter underwear, and went clothed in cotton and her faith, she sometimes wondered if Miss Docker might not be her rival, even though an amateur.

Miss Docker was laughing like a girl.

"If you really *insist* on cutting the grass," the rector said as usual, "I shall go inside and compose my sermon."

Then Miss Docker did something awful, she could not resist. She was pushing the push-mower all the while, clatter and slash, as if to reduce an enormity. Not that truth must ever be reduced. Her misfortune, she knew, was that always, always, she had to introduce the naked truth.

"I can only be frank," Miss Docker admitted. "The trouble with you," she said, "Mr Wakeman, and a serious one in a clergyman"— all the time clatter and slash—"you cannot seem to learn to preach."

The rector was too large to stun. But he stood there holding his buttocks, his jaws working on unformed words, or suspicion confirmed.

"Somehow you do not give yourself to it," Miss Docker pursued, crunching with her foot.

Then Mr Wakeman turned very dark for a blond man. He said: "I cannot argue with you, Miss Docker, on that point. Naturally, you must be the best judge."

"I see that I have touched you on a raw nerve, and am sorry for it," Miss Docker replied.

She had run the mower all along the border. The rector followed out of sense of duty.

"On the contrary," he said. "I am open to criticism. In every way. Otherwise, I should scarcely be fit to serve Our Lord."

"But inspiration," Miss Docker insisted, "where is inspiration?"

"I cannot answer that," said the rector.

Such a strong fellow, too. Deep in the chest.

"A clergyman should have the answers." Miss Docker crashed the mower on a stone. "Even if he makes them up," she only just avoided adding.

Mr Wakeman was gaping wide, smiling whitely.

Then Miss Docker saw, and was oh so cruelly cut. She could have burst into tears. Above the new-mown grass, she smelled the smell of shaving soap. She saw his hands offering the chalice. She loved even his finger-joints.

"Well," she said, "you don't mind me telling the truth. Someone has to."

"I agree," said the rector. "Oh, how I agree with you, Miss Docker," she hoped she heard.

But he went inside at that point, and Miss Docker continued mowing the grass.

"What is it, Gregory?" asked the rector's wife.

Again she noticed the balaclava cap.

"I have come in to write my sermon," he said.

So she closed the door softly, as she did on sermons.

Gregory Wakeman sat, blank. It was his common condition, he realized. He would fail to assist the ghosts of ideas which struggled to escape from his skull. A handsome man, whom ladies loved— spiritually. They brought little presents to him. Who had nothing to offer his divine love. As he sat with his fists further hollowing his hollow eyes, the vision of crimson rhubarb flitted from his wife's kitchen, and the sticks of rhubarb were more articulate in praise than the chaos of his dark mind.

He who had failed to justify himself presently went out.

"What is it, Gregory?" asked his wife.

She had come round the side of the house, along the brick path where the uninitiated often slipped, past the smell from the kitchen outlet.

"Is there anything?" she vaguely asked.

The rector was standing on the tips of his toes. Of his army boots. The seat of his pants was shiny green. There were all those cannas at the back of the rectory. The cannas were rapidly taking over.

Gregory Wakeman stood on his toes, trying to retrieve some elusive object.

She realized, then, the balaclava knitted by Miss Docker was suspended from the crest of the cannas, and that her dearest husband could not reach it.

He turned and looked at her, horrified.

What could she do? Not that he asked anything of her but to suffer alone. She had married him, she was sure, for the wrong reasons, but together they had succeeded, at last, in disembodying themselves. Otherwise they might have clung together, and kissed, in the distressing smell of dishwater, behind the rectory.

Until Miss Docker called:

"Enough for today, Mr Wakeman. I have put the mower in the shed. Hope I have done a decent job."

The balaclava twitching on the cannas.

" 'Bye for now," Miss Docker called.

But she could always be relied on to return.

She would sit in the pews reserved for the choir before the choir had been disbanded. If he had not seen her come and go, an observer might have assumed Miss Docker was rooted there, far less ephemeral than timber, riddled as it was with borer and dry rot, or the crumbly bricks the convicts had baked in the beginning. Miss Docker would sing, her leathery soprano lashing the architraves. She always knew the places where it was traditional to repeat a line, and sometimes added numbers to the board, for the pure glory of singing an extra hymn. Nobody noticed now. Not since the crisis at All Saints, Sarsaparilla.

"You girls ought to come along," Miss Docker would call to the inmates of the Sundown Home. "Do you good. Accepting asylum from them, too, at a nominal rate."

But the old ladies sniggered, and no longer bothered to hide it. Those who were left, that is, for some had discovered nieces willing to take them, while others had simply died of something.

"Why don't you give us a trial, Mrs Custance?" Miss Docker invited from the roadside. "You can show appreciation of your blessings in any shape of church."

"I must," Mrs Custance answered, and smiled.

But didn't.

"Are we all so intellectual, and not intelligent enough, Mr Lickiss?" Miss Docker asked, at the fence.

When she had gone, Mr Lickiss left off cleaning the gutter. He stuck his head over the edge, and answered an invisible wife:

"Yes. It was Her!"

No one more than Mr Wakeman himself was conscious of his failure in his duty towards God, but was unable to discuss the situation with Miss Docker or anybody else. He was scourged by the knowledge, so much so that his wife borrowed a pamphlet on dietetics.

As for the rector, he continued to examine his heart. He walked abroad, no longer amongst his parishioners, hoping rather that obscurity would illuminate his empty mind, discovering in a distant corner some treasure of wisdom he might offer publicly to his Lord. In his stout, army boots, Mr Wakeman was seen to walk. His greenish suit hung looser than before. It was the time of year of black wattles, and he walked in the grove of black wattles. Hoping, by prayer. But leaned his head at last against a trunk, which was oozing those drops of transparent gum.

On a morning in early spring, just such a morning when he should have been wearing Miss Docker's balaclava cap, he asked his wife, who had formed the habit of walking across to the vestry with him:

"How many this morning, Alice?"

Mrs Wakeman peeped out, unseen; she had learnt to do it.

"Oh, the Furzes, and the Bleekers," she said. "And four or five children."

"Oh," she added. "Miss Docker is there."

Presently the rector knelt to ask forgiveness for that personal insufficiency which had finally dispersed his flock, while his wife's rather muscular calves hurried her round to the west door, to take her place amongst the congregation.

As he conducted the service, nobody could have denied the rector his dignity or manliness. No one would have noticed anything amiss.

Miss Docker, naturally, led the responses.

"O Lord have mercy on us!" She lifted her jaw in professional supplication.

"Amen." And again: "Amen." Miss Docker punctuated in stops of lead.

The Furzes and the Bleekers followed, all four notoriously deaf, asking one another to explain the drift, the several children sniffled and whispered, whispered and sniffled, into the pages of their books, the disused organ creaked, in which the borer was working overtime. Only the rector's wife was silent, attempting to prolong her prayer.

When, on that fatal morning, the rector began to ascend the pulpit, his army boot missed the second step. He did not fall, but just failed to bring the pulpit down, the disappointed children reckoned. Mrs Wakeman closed her eyes in pain. It was Miss Docker, though, who barely resisted rushing to her rector's elbow.

Never after was Miss Docker able to remember the text he had chosen for that morning. At the time she was too far gone in a state of extraordinary anticipation, not to say exaltation.

The rector was preaching about sin.

Not surprising. It is always with us.

The sin of goodness, the rector inferred.

Then Miss Docker sat forward in her pew. Mouth open. In despair. Because, not only was Mr Wakeman, poor man, a terrible preacher, he was all mixed up besides.

"Take a pumpkin," the rector preached. "Have you ever noticed an ordinary pumpkin?"

Then Miss Docker did something she had always secretly wanted to do. She sat forward. Heart squelching. She answered a rhetorical question in a sermon.

"Yes, I have," Miss Docker answered. "But why pick on a poor pumpkin? If it had been a gramma," she said. "Ugly shapes! Or choko. All those prickles! But a pumpkin is not what you're looking for."

As, indeed, the rector himself realized at once. Pumpkins will light lamps of splendour perched on iron roofs.

"Not all the sin in the world will persuade me that the pumpkin," Miss Docker pursued.

The rector was hanging over the pulpit. Smiling. As if about to stretch his arguments to reach some distant point of ghastly jollification.

"Take the leaves"—his hands were demonstrating—"on which the tell-tale spores of mildew and blight will settle in the best of summers."

"Not if you spray," Miss Docker corrected. "But people will not take the trouble. I," she said, "if I gave the time to planting pumpkins, would also take the trouble to spray."

The rector's hands were involved with a problem. They had taken over from his mouth.

"Spray, spray!" Miss Docker insisted. "Spray and pray! It is prayer that saves pumpkins, as every clergyman should know and preach."

Children's giggles fell and scattered in and out the empty pews.

But the Furzes and the Bleekers, who were deaf, they were listening to a sermon.

So Miss Docker continued.

"It is all personal. Everything personal. For and against. Take prayer, for instance. Or sin. And God. What I mean is: I am God if I think I am. Only I would not be so bold. And sin. Sin is what you make it. On the cold winter evenings, I am knit up, knit, yes, *knit,* in my warm jacket. That, that is prayer. Don't you see, prayer is protection?"

But nothing could save the rector now.

"Oh, I could tell, if I could tell!" Miss Docker shouted. "But failure is not failure if it is sent to humble. The only failure is not to know."

Illuminated at last, the rector fell forward in a blaze of pumpkins.

The rector's wife was on her knees.

"O Lord, save us!" she prayed aloud in a terrible voice, from under her *Bon Marché* hat. "O Lord, protect us from the powers of darkness."

As the rector lay, lolling on the pulpit's edge.

Sick, Miss Docker saw. Such a powerful man. She was reminded of uncooked rolls of marzipan.

"Hey! Someone! Mrs Wakeman! The rector has taken a turn," Miss Docker cried.

There was a scampering of children, away. Now that the fun was over, now that they were frightened, they remembered how their parents had bullied or bribed them into standing proxy. They remembered the question they would be asked, and were already preparing their sulky answer: Yes, of course, *She* was there.

Miss Docker had reached the parson almost at the same moment as his wife. She would have started to knead the rolls of marzipan, but nobody seemed to expect it of her.

The parson's wife looked out from under her only hat. She spoke very quiet and straight. She said: "Miss Docker, you have killed my saint. Only time will show whether you have killed my God as well."

"Eh?" said Miss Docker.

But the parson's wife was already streaking out of the church, probably towards the telephone.

"So much thanks," Miss Docker said, "for those of us who act in all good faith."

As the church was emptied by now, excepting for the Furzes and the Bleekers, who were listening to a sermon, she began to walk towards the west door, her thoughts still flaming and flying. She walked through the porch, exhaling the love she still had it in her to give.

The wind was careering all along the Northern Road. All along the empty street, behind the shops, and in the homes, the members of the congregation who had accepted the crisis in the church as an excuse to clean that carburettor, clip the hedges, or baste the joint extra good, were by now sitting down to family dinners.

Miss Docker was alone.

Presently she caught sight of a blue cattle-dog she had noticed several times before.

"Bluey!" she called. "Blue? Blue? Blue?"

Although the dog was still at a distance.

"There's a fine dog!" she called. "Come and have a yarn with a poor old woman who never did anything without she was certain it was for someone's good."

The dog advancing stiff-hocked was itself an ageing animal. It paused to examine the source of its summons.

"Ah!" cried Miss Docker. "You are good, Bluey! You are good!"

She looked down into the dog's pumpkin-coloured eyes. She did not touch, however, convinced as she was of a communion of minds.

"Would you come with me, Blue," she asked, "and share my mince collops and bread pudding, at an old persons' home?"

The dog advanced his nose a little. He sniffed at Miss Docker with his dry blackberry of a nose.

"I would allow you every licence, Bluey," she promised. "You would sleep on my bed. We would keep us warm on nights when everything else had failed."

She could look only just so far into the shallow, yellow eyes. But did not altogether give up hope that recognition might germinate.

"Will you, Bluey?" Miss Docker begged, who had always been an optimist.

When the dog turned, and lifted his leg on the suppliant, and walked stiffly off.

The dog went, his tail aslant in the violent wind. The wind tore along the Northern Road, gyrating and swooping, improvising. One exceptionally strenuous gust, on arriving at the hardware, opposite, slapped the plate-glass window so that Miss Docker's reflection began to fluctuate and shudder. Even before her recovery, the wind had burst across the street. It smote the material Miss Docker with all the force of incalculable purpose, but did at least enable her to feel on which one of her best stockings her sentence had been written by a dog.

And dog, she saw for the first time, is God turned round.

Then the tears gushed out of Miss Docker's eyes. It was the wind, of course, the dust, the grit. She must hurry home at once, and bathe, if the little eye-bath had not got lost, and her a martyr to conjunctivitis. She must not let on, though. She was not the kind to spread despondency, encourage grief. Never ever ever ever.

Miss Docker walked along the empty street.

Being Kind to Titina

First Mother went away. Then it was our father, twitching from under our feet the rugs, which formed, he said, a valuable collection. We were alone for a little then. Not really alone, of course, for there was Fräulein Hoffmann, and Mademoiselle Leblanc, and Kyria Smaragda our housekeeper, and Eurydice the cook, and the two maids from Lesbos. The house was full of the whispering of women, and all of us felt melancholy.

Then it was explained to us by Mademoiselle Leblanc that she and Fräulein Hoffmann had gone out and sent a telegram to Smyrna, and soon the aunts would arrive in Egypt. Soon they did: there was our Aunt Ourania, who was less stern than she seemed to be, and Aunt Thalia—she was the artistic one—nobody, said Fräulein Hoffmann, could sing the German *Lieder* with such *Gefühl*.

Soon the house began to live again. There were always people on the stairs. There was a coming and going, and music, in the old house at Schutz. That year my eldest sister Phrosso thought she was in love with an Italian athlete, and my brother Aleko decided he would become a film star. The girls from Lesbos hung out of the upper windows after the dishes had been stacked, and tried to reach the dates which were ripening on the palms. Sometimes there was the sound of dates plopping in the damp garden below. The garden was never so cool and damp as when they brought us back from the beach. The gate creaked, as the governesses let us in through the sand-coloured wall, into the dark-green thicket of leaves.

My eldest sister Phrosso said it was awful, awful—mouldy Alexandria—if only they would let her wear high heels, or take us to Europe, if only she could have a passionate love affair; otherwise, she was going to burst. But it did not occur to me that our life was by any means insufferable. Though I was different. I was the sensible one, said the aunts; Dionysios is a steady boy. Sometimes I felt this bitterly, but I could not alter, and almost always I derived an immense pleasure from the continuous activity of the house: my second sister Agni writing essays at the oval table; the two little ones giving way to tempers; the maids explaining dreams in the attics; and at evening our Aunt Thalia playing the piano in the big *salon* with the gilded mirrors—her interpretation of Schumann was not equalled by that of Frau Klara herself, Fräulein Hoffmann said, not that she had been there. Our aunt was very satisfied. She crossed her wrists more than ever. She sang *une petite chanson spirituelle de votre Duparc* to please Mademoiselle Leblanc, who sat and smiled above her darning-egg. I believe we were at our happiest in the evenings of those days. Though somebody might open a door, threatening to dash the light from the candles on our aunt's piano, the flames soon recovered their shape. Silences were silenter. In those days, it was not uncommon to hear the sound of a camel, treading past, through the dust. There was the smell of camel on the evening air.

Oh yes, we were at our happiest. If my sister Phrosso said it was all awful, awful, it was because she had caught sight of the Italian athlete at the beach, and life had become painful for her.

That year the Stavrides came to live in the house almost opposite.

"Do you know," I informed Aunt Ourania, "these Stavrides are from Smyrna? Eurydice heard it from their cook."

"Yes, I know," our aunt replied rather gravely. "But I do not care for little boys, *Dionysi mou,* to spend so much time in the kitchen."

It hurt me when our aunt spoke like this, because more than any of us I was hers. But I always pretended not to have heard.

"Did you know them?" I had to ask. "These Stavrides, Aunt Ourania?"

"I cannot say I did not *know* them," Aunt Ourania now replied. "Oh, yes," she said, "I *knew* them."

It seemed to me that Aunt Ourania was looking her sternest, but as always on such a transformation, she began to fiddle with my tunic, to stroke my hair.

"Then, shall we know them, too, Aunt Ourania? There is one child, Eurydice says. A little girl. Titina."

But our Aunt Ourania grew sterner still.

"I have not decided," she said at last, "how far we shall commit ourselves. The Stavrides," she said, clearing her throat, "are not altogether desirable."

"How?" I asked.

"Well," she said, "it is difficult to put."

She went on stroking the short stubble of my cropped hair.

"Kyria Stavridi, you see, was the daughter of a chemist. They even lived above her father's shop. It is not that I have anything against Kyria Stavridi," she thought to add. "For all I know, she may be an excellent person by different standards. But we must draw the line. Somewhere. Today."

Then my Aunt Ourania looked away. She was herself such a very good person. She read Goethe every morning, for a quarter of an hour, before her coffee. She kept the Lenten fasts. Very soon after her arrival, she had ordered the hair to be shorn from the heads of all us boys. We were to wear the tunics of ordinary working-class children, because, she said, it was wrong to flaunt ourselves, to pretend we were any different. She herself wore her hair like a man, and gave away her money in secret.

"Still," my Aunt Ourania said, "there is no reason why you children should not be kind to Titina Stavridi, even if her parents are undesirable."

Her eyes had moistened, because she was so tender.

"You, Dionysi," she said, "you are the kindest. You," she said, "must be particularly kind to poor Titina."

For the present, however, nothing further happened.

Our life continued. After the departure of our parents, you could not say anything momentous took place. There were always the minor events, and visits. Our Aunt Calliope, the professor, came from Paris. She made us compose essays, and breathe deep. My brother Aleko wrote for a course on hypnotism; Phrosso forgot her athlete, and began to notice a Rumanian; my second sister Agni won her prize for algebra; and the little ones, Myrto and Paul, each started a money-box. With so many unimportant yet necessary things taking place all the time, it did not occur to me to refer again to the Stavrides. Or perhaps it did cross my mind, and I made no mention of them, because our Aunt Ourania would not have wished it. So the days continued more or less unbroken: the sun working at the street wall; the sea-water salting our skins; the leaves of the ficus sweating in the damp evenings of the old house at Schutz.

When, suddenly, on a Tuesday afternoon, there was Kyria Stavridi herself sitting in Aunt Ourania's favorite chair beside the big window in the *salon*.

"Which one are you, then?" Kyria Stavridi called, showing an awful lot of gold.

"I am the middle one," I replied. "I am Dionysios."

In ordinary circumstances I would have gone away, but now I was fascinated by all that gold.

"Ah," Kyria Stavridi said, and smiled, "often it is the middle ones on whom the responsibilities fall."

It made her somewhat mysterious. She was dressed, besides, in black, and gave the impression, even at a distance of several feet, of being enclosed in a film of steam.

I did not answer Kyria Stavridi, because I did not know what to say, and because I had noticed she was not alone.

"This is my little girl. Titina," Kyria Stavridi said. "Will you be kind to her?"

"Oh," I said. "Yes."

Looking at the unknown child.

Titina Stavridi was standing at her mother's elbow. All in frills. All in white. Wherever she was not stuck with pink satin bows. Now she smiled, out of her oblong face. Some of the teeth appeared to be missing from Titina's smile. She had that banana-coloured skin, those rather pale, large freckles, the paler skin round the edges of

the hair, which suggested to me, I don't know why, that Titina
Stavridi might be a child who had long continued to wet the bed.

Just then my Aunt Ourania came into the room, to which our
maid Aphrodite had called her. She put on her man's voice, and
said: "Well, Kyria Stavridi, who would have expected to see you in
Alexandria!"

Holding out her hand from a distance.

Kyria Stavridi, who had got to her feet, began to steam more than
ever. She was exceptionally broad in her behind. Kyria Stavridi was
bent almost double as she touched my aunt's fingers.

"Ah, Mademoiselle Ourania, such a pleasure!" Kyria Stavridi
was bringing it out by the yard. "To renew acquaintance! And
Mademoiselle Thalia? So distinguished!" Kyria Stavridi said.

Aunt Ourania, I could see, did not know how to reply.

"My sister," she said, finally, "cannot come down. She is
suffering from a headache."

And Kyria Stavridi could not sympathize enough. Her breath
came out in short, agonized rushes.

After that, they spoke about people, which was always boring.

"Dionysi," my aunt said, during a pause, "why don't you take
Titina into the garden? Here there is really nothing for children."

But I did not move. And my aunt did not bother again.

As for Titina Stavridi, she might have been a statue, but an ugly
one. Her legs seemed so very thick and lifeless. All those bows. And
frilly pants. By moving closer I could see she had a kind of little
pock-mark on the side of her lumpy, freckled nose, and her eyes
were a shamefully stupid blue.

"My husband," Kyria Stavridi was saying, "my husband, too,"
she murmured, "does not enjoy the best of health."

"Yes," said my Aunt Ourania, "I remember."

Which somehow made her visitor sad.

Then all the others were pushing and rushing, even Phrosso and
Aleko, the two eldest, all entering to see this Kyria Stavridi from
Smyrna, and her ugly child. Everybody was introduced.

"Then I hope we shall be friends," Kyria Stavridi suggested,
more to us children, because it was obvious even to me that her

hopes of our aunts were not very high. "Dionysios," said Kyria Stavridi, "will be, I feel, Titina's little friend. He has promised me, in fact. They must be the same age, besides."

This made my sister Agni laugh, and Aleko gave me a pinch from behind. But my little brother Paul, who was never in two minds about anything, went straight up to Titina, and undid one of her satin bows. For a moment I thought Titina Stavridi would begin to cry. But she did not. She smiled and smiled. And was still smiling when her mother, who had said all the necessary things, presently led her out.

Then we were all laughing and shouting.

"So that was Kyria Stavridi!" my sister Phrosso shouted. "Did you notice the gap between her front teeth?"

"And the bows on her dreadful Titina!" Agni remarked. "You could dress a bride in all that satin!"

"Do we have to know such very vulgar people?" asked my brother Aleko.

Then our Aunt Ourania replied: "You are the one who is vulgar, Aleko."

And slapped him in the face.

"Aleko, you will go to your room."

This might have shocked us more, Aleko the eldest, already so strong, if Myrto—she was the quiet one who noticed things—had not begun to point and shriek.

"Look! Look!" Myrto shouted. "Titina Stavridi has done it on the floor!"

There, in fact, beside the best chair, was Titina's pool. As if she had been an untrained dog.

At once everyone was pushing to see.

"Such a big girl!" Aunt Ourania sighed.

She rang for Aphrodite, who called to the Arab, who brought a pail.

After that I began to suspect everybody in our house had forgotten the Stavrides. Certainly the two girls from Lesbos had seen the Kyrios Stavridis singing and stumbling at the end of the street. He had put his foot through his straw hat. But nothing was done about Titina, until one hot evening as I searched the garden with a candle, looking for insects for a collection I was about to make, Aunt Ourania called me and said:

"Tomorrow we must do something about Titina. You, Dionysi, shall fetch her."

Several of the others groaned, and our Aunt Thalia, who was playing Schumann in her loveliest dress, of embroidered purple, hunched her shoulders.

"Oh!" I cried. "I?"

But I knew, and my aunt confirmed, it could not have been otherwise. It was I who must be the steadiest, the kindest. Even Kyria Stavridi had said that responsibilities often fell to the middle ones.

On the following afternoon I fetched Titina. We did not speak. But Kyria Stavridi kissed me, and left a wet patch on my cheek.

We were going to the beach, on that, as on almost any other afternoon.

"Oh!" moaned my sister Phrosso. "The old beach! It is so boring!"

And gave Titina a hard pinch.

"What, Titina," asked Agni, "is that?"

For Titina was wearing a blue bead.

"That is to keep away the Eye," said Titina.

"The Eye!"

How they shouted.

"Like an Arab!" cried Myrto.

And we began to chant: *"Titina, Titina, Arapina . . ."* but softly, almost under our breath, in case Mademoiselle should hear.

So Titina came to the beach, on that and other afternoons. Once we took off her pants, and beat her bottom with an empty bottle we found floating in the sea. Then, as always, Titina only smiled, rather watery certainly. We ducked her, and she came up breathless, blinking the sea out of those very stupid, deep blue eyes. When it was wet, her freckly skin shone like a fish's.

"Disgusting!" Phrosso decided, and went away to read a magazine.

You could not torture Titina for long; it became too uninteresting.

But Titina stuck. She stuck to me. It was as if Titina had been told. And once in the garden of our house at Schutz, after showing her my collection of insects, I became desperate. I took Titina's blue bead, and stuck it up her left nostril.

"Titina," I cried, "the holes of your nose are so big I'd expect to see your brain—if you had any," I shouted, "inside."

But Titina Stavridi only smiled, and sneezed the bead into her hand.

In my desperation I continued to shout pure nonsense.

Until my Aunt Thalia came out.

"Wretched, wretched children!" she called. "And *you!* Dionysi!"

During the heat of the afternoon my aunt would recline in a quiet room, nibbling a raw carrot, and copying passages from R. Tagore.

"My headache!" she now protested. "My rest destroyed! Oh, my God! My conjunctivitis!"

On account of the conjunctivitis Aunt Thalia was wearing her bottle-green eye-shade, which made her appear especially tragic. Altogether Aunt Thalia was like a masked figure in a tragedy.

So that I was shocked, and Titina Stavridi even more so.

On the next occasion when I fetched her, her mother took me aside and instructed me in detail.

"Your poor Aunt Thalia!" She sighed. "Night and morning," she made me repeat. "Bathe the eyes. Undiluted."

"What is this bottle you have brought me?" asked Aunt Thalia when I presented it.

She was standing in the big *salon,* and the sleeves fell back from her rather thin but elegant arms.

"It is for the conjunctivitis."

"Yes! Yes! But what is it?"

Aunt Thalia could grow so impatient.

"It is a baby's water," I replied. "Night and morning. Undiluted."

"Oh! Oh!" moaned our Aunt Thalia as she flung the bottle.

It bounced once on the polished floor.

"Disgusting, disgusting creature!"

"It's probably a very *clean* baby," I said.

It sounded reasonable, but Aunt Thalia was not consoled.

Nor did I fetch Titina again. I must say that, even without the episode of Kyria Stavridi's prescription, we should not have been allowed to see Titina. For the Stavrides were always becoming involved in what our aunts considered undignified, not to say repulsive, incidents. For instance, Kyria Stavridi was butted in her broad behind by a piebald goat in the middle of the Rue Goussio. Then there was the thing that happened in our own street as Despo and Aphrodite, the maids from Lesbos, were returning home at dusk. The two girls were panting and giggling when they arrived. We could hear them already as they slammed the gate. What was it, Despo, Aphrodite? we called, running. It was to do with the Kyrios Stavridis, we gathered, who had shown them something in the almost dark. Long afterwards it was a matter for conjecture what the Kyrios Stavridis had shown our maids, though our sister Phrosso insisted from the beginning that she knew.

In any case, Titina Stavridi withdrew from our lives, to a distance of windows, or balconies.

Once indeed, I met her outside the grocer's, when Titina said: "It is sad, Dionysi. You were the one. You were the one I always loved."

So that I experienced a sensation of extreme horror, not to say terror, and ran all the way home with the paperful of sugar for which Kyria Smaragda had sent me.

But I could not escape Titina's face. Its dreadful oblong loomed in memory and at open windows, at dusk especially, as the ripening dates fell from their palms, and a camel grunted past.

So much happened all at once I cannot remember when the Stavrides went away. For we, too, were going. Our Aunt Ourania had paused one evening in doing the accounts, and said it was time to give serious thought to education. So there we were. Packing. Fräulein Hoffmann began to cry.

Once I did happen to remark: "Do you suppose the Stavrides have left already? One sees only shutters."

"That could be," said Aunt Ourania.

And Aunt Thalia added: the Stavrides were famous for moving on.

Anyway, it was unimportant. So many events and faces crowded into the next few years. For we had become Athenians. In the dry, white, merciless light, it was very soon recognized that I was a conscientious, though backward boy. Time was passing, moustaches growing. Often we children were put to shame by the clothes our Aunt Ourania would make us wear, for economy, and to contain our pride.

Most of the other boys had begun to think of going to brothels. Some of them had already been. Their moustaches helped them to it. But I, I mooned about the streets. Once I wrote on a wall with an end of chalk:

I LOVE   I LOVE   I LOVE

And then went off home. And lay on my empty bed. Listening. The nights were never stained with answers.

It was soon the year of the Catastrophe. We moved to the apartment at Patissia then. So as to have the wherewithal to help some of those poor people, our Aunt Ourania explained. For soon the refugees were pouring in from Anatolia. There were cousins sleeping on the tiled floors, and our Aunt Helen and Uncle Constantine in the maids' bedroom; the girls from Lesbos had to be dismissed. Give, give, ordained Aunt Ourania, standing with her arms full of cast-off clothes. My youngest sister Myrto burst into tears. She broke open her money-box with a hammer, and began to spend the money on ices.

Oh, everything was happening at this time. Our eldest brother, who had given up all thought of becoming a film star, was in Cairo being a businessman. Our sister Phrosso had stopped falling in love. She was again in Alexandria, trying for one of several possible husbands. There were the many letters, which filled me with an intolerable longing for damp gardens and ficus leaves. Once I even wrote a poem, but I showed it to no one, and tore it up. It was sometimes sad at home, though Agni might sit down at the piano, and bash out *Un baiser, un baiser, pas sur la bouche* . . . while the aunts were paying calls.

Then it was decided—it was our Aunt Ourania who decided

things—that as Dionysios was an unexceptional, but reliable boy, he should leave school, and go to our Uncle Stepho at the bank. Then there would be so much more to give to those poor people, the refugees from the Turks in Anatolia. It was exciting enough, but only for a little. Soon I was addressing envelopes at the bank. The dry ledgers made me sneeze. And my Uncle Stepho would send for me, and twist my ear, thinking it a huge joke to have me to torture at the bank.

So it was.

Summer had come round again: the eternal, powdery, white Athenian summer. The dust shot out from under my shoes as I trudged along Stadium Street, for although I had intended to spend my holiday at Pelion, Aunt Ourania had at once suggested: will your conscience allow you, with all those refugees sleeping on mattresses in the hall? So I had stayed, and it was intolerable. My clothes were damp rags by eleven o'clock in Stadium Street.

When I heard my name.

"Dionysi! Dionysi?"

It was a young woman. Or girl. Or girl. Who sprang from one of those little marble tables, where she had been eating a water-ice, on the pavement, at Yannaki's.

"Oh," she continued, "I thought. I thought it was *some*one. Dionysios Papapandelidis. Somebody I used to know."

I must have looked so stupid, I had caused this cool, glittering girl to doubt and mumble. She stood sucking in her lips as though to test to what extent her lipstick had been damaged by the ice.

When suddenly I saw, buried deep inside the shell, the remains, something of the pale, oblong face of the child Titina we had known at Schutz.

My surprise must have come pouring out, for at once she was all cries and laughter. She was breathing on me, embracing even, kissing the wretched beginnings of my thin moustache, there in the glare of Stadium Street. I had never felt so idiotic.

"Come," Titina said at last. "We must eat an ice. I have already had several. But Yannaki's ices are so good."

I sat with Titina, but was nervous, for fear I might have to pay for all those previous ices.

But Titina almost immediately said: "I shall invite you, dear Dionysi."

She was so glad. She was so kind. The curious part of it was: as Titina fished in her bag for a cigarette, and fiddled with the stunning little English lighter, and a ball of incalculable notes fell out on the marble table-top, *I* had become the awkward thing of flesh Titina Stavridi used to be.

"Tell me!" she begged; and: "Tell me!"

Dragging on the cigarette, with her rather full, practised lips.

But I, I had nothing to tell.

"And you?" I asked. "Do you live in Athens?"

"Oh, no!" She shook her head. "Never in Athens!"

This goddess was helmeted only in her own hair, black, so black, the lights in it were blue.

"No," she said. "I am here on a short visit. Jean-Louis," she explained, "is an exceptionally kind and generous man."

"Jean-Louis?"

"That is my friend," Titina answered, shaping her mouth in such a way I knew my aunts would have thought it common.

"This person, is he old or young?"

"Well," she said, "he is mature."

"Does your mother know?"

"Oh, Mother! Mother is very satisfied things have arranged themselves so well. She has her own apartment, too. If this is the world, then live in it. That is what Mother has decided."

"And your father?"

"Papa is always there," Titina said, and sighed.

As for myself, I began to fill with desperate longing. Here was Titina, so kind, so close, so skilled, so unimaginable. My clothes tightened on me as I sat.

And Titina talked. All the time her little bracelets thrilled and tinkled. She would turn her eyes this way and that, admiring, or rejecting. She would narrow her eyes in a peculiar way, though perhaps it was simply due to the glare.

"Tell me, Dionysi," she asked, and I experienced the little hairs barely visible on her forearm, "have you ever thought of me? I expect not. I was so horrible! Awful! And you were always so very kind."

The fact was: Titina Stavridi did sincerely believe in her own words, for she had turned upon me her exquisitely contrived face, and I could see at the bottom of her candid eyes, blue as only the Saronic Gulf, I could see, well, I could see the truth.

"There is always so little time," complained Titina, both practical and sad. "Dionysi, are you free? Are you free, say, this afternoon? To take me to the sea? To swim?"

"But this is Greece," I said, "where men and girls have not yet learnt to swim together."

"Pah!" she cried. "They will learn! You and I," she said, "will swim together. If you are free. This afternoon."

And at once time was our private toy. We were laughing and joking expertly as Titina Stavridi pared away the notes, to pay for all those ices we had eaten at Yannaki's.

"First I have an appointment," she announced.

"With whom?" I asked.

I could not bear it.

"Ah!" She laughed. "With a friend of my mother's. An elderly lady, who has a wart."

So I was comforted. There were *youvarlakia** for lunch. Nobody could equal Eurydice at *youvarlakia,* but today, it seemed, sawdust had got into them.

"You will offend Eurydice," Aunt Thalia had begun to moan. "You have left her *youvarlakia.*"

I decided not to tell my two, dear, stuffy aunts of my meeting with Titina Stavridi.

It became the most unbearable secret, and to pass the time—to say nothing of the fact that I should probably have to pay Titina's fare on the rather long journey by bus.

"Oh, no," she was saying at last, there on the steps of the Grande Bretagne. "Call a taxi," Titina insisted, which the man in livery did.

"Money is for spending," she explained.

On the way, as she rootled after the lovely little lighter, I was

* *Youvarlakia:* meatballs.

relieved to see her bag was still stuffed with notes.

For the afternoon she was wearing a bracelet of transparent shells, which jostled together light as walnuts.

"That," Titina said, "is nothing."

"My friend," she added, "advised me to leave my jewels in a safe deposit at the Crédit Lyonnais. One never knows, Jean-Louis says, what may happen in Greece."

I agreed that the Crédit Lyonnais offered greater certainty.

It was like that all the way. As her body cannoned off me, as lightly as her bracelet of shells, Titina revealed a life of sumptuous, yet practical behaviour. She accepted splendour as she did her skin. All along the beach, that rather gritty Attic sand, Titina radiated splendour in godlike armour of nacreous scales, in her little helmet of rubber feathers.

"Do you like my costume?" she asked, after she had done her mouth. "Jean-Louis does not. *Ça me donne un air de putain.* So he says."

At once she ran down into the sea, shimmering in her gorgeous scales. I was glad to find myself inside the water.

Then we swam, in long sweeps of silvery-blue. Bubbles of joy seemed to cling to Titina's lips. Her eyes were the deeper, drowsier, for immersion.

I had asked the taxi to drop us at a certain bay along that still deserted coast. The shore was strewn with earth-coloured rocks. The Attic pines straggled, and struggled, and leaned out over the sea. It was a poor landscape, splendid, too, in its own way, of perfectly fulfilled austerity. I had hoped we should remain unseen. And so we were. Until a party of lads descended half-naked on the rocks. Several of them I had sat beside in school. Now they seated themselves, lips drooping, eyes fixed. They shouted the things one expected. Some of them threw handfuls of water.

But Titina squinted at the sun.

Faced with these gangling louts, of deferred muscle and blubber-lips, anything oafish in myself seemed to have been spent. Was it Titina's presence? My head, set firmly on my neck, had surveyed oceans and continents. I had grown suave, compact, my glistening moustache had thickened, if not to the human eye.

Presently some of the boys I knew plunged in, and were swimming around, calling and laughing in their cracked voices. Their seal-like antics were intended to amuse.

But Titina did not see.

Then, as we were standing in the shallows, squat, yellow Sotiri Papadopoulos attempted to swim between Titina's legs.

"Go away, filthy little boy!"

How she pointed!

Titina's scorn succeeded. Sotiri went. Fortunately. He had often proved himself stronger than I.

Afterwards I sat with Titina, dripping water, under the pines. She told me distantly of the visits to Deauville, Le Touquet, and Cannes. Reservations at the best hotels. I was only lazily impressed. But how immaculate she was. I remembered Agni, her goosy arms, and strings of wet, swinging hair.

Titina produced *fruits glacés*.

"We brought them, Jean-Louis and I, from the Côte d' Azur. Take them," she ordered.

First I offered her the box.

"Ach!" she said. "Eat! I am sick of them. The *fruits glacés!*"

So I sat and stuffed.

For a long time we remained together beneath the pines, she so cool and flawless, myself only hot and clammy. She began to sing— what, I really cannot remember.

"Ah," she exclaimed, lying back, looking up through the branches, "they are stunted, our poor pines."

"That is their way," I told her.

"Yes," she sighed. "They are not stunted."

I walked a short distance, and brought her *vissinada** from a roadside booth. We stained our mouths with the purple *vissinada*. All along the Saronic Gulf the evening had begun to purple. The sand was gritty to the flesh. I believe it was at this point the man with the accordion passed by, playing his five or six notes, as gentle and persuasive as wood-pigeons. Unlike the boys earlier, the man with the accordion did stare. He strolled. I think probably the man was blind.

* *Vissinada:* cherry syrup.

"Ach, Titina! Titina!"

I was breathing my desperation on her.

The darkness was plunging towards us as Titina Stavridi turned her face towards me on the sand. A twig had marked her perfect cheek. She lay looking into me, as though for something she would not find.

"Poor Dionysaki," she said, "at least it is unnecessary to be afraid."

So that I had never felt stronger. As I wrestled with Titina Stavridi on the sand, my arms were turned to sea-serpents. The scales of her nacreous *maillot,* which Jean-Louis had never cared for, were sloughed in a moment by my skilful touch. I was holding in my hands her small, but persistent buttocks, which had been threatening to escape all that afternoon.

"Ach!" she cried, in almost bitter rage, as we heard her teeth strike on mine.

Afterwards Titina remained infinitely kind. The whole darkness was moving with her kindness.

"When will you leave?" I dreaded to ask.

"The day after tomorrow," she replied. "No," she corrected, quick. "Tomorrow."

"Then why did you say: *after* tomorrow?"

"Because," she said, simply, "I forgot."

So my sentence was sealed. All the sea sounds of Attica rose to attack me, as I thrust my lips all over again into Titina's wilted mouth.

"Good-bye, Titina," I said, on the steps of her hotel.

"Good-bye, Dionysi. *Dionysaki!"*

She was so tender, so kind.

But I did not say anything else, as I had begun to understand already that such remarks are idiocy.

All the way to Patissia, the dust was thick and heavy on my shoes.

When I got in, my Aunt Calliope, the professor, had arrived from Paris.

"Our Dionysi!" cried Aunt Calliope. "Almost a man!"

She embraced me quickly, in order to return to politics.

We had never cared for Aunt Calliope, who had made us write essays and things, though her brothers loved her, and would quarrel with her till the white hours over any boring political issue.

"The Catastrophe," my Aunt Calliope had reached the shouting stage, "was the result of public apathy in one of the most backward countries of the world."

My Uncle Stepho was shouting back.

"Hand it over to you and your progressive intellectuals, and we might as well, *all,* decent people, anyway, cut our throats!" bellowed Uncle Stepho, Vice-President of our Whole Bank.

"But let us stick to the Catastrophe!"

"The Generals were to blame!" screamed my Uncle Constantine. "All Royalists! Royalists!"

Aunt Calliope was beating with her fists.

"What can one expect of effete Republicans? Nothing further!"

"Do not blame the Republicans!" Aunt Ourania dared anyone.

"The Royalists have not yet proved themselves."

Aunt Calliope started to cackle unmercifully.

"Better the Devil," thought Constantine.

Aunt Ourania frowned.

"Still, Kosta," she suggested, very gravely, in the voice she adopted for all soothing purposes, "you must admit that when blood flows our poor Greece is regenerated."

My Aunt Thalia, who had been crying, went to the piano. She began to play a piece I remembered. Sweet and sticky, the music flowed from under her always rather tentative hands.

The music gummed the voices up.

Then my Aunt Calliope remarked: "Guess whom I saw?"

Nobody did.

"That little thing, that Titina Stavridi, to whom you were all so kind in the old days at Schutz."

"Living in Athens?" asked Aunt Ourania, though the answer must remain unimportant.

"Not a bit of it," Aunt Calliope said. "I have run into her before. Oh, yes, several times. In Paris." Here Aunt Calliope laughed. "A proper little *thing!* A little whore!"

It was obvious from her expression that Aunt Ourania was taking it upon herself to expiate the sins of the world, while Aunt Thalia forced the music. How it flowed, past the uncles and out of the room, all along the passages of our shrunken apartment, which seldom nowadays lost its smell of *pasta*. The intolerable Schumann pursued me as far as my own room, and farther.

Outside, the lilac-bushes were turned solid in the moonlight. The white music of that dusty night was frozen in the parks and gardens. As I leaned out of the window, and held up my throat to receive the knife, nothing happened. Only my Aunt Thalia continued playing Schumann, and I realized that my extended throat was itself a stiff sword.

Miss Slattery and Her Demon Lover

He stood holding the door just so far. A chain on it too.

"This," she said, "is Better Sales Pty. Ltd." Turning to a fresh page. "Market research," she explained. "We want you to help us, and hope, indirectly, to help you."

She moistened her mouth, easing a threat into an ethical compromise, technique pushed to the point where almost everyone was convinced. Only for herself the page on her pad would glare drearily blank.

Oh dear, do not be difficult, she would have said for choice to some old continental number whose afternoon sleep she had ruined.

"Faht do you vornt?" he asked.

"I want to ask you some questions," she said.

She could be very patient when paid.

"Kvestions?"

Was he going to close the door?

"Not you. Necessarily. The housewife."

She looked down the street, a good one, at the end of which the midday sun was waiting to deal her a blow.

"Housewife?"

At least he was slipping the chain.

"Nho! Nho! Nho!"

At least he was not going to grudge her a look.

"No lady?" she asked. "Of any kind?"

"Nho! Nefer! Nho! I vould not keep any vooman of a permanent description."

"That is frank," she answered. "You don't like them."

Her stilettos were hurting.

"Oh, I *lihke!* How I *lihke!* Zet is *vhy!*"

"Let us get down to business?" she said, looking at her blank pad. "Since there is no lady, do you favour Priceless Pearl? Laundry starch. No. Kwik Kreem Breakfast Treat? Well," she said, "it's a kind of porridge that doesn't get lumps."

"Faht is porritch?"

"It is something the Scotch invented. It is, well, just *porridge,* Mr Tibor."

"Szabo."

"It is Tibor on the bell."

"I am Hoongahrian," he said. "In Hoongary ze nimes are beck to front. Szabo Tibor. You onderstend?"

He could not enlist too much of himself, as if it were necessary to explain all such matters with passionate physical emphasis.

"Yes," she said. "I see. Now."

He had those short, but white teeth. He was not all that old; rather, he had reached a phase where age becomes elastic. His shoes could have cost him a whole week's pay. Altogether, all over, he was rather suède, brown suède, not above her shoulder. And hips. He had hips!

But the hall looked lovely, behind him, in black and white.

"Vinyl tiles?" Her toe pointed. "Or lino?"

After all, she was in business.

"Faht? Hoh! Nho! Zet is all from marble."

"Like in a bank!"

"Yehs."

"Well, now! Where did you find all that?"

"I brought it. Oh, yehs. I bring everysing. Here zere is nossing. Nossing!"

"Oh, come, Mr Tibor—Szabo—we Australians are not all that uncivilized. Not in 1961."

"Civilahsed! I vill learn you faht is civilahsed!"

She had never believed intensely in the advantages of knowledge, so that it was too ridiculous to find herself walking through the marble halls of Tibor Szabo Tibor. But so cool. Hearing the door click, she remembered the women they saw into pieces, and leave in railway cloak-rooms, or dispose of in back yards, or simply dump in the Harbour.

There it was, too. For Szabo Tibor had bought a View. Though at that hour of day the water might have been cut out of zinc, or aluminum, which is sharper.

"You have got it good here," she said.

It was the kind of situation she had thought about, but never quite found herself in, and the strangeness of it made her languid, acting out a part she had seen others play, over-life-size.

"Everysing I hef *mosst* be feuhrst class," Szabo Tibor was explaining. "Faht is your nime, please?"

"Oh," she said. "Slattery. Miss Slattery."

"Zet is too match. Faht little nime else, please?"

Miss Slattery looked sad.

"I hate to tell you," she said. "I was christened Dimity. But my friends," she added, "call me Pete."

"Vitch is veuorse? Faht for a nime is zet? Pete!"

"It is better than going through life with Dimity attached."

"I vill call you nossing," Szabo Tibor announced.

Miss Slattery was walking around in someone else's room, with large, unlikely strides, but it made her feel better. The rugs were so easy, and so very white, she realized she hadn't taken her two-piece to the cleaner.

"A nime is not necessary," Szabo Tibor was saying. "Tike off your het, please; it is not necessary neither."

Miss Slattery did as she was told.

"I am not the hatty type, you know. They have us wear them for business reasons."

She shook out her hair, to which the bottle had contributed, not altogether successfully, though certain lights gave it a look of its own, she hoped: tawnier, luminous, dappled. There was the separate lock, too, which she had persuaded to hang in the way she wanted.

An Australian girl, he saw. Another Australian girl.

Oh dear, he was older perhaps than she had thought. But cuddly. By instinct she was kind. Only wanted to giggle. At some old teddy bear in suède.

Szabo Tibor said: "Sit."

"Funny," she said, running her hands into the depths of the chair, a habit she always meant to get out of, "I have never mixed business and pleasure before."

But Szabo Tibor had brought something very small and sweet, which ran two fiery wires out of her throat and down her nose.

"It is goot. Nho?"

"I don't know about *that*"—she coughed—"Mr Szabo. It's effective, though!"

"In Australien," Mr Szabo said, and he was kneeling now, "peoples call me Tibby."

"Well! Have you a sense of humour!"

"Yehs! Yehs!" he said, and smiled. *"Witz!"*

When men started kneeling she wanted more than ever to giggle.

But Tibby Szabo was growing sterner.

"In Australien," he said, "no *Witz*. Nho! Novair!"

Shaking a forefinger at her. So that she became fascinated. It was so plump, for a finger, banana-coloured, with hackles of little black hairs.

"Do you onderstend?"

"Oh, yes, I understand all right. I am nossing."

She liked it, too.

"Then faht is it?" asked Tibby Szabo, looking at his finger.

"I am always surprised," she answered, "at the part texture plays."

"Are you intellectual girl?"

"My mind," she said, recrossing her legs, "turned to fudge at puberty. Isn't that delicious?"

"Faht is futch?"

"Oh dear," she said, "you're a whale for knowing. Aren't there the things you just accept?"

She made her lock hang, for this old number who wouldn't leave off kneeling by the chair. Not so very old, though. The little gaps between his white teeth left him looking sort of defenceless.

Then Tibby Szabo took her arm, as though it didn't belong to her. The whole thing was pretty peculiar, but not as peculiar as it should have been. He took her arm, as if it were, say, a cob of corn.

As if he had been chewing on a cob of corn. She wanted to giggle, and did. Supposing Mum and Wendy had seen! They would have had a real good laugh.

"You have the funniest ways," she said, "Tib."

As Tibby Szabo kept on going up and down her arm.

When he started on the shoulder, she said: "Stoput! What do you think I *am?*"

He heard enough to alter course.

A man's head in your lap somehow always made you feel it was trying to fool itself—it looked so detached, improbable, and ridiculous.

He turned his eyes on then, as if knowing: here is the greatest sucker for eyes. Oh God, nothing ever went deeper than eyes. She was a goner.

"Oh God," she said, "I am not like this!"

She was nothing like what she thought she was like. So she learned. She was the trampoline queen. She was an enormous, staggery spider. She was a rubber doll.

"You Austrahlian girls are visout *Temperament,*" Tibby Szabo complained. "You are all gickle and talk. Passion is not to resist."

"I just about broke every bone in my body not resisting," Miss Slattery had to protest.

Her body that continued fluctuating overhead.

"Who ever heard of a glass ceiling!"

"Plenty glass ceiling. Zet is to see vis."

"Tibby," she asked, "this wouldn't be—mink?"

"Yehs. Yehs. Meenk beds are goot for ze body."

"I'll say!" she said

She was so relaxed. She was half-dead. When it was possible to lift an arm, the long silken shudders took possession of her skin, and she realized the southerly had come, off the water, in at the window, giving her the goose-flesh.

"We're gunna catch a cold," she warned, and coughed.

"It is goot."

"I am glad to know that something is good," she said, sitting up, destroying the composition in the ceiling. "This sort of thing is all very well, but are you going to let me love you?"

Rounding on him. This fat and hairy man.

"Lof? Faht execkly do you mean?"

"Oh, Tibby!" she said.

Again he was fixing his eyes on her, extinct by now, but even in their dormancy they made her want to die. Or give. Or was it possible to give and live?

"Go to sleep," he ordered.

"Oh, Tibby!"

She fell back floppy whimpery but dozed. Once she looked sideways at his death-mask. She looked at the ceiling, too. It was not unlike those atrocity photographs she had always tried to avoid, in the papers, after the war.

It was incredible, but always had been.

By the time Miss Slattery stepped into the street, carrying her business hat, evening had drenched the good address with the mellower light of ripened pears. She trod through it, tilted, stilted, tentative. Her neck was horribly stiff.

After that there was the Providential, for she did not remain with Better Sales Pty. Ltd.; she was informed that her services would no longer be required. What was it, they asked, had made her so unreliable? She said she had become distracted.

In the circumstances she was fortunate to find the position with the Providential. There, too, she made friends with Phyllis Wimble.

"A Hungarian," Phyllis said, "I never met a Hungarian. Sometimes I think I will work through the nationalities like a girl I knew decided to go through the religions. But gave up at the Occultists."

"Why?"

"She simply got scared. They buried a man alive, one Saturday afternoon, over at Balmoral."

When old Huthnance came out of his office.

"Miss Slattery," he asked, "where is that Dewhurst policy?"

He was rather a sweetie really.

"Oh yes," Miss Slattery said, "I was checking."

"What is there to check?" Huthnance asked.

"Well," Miss Slattery said.

And Huthnance smiled. He was still at the smiling stage.

Thursday evenings Miss Slattery kept for Tibby Szabo. She would go there Saturdays too, usually staying over till Sunday, when they would breakfast in the continental style.

There was the Saturday Miss Slattery decided to give Tibby Szabo a treat. Domesticity jacked her up on her heels; she was full of secrecy and little ways.

When Tibby asked: "Faht is zet?"

"What is what?"

"Zet stench! Zet blue *smoke* you are mecking in my kitchenette. Faht are you prepurring?"

"That is a baked dinner," Miss Slattery answered. "A leg of lamb, with pumpkin and two other veg."

"Lemb?" cried Tibby Szabo. "Lemb! It stinks. Nefer in Budapest did lemb so much as cross ze doorways."

And he opened the oven and tossed the leg into the Harbour.

Miss Slattery cried then, or sat, rather, making her handkerchief into a ball.

Tibby Szabo prepared himself a snack. He had *paprikawurst,* a breast of cold paprika chicken, paprikas in oil, paprika in cream cheese, and finally, she suspected, paprika.

"Eat!" he advised.

"A tiny crumb would choke me."

"You are not crying?" he asked through some remains of paprika.

"I was thinking," she replied.

"So! *Sink*-ing!"

Afterwards he made love to her, and because she had chosen love, she embraced it with a sad abandon, on the mink coverlet, under the glass sky.

Once, certainly, she sat up and said: "It is all so *carnal!*"

"You use zeese intellectual veuords."

He had the paprika chicken in his teeth.

There was the telephone, too, with which Miss Slattery had to contend.

"Igen! *Igen!* IGEN!" Tibby Szabo would shout, and bash the receiver on somebody anonymous.

"All this *iggy* stuff!" she said.

It began to get on her nerves.

"Demn idiots!" Tibby Szabo complained.

"How do you make your money, Tib?" Miss Slattery asked, picking at the mink coverlet.

"I am Hoongahrian," he said. "It come to me over ze telephown."

Presently Szabo Tibor announced he was on his way to inspect several properties he owned around the city.

He had given her a key, at least, so that she might come and go.

"And you have had keys cut," she asked, "for all these other women, for Monday, Tuesday, Wednesday, and Friday, in all these other flats?"

How he laughed.

"At last a real *Witz!* An Austrahlian *Witz!*" he said on going.

It seemed no time before he returned.

"Faht," he said, "you are still here?"

"I am the passive type," she replied.

Indeed, she was so passive she had practically set in her own flesh beneath that glass conscience of a ceiling. Although a mild evening was ready to soothe, she shivered for her more than nakedness. When she stuck her head out the window, there were the rhinestones of Sydney glittering on the neck of darkness. But it was a splendour she saw could only dissolve.

"You Austrahlian girls," observed Tibby Szabo, "ven you are not all gickle, you are all cry."

"Yes," she said. "I know," she said, "it makes things difficult. To be Australian."

And when he popped inside her mouth a kiss like Turkish delight in action, she was less than ever able to take herself in hand.

They drove around in Tibby's Jag. Because naturally Tibby Szabo had a Jag.

"Let us go to Manly," she said. "I have got to look at the Pacific Ocean."

Tibby drove, sometimes in short, disgusted bursts, at others in long, lovely demonstrations of speed, or swooning swirls. His driving was so much the expression of Tibby Szabo himself. He was wearing the little cigar-coloured hat.

"Of course," said Miss Slattery through her hair, "I know you well enough to know that Manly is not Balaton."

"Balaton?"

Tibby jumped a pedestrian crossing.

"Faht do you know about Balaton?"

"I went to school," she said. "I saw it on the map. You had to look at *some*thing. And there it was. A gap in the middle of Hungary."

She never tired of watching his hands. As he drove, the soft, cajoling palms would whiten.

Afterwards when they were drawn up in comfort, inside the sounds of sea and pines, and had bought the paper-bagful of prawns, and the prawn-coloured people were squelching past, Tibby Szabo had to ask: "Are you trying to spy on me viz all zese kvestions of Balaton?"

"All these questions? One bare mention!"

Prawn-shells tinkle as they hit the asphalt.

"I wouldn't open any drawer, not if I had the key. There's only one secret," she said, "I want to know the answer to."

"But Balaton!"

"So blue. Bluer than anything we've got. So everything," she said.

The sand-sprinkled people were going up and down. The soles of their feet were inured to it.

Tibby Szabo spat on the asphalt. It smoked.

"It isn't nice," she said, "to spit."

The tips of her fingers tasted of the salt-sweet prawns. The glassy rollers, uncurling on the sand, might have raked a little farther and swallowed her down, if she had not been engulfed already in deeper, glassier caverns.

"Faht is zis secret?" Tibby asked.

"Oh!"

She had to laugh.

"It is us," she said. "What does it add up to?"

"Faht it edds up to? I give you a hellofa good time. I pay ze electricity end ze gess. I put you in ze vay of cut-price frocks. You hef arranged sings pretty nice."

Suddenly too many prawn-shells were clinging to Miss Slattery's fingers.

"That is not what I mean," she choked. "When you love someone, I mean. I mean it's sort of difficult to put. When you could put your head in the gas oven, and damn who's gunna pay the bill."

Because she did not have the words, she got out her lipstick, and began to persecute her mouth.

Ladies were looking by now into the expensive car. Their glass eyes expressed surprise.

"Lof!" Tibby Szabo laughed. "Lof is viz ze sahoul!" Then he grew very angry; he could have been throwing his hand away. "Faht do zay know of lof?" he shouted. "Here zere is only stike and bodies!"

Then they were looking into each other, each with an expression that suggested they might not arrive beyond a discovery just made.

Miss Slattery lobbed the paper-bag almost into the municipal bin.

"I am sursty," Tibby complained.

Indeed, salt had formed in the corners of his mouth. Could it be that he was going to risk drinking deeper of the dregs?

"This Pacific Ocean," Miss Slattery said, or cried, "is all on the same note. Drive us home, Tibby," she said, "and make love to me."

As he released the brake, the prawn-coloured bodies on the asphalt continued to lumber up and down, regardless.

"Listen," Miss Slattery said, "a girl friend of Phyllis Wimble's called Apple is giving a party in Woolloomooloo. Saturday night, Phyllis says. It's going to be bohemian."

Szabo Tibor drew down his lower lip.

"Austrahlian-bohemian-proveenshul. Zere is nossing veuorse zan bohemian-proveenshul."

"Try it and see," Miss Slattery advised, and bitterly added: "A lot was discovered only by mistake."

"And faht is zis Epple?"

"She is an oxywelder."

"A vooman? Faht does she oxyveld?"

"I dunno. Objects and things. Apple is an artist."

Apple was a big girl in built-up hair and pixie glasses. The night of the party most of her objects had been removed, all except what she said was her major work.

"This is *Hypotenuse of Angst,*" she explained. "It is considered very powerful."

And smiled.

"Will you have claret?" Apple asked. "Or perhaps you prefer Scotch, or gin. That will depend on whoever brings it along."

Apple's party got under way. It was an old house, a large room running in many directions, walls full of Lovely Textures.

"Almost everybody here," Phyllis Wimble confided, "is doing something."

"What have you brought, Phyl?" Miss Slattery asked.

"He is a grazier," Phyllis said, "that a nurse I know got tired of."

"He is all body," Miss Slattery said, now that she had learnt.

"What do you expect?"

Those who had them were tuning their guitars.

"Those are the Spanish guitarists," Phyllis explained. "And these are English teddies off a liner. They are only the atmosphere. It's Apple's friends who are doing things."

"Looks a bit," the grazier hinted.

Phyllis shushed him.

"You are hating it, Tib," Miss Slattery said.

Tibby Szabo drew down his lip.

"I vill get dronk. On Epple's plonk."

She saw that his teeth were ever so slightly decalcified. She saw that he was a little, fat, black man, whom she had loved, and loved still. From habit. Like biting your nails.

I must get out of it, she said. But you didn't, not out of biting your nails, until you forgot; then it was over.

The dancing had begun, and soon the kissing. The twangling of guitars broke the light into splinters. The slurp of claret stained the jokes. The teddies danced. The grazier danced the Spanish dances. His elastic-sides were so authentic. Apple fell upon her bottom.

Not everyone, not yet, had discovered Tibby Szabo was a little, fat, black man, with serrated teeth like a shark's. There was a girl called Felicia who came and sat in Tibby's lap. Though he opened his knees and she shot through, it might not have bothered Miss Slattery if Felicia had stayed.

"They say," Phyllis Wimble whispered, "they are all madly queer."

"Don't you know by now," Miss Slattery said, "that everyone is always queer?"

But Phyllis Wimble could turn narky.

"Everyone, we presume, but Tibby Szabo."

Then Miss Slattery laughed and laughed.

"Tibby Szabo," she laughed, "is just about the queerest thing I've met."

"Faht is zet?" Tibby asked.

"Nossing, darling," Miss Slattery answered. "I love you with all my body, and never my soul."

It was all so *mouvementé,* said one of Apple's friends.

The grazier danced. He danced the Spanish dances. He danced bareheaded, and in his Lesbian hat. He danced in his shirt, and later, without.

"They say," whispered Phyllis Wimble, "there are two men locked in the lavatory together. One is a teddy, but they haven't worked out who the other can be."

"Perhaps he is a social realist," Miss Slattery suggested.

She had a pain.

The brick-red grazier produced a stockwhip, too fresh from the shop, too stiff, but it smelled intoxicatingly of leather.

"Oh," Miss Slattery cried, "stockwhips are never *made,* they were there in the beginning."

As the grazier uncoiled his brand-new whip, the lash fell glisteningly. It flicked a corner of her memory, unrolling a sheet of blazing blue, carpets of dust, cattle rubbing and straining past. She could not have kept it out even if she had wanted to. The electric sun beating on her head. The smell of old, sweaty leather had made her drunker than bulk claret.

"Oh, God, I'm gunna burn up!" Miss Slattery protested.

And took off her top.

She was alarmingly smooth, unscathed. Other skins, she knew, withered in the sun. She remembered the scabs on her dad's knuckles.

She had to get up then.

"Give, George!" she commanded. "You're about the crummiest crack I ever listened to."

Miss Slattery stood with the stockwhip. Her breasts snoozed. Or contemplated. She could have been awaiting inspiration. So Tibby Szabo noticed, leaning forward to follow to its source the faintest blue, of veins explored on previous expeditions.

Then, suddenly, Miss Slattery cracked, scattering the full room. She filled it with shrieks, disgust, and admiration. The horsehair gadfly stung the air. Miss Slattery cracked an abstract painting off the wall. She cracked a cork out of a bottle.

"Brafo, Petuska!" Tibby Szabo shouted. "Vaz you ever in a tseerkoos?"

He was sitting forward.

"Yeah," she said, "a Hungarian one!"

And let the horsehair curl round Tibby's thigh.

He was sitting forward. Tibby Szabo began to sing:

> *"Csak egy kislány*
> *van a világon,*
> *az is az én*
> *drága galambo-o-om!"*

He was sitting forward with his eyes half-closed, clapping and singing.

> "Hooray for love,
> it rots you . . ."

Miss Slattery sang.

She cracked a cigarette out of the grazier's lips.

> *"A jó Isten*
> *de nagyon szeret,"*

sang Tibby Szabo,

> *"hogy nékem adta*
> *a legszebbik-e-e-et!"* *

Then everybody was singing everything they had to sing, guitars disintegrating, for none could compete against the syrup from Tibby Szabo's compulsive violin.

While Miss Slattery cracked. Breasts jumping and frolicking. Her hair was so brittle. Lifted it once again, though, under the tawny sun, hawking dust, drunk on the smell of the tepid canvas waterbags.

Miss Slattery cracked once more, and brought down the sun from out of the sky.

It is not unlikely that the world will end in thunder. From the sound of it, somebody must have overturned *Hypotenuse of Angst*. Professional screamers had begun to scream. The darkness filled with hands.

"Come close, Petuska."

It was Tibby Szabo.

"I vill screen you," he promised, and caressed.

When a Large Person appeared with a candle. She was like a scone.

"These studios," the Large Person announced, "are let for purposes of creative art, and the exchange of intellectual ideas. I am not accustomed to louts—and worse," here she looked at Miss Slattery's upper half, "wrecking the premises," she said. "As there

---

* "Only one little girl
    in the world,
    and she is
    my dear little dove!

"The good God
    must love me indeed
    to have given me
    the most beautiful one!"

has never been any suspicion that this is a Bad House, I must ask you all to leave."

So everybody did, for there was the Large Person's husband behind her, looking as though he might mean business. Everybody shoved and poured, there was a singing, a crumbling of music on the stairs. There was a hugging and a kissing in the street. Somebody had lost his pants. It was raining finely.

Tibby Szabo drove off very quickly, in case a lift might be asked for.

"Put on your top, Petuska," he advised. "You vill ketch a colt."

It sounded reasonable. She was bundling elaborately into armholes.

"Waddayaknow!" Miss Slattery said. "We've come away with the grazier's whip!"

"Hef vee?" Tibby Szabo remarked.

So they drove in Tibby's Jag. They were on a spiral.

"I am so tired," Miss Slattery admitted.

And again: "I am awful tired."

She was staring down at those white rugs in Tibby's flat. The soft, white, serious pile. She was propped on her elbows. Knees apart. Must be looking bloodyawful.

"Petuska," he was trying it out, "vill you perheps do vun more creck of ze whip?"

He could have been addressing a convalescent.

"Oh, but I am tired. I am done," she said.

"Just vun little vun."

Then Miss Slattery got real angry.

"You and this goddam lousy whip! I wish I'd never set eyes on either!"

Nor did she bother where she lashed.

"Ach! Oh! Aÿ-yaÿ-yaÿ! Petuska!"

Miss Slattery cracked.

"What are the people gunna say when they hear you holler like that?"

As she cracked, and slashed.

"Aÿ! It is none of ze people's business. *Pouff! Yaÿ-yaÿ-yaÿ-yaÿ!"* Tibby Szabo cried. "Just vun little vun more!"

And when at last she toppled, he covered her very tenderly where she lay.

"Did anyone ever want you to put on boots?"

"What ever for?" asked Phyllis Wimble.

But Miss Slattery found she had fetched the wrong file.

"Ah, dear," she said, resuming. "It's time I thought about a change," she said. "I'm feeling sort of tired."

"Hair looks dead," said Phyllis Wimble. "That is always the danger signal."

"Try a new rinse."

"A nice strawberry."

Miss Slattery, whose habit had been to keep Thursday evening for Tibby Szabo, could not bear to any more. Saturdays she still went, but at night, for the nights were less spiteful than the days.

"Vair vas you, Petuska, Sursday evening?" Tibby Szabo had begun to ask.

"I sat at home and watched the telly."

"Zen I vill instal ze telly for here!"

"Ah," she said, "the telly is something that requires the maximum of concentration."

"Are you changing, Petuska?" Tibby asked.

"Everything is changing," Miss Slattery said. "It is an axiom of nature."

She laughed rather short.

"That," she said, "is something I think I learned at school. Same time as Balaton."

It was dreadful, really, for everyone concerned, for Tibby Szabo had begun to ring the Providential. With urgent communications for a friend. Would she envisage Tuesday, Vensday, Friday?

However impersonally she might handle the instrument, that old Huthnance would come in and catch her on the phone. Miss Slattery saw that Huthnance and she had almost reached the point of no return.

"No," she replied. "Not Thursday. Or any other day but what was agreed. Saturday, I said."

She slammed it down.

So Miss Slattery would drag through the moist evenings. In which the scarlet hibiscus had furled. No more trumpets. Her hair hung dank, as she trailed through the acid, yellow light, towards the good address at which her lover lived.

"I am developing a muscle," she caught herself saying, and looked round to see if anyone had heard.

It was the same night that Tibby Szabo cried out from the bottom of the pit: "Vhy em I condemned to soffer?"

Stretched on mink, Miss Slattery lay, idly flicking at her varnished toes. Without looking at the view, she knew the rhinestones of Sydney had never glittered so heartlessly.

"Faht for do you *torture* me?"

"But that is what you wanted," she said.

Flicking. Listless.

"Petuska, I vill gif you *any*sink!"

"Nossing," she said. "I am going," she said.

"*Gowing?* Ven vee are so suited to each ozzer!"

Miss Slattery flicked.

"I am sick," she said, "I am sick of cutting a rug out of your fat Hungarian behind."

The horsehair lash slithered and glistened between her toes.

"But faht vill you do visout me?"

"I am going to find myself a thin Australian."

Tibby was on his knees again.

"I am gunna get married," Miss Slattery said, "and have a washing-machine."

"*Yaÿ-yaÿ-yaÿ! Petuska!*"

Then Miss Slattery took a look at Tibby's eyes, and rediscovered a suppliant poodle, seen at the window of an empty house, at dusk. She had never been very doggy, though.

"Are you ze Defel perheps?" cried Tibby Szabo.

"We Australians are not all that unnatural," she said.

And hated herself, just a little.

As for Tibby Szabo, he was licking the back of her hand.

"Vee vill make a finenshul arrangement. Pretty substenshul."

"No go!" Miss Slattery said.

But that is precisely what she did. She got up and pitched the grazier's stockwhip out of the window, and when she had put on her clothes, and licked her lips once or twice, and shuffled her hair together—she went.

The Letters

Mrs Polkinghorn remembered she ought to write a letter of sympathy to Maud. Any illness tended to irritate her, but dear funny old Maud Bles, so loyal, if so colourless, she must really say something about Maud's blood pressure. Or was that Sibyl Farnsworth? No, Sibyl's sounded far more technical.

Mrs Polkinghorn still *enjoyed* sitting down at her marquetry desk in the morning-room, and dashing off a few letters, many of them unnecessary, after her pretence of a breakfast. It seemed, in these days, to uphold her status. She was lucky in having Harriet, who would not last forever, though.

Mrs Polkinghorn's breath caught.

"Charles?" she called, not for any particular reason.

No answer.

She chose a sheet of the second-best writing paper—the lettering was nicely engraved, however:

WISHFORT
SARSAPARILLA, N.S.W.

Then Mrs Polkinghorn was ready.

Dearest Maud,   (*she wrote, in what had been referred to as her bold hand*)

I can think of nothing more *tiresome* than to be told to "go slow"! You can imagine how distressed we, too, shall be, since it will deprive us of your little annual visit. The blossom at "Wishfort" promises to be particularly fine this year, and you do so love it. Still, we must bear our crosses.

I broke the news to Charles, who received it in silence. But I know he will sadly miss the company of his beloved Auntie Maud on the *important occasion*. I did have hopes of coaxing him out to our matinée this year, especially as this will be his *fiftieth* birthday. I cannot believe it! Though of course there is every evidence. Indeed, at times Charles acts so old he makes his poor mother feel positively young!

Here Mrs Polkinghorn was unable to resist a glance. Her eyes could still ravish the glass.

Maud dear, it is not my habit, as you know, to *load* others with my troubles, but your godson has been worrying me more than usual. There is nothing one can *put one's finger on* . . .

For a moment she wondered whether that looked vulgar. She was sorry she had underlined it.

But . . . (*she continued bravely*) . . . the complications do increase. Since his "withdrawal," you will remember I have taken pains to devise little routine occupations to give him an interest in life. My efforts, however, have not always been successful. My plan for him to mow the grass was perhaps an understandable failure. Charles is not mechanical, and grass is so tedious. The grass-mowing did not last for long (Norman had to resume; he is now so deaf and rude, but we are lucky, I expect, to have him). A comparatively recent "brain-wave" on my part was to persuade Charles to walk up to Sarsaparilla and fetch the letters. I rented one of those amusing little private boxes, and Mrs Sugden, the postmistress, is such a decent soul—I knew Charles to have a particular affection for her. All went well for several months, until last week my darling, tiresome son announced he was unable to continue fetching the letters! So now, if you please, the mail is once more delivered at our gate, and I must think of something fresh for Charles.

I do not doubt all this will sound trivial to anyone so far distant as Melbourne. Of course, it is something that concerns *me*, and I would not breathe it to another person, unless to his godmother,

and you do seem to have some influence over him, Maud dear.
I have always been so grateful . . .

Here Mrs Polkinghorn paused again. Funny how dowdy, simple
Maud had known unexpectedly what to do in many a situation.
Was it humility? Oh, but Mrs Polkinghorn had *prayed* for humility. She was frowning hard now, and the glass had grown unkind.

Relax.

Mrs Polkinghorn began to smile, but slackly, but spiritually, as
she had learnt it.

> One last wish for your restored health, dear Maud, and I am
> sure we shall *both* be thinking of you with deepest affection as we
> stroll amongst the blossom at "Wishfort," before Harriet sum-
> mons us to the birthday luncheon.
>
> My very best love—
> URSULA
>
> P.S. If you should write to him, please do not mention any of these
> matters.

When she had sealed the envelope, which tasted rather nasty,
Mrs Polkinghorn went in search.

Charles was sitting in the dining-room, in that big leather arm-
chair, so hideous, but it had belonged to Dickie. Charles was reading something, or so it appeared. She could see the back of his
head, the careful, straw-coloured hair, which he would arrange to
cover as much as possible of that fragile dome. Sometimes the
mother almost expected to see a pulse still beating in her child's
head.

"Charles," she said, gently, going round, "you are reading."

He was, and continued.

"What," she asked, "are you reading, Charles?"

"Rearing of Fowls on the Free Range System."

His small moustache, straw-coloured once, had been dirtied by
the shadow of grey.

"But we have no fowls," she said. "They smell."

He continued reading.

"Or perhaps you would like me to buy you some," she considered. "Half a dozen chickens," she begged. "The grown-up kind. Those little day-old things are such a trouble, and you'd be sure to catch a cold."

Charles said: "No."

He continued reading.

Mrs Polkinghorn could not endure the creaking of that huge leather arm-chair. She was glad of Norman's lawn-mower. With only a little collaboration from her mind, the blast from the machine could destroy almost all other noises, sensations, presences.

"Well," she sighed.

She rearranged her hat. It was the big old straw she wore for the garden, but like all large floppy hats, it suited and pleased Mrs Polkinghorn. The big droopy ones created an atmosphere of weddings.

"Did you go," she remembered, "to the gate, to see whether the postman has brought our letters?"

"No," he answered.

His cheek did twitch just a little. Or was it another of those infinitesimal wrinkles opening in the skin?

"But *why,* darling?"

He was reading, and reading.

Mrs Polkinghorn could not control her irritated breath.

"Then I shall have to fetch them myself. Harriet is busy, and Norman so rude, one hardly dares suggest any longer."

She went out, into the garden she had planned herself, though that landscape creature had claimed the credit. The house, with its little seemly lozenges of leaded panes, set in the Tudor sprawl of shaggy brick, was by now far too big, but when Dickie died she had determined she would make the effort to keep it up. Now she walked along the path, touching the roses of which she was proud. Somewhere jasmine whipped her cheek. You could not say it was a sob that burst from her mouth, but refractory jasmine did recall the contrariety of life.

Nothing but bills, of course. At best, receipts. Two of the more sumptuous circulars for Charles, and the firm's report from Cousin Ken.

After Charles's "withdrawal," Mrs Polkinghorn had arranged—in confidence—with Cousin Ken and Mr Beddoes that the firm's reports be forwarded regularly to her son. *To keep him in the picture,* she said. It pleased Mrs Polkinghorn to collect the idiom of those decades to which she had never succeeded in belonging. Her theft of such phrases made her feel she had entered into conspiracy.

But this morning events seemed to be conspiring against her. She almost tripped near the steps, by slipping her foot into a noose of the couch-grass Norman could never be persuaded to uproot.

She went on, clutching her bills.

Dickie would have attended to bills. Dickie Polkinghorn, a large man, though mild, whom almost everyone had forgotten. Even his widow was sometimes surprised on catching sight of Dickie's face in one of the many silver frames which contained all that was left of him.

But I did, did love darling Dickie.

Thus assured, Mrs Polkinghorn returned to the dining-room with the letters. She did not wish to. It was her duty, however.

"Here are your letters, Charles," she offered.

He took them.

"Are you not going to open them, and see?"

He had put down the pamphlet. He had put his hand to his mouth for a moment. Unlike his father, his bones were fragile.

"There might be something exciting," she coaxed.

"Yes."

But he got up, and shut them in the lacquered box which dominated the mantelpiece.

Mrs Polkinghorn was helpless. If only Maud, now.

"I have just written," she announced, "to Auntie Maud. About her trouble. Who knows when my letter will get posted, though. Norman will refuse to leave the mowing."

When Charles Polkinghorn made a most remarkable offer.

"Give me the letter," he said. "I shall take it to Sarsaparilla."

His mother hardly knew whether to feel gratified or pained. She always experienced a little pang to discover afresh that the wells of human nature were deeper than she was able to plumb.

She gave up the letter, however, and Charles went out with the light, nervous steps of brittle bones, so unlike his father, whose movements had always been attended by a squelch.

Alone with the photograph of Dickie, she remembered those other men whose company she had enjoyed. English tweed went to her head, and the gloss on the toe-cap of a well-shod foot. She would glance at a man's wrist, while fanning his vanity with what he supposed to be her attention. She was very expert. The lips of many congested, jolly, tweedy men would still droop open at the recollection of Ursula Polkinghorn's smile.

Now she walked through her house—it was unmistakably *her* walk—trailing the garments which clothed her spirit, while in fact wearing some she did not particularly care for. Ursula Polkinghorn (one of the Annesley Russells of Toorak) had always favoured the trailing dresses, weeping sleeves, stoles tipped with feather, to throw casually round her throat. That throat! Whenever she had made her entrance, at weddings, for instance, smoothing the long kid gloves, or hand barely passing through the faint effulgence of her pale hair, everybody forgot the bride. Yet her eyes hardly encouraged them, for of course she had never trifled with *any*body's affections. She had *adored* her Dickie. Though her mouth would smile for someone she might never confess.

Involved in a kind of composite of all the weddings at which she had assisted, Mrs Polkinghorn made for the pantry, where she still did the flowers, every morning, after the ritual of her desk. Harriet had found the scissors, so easily lost, and stood a wrong selection of vases.

For Mrs Polkinghorn to preside.

"Lovely, lovely roses!"

But this morning something was eating the roses.

Her rings clashed. She never took off her rings by day, unless to demonstrate to Harriet the number of folds for rough puff. Which Harriet secretly knew.

But today the rings were brutal.

Nor could she resist one quick look out of the window—she always took the greatest precautions—before treading smoothly

back, into the dining-room. It was empty. Breathless. Presences
still lingered there. She almost expected Dickie's leather arm-chair
to creak.

Mrs Polkinghorn opened the lacquered box. There was quite
a bundle of letters inside. All unopened. Several days of them.

At that point she began to dread something she might not be
capable of understanding.

The first moment after stepping outside into the brilliant, fleshy
garden, Charles Russell Polkinghorn had sidled rather. The light
blinded his sandy eyes. He held on to the letter, though.

The morning had grown silent in which old Norman squatted,
to fiddle with the mowing-machine.

Charles paused, because one did.

"What is it, Norman?" he asked. "A cog?"

Norman never looked up for Charles.

"Cog! It's the bloody maggy!"

Charles Polkinghorn might have been relieved.

"Patch it up!" Norman complained. "Patch up the bloody
maggy!"

Because, she had said, I shall spend nothing further on the
mower. Horrid thing. If it had been something attractive.

Charles Polkinghorn continued on through what his mother was
pleased to call the Great Eastern Shrubbery. He was picking at the
sliver of dry skin which grew alongside one of his nails. As a little
golden boy he had begun to take an interest in those pieces of
dead-seeming skin, often fraying them till he bled. He would stand
beside the wood-shed, or slip inside the shrubberies, to pick.

"Don't you find them interesting, Auntie Maud? The corners of
skin. Except you sometimes pick too hard."

To Maud Bles her godson was a most fanciful little boy.

"Yes," she said.

And touched his hair.

Married to a poor clergyman of acceptable family she had failed
to reproduce.

Charles Polkinghorn walked up the road to Sarsaparilla. It was *his* road, though nobody knew. Although his shoulders were narrow, and his waist thin, in the black pin-stripe he was wearing out, he walked purposefully now. Nor did he turn his head, though suspecting faces. There were, too. Ladies would pause, in their dusting or conversation, to observe "that Mr Polkinghorn."

Who arrived at last. And skirted round. To slip the letter, quietly, deftly, into the box.

As soon as done, he escaped. Not even the postmistress had seen: Mrs Sugden, of straight, upstanding hair, for whom he had the affection.

Not a bad lot this morning, a pretty respectable bunch, Mrs Sugden used to remark in the days when Charles fetched the letters from their private box.

Charles Russell Polkinghorn was returning jauntier than he had come.

He had been to the circus with his Auntie Maud. The clowns began to terrify, especially the one who broke his neck. Poor, poor Charles, she comforted; now you may look, it was nothing, only horseplay. Horseplay? There hadn't been any horses, only terrifying clowns. Just a lot of silly nonsense, she reassured. He raised his head slowly from her breast. She smelled of nothing, he was surprised to find. But kindness. Her hand, chafing his skin, looked so natural, he continued staring at it after the clowns and his terror had vanished.

It wasn't real, she explained; it wasn't meant.

Charles Russell Polkinghorn had often wondered what is meant. Now he whimpered a little going down the hill.

"Good morning, Mr Polkinghorn," said old Miss Langlands.

"Good morning, Miss Langlands. You are looking well."

Could it be that she liked him?

Entered for the right school, Polkinghorn had acquired manners. That he distinguished himself scholastically, people had forgotten. His mother would sit below the dais, waiting for afterwards, waiting for him to heap the prizes in her arms.

They sent him over to Cambridge, too. Dad had agreed. Polkinghorn trod warily at first. In his second year he had invited two

or three men to tea and crumpets. They had not come again. But
Charles was immersed in all that he had discovered. He took a
degree, with honours. Only a second, it must be admitted. If that
hour of amnesia hadn't occurred in the course of his final paper,
his tutor considered he might have managed a first. Charles was
quietly crushed. He had cherished the prospect of a prolonged affair with the Romance languages in some academic backwater.
Curiously enough, languages enabled him to communicate—discreetly, though—with other people.

But all that would have been impossible, of course. For other
reasons.

His mother had written:

. . . did not cable, because I understand the greater shock cables
can give. You will be happy at least to know, dear, that Dad
died painlessly, in his sleep. Only the suddenness of it! I expect it
will take me quite a time to recover, but I shall throw myself into
as much as I can. There is always the Firm to consider. Cousin Ken
and Mr Beddoes are, mercifully, towers of strength. Dad had the
greatest confidence in them, but Charles, darling, it was always his
dearest wish that his son . . .

Charles returned.

She was not at the boat to meet him, preferring to stage their
reunion away from the hurly-burly, in the setting they both loved.

She had come down the steps towards him, offering her face
which tears had tightened. Her eyes astonished by their blueness.
She patted his arm, lingering on it for a moment to enjoy the texture of English tweed.

Charles Polkinghorn at that stage was what is called a dapper
little man, with his small, evenly-divided moustache, discretion
in his clothes and cuff-links. In those days he could still tell a story.
Cigarette smoke acted as a screen. The music had not begun to
throb. One or two girls had even looked him over at dances.

"Tell me," his mother asked, offering her face, "there must be
someone."

"Someone? Who?"

"Why," she laughed, "you silly old boy! Some charming girl!"

Charles Polkinghorn was thunderstruck.

"But," he said, "I thought I had done everything that was required of me."

On leaving the room he mopped his forehead with a handkerchief.

His mother had to wet her lips. And to return on frequent occasions to the inquisition. Her eyes were at their bluest then.

"Surely," she said, "I cannot believe there isn't some lovely girl. Otherwise it just isn't natural."

She watched his mouth as it tried out shapes.

"There is no one," he said.

And stuck to it.

Considered from certain angles the situation was unfortunate, Mrs Polkinghorn told Miss Langlands. But she and Charles were very happy together. They had so many interests in common.

In those days Charles Russell Polkinghorn was scrupulously observant once he had made up his mind to a thing. Caught the train every morning to the works. Cousin Ken had explained the plant. The men acted hearty, while they thought it was expected of them. Charles was given an office, not the one which had been his father's —Cousin Ken had taken over that—but a smaller, no less airy, well-equipped room. At intervals during the day, secretaries placed papers in his tray. Miss Gregson smelled of Ashes-of-Roses. Charles Russell Polkinghorn would take the papers out of his tray, and examine them gravely.

It was the noise which began to worry him. Sometimes Miss Gregson's lips would move without sound. It was the machinery, at which he never learned to look without wanting to avert his face.

There was the annual dinner and dance, at which his mother put in an appearance. Mr Beddoes would hand her through the waltzes. His wrist-watch was far too small for him.

"Do you care for Greta Garbo, Mr Polkinghorn?" Miss Gregson inquired.

"Enjoying yourself, darling?" his mother asked.

She, at least, never failed in her performance.

After the first year or two, somebody hit on the idea of introducing paper caps and streamers. To make the dance jollier like.

Charles Polkinghorn suspected a private joke, the point of which he would never see.

Yet, there was his mother, dancing with the toolmakers, too.

He began, worse, to suspect the machinery. How it belted, as he sat examining Miss Gregson's papers. Voices did not carry. That had a certain advantage. Or most voices would not.

There was that Badgery, though, of Thompson Johnson Constructions.

"Everything running smoothly, Ken?"

Throwing his gravel into the machines.

"Smoothly? Couldn't be smoother. Even with our extra cog!"

The bits almost flew off then, the oily fragments, into Charles Polkinghorn's office. He put Miss Gregson's papers into the wrong tray.

On returning home that evening, Polkinghorn stayed away for a week.

"I must tell you, Ken, in confidence, though," his mother rang up the office, "Charles is suffering from a slight breakdown. . . . Yes, rest is what he needs. . . . I shall keep in touch. . . . Thank you, Ken, dear. You're a brick. . . ."

But Charles returned at the end of the week. He would sit it out.

They allowed him to keep his office. He continued to go there to read the *Herald,* until finally, as Mrs Polkinghorn herself put it, Charles "withdrew."

At "Wishfort" the years turned over quite as regularly as the most merciless machine; the difference was they were oiled with silence. Although he had given up reading, excepting the pamphlets and the circulars, there were lines that troubled Charles Polkinghorn still. *De l'amour j'ai toutes les fureurs* . . . might sound its muffled trumpet. He would slip out into the shrubberies, there to pick at his more placid thoughts, or the skin that had died at the sides of his nails. Sometimes the knots in his throat would almost soften into words of wonder, images almost crystallize somewhere at the back of his eyes.

Sometimes his mother would call to him, but he only answered when it suited.

On the morning of his fiftieth birthday Charles Polkinghorn woke early, aware that something had to be done. It could have been the presents; presents still gave him a thrill, though he was clever at finding out in advance.

His mother came, bringing the half-dozen Swiss voile shirts embroidered with his monogram. In all the house, she always rose the earliest. She kissed him. Her cheek, of legendary complexion, had the taste of icy water.

"Many happy returns, dear Charles!" she said, so brightly, she could have been speaking through falling water.

"Aren't they lovely?" she prompted. "Feel."

"Yes," he said.

He looked at them.

Presently she went down into the garden, into the dew and spider-webs. She liked to visit it before the heat, to sever the heads of roses. Thorns would tear at her silken wings, of a rose colour too, but she always won in the end.

The day was already promising a blue blaze, in which the new, feverish leaves would do little to allay apprehensions. Still, Charles was prepared for it: the tufts of blossom blowing brown in a withering wind. This year Auntie Maud would not be there to share his distress. In other details the programme promised to be much the same: roast chicken, and chocolate mousse; Harriet had iced a cake—Harriet, whose wizened face was one of those perennial loyalties he dared not look directly in the eye.

Charles went down. After breakfast, which his mother's figure did not allow her to share, he knew for certain there was something. Thumping. At times, his heart would sound like a man approaching in crêpe-rubber soles along a linoleum corridor.

He realized then; sleep perhaps had planted in him the necessity for correcting a mistake. It was the boxful of unopened letters. The lacquered box on the mantelpiece.

Could it be that the sealed letters might breed the dangers he thought to escape, secrets stirring, gases expanding, poisons maturing? His rubbery heart was maddening him. And towards nine, the postman would arrive with more.

At nine, precisely, he did. Clocks accompanied the event. Charles, who was watching, noticed the peak of a cap glinting through the cotoneasters.

Inspiration drove him down the path. To liberate. The flaps of his hacking-jacket flew.

There was something this morning disguised as a bill. Something more innocent-dangerous. And—might he thank Heaven? —a letter from Auntie Maud.

Charles Polkinghorn returned quickly to the dining-room, to decide, but not quickly enough, which letters to open first. To repair. To avert. The box tumbled the whole collection out on the table, into the marmalade, amongst the crumbs.

Then he opened. One.

> . . . this machine will cut closer, wear better than any other on the market. It will demolish the worst growth of Paddy's lucerne, Paterson's Curse, paspalum, or that most stubborn invader of the home lot, Kikuyu grass.
>
> The rotator's cut . . .

Charles Polkinghorn recoiled. Almost mown by the wind the machine made in passing, he kept his balance with difficulty. Once, he remembered to have read, a blade had become detached, and embedded itself in a human eye.

But a certain minutia of evil had been dispersed simply by the opening of an envelope. His hands faltered in search of increased relief. To do his duty. If it was not—for he could not claim to be noble—to save his own skin.

He had opened, again, at last.

> . . . *otherwise* (the next threat ran) *your supply may be disconnected without further warning* . . .

So that his neck was straining, his eyes grew polypous, his veins shrank until it seemed they might fail altogether to convey the flow.

Then Charles Polkinghorn remembered his godmother. Auntie Maud, he was convinced, must save. If his swollen tongue had not choked him before he tore the envelope.

My dear Charles,   (*it was herself speaking*)

   This is just a note to wish you the happiest of birthdays. I am truly disappointed not to be with you on the occasion. But the doctor forbids me to attempt it since my "turn."

   Dear Charles, I want you to know what very great happiness you have given me, almost as though you were my own son. I have been an unsatisfactory godmother, I admit, what with the actual distance that has always separated us—and, well, just my own inadequacy. My only consolation is a belief that it is not possible to discuss things of the spirit without their losing something of their purity. Will you, too, my dear, console yourself in realizing this? I have always liked to think we have brought each other comfort of a kind.

   Now, Charles, I must take you into my confidence—that is to say: I do not wish to upset your mother—but there is every possibility that I may not last so very much longer. The truth is always a risk, but at some points one has to risk it. I asked, and I was told. In the meantime, I shall pray that I remain with you, *always, always,* in the spirit.

   I am sending you a little package for your birthday. If it should arrive beforehand, I ask you to keep it until the day for which it is intended.

                                Your loving godmother—
                                MAUD BLES

   Then Charles Polkinghorn had to cry out. *Blessés!* The two— or was it the three of them?

   But was not Auntie Maud aware that packages contain the worst of dangers, threatening the lives of politicians, diplomats, film stars, all people of importance? At least the package had not arrived. Or had they put it away, and forgotten it was thriving and throbbing in the dark of some unvisited cupboard?

   He began to go round the room. The windows were open. Through them he suddenly heard the approach of animals above the gibbering of Norman's mower. The soft, but insidious animals. Or rain? It was the first enormous drops of rain padding through the mulberry leaves. None the less, he closed the windows.

But could not shut out his own heart.

"What is it?" his mother asked very quickly on coming in. "Ah, you have opened the letters! I am so glad! Did you find anything of interest?"

Did he!

Mrs Polkinghorn saw that it had happened.

"Charles," she said, "we must not give way."

She was trembling, though.

As for Charles Polkinghorn, the walls had started screeching.

When she bore down on him, her face had become a circular saw, teeth whirling, eyes blurred into the steel disk.

He screamed back.

"Darling," she cried, "what has been done to us? We must, we *must* be *strong!*"

After that, they were seated on the sofa, their knees trembling in the same piece. He, no longer so very frightened. Crying, though, because he had forgotten how to stop. By now she had compressed her face into a lump of the marshmallow he used to love, and even now he might have popped it into his mouth, if the white mass had not been smeared so palpably with blood.

He continued crying for all they had forfeited, or never found.

"Strong, *strong!*" Mrs Polkinghorn commanded.

Was this her son? This bunch of twigs she held in her hands? She could almost have snapped the brittle stuff.

But caught sight: the old, slanting teeth set in the remnants of her own face.

"Remember, remember," she uttered, fainter, "I shall always be at your side."

It did not stop him.

Though he did, at least, remember. She was standing at the foot of the stairs. In white satin. *Remember,* she said, *Charles,* as he slowly descended, paying out the smooth rail through his hand, *remember you are of an age where you must not open letters. Other people's affairs are their own. Besides,* she added, *you might discover something to hurt you. Always remember that.*

Remumber. Oh, Mum, Mum, Mum, oh, Mummy!

"I shall help you," his mother was saying, "if you will let, if you will trust me."

She was holding his head against her brooch. Sapphires were threatening to gouge his eye.

"Oh, yes! Yes, yes!" he cried, or mumbled.

Descending still farther on the spiral, into the remoter, satiny depths, he stooped to pick up her voice, its shell. *Isn't he an angel? Look, Dickie! A cherub off a palace ceiling! He is mine! My angel!* Oh, delicious persuasions! And when she touched, flooding him with satin.

"Charles! CHARLES!" Ursula Polkinghorn had begun to rattle.

"Oh, God help us!" she called.

If Charles had been less involved, he might have heard the pennies drop. But must push past, ever deeper, past the sapphires and the wrinkles, in search of darkness.

"Oh, horrible! Oh, Charles!"

As soon as he began to nuzzle at her, Mrs Polkinghorn threw him off. How did she deserve? Ever! Her beastly, her unnatural child!

The Woman Who
Wasn't Allowed to Keep Cats

By the time the Hajistavri reached the Alexious' door they were in a state of petulance, if not actual anger.

"If you ask me," Spiro Hajistavros said, "we did a crazy thing setting out before the food had settled in our stomachs. You've gotta take the climate into account."

Then he burped. His wife did not let herself hear it, for she did not want to feel humiliated.

"Yes, sir!" Spiro said, and burped, and plodded.

"It's *our* climate, isn't it?" Maro Hajistavrou found her voice.

"Sure, but you forget," Spiro said.

He was one of those who cling to their adopted language until forced out of it. Success had not come to him in Greek.

"And *my* friends. I believe you begrudge me my friendship for Kikitsa Alexiou," Maro complained.

"What would I have against you and this Mrs Alexiou being friends?" her husband asked. "Sure you're friends. Old friends. So old they forgot to come and meet you at the airport."

Maro Hajistavrou might have cried, only then she would have arrived looking a sight.

"Oh, but Kikitsa was always such a lovely person! The prettiest thing. Smart as paint. I can't tell you. She had bronze hair. And always so lively. And legs. Greek women have thick legs on the whole."

Spiro grunted.

Maro wondered whether he had kept mistresses. For the moment she did not altogether care. As she climbed the hill in his footsteps, she could not see her husband's face, only the cropped lines of his rather thick, bull's neck, and the wings of his too perfect, silver hair. She thought she hated what she saw. It was what she had needed, though, and married, and even loved at times.

There is nothing in this man to which one can object, her Aunt Cecaumenou had decided already so many years ago. In that exquisitely reasonable voice the "nothing" suggested "everything." It is not the restaurants, the Aunt Cecaumenou had concluded, and her niece was more than ever reminded of an icon, restored admittedly by Schiaparelli; no girl in her right mind would turn up her nose at a chain of restaurants in seven cities, and the man himself is by any standards honest, it is only that his food is, well, so horribly indifferent.

Maro Mauroleondos, thin and brittle even as a girl, had married Spiro Hajistavros almost twenty years ago. In their progress through a series of increasingly desirable apartments the Hajistavri had grown together like two luxurious indoor plants. Different in habit and variety, they relied upon each other for support; he for the thorny traditions of her class which she brought to bear on daily life, she for the succulence on which her parasitic nature fed. On recognizing the value of her find, Maro Mauroleondos would have risked any aunt's overt opposition. If she had hesitated at the time, it was for imagining what her friend, Kikitsa Andragora, undoubtedly would think and say.

Now, as the Hajistavri continued plodding through present dust, negotiating the cracks in the paving, skirting the corpse of a piebald cat, Hajistavros turned to spit.

"Athens 1949!"

His wife refused to comment, but very briefly touched her pearls. Since arriving in the city several hours earlier Maro Hajistavrou had been feeling a little ashamed of the pearls.

"You have never liked my friends the Alexious," she began again, high and querulous. "Never for a moment, Spiro."

"Ba!" He almost spat a second time, but lapsed instead into his rejected native tongue. "Who am I to crab somebody we haven't even met?"

It was partly true. She had not met Aleko Alexiou.

"But Kikitsa!"

Dry at the best of times, Maro droned against the dust. Sensing her husband to be afraid of the Alexious made her even drier. That she was afraid of Kikitsa's husband she thought Spiro did not know.

"Your fine friends are your own affair," Spiro mumbled above their footsteps.

That they should approach important issues along class levels was something he took for granted.

"My fine friends?" Maro cried piteously. "They are poor, I gather. And intellectual."

"Intellectuals!" Spiro said, arranging what she knew from behind must be his monogrammed handkerchief. "I know no intellectuals," he said, "but soon shall. Unless they have gone to the sea."

Maro Hajistavrou, in her irritation, did not pay attention enough, and almost tripped on the uneven paving.

"Oh, but Kikitsa is not a bit like what you persist in thinking she is," she recovered herself and babbled. "She is not at all *dreary*. If anything I was the uninteresting one."

When anybody roused her stubbornness, her loyalty became excessive. If only she could have invoked the past, and allowed it to reflect her shining friend. But in the heat of the street she could not have conveyed its virtues, like a spring of mountain water, at which two girls had knelt to plunge their cupped hands.

"It is no use, I see," she muttered.

Impatience brought her level, and for a moment he put his arm through hers, and she felt its thickness, its rubbery solidity. Then she let fall one of those little grudging smiles which were always her final answer to anyone's implied criticism of her husband.

But would Kikitsa Alexiou recognize that it was more than a material necessity which had forced Maro Mauroleondos into marriage with a common Peloponnesian *restaurateur*?

For several months after landing in New York the thin girl had continued to measure, not so much after the standards of her Aunt Cecaumenou, so adept at bullying Americans into not following their own taste, but according to those vaguer, hence more desirable, even when agonizing, standards of Kikitsa Andragora.

Kikitsa had written regularly at first.

Dearest Maro,
    I wonder, and pity! All those Americans! How do they react? And the Aunt Cecaumenou, whose nails break from central heat! Perhaps when it is autumn I shall write a novel. Just at present I am quite spasmodic—suffering from too much summer. How I would love to make love on marble, beside the rose-coloured ramparts, under a pomegranate tree, looking seawards . . .

Maro tied Kikitsa's letters and kept them under her writing-paper.

Kikitsa wrote:

Dear, dear Maro,
    There are times when I find men reasonably fascinating. When, for example, they scoop the balls off a tennis court, and present them on a racket, like something formal on a dish. There is one creature in particular I shall refer to as A. for the time being—or as long as he remains anonymous!

Maro Mauroleondos had grown thinner, paler, in the aunt's Byzantine apartment, in the Park Avenue Gothic spire.

I assure you, Maro, the Aunt Cecaumenou said, the attitude is different, the pace brisker over here. It is quite in order for young girls to carry contraceptives in their hand-bags. Though, of course, connections should be taken into account. Not every date is desirable.

Maro Mauroleondos had locked herself in the lavatory, and remained there several hours.

Kikitsa wrote:

Dear Maro,
    I am engaged to Aleko Alexiou. He is an intellectual! Of good, but impoverished family, however. I am so excited! I have

always felt that anything of consequence must be short, sharp, stunning. It will not be long before we are married . . .

Maro Mauroleondos had walked in the rain, in a mackintosh, on Lexington. In a restaurant near Fifty-second, which fate had chosen for her, she ordered food when it was time. Nothing would have caused her to remember a luxury muted by discretion, if the proprietor had not approached. You are a Greek, she found him accusing her. How, she asked, could he have known? You are black enough, *moree,* the proprietor had said. When she had always prided herself. After dismissing her order of Manhattan chowder and cole-slaw, he called for *soudzoukakia,* and fed her, literally, off the fork. As he told her the story of his inevitably poor boyhood and eventual success, his gravity prevailed over his somewhat gorgeous clothes. Maro Mauroleondos allowed herself to become fascinated by the blunt fingers of the black Greek forking the *soudzoukakia* into her mouth. The action made her drowsy at last. She would not have been surprised to find herself sinking, in childlike trust, into the receptive carpet. He was, in fact, she discovered later, more than ten years her senior. But what did it matter? Unhappiness in the beginning made it even desirable, and that he should escort her afterwards, between an umbrella and the plate-glass windows, back to the Gothic tower. Safe. His name, he told her, was Hajistavros.

It was over twenty years since Mrs Hajistavrou had left Athens for her aunt's patronage in New York, it was over thirty since Hajistavros had reached Piraeus from Taygetos. Not surprising that neither of them now belonged.

"You gotta admit, Maro, it's scenic. A paradise for tourists." Mr Hajistavros panted on the slope. "Whichever direction. Take the Parthenon. Take Hymettus."

"Ah, I do not care for Hymettus!" cried his wife, and frowned. "It's so ugly. They cut down the trees during the Occupation. But even before they cut down the trees Hymettus was ugly. Irregular."

Deliberately she averted her face, thus to prevent herself seeing anything so distasteful. It was almost as though the sharp edge of the irregular mass had left a wound somewhere in Mrs Haji-stavrou's mind.

"At least," she said, "I believe this is the block."

Again consulting the envelope.

It was one of the beige blocks of Kolonaki in which the bullet holes had never healed.

Mr Hajistavros grunted.

"It is not *bad,*" his wife persuaded.

The doorkeeper pointed at the sky, and insisted on answering the Americans in English.

"Up! Up! Yes! To the roof! No work *ascenseur*. Tomorrow!"

"Drama! Drama!" Mrs Hajistavrou was less jaunty than she tried to sound.

The small old man clapped Mr Hajistavros on the back.

"Bravo, Amerikani!"

The Americans picked their way, apprehensive for their clothes.

"The address is a good one," Maro continued to insist in whispers, as if she alone would have recognized it.

Her husband burst one of the large, dried paint blisters on the wall. She knew, but ignored what Spiro meant.

And so they ascended. And as they did, careful of their American hearts, the excellent materials of their French and English clothes seemed to be slipping from them, together with Mrs Hajistavrou's breeding and Mr Hajistavros' seven restaurants, the two Cadillacs, the apartment in New York, all eventually superfluous, as the victims were reduced again to Maro and Spiro, a couple of Greeks. So they climbed. There was a smell of beans from under one door, there was the sound of an educated quarrel through another. If the stairs had not been so narrow, the visitants might once again have taken each other by the arm, to reconcile themselves to the thought that over all those years, in spite of the plans and discussions, it had perhaps been fear of the Alexious which had prevented a return to their native land.

Till there, at the top, was the woman standing in the doorway, in the draught which was blowing that post-war nylon stuff hither and thither between her thighs. The rather slack, mature figure, innocent of girdle. Eyes inquisitive amongst the fat.

"Kyria Alexiou," Maro began, so tentative it sounded false.

She had realized, of course, but was compelled to hold off her realization as long as it was possible.

Only Kikitsa Andragora would not allow. Could she have been expecting them?

"Maroula mou! Chrysoula mou!"

Momentarily the twenty years' fastidious aridity to which hair-dressers, manicurists, *couturiers,* and milliners had reduced Maro Mauroleondos was clasped to the steamy body of her friend.

Maro made the little, dry, gasping mouths of neat, middle-aged gentlewomen. To express what is, technically, their pleasure.

"Hi! Come right in, folks!"

Kikitsa should have shouted, but for some reason, she encouraged *sotto voce*.

"Why does this Mrs Alexiou speak like this?" Spiro would ask later on.

And Maro would reply: "She likes to think it has a kind of chic. That is Kikitsa all over."

"So very common?" Spiro would ask fastidiously.

"She can afford to be. Kikitsa is of such good family."

Spiro could not understand.

"Does it stink? Come on in!" Kikitsa was briskly sweeping off some crumbs. "Straight out of *The New Yorker* into the stench of *kephtedakia!* My God and little Virgin!"

The Hajistavri were making the difficult adjustment. They had begun to tremble their way across the threshold.

"And this is the man?"

Kikitsa had always been deliberate. She was peering out of all that fat. Maro remembered how her friend had always noticed more than she.

Then Kikitsa bared her teeth, and when her eyes were positively splintering, she went straight up to Hajistavros, and felt him, as though he had been a piece of expensive material.

"Lovely, Maro!" she pronounced.

Maro could not remember having seen Kikitsa's eyes quite so golden, or quite so reckless.

"You must admit, Maro darling, men are really rather lovely."

When they were all three seated in the very small living-room, in the draught which, blowing off the roof, appeared mercifully to make a fourth, Kikitsa resumed: "This is my home. *Homette* no doubt you Americans would call it. Aren't you fascinated the way so much *-ette* has crept into life?"

Spiro Hajistavros made an extra chin.

Kikitsa did not pause, however. Maro remembered with gratitude that Kikitsa very seldom paused.

"I expect that is of some sociological—or is it anthropological? —significance," Kikitsa continued. "We'll have to ask Aleko. When he comes in."

Would they escape Aleko? Spiro began to wonder and hope.

"And these are my cats," Kikitsa was explaining. "This is Hairy —Ronron—and—where—where—is Apricot?"

Spiro Hajistavros saw that this crazy thing, this Mrs Alexiou, seemed in some distress about her cat. Her over-generous bust began to jump. Little, noticeable points of steel glittered on her temples and her upper lip.

"Mish-mish-mish? Ver-i-kok-ko! *Poon doh? Poon doh?*" Mrs Alexiou called, but always in an undertone.

"Ah, there! Kikitsa whispered. "There!" She drew them gently after. "There is my bad Apricock! Look! Look! In my kitchen! Or is it *-ette?* You should know."

There was no doubt. The kitchen was minute.

But what was this Kikitsa trying to put over them? Spiro Hajistavros had to wonder. There, in fact, was her orange, ugly cat, stretched out on the kitchen slab between the *bourekakia* and a pair of Mrs Alexiou's shoes.

"One day you shall taste my *bourekakia, Monsieur le Restaurateur!*" Kikitsa laughed and promised.

For the present she merely broke off a leaf of pastry with which to tempt her bored cat.

But the great matted Apricock chose to turn his nose away. His great tail dangled, lollop and twitch, lollop and twitch.

"One day," Kikitsa smiled and mused, "when the pastry's nice and fresh."

"I shall be very interested," Mr Hajistavros murmured, and

withdrew his sleeve out of reach of a boiled fowl's detached claw.

Mrs Alexiou seemed to notice nothing, or if she did, she did not care. She was so in love with Apricot. And when one of her shoes toppled off the marble slab, where it had been lying, into a pan of *béchamel,* again she did not seem to care. But buried her face in the orange fur.

"Sometimes my Mish-mish refuses to recognize. Sometimes," she sighed, "I think my Kok-kos has a fever."

When she could no longer bear it Maro Hajistavrou slipped out into the living-room, though without escaping what had established itself as a permanent smell of cat. Now at least she would be able to look out of the window, and on this side of the apartment Hymettus could not be seen—there was the Parthenon instead.

"Oh," she now exclaimed, "is that your husband?"

For there on the tessellated roof was the head of a man lolling and drooping from a deck-chair.

Kikitsa Alexiou immediately rushed into the living-room as though she had neglected ritual. Laying a finger against her lips she took up the rites expertly at the point where they had been broken off.

"Sshhh!" she whispered.

"Oh, I am sorry! The siesta!"

"Didn't I tell you, Maro?" Hajistavros said, and laughed. "My wife must always have her way."

He sounded bitterly justified, and even Maro felt herself inwardly recoil.

"Oh, no! Not the siesta! The siesta comes afterwards. He is thinking now!" Kikitsa explained.

Hajistavros looked over the shoulders of the two women at this intellectual who had troubled him so sorely in advance, and who would doubtless never contribute to his ease. Hajistavros would have liked to live at peace with all men, but was continually brought to a halt on the edge of a hostile country, partly obscure, partly lambent, which he would end by recognizing as the human mind. Yet here was Alexiou at once identifiable: the yellow beads of the *komboloyi* trailing, just, through his open fingers, the silken tassel stirring in the breeze, and beside him the little cupful of dregs, the none-too-polished copper *briki*. In the circumstances Alexiou looked as though he had been scooped up, intellect and all, from under the plane-tree in the village square, and dumped down on the roof in Athens.

"At least he is a good Greek," Hajistavros remarked.

But Kikitsa Alexiou did not hear.

"This is the way it is," she said.

She had sunk down, in a state of complete beatitude, and was explaining rapidly, though muted, to her friends.

"One has to respect the minds of exceptional men. Sometimes he will take a sheet of paper. But that does not mean he will begin to write. No! Oh, no!" She wagged a finger. "Have you ever noticed that a clean white sheet of paper is what provokes the deepest thoughts? Scribble on it, and the flow dries up."

She sounded awful.

"Though Aleko is a writer too."

"You never told us," Maro realized, "what he has written."

"Books," Hajistavros dared suppose.

"Oh, no!"

Kikitsa Alexiou shook her head. She was scornful. She was ashen.

"He is not yet ripe," she said. "He writes," she said, "little pieces for the newspapers. But when I say little, I do not mean *little*. They are so concentrated! *Ach*," Kikitsa said, and smiled, "they are so nice, the little articles!"

At this point there was a grating on the tessellated terrace. Something rose, something loomed.

At once its controlling strings whirled into action the melting masses of Kikitsa Alexiou's waxlike flesh.

"See?" she almost spat. "He's coming to us! Wait!"

Revolving and jerking, opening doors, she worked as though to prepare an entrance down a never-ending corridor. Until she did create something of the necessary illusion. Aleko Alexiou emerged out of his wife's skilful *trompe l'œil*. Slowly he began to fill the room. His head appeared immense, even noble, an Anatolian Beethoven, as Kikitsa flew at him, to support, to present, to rough up the hair just so much.

"These are the friends, *Aleko mou*. I told you. The Americans."

But Aleko Alexiou was still inspired.

"I am so sorry, I forgot," he apologized, and smiled.

But most amiable. In his stringy tie, in his rather crushed linen suit, a little stained, as well as half-open at the fly, Hajistavros could not help noticing.

Massive, but crumbly, Maro saw. Whereas, if his wife could have had him in granite, how she would have polished the brow.

Instead, Kikitsa Alexiou had taken her husband, but literally, by the nose.

"At least he has a nose!" she screamed. "Heh? You old big-nosy thing!"

She had plastered herself upon him, and he was accepting it with such good grace Spiro Hajistavros stepped forward, and offered his hand with the kind of spontaneous and manly firmness which would rouse in Maro a shiver of pleasure on recognizing it once again in her usually imperfect husband.

"How are you, Mr Alexiou?" Hajistavros asked quite simply, as though his host had been in business.

But the great man appeared to be groping after something.

And his wife's mouth, suddenly split from its corners to the jaw, moved as agonizingly as that of a ventriloquist's dummy as it snapped at words.

"He is so—he is so—" Kikitsa clicked.

"I am so—" Aleko Alexiou sighed, "I am so *tired!*"

Then he collapsed on a chair. From which he continued smiling and imploring.

"It is the time of year," Kikitsa hurried to explain. "But after the heat breaks, when the rain falls at the end of August, the mind is at once refreshed. So much thinking"—here she fell to boring her own skull with naked finger—"takes it out of one. The siesta even, you'll see, makes all the difference."

Suddenly everyone had collapsed. They were all sitting on the little, uncomfortable Skyros chairs. Each had realized what it is to be a Greek. A gentle timeless melancholy, lapping and flowing between their islands, had reached one of the more easily accessible shores. Maro remembered certain dusty courtyards aching through the vines with exquisite silence. Spiro's lips had grown glutinous.

The immense warm stone with which sleep had so often almost erased him in summer was again weighing on him, and he would have accepted for ever, if waking had not promised a scent of crushed pine-needles. As for the Alexious, they had never been expected to forget. They were lolling against each other with professional luxuriance. They were smiling at the Hajistavri from under benevolent lids. In each of four material envelopes, whether the buttered Athenian pastry-cases, or the oiled, the meticulously serviced, American machines, a tormented soul was temporarily blessed. Each of the bodies was wearing for a moment the same, brown, Byzantine face.

Spiro Hajistavros was so moved he suddenly realized: "I guess I might take a picture."

And began to unstrap his Hasselblad.

"Not this afternoon," his wife objected coldly. "Don't forget we are here on an extended visit."

Maro had begun again to remember she was American as well. She was very glad she had that to cling to.

"And we shall be taking them for drives," she announced, making *them* her property. "Just as soon as we have located the car."

For the second Cadillac had been shipped over in advance.

"My God!" Kikitsa said.

"We Athenians," Alexiou added, "expect to *suffer* for our pleasures."

With the result that Hajistavros was again resentful.

"My God!" said Kikitsa. "Long live all returned millionaires! But what shall I do with my darling cats? While I go gadding pneumatically! Eh, husband *mou* what about cats?"

Here she pinched her Aleko, and might have gone right through, if his smile had not been more resistant than it looked.

Then she forgot for a moment, or remembered, for scrambling up, she began to grasp at the air, and cry: "Hymettus, Maroula! They say the convent at Ayia Varvara has been done up. The nuns are no longer there. Some of them were rather dirty, poor things. The nuns, Maroula, who gave us the milk."

Maro Hajistavrou drew on her gloves.

"Nuns!" she said, and shivered. "But monks are usually dirtier."

"They say the garden of the convent is so well kept. And the road that runs. You remember, Maroula, the Sunday we walked? But over the mountain. Resting in the heather. How we used to walk!"

So that again two girls were plunging their arms in mountain water, they were wiping off their moustaches of milk.

But Maro tossed her head.

"I never cared for Hymettus."

She was rich enough to afford unreasonable dislikes.

"I thought perhaps Sounion," she said. "Anyway, for a start."

"*Ach, Soun*-ion!" Kikitsa swooned.

"*Ach,* Verikokko!" she quickly added. "What shall we do with Apricock? Eh? My lovely orange cat?"

She would have stuffed him in her bosom. But the great cat, after entering the room fastuously, trying out his eyes, his claws, had begun to back against the furniture, his thrilling tail perfectly erect.

Everybody was fascinated.

"*Ach,* Verikokko!" Kikitsa shrieked. "Look, he's done it on the bookcase!"

Aleko Alexiou sat and smiled.

"My wife is fond of cats," he said.

Maro Hajistavrou decided she was not aware that anything had happened.

"But understanding," Kikitsa cried. "To *love* is unimportant in itself. Understanding is what really matters."

Alexiou had sat forward. He was masticating his lower lip.

"It is important," he said, addressing the room, "to distinguish between the instinctive and the rational."

The climate no longer favoured abstraction. Nor was his wife, in the grip of her very personal passion, able to nurture or even notice. So he sank back.

"You, Maro," Kikitsa moaned, "quite liked but never understood a cat."

"We shall leave you to your siesta," Maro Hajistavrou said, and laughed.

"Don't you indulge?" asked Alexiou out of a yawn.

"Such a long time. We had forgotten," Maro murmured, looking for the step.

"But you shall see!" Kikitsa screamed and followed. "My Apricockle is not like this. It is the summer. And my darling husband. We shall all be the better for autumn."

Hajistavros looked back to where the Alexious stood propping each other in the doorway. Mrs Alexiou was indolently paddling a hand in her husband's unresisting flesh.

Then the Americans began to go down, down, down, concentrating on their toes. They were both suffering from the physical impact which rocks those who return to Greece.

The Alexious were so happy. Kikitsa Alexiou saw to that. When necessary she would button up his pants; life, it seemed, was heavier for men to bear. Her own constitution was excellent. Had she not almost literally carried off Aleko from a series of day-beds and deck-chairs? Nor could anyone deny that Kyria Alexiou was strong-minded. If she yielded, it was to mollify. At least, that was how she saw it—and how she told others that it was.

Some of her acquaintances laughed at Kyria Alexiou's cats. But everyone is in need of something in addition to another human being. For she had her husband, of course. Some people kept their religion, or collected gold sovereigns, or cultivated sensuality, but Kyria Alexiou needed cats: there was Hairy, who had never appeared interested, and Ronron—was she beginning again?—and the arrogant Apricot. Sometimes the latter would turn and scratch, quite lightly, though unmistakably, as she held him in her arms, as she made yet another attempt to possess. Then Kyria Alexiou would have found it difficult to explain to any third person the efficacy, or even the reality, of possession.

But there was seldom that third person, for the simple reason the Alexious were not in need of one. Certainly there were the Party members, but that was different, in other surroundings. For naturally Alexiou was a member of the Party. How, otherwise, could he have claimed to be an intellectual? So Alexiou sat in the Party rooms, drinking the little cups of coffee, and his wife, who might have grown jealous, was not, because her breeding and the dictates of chic convinced Kyria Alexiou that truth could only flower in their country after some kind of, well, metamorphosis—to call it by a comfortingly abstract, Greek word. So, she accepted curfews, and travel permits, not to mention his forced absence on the Island. Not even when Alexiou paid the Official Visit together with other chosen members, was Kyria Alexiou more than incidentally put out. Did she not always have her cats? And when Aleko returned, with the fountain pen they had given him, and the astrakhan cap which he wore on winter occasions, in spite of the seam which ate into his forehead, she was delighted for him.

Sometimes joy and thankfulness for the almost miraculous fact of their union would boil over, and she would begin to prowl about the roof, as though to give expression to the tumult of her feelings. At dusk, after the purples had fled out of Athens, leaving its white cubes a grey rubble of extinct gas-fires, or on the browner, brooding nights of August, when the burnt fields had invaded the streets, and a wind was blowing out of Africa, then it would sound as though Kyria Alexiou on her platform was particularly aware, yet unable to communicate. As she prowled, and hummed in little bursts. As she leaned out over the parapet addressing anyone who might hear.

"My God!" she would mutter. *"Kaymenes!* How fortunate that where one of us exists, a second has almost always been created. Otherwise it would be unbearable."

The perspiration streamed out of Kyria Alexiou's porous skin.

Or she would lean out over the parapet, and call back to her husband, who would almost certainly be in bed: "Aleko? They are at it! Those Kolokithopouli! *Po-po-po! Quelle horreur!* You can hear, Aleko, I swear you can hear the springs!"

Kyria Alexiou would prowl and hum.

"Zing zing!" she would hiss and laugh.

Her slippers went slit slat across the still overheated tiles.

Or again, she would lean out over the parapet, and call back: "Plumpy thing! You should see, Aleko. A real Turk's delight!"

But the Kyrios Alexiou had turned out the light. The summer nights exhausted him.

Sometimes, however, and at last, he might appear in the doorway, his greatness gone, a grey shape in pyjama pants. He would call back: "*Ach,* Kikitsa! Come to bed! People will say you are a maniac!"

"What is mania?" Kyria Alexiou would shout. "Life is mania?"

It made her laugh.

"Trumpeting over the rooftops like the radio!" her husband complained.

"It is all good popular Greek," she grumbled.

"Come to bed, Kikitsa," he coaxed. "Act a little sensibly!"

Then she grew very quiet and meek.

"Yes, husband *mou*," she said. "I cannot act sensibly, because I am not sensible in any way, but will come to bed if you wish it."

At once she was a little obedient girl with a bow in her hair. Kyria Alexiou almost toddled.

"*Rouli, rouli, rouli mou!*" she cooed and drooled when they were arranged.

The disorder of her hair appeared the damper, the streakier for the drizzled light from the electric bulb. They lay in bed. The Kyrios Alexiou would sweat quite desperately on being touched by the tips of his wife's abandoned hair.

"*Ach,* Kikitsa!" he complained. "I am exhausted!"

"Yes, my darling husband," she agreed.

Then, when they were extinguished, she would encircle him instead as though he had been a cat. Her moist skin would lap at his. But after she had fallen, into sleep, and the bottomless depths of her affection, he would extricate himself from the cat's-cradle of anatomy to which he had been subjected. It was only that he felt so tired, not that he did not love her. In fact, gratitude would carry him so far as to free her from the suffocating curtain of her own hair, as she lay sleeping, while there was no possibility that his gratitude might be returned.

The drive to Sounion had not yet taken place, for no very adequate reason, except that one week Maro Hajistavrou had felt off colour, suffering from that migraine of hers. As the agreement remained unfulfilled, her husband finally remarked on it.

"What about these friends of yours, these Alexious you were bellyaching to see? How come we haven't taken them for some of the rides you promised?"

"Yes. Yes, we must invite the Alexious," Maro answered, but as though she were being victimized.

The situation might have continued unresolved, if she had not run into Kikitsa Alexiou in the doorway of a grocer's off Kolonaki Square.

Then Maro Hajistavrou had to exclaim: "Well now, Kikitsa, you might almost say I was on my way to look you up."

"Yes, Maro, I know," Kikitsa answered. "I am quite half to blame."

She gave Maro one of her looks which, in their youth, would have penetrated uncomfortably deep, but today became deflected on other errands, by other cares. Kikitsa was visibly distracted.

"We must make a date," she said. "I am late, you see. Though Anthoula will be there."

"Anthoula?"

"An old servant we had, who went, but returned. She is no great shakes as a servant. But she tolerates cats. Is firm but kind. She gets him his meal if I turn up late. Fancy, Maro, Anthoula has a beard. She shaves it every second day. I must say she is what you would call slovenly. And has an arrangement with the tradesmen. But is invaluable when I am held up."

Kikitsa Alexiou appeared positively *affairée*. So that it was the turn of Maro Hajistavrou to peer below the surface.

"I should tell you," Kikitsa said, not before looking over her shoulder, "I have taken a little morning job. You see, I am quite fast on the typewriter, if not always accurate, from copying Aleko's work. So there is really no reason why I should not help a little in other ways as well."

"No reason," Maro agreed.

Poor Kikitsa was too distracted.

"It is a privilege to play a part," she said, "in such an exceptional man's life."

She looked over her shoulder again, and smiled on seeing the empty street. Everyone had gone to lunch.

"Remind me some time," she said, "to tell you Anthoula's story. It is of no importance, but rather nice."

Maro promised she would, and only remembered years afterwards that Kikitsa had forgotten to tell.

"And now," the latter said, "I must run. Because *he* will be anxious."

"Then shall we say Sounion Wednesday afternoon?" Maro asked tentatively, because she had to.

"Heavenly, Maroula!" Kikitsa answered. "Now I must really go and see what that girl is doing to my man. Fancy, Anthoula has lovers. Beard and all. And fifty if a day. It appears that men like to be rubbed up the wrong way."

So Kikitsa ran, an irregular and bumpy motion on account of her many oily parcels, and as she did so it pleased her to remember old Anthoula's life.

The old thing had come from a village of the Mesoyia. If it had not been for her complexion, she might have been moulded out of clay—formally she was so archaic. But her complexion, it was porcelain. Under the stubble she remained a delicate blush colour, rather blue at times to be sure, from a collaboration of bristle with the white powder that she used. But Anthoula's eye would not have disgraced the Panayia. Of such a candour, of such a truly pure blue. It must, in fact, have been her appearance of chastity which appealed so very much to the men. For there had been Kyr Spyrakopoulos, the caretaker at Sixty-one, and Kyr Hondros of the Three Lemontrees, and Manolis of the laundry, to name a few. There had been Vangelaki, the gendarme at Ayia Paraskevi, who was the reason why she had returned to her village and kept the little sweetshop for the nuns. Anthoula had sold bon-bons, and mineral waters, and postcards of the mosaics, and of course the embroideries the nuns themselves had worked. It should have turned out an admirable arrangement if it had not been for Vangelaki. Who would come. And sit. It grew into quite a scandal, Vangelaki's boots lying at the door. Such a ruddy young man, it must have been his Albanian blood. Anthoula loved him. She could have eaten every particle of the burnt earth from which her Vangelaki was baked. Even when he brought disaster. First, it was the nuns. The *diavolopoutanes* had packed her off. Then, it was her savings. Of course, she said, I knew Vangelaki was after my money. She had lived for a time after the disaster at Pancrati, with a little cat, and swept the floors of public institutions for a crust of bread. Till the cat had wandered. As some cats will. Then Anthoula had returned to a former mistress, Kyria Alexiou.

"I might have known," Anthoula said. "A cat is never more than a cat."

"Oh, but you must experiment," her mistress assured her, "you must try, Anthoula, until you have found the cat that suits you."

"I'll not try," Anthoula grunted, "here where there are cats for all."

"But you're fond of them, aren't you?" the mistress insisted.

"It's an effort that doesn't cost," Anthoula said, and sighed.

On returning home Kyria Alexiou could never congratulate herself enough for recovering the services of old Anthoula.

She would hear: "There! Stick this inside, and grow into a big strong man!"

"*Ach,* but Anthoula, I am too *tired,* it is too hot to think about food!"

"I don't know what else a man would think about at midday, unless he is the randy sort."

Then Kyria Alexiou would peep in—she was so pleased to hear such a flow of language, of truly popular speech—and there would be Aleko her husband still in his pyjama pants. She did not notice how he sagged, only the full fork with which Anthoula was threatening further refusal from her important husband's lips.

"And my cats?" she would inquire. "Have my cats eaten?"

"The cats have eaten," Anthoula would answer, sweet, but stern. She did not add: They have eaten my foot.

Because Anthoula knew that, even though she might put the boot into Kyria Alexiou's cats, it was really a soft felt slipper.

So Kyria Alexiou was most relieved. She kissed her husband with a great smack.

"I know you will never forget, Anthoula. One must cherish one's

cats," Kyria Alexiou insisted. "They are almost," she said, "human
beings."

"This Ronron," Anthoula said, "this ugly, spotted whore has had
her kittens in the blankets."

Spiro Hajistavros was a different man in control of the second Cadillac. He could have driven head-on at far more ominous situations
than the Alexious presented. Or did the Alexious present a situation
after all?

"Bravo the Americans!" Kikitsa Alexiou cried. "Is this the
Prophet Elias already?"

Kikitsa lolled. She was dressed *pour le sport,* in a leather jacket,
and a little hat with a breast-feather in crimson. My college hat,
Kikitsa explained. It was a joke.

Hajistavros frowned and drove.

"Spiro hates to be disturbed," his wife was forced finally to call.

For, on the drive to Sounion, the couples were separated to the
extent that Kikitsa sat with Spiro in front, Maro and Aleko were
disposed of behind.

The car ran so smoothly it put the distance to shame. We shall
be there too soon, Maro thought almost with horror.

"Our poor Greece!" Kikitsa sighed. "Our rundown, dilapidated,
little, cosmic mess! How I love you! Long live Hellas!"

Aleko Alexiou looked out of the window. Always when his wife
exasperated him most he looked out of the window, and dilated his
nostrils, as though the mucus inside them had turned bad. Otherwise Alexiou was pretty comfortable. His thighs had adapted themselves to the shape and motion of the well-upholstered car. After
all, he had been born to ease, even if greatness, poverty, and the
Party had ended by taking possession of him.

"This is Phaneromeni," Kikitsa said. "It was not the Germans,
but the Black Reaction who marched two-thirds of the inhabitants
out of the village and shot them in a field. Tell them, Aleko. It is
quite a story."

"Oh," he complained, "the story is far too long."

He sat dilating his nostrils as if by numbers.

"It is all that," Kikitsa agreed. "It is the story of the Black Re-action."

Aleko looked over his shoulder. If he had been wearing a hat he would have pulled it down about his ears. Except in the abstract, his affiliations embarrassed Alexiou.

Maro, too, was embarrassed. She did not doubt that *she* was the Black Reaction. She looked at her ankles, slim and silken, and wondered how she had ever conceived the character of Kikitsa Andragora. The lost radiance transferred itself to a landscape seldom far from the ideal.

The heat had lifted from Attica. Autumn hung a swag of gold from the poles of the horizon. If the car had pulled up, all knew that the silence would have been too much for them, the ground too hard under the olive trees. So they drove on, and nostalgia grated on their minds, like a withered olive grating and turning between the cheek and an earthy pillow.

They drove down amongst the empty shells, the gaping foundries of Lavrion, where the colour of the sea, for the first time in their lives, it seemed, rose up and smote them in the faces.

"Drive on!" Kikitsa commanded. "Lavrion is bad!"

It could have been. In the manner of predominantly masculine men, Spiro drove with that air of clinging to a few simple convictions. His instincts did perhaps sense something of evil in the derelict village of Lavrion, but his principles would not have allowed him to admit it to such a person as Kyria Alexiou.

"You are quiet, aren't you?" Kikitsa remarked.

"Leave him alone!" Maro warned.

"Is he a lion?" Kikitsa asked.

Aleko looked more desperately than ever out of the window, in search of something, form or symbol, which might save him from humiliation in the face of the inexpressible.

"I should understand," Kikitsa was saying. "A lion is only a different kind of cat. I have been practically inside their skins."

Then she drew a deep breath.

"Such air!" she moaned. "Under our Greek sky! Look! A little sheep. *Provataki! Provataki!*" Kikitsa Alexiou called. "It is no use," she murmured at last.

She worked herself deeper into the upholstery. She began to declaim Solomos, and hesitatingly, Palamas, and might have unpicked a line or two of Sikelianos, when the car leaped at the promontory, and there was Sounion out in the blue.

Nobody doubted that this was the original blue.

Then, when they had left the car, and climbed with grudging, almost fearful steps upon what remained of the little temple, Kikitsa asked a vaster audience: "What do you say if I dance?"

It was not surprising nobody answered, though Maro was surprised and grateful that, despite discouragement, her friend did not choose to begin. Instead, she flopped down. Against a column. A fat woman, in middle age, and a mackintosh with a grease-mark on it.

Maro Hajistavrou wished she could think of something to say in some way worthy of their setting. But she could not.

"Do you come here often?" she asked Kikitsa's great man with a dryness she suspected people might consider typical of her.

"We have other ruins closer at hand," he answered rather crossly. "It is all ruins, ruins!"

"But what is Greece without its ruins?"

"Exactly! Then we should be left with the keepers of them."

Professional masochism deterred Maro, who had always remained an amateur. She was glad to watch her husband exploring the terrain, in clothes far too young for him. Though Spiro was younger than his grey head. She noticed on his arms the dark hair, which theoretically she should have abhorred, but which secretly she rather admired.

"Spiro! Don't you think you ought to take a picture?" she called to him in gratitude.

And Spiro Hajistavros was only too glad. He had brought with him his Hasselblad, though nobody, not even his wife, realized exactly what that meant. He was dangling the full gadget bag, which bumped against his sturdy calf, and bumped again, and reassured.

"A picture would be nice for them to have," Maro decided.

"Sure," Spiro said, and smiled.

Founded in early poverty, his teeth had always dazzled her.

"Provataki, provataki . . ." Kikitsa sang, and suddenly trans-

posed into the darker key of the midnight alleys: *"To ga-ta-ki MOU!"*

Then, with equal facility, she began to laugh, and said in her hoarser tone of voice: "You and Aleko have got together in such an ungainly group, *chère Marouline*. You are all elbows, all angles. Your legs make an ugly tripod."

Suddenly Maro saw how Kikitsa's eyes, looking from between the fat, were the eyes of the girl she herself had created, and feared as much as loved.

But at once Kikitsa was poured back into the channel of her own complacency.

"I shall tell you about my cats," she announced.

Spiro was fitting up his little tripod. He was as totally absorbed as masculine men are able to become. If he was the least bit distracted it was the rich man wondering whether those present could take him seriously enough, whether they would appreciate his expertise. In any case, his muscular, not yet aged hands managed the tripod masterfully.

"I shall tell you about my cats," Kikitsa Alexiou repeated, sinking her chin to emphasize.

Spiro began to motion with his hands.

"Come along now," his assistant ordered.

Playing this expensive, adult game, Maro, too, was expert in her way, at the same time sensible, for she realized the limits of her powers, the point at which she must give in. So now she said: "Aleko and I shall group ourselves around Kikitsa. Since she has made herself comfortable."

Spiro was looking down into his camera. She could see his very accurate parting.

"There is Hairy. He came first," Kikitsa was telling. "And I do not love Hairy. Not as I ought. But try. There is nothing so sad as a cat that isn't loved."

Maro felt she could begin to scream. She could feel the tic in her left eyelid.

Spiro had walked up and was taking a reading on the exposure meter. His subject might have been a heap of stones.

"That devil, Ronron, she doesn't count, she is herself, or

seven others pulling at her teats. *Epta, vre!* And only one of them apricot!"

"All his work is in Ektachrome," Maro whispered.

Spiro had walked back to the camera. There was tension in his shoulder-blades.

"Do you want me to stop talking?" Kikitsa asked. "But of course it's different when they take a picture nowadays. They used to put your neck in a vice. Now you can do anything you like."

A little boy had approached, and was offering them rose tomatoes the size of large cherries.

"Vlepete!" Kikitsa exclaimed. "A gift of the people! A true love-offering!"

If her mind had not been otherwise involved, she might have enjoyed tears.

"But Apricot," she said, "I had got to Apricot."

This could have been the moment Spiro Hajistavros had waited for, to prove an unimpaired dexterity. There was no trace of elderliness in the stance of his rather springy legs.

"Apricot," Kikitsa continued, "he is the mystery cat."

Aleko Alexiou was staring out to sea. He had allowed wind and sunlight to prepare his head for sacrifice.

"Take nature," Alexiou said.

His hand was helping him extract, or mould, a painfully refractory object.

"Nature is so—so—*un*cooperative, ultimately so *unreal!*"

Then his hand fell, and with it his failure, while the illusory light continued to cascade into a spurious sea.

Spiro was looking and looking, straight, then down.

"I do not say," said Kikitsa, "that I do not understand. Because with my great experience of cats it is not possible not to understand."

The tomato-boy sat at their feet picking his nose.

"But look at this charming, natural boy!" Kikitsa rejoiced. "Has Spiro pressed? Has he clicked, or whatever he does? Are we *in the picture?*" she asked, suddenly almost hysterical. "Spiro," she called, "some day will you—as a special favour—will you snap my Apricock?"

Spiro Hajistavros, his wife saw, was compressed. His strong, rather yellow fingers were trembling.

"*Ach,* Kikitsa!" her husband begged. "It is too tiring!"

When a cat appeared, low against the ground, rounding the temple's marble plinth.

"My God!" Kikitsa cried. "A cat!"

The flat grey cat flattened flatter against the marble.

"Starved!" Kikitsa Alexiou cried.

"It is nobody's cat," explained the apathetic boy. "It is no good. They do not want it."

But Kikitsa Alexiou had begun to stalk the cat.

The boy laughed. Her mackintosh had rucked up. Maro Hajistavrou had to admit to Kikitsa's lumpy calves.

When she returned, empty-armed, Kikitsa Alexiou had broken a nail. Marble had powdered her broad behind.

"The trouble with Greeks," she bemoaned, "they are not cat-lovers. They are themselves too egotistical, quarrelsome, lazy, and gluttonous to understand the force of love. That love is something more than pouncing in the dark, or waiting to be pounced on."

She had laid her arms across her breasts. She might have been preparing to recite some love poems she had composed, of such poignancy she would never be able to get it all out.

"Poor starving soul! If only you understood!" she did at least make the attempt. "I would feed you on red mullet. And quail."

The boy was gulping down his laughter.

"Love," she said, and her voice trembled.

Then Alexiou drew in his breath from so far it sounded like an aluminium tape-measure.

"You are crazy!" he hissed. "Idiotic! Crazy! Let us get into the car, and ask them to drive us home."

Not that he succeeded in breaking the spell which Kikitsa Alexiou had wilfully laid upon herself.

"You must not take any notice of Aleko," she advised with apparent satisfaction after he had started down the hill. "There are times when it is good for him to give way to his temperament."

So she began to rock and hobble down the slope, carrying her unborn poem, and the form of the escaped, unwanting cat.

"Did you manage to take the picture?" Maro Hajistavrou whispered, as she slipped her arm inside her husband's.

Spiro was too furious to answer.

So Maro got inside the car beside her husband and, for the return journey, allowed the Alexious to have the back.

The sea was purpler than before.

"Aleko will write something very nice about it all. You will see," Kikitsa promised rapturously.

Glancing in the driver's mirror, Maro could see that Kikitsa would gather up the pieces of her crumbly genius, and at least for herself, fit them together again.

Not long after that the call of business made it necessary for the Hajistavri to return to New York. Probably they saw the Alexious again, on the other hand there may not have been time. A hasty packing. And about that period Aleko Alexiou fell temporarily ill. In any case, Maro was so glad to be returning to all that material superfluity which had become her substitute for life. Whether Spiro felt the same way, she never thought to ask, for she suspected an absence of education might have prevented him from understanding, or at least, from answering. Not that she was critical. She no longer expected so much of anybody, herself included.

In a little over two years the Hajistavri returned. Their reasons for boycotting Greece throughout their earlier married life no longer seemed valid. Sometimes now they laughed together at the expense of their friends the Alexious.

"Perhaps Kikitsa's Aleko will have ripened," Maro Hajistavrou would venture.

For Kikitsa and she corresponded infrequently now.

"He's been waiting for the Party word," Spiro would suggest.

"Do you believe Aleko is a genuine red?"

"A washed-out pink. Aleko is so very, very tired."

As their plane bumped around above the airport Maro Haji-stavrou peered out and saw Hymettus. Because it was spring, that rather forbidding, morose ridge was greening over from its mauves and browns. It is still ugly, she told herself, but fascinating, un-avoidable, something of me was hatched on it.

"Did we bring presents for the Alexious?" Spiro asked, as they sat there those last moments, holding their lumped-together coats and furs.

"No," said Maro. "I thought about it."

Again their friends were not at the airport to meet them, but this time Mrs Hajistavrou did not resent, because she no longer expected it.

When they had settled in, Maro decided she was strong enough to visit Kikitsa. A spasm of guilt drove her. This time she went there on her own. She even mounted the Kolonaki hill with very little thought for her heart.

"Alexious?" replied that small, unpleasant old caretaker who insisted on addressing in English. "Gone. Gone. Too much money. Very changed. The rich forget," the caretaker accused.

After he had run inside, and returned with an address dashed across a corner of paper, Maro took a taxi, and was driven to a block on what was now the outskirts of the city. Fields still straggled round the marble towers, but already she could smell Athenian dust competing against the scent of stocks.

A woman with an exceptionally large behind and an apparently approving smile answered yes, Alexious lived in an apartment on the roof.

"Welcome," said Anthoula, directing that virginal smile from above her razed beard onto the returned traveller. The *kyria,* she said, and pointed, was at home and on the terrace.

There, indeed, was Kikitsa, leaning out over the parapet.

Maro approached her through the white light of marble, still not a glare, for it was only spring.

". . . beside the rose-coloured ramparts, under a pomegranate tree, looking seawards . . ." Maro quoted from memory.

"What a disease alliteration used to be!"

The two friends embraced with a formal tenderness. Maro was surprised to encounter the bones of Kikitsa Alexiou's cheek.

"This time one can see Hymettus," the visitor remarked.

"Hymettus? Everything! Everything! Just like before."

She led Maro across the marble tesserae, everywhere, everywhere.

"It is nice?"

Maro realized she was still holding Kikitsa's hand.

Then when they had gone in, into the little *saloni,* like a cabin on board the ship of the world, and Anthoula had brought cold water and green figs, and the two women had seated themselves on a coarse-covered, intimate sofa, Kikitsa said: "So you see it is the same. Only different.

She was certainly thinner, almost young, almost lithe.

"It is certainly more complicated than that," Maro Hajistavrou replied.

"It is quite a mosaic," Kikitsa said. "First—you will remember I had taken a job—the amiable old creature died, and left me a little something." She blushed. "Virtuous relationships are always the most difficult to explain. But there it is. Or was. At the same time Aleko wrote his book, his great work which he had always been planning, which he had started already while you were here, his *Sacrifices to Independence.* The War of Independence, you know, told strictly from *our* point of view." Here, at least, Kikitsa lowered her eyes, and closed one of the many meticulous pleats in her raw-silk skirt. "So, putting one thing and another together, we were able to take this apartment. Here we are!"

She laughed. Rather sadly.

"It is lovely!" Maro said, and laughed.

"More convenient. Much more space."

"And Aleko is out?"

"Aleko is at the library. He is writing somebody's life. Oh, some Greek. Someone historic. There will be others. It pays."

"Then Aleko is successful!"

"Yes. You must not think that because it has happened, he has given up any of his ideals. His style has remained perfect. The purest of all popular Greek."

"And do they understand?"

"Well, anyone is at liberty to put his own interpretation on the written word."

Maro had discovered a fig seed between her teeth.

"And the cats?" she asked, because she ought to.

"There are no cats."

"No cats!"

"Aleko refused to let me keep my cats."

It was Kikitsa who discovered the half-built apartment block on the edge of the city. A winter sunshine flowered for a moment on the empty shelves, and fluttered to earth amongst the marble chips. She had run about the roof with the ungainly, little-girl's action she affected under the influence of emotion. From under their dusting of marble the workmen had laughed at the crazy thing.

But Kikitsa was too obsessed to notice.

"The roof," she told Aleko on returning, "is the most splendid of all roofs."

The roof was all-important, for was not practically the whole of life spent prowling on a roof, peering at windows, following the coloured slides which light imposed in rotation on the Attic coast, calling to, pouncing on, fondling cats?

"It will be perfect for the cats," she told her husband.

"It will be an extravagance," he said. "Also, perhaps, an embarrassment."

He was, she knew, thinking of the Party.

"Dearest Aleko," she said, "you owe it to your eminence."

And took his head, as though she intended to smooth fur.

"We are the ones who have preached," he said.

"Ba," she answered, "we shall preach all the better when we have experienced freedom."

She knew it was outrageous, shamefully unorthodox. Of course her origins were raising their head, nor did she regret it.

And Aleko was perhaps a little drunker for temptation. His rather grey skin had coloured along the cheek-bones, his lips had opened in which she put the mere tip of her expert tongue.

"There," she said, and knew for certain.

From then on Kikitsa Alexiou could not cover quick enough all the ground that had to be covered. She was ever running. To the furniture removers, long before their time, to the electrician, or the seamstress, to Kyr Leon Zimbal, the Jew of Odos Ispanias, who had promised to make her a strong wooden box in which to transport her cats.

"There will be many other uses," she decided, "to which we can put our cats' box."

The possessive pronoun in the plural would issue from her mouth uniting her even more closely with the husband to whom she was devoted.

When Aleko Alexiou announced, leaning against a wall for support—it was a night in January, she would remember: "There shall be no cats, Kikitsa."

His wife did not reply, because reply was not possible. The room was straining round them. Outside, rain had begun to slash at the terrace.

Then Alexiou had to make an effort to justify himself.

"I am drenched with cats!" he shouted.

He went out into the bathroom, skidding on a sliver of catshit, which should have reinforced his argument, only it didn't.

Kikitsa Alexiou had continued standing in the room even after realizing she must move from there eventually.

As it happened, the wooden box which Kyr Leon Zimbal had already begun was used for a practical purpose. Anthoula had consulted with Kyra Photini, the caretaker at the new flats, and a plan of kinds was formed. Opposite the block was a diminished wood of dusty pine-trees, and a piece of land to which families, not yet altogether urban, no longer quite peasant, came on Sunday afternoons to cultivate a sprawl of tomatoes and rows of struggling vines. There in the wood, on the edge of this surviving vineyard, Anthoula and the caretaker decided the *kyria* should set up her cat-hutch. Already amongst the trees there was a black goat on a chain.

"Ba," cried Kyria Alexiou, "what else can a creature do?"

The two other ladies cried a little for their poor burnt one, who was herself dry of tears.

She put bowls of milk and fish for her cats, there amongst the trees, and stumps, for during the Occupation some of the pines had fallen to the axe. While the cats preened and arched, and with their claws drew resin from the scaly bark, and curled in the sand and wiry grass. Though their box was lined with wool.

From the marble ramparts Kyria Alexiou watched the life which had slipped away from her. She watched her cats coming and going, coming and going. Or going. Or going.

Hairy was the first, who had never been interested. Hairy sidled by daylight in amongst the rose tomatoes, and was not seen afterwards. It was Ronron who let out a shriek by night. (How could she fail to identify her own cats, even at a distance, and under cover of darkness?) Ronron was never seen again. But Apricot, her most insolent, he remained, licking and rubbing, looking, or turned to stone upon a bed of needles.

She would go down and talk to her cat, in the long clear accents of tragedy. Though the cat himself would not be coaxed into playing a positive part. And once drew blood from her breast, causing in her a certain melancholy satisfaction.

"Even the cats are Greek," Kyria Alexiou told herself.

When on a morning of rain Anthoula announced: "There is a little white *poutana* of a cat. So lovely. So nice. Rubbing against the side of the box. Her little nose so pink."

Kyria Alexiou rushed down.

"My Apricockle! My Apricock!"

The two cats were watching each other. Head to head. Their identical positions were as severe as stone.

Kyria Alexiou came and went. Her movements were quite distracted now.

"What is it, Kikitsa?" her husband asked later in the day.

She had heard his key, of course, but was not to be influenced, neither by the silk bow-tie, nor the pressed suit of imported tweed. Kyrios Alexiou would sit tossing his ankle. The cooler seasons were in his favour, and this one in particular.

"You have grown thinner, Kikitsa," he remarked.

Then she had clapped her hands to her cheeks. She had, she thought, the look of a starved, a flattening cat. Her eyes were larger than before.

So she ran down quickly at dusk. She took the dish of mullets' heads, in death still exquisitely coralline.

"Ver-i-kok-ko!" she called. "My Apricock!"

But without heart.

The orange cat was standing on a stump from which the resinous blood had run. He suddenly leaped, into space.

"The white whore! The white devil!" Kyria Alexiou cried.

"It is her, the poor burnt one, who should have our sympathy." Old Anthoula had come up behind through the screening trees. "Who will bleed, but the woman? It is in her nature!"

Certainly the orange tom's teeth appeared to be fastened in the nape of white fur. His tail was thrashing the dead-coloured grass.

"Vromogatos!" Kyria Alexiou cried.

Whose passion was bruising her.

"Good appetite!" Old Anthoula laughed.

Then the servant led her mistress away. In the late light the old woman's young skin had the blue translucence of porcelain.

"What was it, Kikitsa?" Aleko Alexiou asked, because at least they shared a roof.

But his wife sat and crumbled bread.

And again a cat was gone. Rain beat into the empty box. The particles of soil set at a visible level on the empty dishes. Kyria Alexiou continued mooning in the empty wood. There was still the goat, certainly, whose name, Kyra Photini had learnt, was Arapina. Kyria Alexiou lowered her face on one occasion to the wooden mask of the black goat, but was unable to see into the eyes.

So the bereft kept to her roof. Her clothes were drabber than before, and hung. She could not bear the encumbrance of her drab, pricking clothes. She bought the raw-silk dresses which suddenly had caught her eye, and would dress herself listlessly in the accommodating garments, which moved so naturally with her body as she prowled about the marble roof, barefoot more often than not. The tones of evening would slant her eyes in heavy violet, morning gilded the refractory down at the nape of her neck, as Kyria Alexiou stood resting her fingertips on the polished parapet.

"Silk flatters!" Anthoula laughed.

She lowered her eyes from her mistress's, which had grown uncommunicative.

Anthoula would bring bowls of warmed milk.

"The milk is good. Drink," she advised. "It soothes."

But Anthoula was crueller than she thought.

Some of it Kikitsa Alexiou told her friend Maro Hajistavrou as they sat in the *saloni* of her marble ship afloat on the light of Attica.

"A tragic story," Maro Hajistavrou declared.

For one so remote, she even felt faintly moved. She could not resist peeping into the cleft between Kikitsa's breasts, at the bluish lights which drowsed in the folds of the subtle dress.

Then Kikitsa cried out: "Less tragic if it had not been necessary!"

Her nails, her friend noticed for a moment, were embedded in the weave of the linen sofa. But only for a moment. For almost at once Maro Hajistavrou was overwhelmed by a gust of unspeakable joy or fear: Hymettus reeling mottled through the window beyond Kikitsa Alexiou's shoulder.

"Maroula! Marou-*lina!* Don't you remember?"

Maro Hajistavrou was drunk with the scent of flesh. Or heather.

"No! No!" she protested. "What should I remember?"

What indeed? It had been so strange. The two girls resting in the pocket between the cushions of rough heather.

"Take love," Kikitsa Andragora had begun, drawing in the air with a blade of grass. "I could put a ring round it. But would you, too, accept what I had enclosed?"

Maro had been impressed, but terrified by what she only partly understood.

"Or sky." Again Kikitsa described a circle with her blade of grass. "I would not dare suggest 'heaven.' 'Heaven' is so personal."

Then Kikitsa had started laughing.

"Don't worry"—she laughed—"I shall not make any attempt on infinity today! Today is a day of little *cats'* tongues!"

After that Kikitsa did something so extraordinary it was difficult to recall in detail, only as a scurry of bronze, of furred light, and the crackle of dried heather twigs.

"See?" Kikitsa breathed as soon as she had withdrawn. "A little, thin, cat's tongue!"

Maro's mouth had melted for a moment in the sun.

"And you, *chrysoula*," murmured Kikitsa through her teeth, "are a kind of little, thin cat."

For a second, locked together, their thighs had something of the duplicity, the elasticity, of softest cat-flesh bundled together in the sun.

At once the two girls sat up, and began to arrange their hair slightly.

Kikitsa had pointed out that it was perhaps a kilo to the convent at Ayia Varvara, where they might persuade a nun to give them milk.

Maro had followed drowsily.

But was now protesting, a middle-aged woman in a hat.

"*Ach,* Ki-ki-tsa!"

Her heart was jumping alarmingly inside her Saks Fifth Avenue dress.

Then Maro Hajistavrou was shocked to find she had drawn blood on her friend Kikitsa Alexiou's arm.

Kikitsa laughed, smoothing her mouth. Her eyes were positively fragmentary.

"Lick it, Maro!" she invited.

Mrs Hajistavrou had never been so horrified. While drawn to the beads of crimson blood in the golden down of Kyria Alexiou's arm.

"Are we crazy?"

"Who shall answer?"

Just then Aleko Alexiou came in, the great man himself, with a considerable thickness of manuscript beneath his arm. Maro Hajistavrou did not remember to have seen him kempt, not to say downright handsome before.

"Oh," she said at once, "I have to congratulate you, Aleko, on your great success."

"Success of a kind," he replied with a nonchalance she did not associate with Aleko. "At least we have this apartment," he said.

"May we offer you an *ouzo*?" Kikitsa asked.

Maro did not think she would take an *ouzo*. She was drunk enough already. Her heart bumping. She could smell, she was convinced, the scent of Aleko Alexiou's tweed. Or was it heather?

"What does it feel like to be a successful man?"

She heard her voice begin to nicker foolishly.

But Aleko Alexiou had been prudent enough to leave the room, and all she could do was try to remember the details of his magnificent head. She had even failed to inquire which of the heroes of the Independence he was engaged in writing about.

"Is it Capo d'Istria?" she babbled.

Kikitsa was looking down the front of her dress.

"It is not." She smiled.

Neither bothered. Mrs Hajistavrou was gathering up her gloves.

"We must arrange," she said.

"You may ring me now. We have the telephone."

Kikitsa was smiling with the corners of her mouth.

"Yes, I shall call you."

Though, for the moment, she had not the slightest intention.

Kyria Alexiou took Mrs Hajistavrou across the apartment to the door. The sound of silk accompanied them.

Then Mrs Hajistavrou fled.

Just for a moment, as she fell from sight in the cage of the stuffy little lift, Maro looked back through the grille to where Kikitsa leaned against the frame of her door. The classic folds of the silk dress had been turned to immemorial stone. Maro knew that Kikitsa's image must last in her mind much longer than the actual, ephemeral image of Kikitsa standing in her doorway. Then the lift continued to sink the traveller in the limbo of the darker building. Light flickered and flackered at passing instants. And the scintillating, fragmentary eyes. And the quirks at the corners of the rather thin, dark lips.

Mrs Hajistavrou was panting like a stringy fowl by the time the

lift released her at ground level. She went away panting and gasping, on her thin, brittle legs, in their impeccable American stockings.
As other pedestrians passed her she averted her face, in case, by
some distasteful chance, the episode she had experienced might
flow out of her frightened eyes in identifiably sensuous waves.

"You are not seeing much of your Hajistavri," Aleko Alexiou had
to comment.

"No."

Kikitsa would sit stroking her forearms as though to discover
some still-to-be-experienced sensation.

"Probably," she said, "Maro and I have given each other all we
had to give."

Aleko laughed.

His wife did not seem to think it worth the trouble to ask him
why.

Aleko Alexiou, normally unconscious of a woman's contours or
the tics of her peculiar mind, noticed that the lines of Kikitsa's face
had been rejuvenated by some process of mentality or light. Once
an acquaintance, a *coureur de femmes,* had pointed out to him in
the street a face which he said he knew for certain—it was a famous, international face—had been lifted by surgery. Now it was
quite unthinkable, in Athens, that a woman of Kikitsa's class and
mind should have resorted to such an expedient, her husband was
complacent enough to believe. It was simply that Kikitsa's face had
undergone a change, the way faces will, by joy, or suffering. Alexiou
immediately turned away because he did not wish to think about it.
He tried to remember a fact he had culled that morning from a
manuscript in the library, and which continued to elude him
throughout the evening.

Kikitsa was soon strolling on the terrace. They had eaten, and
she drew him out there, slipping her arm through the angle of his.
The lisping silk fretted against the rather rough tweed. At first he
would have liked to throw her off, but continued strolling, awk-
wardly easing one of his legs. At least she did not chatter now, or

shriek, and he hoped under the blandishment of silence his mind might solve its more pressing problems.

So the Alexious dawdled in the furry darkness.

It had become Kikitsa Alexiou's practice to pursue a kind of recitative, which soothed extraordinarily, he had to admit, as she made their motion and the passage of time rub upon his senses.

"You should have seen the last light this evening," Kikitsa's voice would soothe, "you should have seen the dove-coloured light, *chryso mou,* all the doves in the world huddling together on the shores of the Gulf. And the violet shadows. Athens is ashes and violets at dusk. Before it is burnt right out. Have you looked? Have you ever noticed?"

She did not altogether care. In any case, she was telling him. As they strolled she would twitch the silk of her trailing skirt.

Then there were the moments when Kikitsa's voice would rasp out harsh, thrillingly, across Aleko's mind. There were the days when she would decide: "We cannot afford not to go out."

The light was almost verdant.

"Somewhere. Into the country," she mumbled.

On such occasions Kikitsa would be roaming round the rooms, her mouth full of pins, binding her hair with a scarf.

But restless.

Once she surprised herself calling: "In case we are late, Anthoula, see that you put their milk."

Immediately she retrieved her voice, but not before shocking, even frightening her husband. She herself was palpitating.

Ordinarily the Alexious made their way uneventfully by bus to the villages which lie behind the seashore. They walked by the gritty paths and lanes. Reeds clattered, and the black cypress pointed a finger at the last way of escape. Whitewash was scaling from the walls. Sometimes voices hung suspended in the air, singing.

Or the people would come out of doorways: old, benevolent women, their pregnant daughters-in-law, old men whose faces had been cured for ever in brine. The old people would call caressingly to the couple strolling in the byways, almost as though they hoped to coax the strangers to remain.

"Come," the villagers would call, "here we have the purest water."

Sometimes there were strips of bitter orange, or glasses of black wine.

Then the two strangers would advance lazily, nonchalantly—it was their right, it seemed—between the rows of stocks, always rubbing against each other. The woman's skirt would brush against the club-headed stocks, dragging the perfume out of them. Nothing could have made drunker. The man and woman were more than ever in need of each other's support.

The villagers were so pleased, they would caress the travellers with civility and glances.

On one occasion, emerging on a road, the Alexious came across a car hesitating at a turn. The big parti-coloured monster was so unmistakable, it was surprising the linked couple stood there staring at it with a certain indecision.

"Fancy their finding their way out here," Kikitsa remarked.

"They have covered all the roads in Greece. Now they are combing the lanes," Aleko suggested.

The great car backed, advanced, slithered, and almost jumped. The Attic light was threatening its ephemeral shell.

"Well, there are your Alexious," Spiro said. "Our thoughts have taken shape."

But Maro was annoyed.

"Speak for yourself, Spiro," she said. "Nothing was farther from my thoughts than the Alexious."

She was irritated, too, by the irregular motion of the car. Her husband might have lost his skill.

"Seeing they're here, we can hardly avoid them." Spiro was always so right, it hurt her.

"No," she said. "Well," she said. "Certainly they are *there!*"

An aeroplane flew into the sky. It wrote in vapour, advertising NESCAFÉ for Greeks.

"Is it our move?" Alexiou asked.

"I have lost count!" His wife laughed.

"We may come if we are called."

"If we are called, we shall make up our minds."

Suddenly the great car gave an unexpected toot, for the driver's hand had made unintentional contact with the horn.

"Oh, Spiro! You do embarrass me!" Maro cried; she had to blame someone.

The Alexious were actually laughing, or so their mouths seemed to suggest by their long, lazy lines.

The car's enormous glass and metal shell should have offered some protection, but the Hajistavri had their doubts. Only America was certain.

"I guess these Alexious are nobody's yardstick after all," Spiro Hajistavros said.

He began to turn, in a vast, though jerky sweep. The rear wheels bit into a ditch.

"No. Oh, no!" Maro cried, and bumped. "They were never that, were they? Or were they? As I see it, one can't bear to reject the past. Even the hateful parts of it."

Spiro Hajistavros would ignore his wife when she opened up in that strain. Now he carried on. Already the great car was driving in the direction of America. Maro Hajistavrou's eyes were watering with annoyance and pain.

The Alexious returned home before the rain began. Only a scurry, but it belted at the windows of the elevated flat, and in at those which were half-open. The smell of rain was overpowering, for it was the cold kind which blows through sticky shoots and opening buds.

"Aleko," she said, "let us go out."

"We have just come in."

But her bare arms were so compelling he no longer gave his objections a thought. Just as her softly beshawled arms completed the act of blandishment. It seemed only natural to obey and follow.

When they went down Anthoula and Kyra Photini were standing as almost always in the doorway, and squeezed against the frame to allow their gentry to pass. The old women looked at, or down

upon them, with a sly, caressing possessiveness. Kyria Kikitsa, they
saw, had sleeked down her hair to the point where it reflected the
light.

"Rejoice!" the fat janitress mumbled conventionally as they
passed.

It had stopped raining, though the pine-wood was still tingling
with its load of drops. The air smelled of resin, moisture, and a
goat's dung. Beyond the straggle of tomato vines the lights of human habitation did not interfere with darkness.

Were the gentry discussing? There was a drizzle of voices. Or it
could have been a distant traffic.

The night was such that the two old women were driven to follow. Their slippers were silent in the wet needles.

"My God," protested Kyra Photini, "we shall catch our deaths!"
But Anthoula did not have time to consider.

The moon, the clouds were tearing at space through the branches
of the trees. The goat called. Darkness chafed the skin with a
roughness of bark.

Was it the Kyria Alexiou, then, who suddenly sprang on the
stump of one of the martyred trees? Her teeth glittered in the
moonlight.

Long, long moments passed.

Then it was the Kyrios Alexiou who sprang. The scents, the
cold draughts of air were quite intoxicating. The Kyrios sprang
as though he had been wound up for it. How his trouser-legs
streamed black in his wake. As the Kyria Kikitsa leaped away, as
white by moonlight as the stump from which the resin had run,
Anthoula did not exactly see, but knew he had fastened his teeth
in the nape of the white neck.

Beyond, where the moonlight was dappled with darkness, all
was a wrestling of light with dark.

Did Kyria Alexiou shriek?

Kyra Photini began to pant.

"Did you see? Did you hear, Anthoula? What is happening?"

But Anthoula turned. She shuffled in her felt slippers.

"What is it?" Kyra Photini followed moaning. "Tell, Anthoula
mou! Why shouldn't you tell?"

Kyra Photini's buttocks went jiggle joggle as she ran to keep up. But Anthoula laughed. She scuttled in her felt slippers.

"How is a creature to know?" Kyra Photini complained.

And her buttocks went plop plop.

Anthoula laughed and laughed.

"Some people," she said, more for herself than her companion, "some people find the cat that suits them."

There the two old women crossed the street, and the familiar doorway received them.

When the Hajistavri were ready to leave, their faces grew grave simultaneously.

"Do you think we ought?" Maro reconsidered.

"It is up to you, sugar."

She frowned her husband's distasteful endearment off, and the face in the mirror supported her. She had had her hair set that morning by a girl who had not yet learnt how.

"Surely it is our duty to take our leave?" Maro Hajistavrou persisted.

"If that is how you feel, Maro, then have them call a cab. You know I am always with you. I just ask myself whether we shall make ourselves look ridiculous. The only occasion I personally set eyes on the Alexious during our present visit was way down a country road."

Because Maro Hajistavrou had never been made look ridiculous, they took a taxi out to the Alexious. (The second Cadillac had been shipped home in advance.) It was at an hour when the traffic alone suggested the siesta had been slept out.

"Yes, the *kyrii* are above," the janitress answered, while looking down, while addressing the visitors as though they had been foreigners.

Greeks can be so very annoying.

"Anthoula must be out," Maro remarked when nobody responded to the bell.

Her hair was simply maddening her.

"Or everybody," she said at last, "everybody could be out."

Spiro was holding his ear to the door.

"No," he said.

"Can you really hear?"

Because he couldn't, he did not answer.

"I'm gonna take a look," he said. "From the terrace."

He began to walk across the roof.

"Ah, no, Spiro! Spiro! It isn't done to invade other people's privacy!"

But she had such limited control of him. Alone, she asked, as so many times before, for what reason had she married her husband, and concluded, as always, she needed him to keep her company as she stood on the edge of life.

When Spiro returned he did not answer. He was walking with his strong, rubbery step.

"But were they in? What did you find?" she persisted in the sighing lift.

"They were in bed," he said.

"Still!" she cried. "You don't mean to say they hadn't finished the siesta?"

"I guess they hadn't begun."

Then Maro Hajistavrou hated—was it her husband? was it the Alexious?—in any case, she hated.

"Some people are like animals!" she gasped; it was so hateful.

"The hour won't always wait, neither for human beings," Spiro Hajistavros said.

Mrs Hajistavrou tried, briefly, discreetly, to calculate whether in all the history of their relationship the hour had not waited for her husband.

When the lift released them it was the hour of gold. Hymettus was purest red gold. The columns of the Parthenon glittered with openly revealed veins. Only the goddess was absent. Mrs Hajistavrou, who was walking with those quick, controlled steps, looking for the cab which would not come to carry them away, was submitted to Greece as never before. But she would not, would not allow herself to disintegrate. She closed her eyes against present and past. How glad she was, really, to be in a position to look forward to America. Even the distress of the Atlantic flight, the constriction, anxiety, the pills which would not work, struck her as desirable, and to walk at last inside their own apartment door, to discover whether she had been dreaming, or whether her india-rubber tree had died.

Down at the Dump

"Hi!"

He called from out of the house, and she went on chopping in the yard. Her right arm swung, firm still, muscular, though parts of her were beginning to sag. She swung with her right, and her left arm hung free. She chipped at the log, left right. She was expert with the axe.

Because you had to be. You couldn't expect all that much from a man.

"Hi!" It was Wal Whalley calling again from out of the home.

He came to the door then, in that dirty old baseball cap he had shook off the Yankee disposals. Still a fairly appetizing male, though his belly had begun to push against the belt.

"Puttin' on yer act?" he asked, easing the singlet under his armpits; easy was policy at Whalleys' place.

" 'Ere!" she protested. "Whaddaya make me out ter be? A lump of wood?"

Her eyes were of that blazing blue, her skin that of a brown peach. But whenever she smiled, something would happen, her mouth opening on watery sockets and the jags of brown, rotting stumps.

"A woman likes to be addressed," she said.

No one had ever heard Wal address his wife by her first name. Nobody had ever heard her name, though it was printed in the electoral roll. It was, in fact, Isba.

"Don't know about a dress," said Wal. "I got a idea, though."

His wife stood tossing her hair. It was natural at least; the sun had done it. All the kids had inherited their mother's colour, and when they stood together, golden-skinned, tossing back their unmanageable hair, you would have said a mob of taffy brumbies.

"What is the bloody idea?" she asked, because she couldn't go on standing there.

"Pick up a coupla cold bottles, and spend the mornun at the dump."

"But that's the same old idea," she grumbled.

"No, it ain't. Not our own dump. We ain't done Sarsaparilla since Christmas."

She began to grumble her way across the yard and into the house. A smell of sink strayed out of grey, unpainted weatherboard, to oppose the stench of crushed boggabri and cotton pear. Perhaps because Whalleys were in the bits-and-pieces trade their home was threatening to give in to them.

Wal Whalley did the dumps. Of course there were the other lurks besides. But no one had an eye like Wal for the things a person needs: dead batteries and musical bedsteads, a carpet you wouldn't notice was stained, wire, and again wire, clocks only waiting to jump back into the race of time. Objects of commerce and mystery littered Whalleys' back yard. Best of all, a rusty boiler into which the twins would climb to play at cubby.

"Eh? Waddaboutut?" Wal shouted, and pushed against his wife with his side.

She almost put her foot through the hole that had come in the kitchen boards.

"Waddabout what?"

Half-suspecting, she half-sniggered. Because Wal knew how to play on her weakness.

"The fuckun *idea!*"

So that she began again to grumble. As she slopped through the house her clothes irritated her skin. The sunlight fell yellow on the grey masses of the unmade beds, turned the fluff in the corners of the rooms to gold. Something was nagging at her, something heavy continued to weigh her down.

Of course. It was the funeral.

"Why, Wal," she said, the way she would suddenly come round, "you could certainly of thought of a worse idea. It'll keep the kids out of mischief. Wonder if that bloody Lummy's gunna decide to honour us?"

"One day I'll knock 'is block off," said Wal.

"He's only at the awkward age."

She stood at the window, looking as though she might know the hell of a lot. It was the funeral made her feel solemn. Brought the goose-flesh out on her.

"Good job you thought about the dump," she said, outstaring a red-brick propriety the other side of the road. "If there's anythun gets me down, it's havin' ter watch a funeral pass."

"Won't be from 'ere," he consoled. "They took 'er away same evenun. It's gunna start from Jackson's Personal Service."

"Good job she popped off at the beginnun of the week. They're not so personal at the week-end."

She began to prepare for the journey to the dump. Pulled her frock down a bit. Slipped on a pair of shoes.

"Bet *She*'ll be relieved. Wouldn't show it, though. Not about 'er sister. I bet Daise stuck in 'er fuckun guts."

Then Mrs Whalley was compelled to return to the window. As if her instinct. And sure enough there She was. Looking inside the letter-box, as if she hadn't collected already. Bent above the brick pillar in which the letter-box had been cemented, Mrs Hogben's face wore all that people expect of the bereaved.

"Daise was all right," said Wal.

"Daise was all right," agreed his wife.

Suddenly she wondered: What if Wal, if Wal had ever . . . ?

Mrs Whalley settled her hair. If she hadn't been all that satisfied at home—and she *was* satisfied, her recollective eyes would admit—she too might have done a line like Daise Morrow.

Over the road Mrs Hogben was calling.

"Meg?" she called. "Mar*gret*?"

Though from pure habit, without direction. Her voice sounded thinner today.

Then Mrs Hogben went away.

"Once I got took to a funeral," Mrs Whalley said. "They made me look in the coffun. It was the bloke's wife. He was that cut up."

"Did yer have a squint?"

"Pretended to."

Wal Whalley was breathing hard in the airless room.

"How soon do yer reckon they begin ter smell?"

"Smell? They wouldn't let 'em!" his wife said very definite. "You're the one that smells, Wal. I wonder you don't think of takin' a bath."

But she liked his smell, for all that. It followed her out of the shadow into the strong shaft of light. Looking at each other their two bodies asserted themselves. Their faces were lit by the certainty of life.

Wal tweaked her left nipple.

"We'll slip inter the Bull on the way, and pick up those cold bottles."

He spoke soft for him.

Mrs Hogben called another once or twice. Inside the brick entrance the cool of the house struck at her. She liked it cool, but not cold, and this was if not exactly cold, anyway, too sudden. So now she whimpered, very faintly, for everything you have to suffer, and death on top of all. Although it was her sister Daise who had died, Mrs Hogben was crying for the death which was waiting to carry her off in turn. She called: "Me-ehg?" But no one ever came to your rescue. She stopped to loosen the soil round the roots of the aluminium plant. She always had to be doing something. It made her feel better.

Meg did not hear, of course. She was standing amongst the fuchsia bushes, looking out from their greenish shade. She was thin and freckly. She looked awful, because Mum had made her wear her uniform, because it was sort of a formal occasion, to Auntie Daise's funeral. In the circumstances she not only looked, but was thin. That Mrs Ireland who was all for sport had told her she must turn her toes out, and watch out—she might grow up knock-kneed besides.

So Meg Hogben was, and felt, altogether awful. Her skin was green, except when the war between light and shade worried her face into scraps, and the fuchsia tassels, trembling against her unknowing cheek, infused something of their own blood, brindled her with shifting crimson. Only her eyes resisted. They were not exactly an ordinary grey. Lorrae Jensen, who was blue, said they were the eyes of a mopey cat.

A bunch of six or seven kids from second-grade, Lorrae, Edna, Val, Sherry, Sue Smith, and Sue Goldstien, stuck together in the holidays, though Meg sometimes wondered why. The others had come around to Hogben's Tuesday evening.

Lorrae said: "We're going down to Barranugli pool Thursday. There's some boys Sherry knows with a couple of Gs. They've promised to take us for a run after we come out."

Meg did not know whether she was glad or ashamed.

"I can't," she said. "My auntie's died."

"Arrr!" their voices trailed.

They couldn't get away too quick, as if it had been something contagious.

But murmuring.

Meg sensed she had become temporarily important.

So now she was alone with her dead importance, in the fuchsia bushes, on the day of Auntie Daise's funeral. She had turned fourteen. She remembered the ring in plaited gold Auntie Daise had promised her. When I am gone, her aunt had said. And now it had really happened. Without rancour Meg suspected there hadn't been time to think about the ring, and Mum would grab it, to add to all the other things she had.

Then that Lummy Whalley showed up, amongst the camphor laurels opposite, tossing his head of bleached hair. She hated boys with white hair. For that matter she hated boys, or any intrusion on her privacy. She hated Lum most of all. The day he threw the dog poo at her. It made the gristle come in her neck. Ugh! Although the old poo had only skittered over her skin, too dry to

really matter, she had gone in and cried because, well, there were
times when she cultivated dignity.

Now Meg Hogben and Lummy Whalley did not notice each
other even when they looked.

> "Who wants Meg Skinny-leg?
> I'd rather take the clothes-peg . . ."

Lum Whalley vibrated like a comb-and-paper over amongst the
camphor laurels they lopped back every so many years for fire-
wood. He slashed with his knife into bark. Once in a hot dusk he
had carved I LOVE MEG, because that was something you did, like
on lavatory walls, and in the trains, but it didn't mean anything of
course. Afterwards he slashed the darkness as if it had been a train
seat.

Lum Whalley pretended not to watch Meg Hogben skulking in
the fuchsia bushes. Wearing her brown uniform. Stiffer, browner
than for school, because it was her auntie's funeral.

"Me-ehg?" called Mrs Hogben. "Meg!"

"Lummy! Where the devil are yer?" called his mum.

She was calling all around, in the woodshed, behind the dunny.
Let her!

"Lum? Lummy, for Chris*sake!*" she called.

He hated that. Like some bloody kid. At school he had got them
to call him Bill, halfway between, not so shameful as Lum, nor
yet as awful as William.

Mrs Whalley came round the corner.

"Shoutin' me bloody lungs up!" she said. "When your dad's got
a nice idea. We're goin' down to Sarsaparilla dump."

"Arr!" he said.

But didn't spit.

"What gets inter you?" she asked.

Even at their most inaccessible Mrs Whalley liked to finger her
children. Touch often assisted thought. But she liked the feel of
them as well. She was glad she hadn't had girls. Boys turned into
men, and you couldn't do without men, even when they took you
for a mug, or got shickered, or bashed you up.

So she put her hand on Lummy, tried to get through to him. He was dressed, but might not have been. Lummy's kind was never ever born for clothes. At fourteen he looked more.

"Well," she said, sourer than she felt, "I'm not gunna cry over any sulky boy. Suit yourself."

She moved off.

As Dad had got out the old rattle-bones by now, Lum begun to clamber up. The back of the ute was at least private, though it wasn't no Customline.

The fact that Whalleys ran a Customline as well puzzled more unreasonable minds. Drawn up amongst the paspalum in front of Whalleys' shack, it looked stolen, and almost was—the third payment overdue. But would slither with ease a little longer to Barranugli, and snooze outside the Northern Hotel. Lum could have stood all day to admire their own two-tone car. Or would stretch out inside, his fingers at work on plastic flesh.

Now it was the ute for business. The bones of his buttocks bit into the boards. His father's meaty arm stuck out at the window, disgusting him. And soon the twins were squeezing from the rusty boiler. The taffy Gary—or was it Barry?—had fallen down and barked his knee.

"For Chrissake!" Mrs Whalley shrieked, and tossed her identical taffy hair.

Mrs Hogben watched those Whalleys leave.

"In a brick area, I wouldn't of thought," she remarked to her husband once again.

"All in good time, Myrtle," Councillor Hogben replied as before.

"Of course," she said, "if there are *reasons*."

Because councillors, she knew, did have reasons.

"But that home! And a Customline!"

The saliva of bitterness came in her mouth.

It was Daise who had said: I'm going to enjoy the good things of life—and died in that poky little hutch, with only a cotton frock to her back. While Myrtle had the liver-coloured brick home—not a single dampmark on the ceilings—she had the washing-machine, the septic, the TV, and the cream Holden Special, not to forget her husband. Les Hogben, the councillor. A builder into the bargain.

Now Myrtle stood amongst her things, and would have continued to regret the Ford the Whalleys hadn't paid for, if she hadn't been regretting Daise. It was not so much her sister's death as her life Mrs Hogben deplored. Still, everybody knew, and there was nothing you could do about it.

"Do you think anybody will come?" Mrs Hogben asked.

"What do you take me for?" her husband replied. "One of these cleervoyants?"

Mrs Hogben did not hear.

After giving the matter consideration she had advertised the death in the *Herald*:

> Morrow, Daisy (Mrs), suddenly, at her residence,
> Showground Road, Sarsaparilla.

There was nothing more you could put. It wasn't fair on Les, a public servant, to rake up relationships. And the *Mrs*—well, everyone had got into the habit when Daise started going with Cunningham. It seemed sort of natural as things dragged on and on. Don't work yourself up, Myrt, Daise used to say; Jack will when his wife dies. But it was Jack Cunningham who died first. Daise said: It's the way it happened, that's all.

"Do you think Ossie will come?" Councillor Hogben asked his wife slower than she liked.

"I hadn't thought about it," she said.

Which meant she had. She had, in fact, woken in the night, and lain there cold and stiff, as her mind's eye focused on Ossie's runny nose.

Mrs Hogben rushed at a drawer which somebody—never herself—had left hanging out. She was a thin woman, but wiry.

"Meg?" she called. "Did you polish your shoes?"

Les Hogben laughed behind his closed mouth. He always did when he thought of Daise's parting folly: to take up with that old scabby deadbeat Ossie from down at the showground. But who cared?

No one, unless her family.

Mrs Hogben dreaded the possibility of Ossie, a Roman Catholic for extra value, standing beside Daise's grave, even if nobody, even if only Mr Brickle saw.

Whenever the thought of Ossie Coogan crossed Councillor Hogben's mind he would twist the knife in his sister-in-law. Perhaps, now, he was glad she had died. A small woman, smaller than his wife, Daise Morrow was large by nature. Whenever she dropped in she was all around the place. Yarn her head off if she got the chance. It got so as Les Hogben could not stand hearing her laugh. Pressed against her in the hall once. He had forgotten that, or almost. How Daise laughed then. *I'm not so short of men I'd pick me own brother-in-law.* Had he pressed? Not all that much, not intentional, anyway. So the incident had been allowed to fade, dim as the brown-linoleum hall, in Councillor Hogben's mind.

"There's the phone, Leslie."

It was his wife.

"I'm too upset," she said, "to answer."

And began to cry.

Easing his crutch Councillor Hogben went into the hall.

It was good old Horrie Last.

"Yairs . . . yairs . . ." said Mr Hogben, speaking into the telephone which his wife kept swabbed with Breath-o'-Pine. "Yairs . . . Eleven, Horrie . . . from Barranugli . . . from Jackson's Personal . . . Yairs, that's decent of you, Horrie."

"Horrie Last," Councillor Hogben reported to his wife, "is gunna put in an appearance."

If no one else, a second councillor for Daise. Myrtle Hogben was consoled.

What could you do? Horrie Last put down the phone. He and Les had stuck together. Teamed up to catch the more progressive vote. Hogben and Last had developed the shire. Les had built Horrie's home, Lasts had sold Hogbens theirs. If certain people were spreading the rumour that Last and Hogben had caused a contraction of the Green Belt, then certain people failed to realize the term itself implied flexibility.

"What did you tell them?" asked Mrs Last.

"Said I'd go," her husband said, doing things to the change in his pocket.

He was a short man, given to standing with his legs apart.

Georgina Last withheld her reply. Formally of interest, her shape suggested she had been made out of several scones joined together in the baking.

"Daise Morrow," said Horrie Last, "wasn't such a bad sort."

Mrs Last did not answer.

So he stirred the money in his pocket harder, hoping perhaps it would emulsify. He wasn't irritated, mind you, by his wife—who had brought him a parcel of property, as well as a flair for real estate—but had often felt he might have done a dash with Daise Morrow on the side. Wouldn't have minded betting old Les Hogben had tinkered a bit with his wife's sister. Helped her buy her home, they said. Always lights on at Daise's place after dark. Postman left her mail on the veranda instead of in the box. In summer, when the men went round to read the meters, she'd ask them in for a glass of beer. Daise knew how to get service.

Georgina Last cleared her throat.

"Funerals are not for women," she declared, and took up a cardigan she was knitting for a cousin.

"You didn't do your shoes!" Mrs Hogben protested.

"I did," said Meg. "It's the dust. Don't know why we bother to clean shoes at all. They always get dirty again."

She stood there looking awful in the awful school uniform. Her cheeks were hollow from what she read could only be despair.

"A person must keep to her principles," Mrs Hogben said, and added: "Dadda is bringing round the car. Where's your hat, dear? We'll be ready to leave in two minutes."

"Arr, Mum! The hat?"

That old school hat. It had shrunk already a year ago, but had to see her through.

"You wear it to church, don't you?"

"But this isn't church!"

"It's as good as. Besides, you owe it to your aunt," Mrs Hogben said, to win.

Meg went and got her hat. They were going out through the fuchsia bushes, past the plaster pixies, which Mrs Hogben had trained her child to cover with plastic at the first drops of rain. Meg Hogben hated the sight of those corny old pixies, even after the plastic cones had snuffed them out.

It was sad in the car, dreamier. As she sat looking out through the window, the tight panama perched on her head lost its power to humiliate. Her always persistent, grey eyes, under the line of dark fringe, had taken up the search again: she had never yet looked enough. Along the road they passed the house in which her aunt, they told her, had died. The small, pink tilted house, standing amongst the carnation plants, had certainly lost some of its life. Or the glare had drained the colour from it. How the mornings used to sparkle in which Aunt Daise went up and down between the rows, her gown dragging heavy with dew, binding with bast the fuzzy flowers by handfuls and handfuls. Auntie's voice clear as morning. No one, she called, could argue they look stiff when they're bunched tight eh Meg what would you say they remind you of? But you never knew the answers to the sort of things people asked. Frozen fireworks, Daise suggested. Meg loved the idea of it, she loved Daise. Not so frozen either, she dared. The sun getting at the wet flowers broke them up and made them spin.

And the clovy scent rose up in the stale-smelling car, and smote Meg Hogben, out of the reeling heads of flowers, their cold stalks dusted with blue. Then she knew she would write a poem about Aunt Daise and the carnations. She wondered she hadn't thought of it before.

At that point the passengers were used most brutally as the car entered on a chain of potholes. For once Mrs Hogben failed to invoke the Main Roads Board. She was asking herself whether Ossie could be hiding in there behind the blinds. Or whether, whether.

She fished for her second handkerchief. Prudence had induced her to bring two—the good one with the lace insertion for use beside the grave.

"The weeds will grow like one thing," her voice blared, "now that they'll have their way."

Then she began to unfold the less important of her handkerchiefs.

Myrtle Morrow had always been the sensitive one. Myrtle had understood the Bible. Her needlework, her crochet doilies had taken prizes at country shows. No one had fiddled such pathos out of the pianola. It was Daise who loved flowers, though. It's a moss-rose, Daise had said, sort of rolling it round on her tongue, while she was still a little thing.

When she had had her cry, Mrs Hogben remarked: "Girls don't know they're happy until it's too late."

Thus addressed, the other occupants of the car did not answer. They knew they were not expected to.

Councillor Hogben drove in the direction of Barranugli. He had arranged his hat before leaving. He removed a smile the mirror reminded him was there. Although he no longer took any risks in a re-election photograph by venturing out of the past, he often succeeded in the fleshy present. But now, in difficult circumstances, he was exercising his sense of duty. He drove, he drove, past the retinosperas, heavy with their own gold, past the lagerstroemias, their pink sugar running into mildew.

Down at the dump Whalleys were having an argument about whether the beer was to be drunk on arrival or after they had developed a thirst.

"Keep it, then!" Mum Whalley turned her back. "What was the point of buyin' it cold if you gotta wait till it hots up? Anyways," she said, "I thought the beer was an excuse for comin'."

"Arr, stuff it!" says Wal. "A dump's business, ain't it? With or without beer. Ain't it? Any day of the week."

He saw she had begun to sulk. He saw her rather long breasts floating around inside her dress. Silly cow! He laughed. But cracked a bottle.

Barry said he wanted a drink.

You could hear the sound of angry suction as his mum's lips called off a swig.

"I'm not gunna stand by and watch any kid of mine," said the wet lips, "turn 'isself into a bloody dipso!"

Her eyes were at their blazing bluest. Perhaps it was because Wal Whalley admired his wife that he continued to desire her.

But Lummy pushed off on his own. When his mum went crook, and swore, he was too aware of the stumps of teeth, the rotting brown of nastiness. It was different, of course, if you swore yourself. Sometimes it was unavoidable.

Now he avoided by slipping away, between the old mattresses, and boots the sun had buckled up. Pitfalls abounded: the rusty traps of open tins lay in wait for guiltless ankles, the necks of broken bottles might have been prepared to gash a face. So he went thoughtfully, his feet scuffing the leaves of stained asbestos, crunching the torso of a celluloid doll. Here and there it appeared as though trash might win. The onslaught of metal was pushing the scrub into the gully. But in many secret, steamy pockets, a rout was in progress: seeds had been sown in the lumps of grey, disintegrating kapok and the laps of burst chairs, the coils of springs, locked in the spirals of wirier vines, had surrendered to superior resilience. Somewhere on the edge of the whole shambles a human ally, before retiring, had lit a fire, which by now the green had almost choked, leaving a stench of smoke to compete with the sicklier one of slow corruption.

Lum Whalley walked with a grace of which he himself had never been aware. He had had about enough of this rubbish jazz. He would have liked to know how to live neat. Like Darkie Black. Everything in its place in the cabin of Darkie's trailer. Suddenly his throat yearned for Darkie's company. Darkie's hands, twisting the wheel, appeared to control the whole world.

A couple of strands of barbed wire separated Sarsaparilla dump from Sarsaparilla cemetery. The denominations were separated too, but there you had to tell by the names, or by the angels and things the RIPs went in for. Over in what must have been the Church of England Alf Herbert was finishing Mrs Morrow's grave. He had reached the clay, and the going was heavy. The clods fell resentfully.

If what they said about Mrs Morrow was true, then she had lived it up all right. Lum Whalley wondered what, supposing he had met her walking towards him down a bush track, smiling. His skin tingled. Lummy had never done a girl, although he pretended he had, so as to hold his own with the kids. He wondered if a girl, if that sourpuss Meg Hogben. Would of bitten as likely as not. Lummy felt a bit afraid, and returned to thinking of Darkie Black, who never talked about things like that.

Presently he moved away. Alf Herbert, leaning on his shovel, could have been in need of a yarn. Lummy was not prepared to yarn. He turned back into the speckled bush, into the pretences of a shade. He lay down under a banksia, and opened his fly to look at himself. But pretty soon got sick of it.

The procession from Barranugli back to Sarsaparilla was hardly what you would have called a procession: the Reverend Brickle, the Hogbens' Holden, Horrie's Holden, following the smaller of Jackson's hearses. In the circumstances they were doing things cheap—there was no reason for splashing it around. At Sarsaparilla Mr Gill joined in, sitting high in that old Chev. It would have been practical, Councillor Hogben sighed, to join the hearse at Sarsaparilla. Old Gill was only there on account of Daise being his customer for years. A grocer lacking in enterprise, Daise had stuck to him, she said, because she liked him. Well, if that was what you put first, but where did it get you?

At the last dip before the cemetery a disembowelled mattress from the dump had begun to writhe across the road. It looked like a kind of monster from out of the depths of somebody's mind, the part a decent person ignored.

"Ah, dear! At the cemetery too!" Mrs Hogben protested. "I wonder the Council," she added, in spite of her husband.

"All right, Myrtle," he said between his teeth. "I made a mental note."

Councillor Hogben was good at that.

"And the Whalleys on your own doorstep," Mrs Hogben moaned.

The things she had seen on hot days, in front of their kiddies too.

The hearse had entered the cemetery gate. They had reached the bumpy stage, toppling over the paspalum clumps, before the thinner, bush grass. All around, the leaves of the trees presented so many grey blades. Not even a magpie to put heart into a Christian. But Alf Herbert came forward, his hands dusted with yellow clay, to guide the hearse between the Methoes and the Presbyterians, onto Church of England ground.

Jolting had shaken Mrs Hogben's grief up to the surface again. Mr Brickle was impressed. He spoke for a moment of the near and dear. His hands were kind and professional in helping her out.

But Meg jumped. And landed. It was a shock to hear a stick crack so loud. Perhaps it was what Mum would have called irreverent. At the same time her banana-coloured panama fell off her head into the tussocks.

It was really a bit confusing at the grave. Some of the men helped with the coffin, and Councillor Last was far too short.

Then Mrs Hogben saw, she saw, from out of the lace handkerchief, it was that Ossie Coogan she saw, standing the other side of the grave. Had old Gill given him a lift? Ossie, only indifferently buttoned, stood snivelling behind the mound of yellow clay.

Nothing would have stopped his nose. Daise used to say: You don't want to be frightened, Ossie, not when I'm here, see? But she wasn't any longer. So now he was afraid. Excepting Daise, Protestants had always frightened him. Well, I'm nothing, she used to say, nothing that you could pigeonhole, but love what we are given to love.

Myrtle Hogben was ropable, if only because of what Councillor Last must think. She would have liked to express her feelings in words, if she could have done so without giving offence to God.

Then the ants ran up her legs, for she was standing on a nest, and her body cringed before the teeming injustices.

Daise, she had protested the day it all began, whatever has come over you? The sight of her sister had made her run out leaving the white sauce to burn. Wherever will you take him? He's sick, said Daise. *But you can't,* Myrtle Hogben cried. For there was her sister Daise pushing some old deadbeat in a barrow. All along Showground Road people had come out of homes to look. Daise appeared smaller pushing the wheelbarrow down the hollow and up the hill. Her hair was half uncoiled. *You can't! You can't!* Myrtle called. But Daise could, and did.

When all the few people were assembled at the graveside in their good clothes, Mr Brickle opened the book, though his voice soon suggested he needn't have.

"I am the resurrection and the life," he said.

And Ossie cried. Because he didn't believe it, not when it came to the real thing.

He looked down at the coffin, which was what remained of what he knew. He remembered eating a baked apple, very slowly, the toffee on it. And again the dark of the horse-stall swallowed him up, where he lay hopeless amongst the shit, and her coming at him with the barrow. What do you want? he asked straight out. I came down to the showground, she said, for a bit of honest-to-God manure, I've had those fertilizers, she said, and what are you, are you sick? I live 'ere, he said. And began to cry, and rub the snot from his snivelly nose. After a bit Daise said: We're going back to my place, What's-yer-name—Ossie. The way she spoke he knew it was true. All the way up the hill in the barrow the wind was giving his eyes gyp, and blowing his thin hair apart. Over the years he had come across one or two lice in his hair, but thought, or hoped he had got rid of them by the time Daise took him up. As she pushed and struggled with the barrow, sometimes she would lean forward, and he felt her warmth, her firm diddies pressed against his back.

"Lord, let me know mine end, and the number of my days: that I may be certified how long I have to live," Mr Brickle read.

Certified was the word, decided Councillor Hogben looking at that old Ossie.

Who stood there mumbling a few Aspirations, very quiet, on the strength of what they had taught him as a boy.

When all this was under way, all these words of which, she knew, her Auntie Daise would not have approved, Meg Hogben went and got beneath the strands of wire separating the cemetery from the dump. She had never been to the dump before, and her heart was lively in her side. She walked shyly through the bush. She came across an old suspender-belt. She stumbled over a blackened primus.

She saw Lummy Whalley then. He was standing under a banksia, twisting at one of its dead heads.

Suddenly they knew there was something neither of them could continue to avoid.

"I came here to the funeral," she said.

She sounded, well, almost relieved.

"Do you come here often?" she asked.

"Nah," he answered, hoarse. "Not here. To dumps, yes."

But her intrusion had destroyed the predetermined ceremony of his life, and caused a trembling in his hand.

"Is there anything to see?" she asked.

"Junk," he said. "Same old junk."

"Have you ever looked at a dead person?"

Because she noticed the trembling of his hand.

"No," he said. "Have you?"

She hadn't. Nor did it seem probable that she would have to now. Not as they began breathing evenly again.

"What do you do with yourself?" he asked.

Then, even though she would have liked to stop herself, she could not. She said: "I write poems. I'm going to write one about my Aunt Daise, like she was, gathering carnations early in the dew."

"What'll you get out of that?"

"Nothing," she said, "I suppose."

But it did not matter.

"What other sorts of pomes do you write?" he asked, twisting at last the dead head of the banksia off.

"I wrote one," she said, "about the things in a cupboard. I wrote about a dream I had. And the smell of rain. That was a bit too short."

He began to look at her then. He had never looked into the eyes of a girl. They were grey and cool, unlike the hot or burnt-out eyes of women.

"What are you going to be?" she asked.

"I dunno."

"You're not a white-collar type."

"Eh?"

"I mean, you're not for figures, and books, and banks and of-fices," she said.

He was too disgusted to agree.

"I'm gunna have me own truck. Like Mr Black. Darkie's got a trailer."

"What?"

"Well," he said, "a semi-trailer."

"Oh," she said, more diffident.

"Darkie took me on a trip to Maryborough. It was pretty tough goin'. Sometimes we drove right through the night. Sometimes we slept on the road. Or in places where you get rooms. Gee, it was good though, shootin' through the country towns at night."

She saw it. She saw the people standing at their doors, frozen in the blocks of yellow light. The rushing of the night made the fig-ures forever still. All around she could feel the furry darkness, as the semi-trailer roared and bucked, its skeleton of coloured lights. While in the cabin, in which they sat, all was stability and order. If she glanced sideways she could see how his taffy hair shone when raked by the bursts of electric light. They had brought cases with tooth-brushes, combs, one or two things—the pad on which she would write the poem somewhere when they stopped in the smell of sunlight dust ants. But his hands had acquired such mastery over the wheel, it appeared this might never happen. Nor did she care.

"This Mr Black" she said, her mouth getting thinner, "does he take you with him often?"

"Only once interstate," said Lummy, pitching the banksia head away. "Once in a while short trips."

As they drove they rocked together. He had never been closer to anyone than when bumping against Darkie's ribs. He waited to experience again the little spasm of gratitude and pleasure. He would have liked to wear, and would in time, a striped sweatshirt like Darkie wore.

"I'd like to go in with Darkie," he said, "when I get a trailer of me own. Darkie's the best friend I got."

With a drawnout shiver of distrust she saw the darker hands, the little black hairs on the backs of the fingers.

"Oh, well," she said, withdrawn, "praps you will in the end," she said.

On the surrounding graves the brown flowers stood in their jars of browner water. The more top-heavy, plastic bunches had been slapped down by a westerly, but had not come to worse grief than to lie strewn in pale disorder on the uncharitable granite chips.

The heat made Councillor Last yawn. He began to read the carved names, those within sight at least, some of which he had just about forgot. He almost laughed once. If the dead could have sat up in their graves there would have been an argument or two.

"In the midst of life we are in death," said the parson bloke.

JACK CUNNINGHAM
BELOVED HUSBAND OF FLORENCE MARY,

read Horrie Last.

Who would have thought Cunningham, straight as a silky-oak, would fall going up the path to Daise Morrow's place. Horrie

used to watch them together, sitting awhile on the veranda before
going in to their tea. They made no bones about it, because everybody knew. Good teeth Cunningham had. Always a white, well-
ironed shirt. Wonder which of the ladies did the laundry. Florence Mary was an invalid, they said. Daise Morrow liked to laugh
with men, but for Jack Cunningham she had a silence, promising
intimacies at which Horrie Last could only guess, whose own private life had been lived in almost total darkness.

Good Christ, and then there was Ossie. The woman could only
have been at heart a perv of a kind you hadn't heard about.

*"Forasmuch as it hath pleased Almighty God of his great mercy
to take unto himself the soul . . ."* read Mr Brickle.

As it was doubtful who should cast the earth, Mr Gill the grocer
did. They heard the handful rattle on the coffin.

Then the tears truly ran out of Ossie's scaly eyes. Out of darkness. Out of darkness Daise had called: What's up, Ossie, you
don't wanta cry. I got the cramps, he answered. They were twisting
him. The cramps? she said drowsily. Or do you imagine? If it isn't
the cramps it's something else. Could have been. He'd take Daise's
word for it. He was never all that bright since he had the menin-
gitis. Tell you what, Daise said, you come in here, into my bed,
I'll warm you, Os, in a jiffy. He listened in the dark to his own
snivelling. Arr, Daise, I couldn't, he said, I couldn't get a stand,
not if you was to give me the jackpot, he said. She sounded very
still then. He lay and counted the throbbing of the darkness.
Not like that, she said—she didn't laugh at him as he had half expected—besides, she said, it only ever really comes to you once.
That way. And at once he was parting the darkness, bumping and
shambling, to get to her. He had never known it so gentle. Because
Daise wasn't afraid. She ran her hands through his hair, on and on
like water flowing. She soothed the cramps out of his legs. Until
in the end they were breathing in time. Dozing. Then the lad Ossie
Coogan rode again down from the mountain, the sound of the
snaffle in the blue air, the smell of sweat from under the saddle-
cloth, towards the great, flowing river. He rocked and flowed with
the motion of the strong, never-ending river, burying his mouth in
brown cool water, to drown would have been worth it.

Once during the night Ossie had woken, afraid the distance might have come between them. But Daise was still holding him against her breast. If he had been different, say. Ossie's throat had begun to wobble. Only then, Daise, Daise might have turned different. So he nuzzled against the warm darkness, and was again received.

"If you want to enough, you can do what you want," Meg Hogben insisted.

She had read it in a book, and wasn't altogether convinced, but theories sometimes come to the rescue.

"If you want," she said, kicking a hole in the stony ground.

"Not everything you can't."

"You can!" she said. "But you can!"

She who had never looked at a boy, not right into one, was looking at him as never before.

"That's a lot of crap," he said.

"Well," she admitted, "there are limits."

It made him frown. He was again suspicious. She was acting clever. All those pomes.

But to reach understanding she would have surrendered her cleverness. She was no longer proud of it.

"And what'll happen if you get married? Riding around the country in a truck. How'll your wife like it? Stuck at home with a lot of kids."

"Some of 'em take the wife along. Darkie takes his missus and kids. Not always, like. But now and again. On short runs."

"You didn't tell me Mr Black was married."

"Can't tell you everything, can I? Not at once."

The women who sat in the drivers' cabins of the semi-trailers he saw as predominantly thin and dark. They seldom returned glances, but wiped their hands on Kleenex, and peered into little mirrors, waiting for their men to show up again. Which in time they had to. So he walked across from the service station, to take possession of his property. Sauntering, frowning slightly, touching the yellow stubble on his chin, he did not bother to look. Glanced sideways perhaps. She was the thinnest, the darkest he knew, the coolest of all the women who sat looking out from the cabin windows of the semi-trailers.

In the meantime they strolled a bit, amongst the rusty tins at Sarsaparilla dump. He broke a few sticks and threw away the pieces. She tore off a narrow leaf and smelled it. She would have liked to smell Lummy's hair.

"Gee, you're fair," she had to say.

"Some are born fair," he admitted.

He began pelting a rock with stones. He was strong, she saw. So many discoveries in a short while were making her tremble at the knees.

And as they rushed through the brilliant light, roaring and lurching, the cabin filled with fair-skinned, taffy children, the youngest of whom she was protecting by holding the palm of her hand behind his neck, as she had noticed women do. Occupied in this way, she almost forgot Lum at times, who would pull up, and she would climb down, to rinse the nappies in tepid water, and hang them on a bush to dry.

"All these pomes and things," he said, "I never knew a clever person before."

"But clever isn't any different," she begged, afraid he might not accept her peculiarity and power.

She would go with a desperate wariness from now. She sensed that, if not in years, she was older than Lum, but this was the secret he must never guess: that for all his strength, all his beauty, she was, and must remain the stronger.

"What's that?" he asked, and touched.

But drew back his hand in self-protection.

"A scar," she said. "I cut my wrist opening a tin of condensed milk."

For once she was glad of the paler seam in her freckled skin, hoping that it might heal a breach.

And he looked at her out of his hard blue Whalley eyes. He liked her. Although she was ugly, and clever, and a girl.

"Condensed milk on bread," he said, "that's something I could eat till I bust."

"Oh, yes!" she agreed.

She did honestly believe, although she had never thought of it before.

Flies clustered in irregular jet embroideries on the backs of best suits. Nobody bothered any longer to shrug them off. As Alf Herbert grunted against the shovelfuls, dust clogged increasingly, promises settled thicker. Although they had been told they might expect Christ to redeem, it would have been no less incongruous if He had appeared out of the scrub to perform on altars of burning sandstone a sacrifice for which nobody had prepared them. In any case, the mourners waited—they had been taught to accept whatever might be imposed—while the heat stupefied the remnants of their minds, and inflated their Australian fingers into foreign-looking sausages.

Myrtle Hogben was the first to protest. She broke down—into the wrong handkerchief. *Who shall change our vile body?* The words were more than her decency could bear.

"Easy on it," her husband whispered, putting a finger under her elbow.

She submitted to his sympathy, just as in their life together she had submitted to his darker wishes. Never wanting more than peace, and one or two perquisites.

A thin woman, Mrs Hogben continued to cry for all the wrongs that had been done her. For Daise had only made things viler. While understanding, yes, at moments. It was girls who really understood, not even women—sisters, sisters. Before events whirled them apart. So Myrtle Morrow was again walking through the orchard, and Daise Morrow twined her arm around her sister; confession filled the air, together with a scent of crushed, fermenting apples. Myrtle said: Daise, there's something I'd like to do, I'd like to chuck a lemon into a Salvation Army tuba. Daise giggled. You're a nut, Myrt, she said. But never *vile*. So Myrtle Hogben cried. Once, only once she had thought how she'd like to push someone off a cliff, and watch their expression as it happened. But Myrtle had not confessed that.

So Mrs Hogben cried, for those things she was unable to confess, for anything she might not be able to control.

As the blander words had begun falling, *Our Father,* that she knew by heart, *our daily bread,* she should have felt comforted. She should of. Should of.

Where was Meg, though?

Mrs Hogben separated herself from the others. Walking stiffly. If any of the men noticed, they took it for granted she had been overcome, or wanted to relieve herself.

She would have liked to relieve herself by calling: "Margaret Meg wherever don't you hear me Me-ehg?" drawing it out thin in anger. But could not cut across a clergyman's words. So she stalked. She was not unlike a guinea-hen, its spotted silk catching on a strand of barbed-wire.

When they had walked a little farther, round and about, anywhere, they overheard voices.

"What's that?" asked Meg.

"Me mum and dad," Lummy said. "Rousin' about somethun or other."

Mum Whalley had just found two bottles of unopened beer. Down at the dump. Waddayaknow. Must be something screwy somewhere.

"Could of put poison in it," her husband warned.

"Poison? My arse!" she shouted. "That's because *I* found it!"

"Whoever found it," he said, "who's gunna drink a coupla bottlesa hot beer?"

"I am!" she said.

"When what we brought was good an' cold?"

He too was shouting a bit. She behaved unreasonable at times.

"Who wanted ter keep what we brought? Till it got good an' hot!" she shrieked.

Sweat was running down both the Whalleys.

Suddenly Lum felt he wanted to lead this girl out of earshot. He had just about had the drunken sods. He would have liked to find himself walking with his girl over mown lawn, like at the Botanical Gardens, a green turf giving beneath their leisured feet. Statues pointed a way through the glare, to where they finally sat, under enormous shiny leaves, looking out at boats on water. They unpacked their cut lunch from its layers of fresh tissue-paper.

"They're rough as bags," Lummy explained.

"I don't care," Meg Hogben assured.

Nothing on earth could make her care—was it more, or was it less?

She walked giddily behind him, past a rusted fuel-stove, over a field of deathly feltex. Or ran, or slid, to keep up. Flowers would have wilted in her hands, if she hadn't crushed them brutally, to keep her balance. Somewhere in their private labyrinth Meg Hogben had lost her hat.

When they were farther from the scene of anger, and a silence of heat had descended again, he took her little finger, because it seemed natural to do so, after all they had experienced. They swung hands for a while, according to some special law of motion.

Till Lum Whalley frowned, and threw the girl's hand away.

If she accepted his behaviour it was because she no longer believed in what he did, only in what she knew he felt. That might have been the trouble. She was so horribly sure, he would have to resist to the last moment of all. As a bird, singing in the prickly tree under which they found themselves standing, seemed to cling to the air. Then his fingers took control. She was amazed at the hardness of his boy's body. The tremors of her flinty skin, the membrane of the white sky appalled him. Before fright and expectation melted their mouths. And they took little grateful sips of each other. Holding up their throats in between. Like birds drinking.

Ossie could no longer see Alf Herbert's shovel working at the earth.

"Never knew a man cry at a funeral," Councillor Hogben complained, very low, although he was ripe enough to burst.

If you could count Ossie as a man, Councillor Last suggested in a couple of noises.

But Ossie could not see or hear, only Daise, still lying on that

upheaval of a bed. Seemed she must have burst a button, for her
breasts stood out from her. He would never forget how they la-
boured against the heavy yellow morning light. In the early light,
the flesh turned yellow, sluggish. What's gunna happen to me,
Daisy? It'll be decided, Os, she said, like it is for any of us. I ought
to know, she said, to tell you, but give me time to rest a bit, to get
me breath. Then he got down on his painful knees. He put his
mouth to Daise's neck. Her skin tasted terrible bitter. The great
glistening river, to which the lad Ossie Coogan had ridden jingling
down from the mountain, was slowing into thick, yellow mud.
Himself an old, scabby man attempting to refresh his forehead
in the last pothole.

Mr Brickle said: *"We give thee hearty thanks for that it hath
pleased thee to deliver this our sister out of the miseries of this sin-
ful world."*

"No! No!" Ossie protested, so choked nobody heard, though it
was vehement enough in its intention.

As far as he could understand, nobody wanted to be delivered.
Not him, not Daise, anyways. When you could sit together by the
fire on winter nights baking potatoes under the ashes.

It took Mrs Hogben some little while to free her *crêpe de Chine*
from the wire. It was her nerves, not to mention Meg on her mind.
In the circumstances she tore herself worse, and looked up to see
her child, just over there, without shame, in a rubbish tip, kissing
with the Whalley boy. What if Meg was another of Daise? It was
in the blood, you couldn't deny.

Mrs Hogben did not exactly call, but released some kind of
noise from her extended throat. Her mouth was too full of tongue
to find room for words as well.

Then Meg looked. She was smiling.

She said: "Yes, Mother."

She came and got through the wire, tearing herself also a little.

Mrs Hogben said, and her teeth clicked: "You chose the like-
liest time. Your aunt hardly in her grave. Though, of course, it
is only your aunt, if anyone, to blame."

The accusations were falling fast. Meg could not answer. Since joy had laid her open, she had forgotten how to defend herself.

"If you were a little bit younger"—Mrs Hogben lowered her voice because they had begun to approach the parson—"I'd break a stick on you, my girl."

Meg tried to close her face, so that nobody would see inside.

"What will they say?" Mrs Hogben moaned. "What ever will happen to us?"

"What, Mother?" Meg asked.

"You're the only one can answer that. And someone else."

Then Meg looked over her shoulder and recognized the hate which, for a while, she had forgotten existed. And at once her face closed up tight, like a fist. She was ready to protect whatever justly needed her protection.

Even if their rage, grief, contempt, boredom, apathy, and sense of injustice had not occupied the mourners, it is doubtful whether they would have realized the dead woman was standing amongst them. The risen dead—that was something which happened, or didn't happen, in the Bible. Fanfares of light did not blare for a loose woman in floral cotton. Those who had known her remembered her by now only fitfully in some of the wooden attitudes of life. How could they have heard, let alone believed in, her affirmation? Yet Daise Morrow continued to proclaim.

Listen, all of you, I'm not leaving, except those who want to be left, and even those aren't so sure—they might be parting with a bit of themselves. Listen to me, all you successful no-hopers, all of you who wake in the night, jittery because something may be escaping you, or terrified to think there may never have been anything to find. Come to me, you sour women, public servants, anxious children, and old scabby, desperate men. . . .

Physically small, words had seemed too big for her. She would push back her hair in exasperation. And take refuge in acts. Because her feet had been planted in the earth, she would have been the last to resent its pressure now, while her always rather hoarse voice continued to exhort in borrowed syllables of dust.

Truly, we needn't experience tortures, unless we build chambers in our minds to house instruments of hatred in. Don't you know, my darling creatures, that death isn't death, unless it's the death of love? Love should be the greatest explosion it is reasonable to expect. Which sends us whirling, spinning, creating millions of other worlds. Never destroying.

From the fresh mound which they had formed unimaginatively in the shape of her earthly body, she persisted in appealing to them.

I will comfort you. If you will let me. Do you understand?

But nobody did, as they were only human.

For ever and ever. And ever.

Leaves quivered lifted in the first suggestion of a breeze.

So the aspirations of Daise Morrow were laid alongside her small-boned wrists, smooth thighs and pretty ankles. She surrendered at last to the formal crumbling which, it was hoped, would make an honest woman of her.

But had not altogether died.

Meg Hogben had never exactly succeeded in interpreting her aunt's messages, nor could she have witnessed the last moments of the burial, because the sun was dazzling her. She did experience, however, along with a shiver of recollected joy, the down laid against her cheek, a little breeze trickling through the moist roots of her hair, as she got inside the car, and waited for whatever next.

Well, they had dumped Daise.

Somewhere the other side of the wire there was the sound of smashed glass and discussion.

Councillor Hogben went across to the parson and said the right kind of things. Half-turning his back he took a note or two from his wallet, and immediately felt disengaged. If Horrie Last had been there Les Hogben would have gone back at this point and put an arm around his mate's shoulder, to feel whether he was forgiven for unorthodox behaviour in a certain individual—no relation, mind you, but. In any case Horrie had driven away.

Horrie drove, or flew, across the dip in which the dump joined the cemetery. For a second Ossie Coogan's back flickered inside a spiral of dust.

Ought to give the coot a lift, Councillor Last suspected, and wondered, as he drove on, whether a man's better intentions were worth, say, half a mark in the event of their remaining unfulfilled. For by now it was far too late to stop, and there was that Ossie, in the mirror, turning off the road towards the dump, where, after all, the bugger belonged.

All along the road, stones, dust, and leaves, were settling back into normally unemotional focus. Seated in his high Chev, Gill the grocer, a slow man, who carried his change in a little, soiled canvas bag, looked ahead through thick lenses. He was relieved to realize he would reach home almost on the dot of three-thirty, and his wife pour him his cup of tea. Whatever he understood was punctual, decent, docketed.

As he drove, prudently, he avoided the mattress the dump had spewed, from under the wire, half across the road. Strange things had happened at the dump on and off, the grocer recollected. Screaming girls, their long tight pants ripped to tatters. An arm in a sugar-bag, and not a sign of the body that went with it. Yet some found peace amongst the refuse: elderly derelict men, whose pale, dead, fish eyes never divulged anything of what they had lived, and women with blue, metho skins, hanging around the doors of shacks put together from sheets of bark and rusty iron. Once an old downandout had crawled amongst the rubbish apparently to rot, and did, before they sent for the constable, to examine what seemed at first a bundle of stinking rags.

Mr Gill accelerated judiciously.

They were driving. They were driving.

Alone in the back of the ute, Lum Whalley sat forward on the empty crate, locking his hands between his knees, as he forgot having seen Darkie do. He was completely independent now. His face had been reshaped by the wind. He liked that. It felt good. He no longer resented the junk they were dragging home, the rust flaking off at his feet, the roll of mouldy feltex trying to fur his nostrils up. Nor his family—discussing, or quarrelling, you could never tell—behind him in the cabin.

The Whalleys were in fact singing. One of their own versions. They always sang their own versions, the two little boys joining in.

"Show me the way to go home,
    I'm not too tired for bed.
    I had a little drink about an hour ago,
    And it put ideas in me head . . ."

Suddenly Mum Whalley began belting into young Gary—or was it Barry?

"Wadda *you* know, eh? Wadda *you?*"

"What's bitten yer?" her husband shouted. "Can't touch a drop without yer turn nasty!"

She didn't answer. He could tell a grouse was coming, though. The little boy had started to cry, but only as a formality.

"It's that bloody Lummy," Mrs Whalley complained.

"Why pick on Lum?"

"Give a kid all the love and affection, and waddayaget?"

Wal grunted. Abstractions always embarrassed him.

Mum Whalley spat out of the window, and the spit came back at her.

"Arrrr!" she protested.

And fell silenter. It was not strictly Lum, not if you was honest. It was nothing. Or everything. The grog. You was never ever gunna touch it no more. Until you did. And that bloody Lummy, what with the caesar and all, you was never ever going again with a man.

"That's somethink a man don't understand."

"What?" asked Wal.

"A caesar."

"Eh?"

You just couldn't discuss with a man. So you had to get into bed with him. Grogged up half the time. That was how she copped the twins, after she had said never ever.

"Stop cryun, for Chrissake!" Mum Whalley coaxed, touching the little boy's blowing hair.

Everything was sad.

"Wonder how often they bury someone alive," she said.

Taking a corner in his cream Holden Councillor Hogben felt quite rakish, but would restrain himself at the critical moment from skidding the wrong side of the law.

They were driving and driving, in long, lovely bursts, and at the corners, in semicircular swirls.

On those occasions in her life when she tried to pray, begging for an experience, Meg Hogben would fail, but return to the attempt with clenched teeth. Now she did so want to think of her dead aunt with love, and the image blurred repeatedly. She was superficial, that was it. Yet, each time she failed, the landscape leaped lovingly. They were driving under the telephone wires. She could have translated any message into the language of peace. The wind burning, whenever it did not cut cold, left the stable things alone: the wooden houses stuck beside the road, the trunks of willows standing round the brown saucer of a dam. Her too candid, grey eyes seemed to have deepened, as though to accommodate all she still had to see, feel.

It was lovely curled on the back seat, even with Mum and Dad in front.

"I haven't forgotten, Margret," Mum called over her shoulder.

Fortunately Dadda wasn't interested enough to inquire.

"Did Daise owe anything on the home?" Mrs Hogben asked. "She was never at all practical."

Councillor Hogben cleared his throat.

"Give us time to find out," he said.

Mrs Hogben respected her husband for the things which she, secretly, did not understand: Time the mysterious, for instance, Business, and worst of all, the Valuer General.

"I wonder Jack Cunningham," she said, "took up with Daise. He was a fine man. Though Daise had a way with her."

They were driving. They were driving.

When Mrs Hogben remembered the little ring in plaited gold.

"Do you think those undertakers are honest?"

"Honest?" her husband repeated.

A dubious word.

"Yes," she said. "That ring that Daise."

You couldn't very well accuse. When she had plucked up the courage she would go down to the closed house. The thought of it made her chest tighten. She would go inside, and feel her way into the back corners of drawers, where perhaps a twist of tissue-paper. But the closed houses of the dead frightened Mrs Hogben, she had to admit. The stuffiness, the light strained through brown holland. It was as if you were stealing, though you weren't.

And then those Whalleys creeping up.

They were driving and driving, the ute and the sedan almost rubbing on each other.

"No one who hasn't had a migraine," cried Mrs Hogben, averting her face, "can guess what it feels like."

Her husband had heard that before.

"It's a wonder it don't leave you," he said. "They say it does when you've passed a certain age."

Though they weren't passing the Whalleys he would make every effort to throw the situation off. Wal Whalley leaning forward, though not so far you couldn't see the hair bursting out of the front of his shirt. His wife thumping his shoulder. They were singing one of their own versions. Her gums all watery.

So they drove and drove.

"I could sick up, Leslie," Mrs Hogben gulped, and fished for her lesser handkerchief.

The Whalley twins were laughing through their taffy forelocks.

At the back of the ute that sulky Lum turned towards the opposite direction. Meg Hogben was looking her farthest off. Any sign of acknowledgment had been so faint the wind had immediately blown it off their faces. As Meg and Lummy sat, they held their sharp, but comforting knees. They sank their chins as low as they would go. They lowered their eyes, as if they had seen enough for the present, and wished to cherish what they knew.

The warm core of certainty settled stiller as driving faster the wind payed out the telephone wires the fences fences the flattened heads of grey grass always raising themselves again again again